I0598799

HUNTER'S MOON

This book is a work of fiction. The characters, incidents, and dialogue are drawn from the author's imagination and are not to be construed as real. Any resemblance to actual events or persons, living or dead, is entirely coincidental.

HUNTER'S MOON
Copyright © 2020 by Sarah M. Awa.

Cover design by Nada Orlic.

All rights reserved. In accordance with the U.S. Copyright Act of 1976, the scanning, uploading, and electronic sharing of any part of this book without the permission of the publisher constitute unlawful piracy and theft of the author's intellectual property. If you would like to use material from this book (other than for review purposes), prior written permission must be obtained by contacting the publisher at contact@thinklingsbooks.com. Thank you for your support of the author's rights.

Thinklings Books
1400 Lloyd Rd. #279
Wickliffe, OH 44092
thinklingsbooks.com

The author thanks:

My fellow Thinklings, Jeannie and Deborah, without whom this book would not be finished and publishable.

My husband, Oscar, for always believing in me and encouraging me, for helping me hold back the darkness. *Itsumo aishiteru yo.*

Dr. Don Williams, a.k.a. Gandalf, for your wit, wisdom, and investment in me, in and beyond the ten courses I took with you.

My parents and family, for much more love and support than I am aware of.

SDG.

HUNTER'S MOON

The Wolves of Wellsboro, Book 1

Sarah M. Awa

Thinklings

Thinklings Books, LLC
Wickliffe, OH

Contents

Prologue

His breath came in great ragged gasps as he half-ran, half-stumbled through the forest, desperate to get to the cave in time. He cursed the underbrush that grabbed at his feet, tripping him. *I'm getting too old for this.*

He was almost out of time; the sun had already set. He was late tonight. A series of trivial annoyances had delayed him, and he'd been unable to escape to the national forest until the sun was brushing the tree-lined Pennsylvania horizon.

Where is that blasted cave? he thought frantically, eyes darting every which way, searching for the large outcropping of rocks. He should have reached the spot by now.

His aching sides and heaving chest felt about to collapse, and not only from running: The first small, tingling waves of pain had begun. The all-too-familiar sensation spurred him to even greater speed, practically blinding him with panic.

If he couldn't reach the cave in time, at least he could lose himself deep within this forest, as far away from human beings and their cozy little campsites as he could manage.

Although maybe they'd have the decency to shoot me, he thought bitterly. *It would be just payment—fair recompense for what I owe.*

He pressed on through the woods, past countless blurs of trees. How much farther could he run?

There—up ahead! The rock formation. He crashed through the final yards of underbrush and into inky blackness.

Water dripped from stalactites, echoing eerily around him. Loose pebbles rolled under his feet. Every twenty yards or so, a shaft of dim light filtered down from a hole in the roof, allowing him to see shelf

1

mushrooms and the vague forms of naturally carved stone.

His legs buckled, and he pitched forward onto hard, damp stone. Was he far enough? Would the monster be able to find its way out of the cavern?

Tump, tump. His head jerked up, and his muscles tensed at the distant footsteps.

Tump, tump, tump, the footfalls continued, louder and louder, nearer and nearer. *No!* he cried inside his mind, even as pain seized him in its iron grip. *Stop! Stay away!*

But he knew, deep down, that it was already too late.

1

Pine Groves

Somewhere beyond the dense tangle of treetops, the sun was sinking—soon it would crouch behind the Appalachian foothills. Although full darkness hadn't yet descended, the forest gloom was deceptive. It wasn't quite seven o'clock.

For the moment, Pam's cheerful chatter kept Mel's nervousness at bay. "Hey, did you hear that a bunch of guys from Van Zeelen Hall are here this weekend too?" Her gray eyes brightened, and a touch of excitement curved her lips.

"No." Frowning, Melanie Caldwell tried to recall which of their classmates lived in that dorm.

"Seriously, Mel? You work for the school paper. You're supposed to know about everything that goes on at good ol' Wellsboro U. What happened to those English-major psychic powers you were talking about the other day?"

Melanie smirked. "Doesn't mean I read the entire paper."

"Oh yeah, you prefer those Agatha Christie novels."

Mel hoped she didn't find any Christie-style bodies out in these woods. *That'd make it a memorable camping trip.* She sneaked a glance around but saw only foliage.

The cool scent of pine rode the breeze, and the crickets' chorus was in full swing. Occasionally, an owl hooted high above. The narrow trail the girls followed wound between towering oaks, copses of younger birches, and scattered evergreens. The pathway branched off in many places, leading who knew where. Mel and Pam had no clue where the main trail was headed, either, but at every crossroads they made sure to score a deep arrow mark in the dirt.

"Which floor?" Mel asked suddenly.

3

"What?"

"Of Van Zeelen. Is it guys from a certain hallway?"

"I heard second floor, south wing." Pam Grazziano's smile faded, then returned. "But maybe some from first floor too?"

Raising an eyebrow, Mel said innocently, "Perhaps a certain Mr. Aaron Gates?"

Pam's blush was barely noticeable in the darkness. "Hey, what about Luis Vargas?" she countered—and heat crept into Mel's own cheeks. "He seems to have a thing for you."

"We just work together."

"Yeah, sure . . . 'tutoring.'" Pam made air quotes with her free hand and winked. "I envy you—getting paid to flirt."

Mel slapped her playfully on the arm, and Pam broke into a fit of giggles. At the glint in Mel's eye, though, she raised her hands in surrender. "All right, all right, don't shoot."

Mel grinned up at the taller girl. "You sure gave up quickly. I must be quite intimidating."

"A terror to behold."

Their laughter echoed between the trees, but conversation dwindled as they ventured deeper into the forest's gnarled heart. Silence pressed thickly around them, almost a palpable presence.

The darkness was complete now, outside the flashlight beams. Every so often a bush beside the girls rustled, and one or both of them jumped. "It's only the wind," Mel said, trying to keep her voice steady.

"Yep. Wind," Pam echoed with a weak smile.

Don't let your imagination take over, Melanie warned herself. *No bears, wolves, or bobcats are going to jump out at you.* If she gave in to it, she knew that she would find herself running back down the trail.

Why'd we dare ourselves to do this again? We should've stayed in camp and roasted marshmallows.

The breeze was picking up; soon, strong gusts howled around the girls. The trees shivered and dropped dead leaves that crunched under their feet. Mel thought she felt a drop of rain. Thick gray clouds had converged, covering the sky, and the low rumble of distant thunder rushed over the forest.

"There wasn't a storm in the forecast," Mel said.

"We'd better get back to camp." Pam looked skyward. "Please don't rain till we're in the tent." Reflexively, she ran a hand through her short light-brown hair.

Mel hid a grin. She was still surprised that stylish, sophisticated Pam had wanted to come here to Pine Groves. Neither of the pair was very outdoorsy, and Pam usually spent even weekend days in the music building, practicing.

As the girls hurried along, their ears picked up another sound: the opening strains of Vivaldi's *Spring*, the gloriously tinny version serving as Pam's ringtone.

Pam slowed down and scrambled to pull the phone out of her pocket. "Hello?" she said breathlessly, giving Mel an apologetic look.

Melanie stifled a sigh and matched her friend's slower pace while Pam chatted away. Finally, Pam informed her caller that she was out camping with a friend but, "You can call back tomorrow night if you want. Uh-huh. Okay, that sounds great. Talk to you then. 'Bye."

"Important business?" asked Mel as Pam stashed her phone.

Pam shrugged. "Nah, it was just some guy I went to high school with. Sorry about that. Gosh, I haven't talked to Bryce in ages."

"Ah," said Melanie with a nod. She was used to it by now, since she'd roomed with Pam since sophomore year, but at first she'd been astonished at how many phone calls like that her friend received. Pam's social network reminded Mel of the kudzu vines rapidly taking over the Southern United States.

The call also reminded her that she'd brought her own cell phone along, just because it felt weird not to have it. Mel couldn't imagine anyone calling her this weekend, but she decided to check for messages anyway.

She felt for it in her jacket pocket. Then her other jacket pocket. Then the back pockets of her shorts. Then the front pockets. Then the jacket pockets again, just in case she'd missed it the first time.

"Crap," she said, halting in her tracks. "My phone's gone."

"What? Are you sure you brought it?"

"Yes, I'm positive. I remember sticking it in my jacket after lunch. I must have dropped it somewhere out here.... Wait, do you think I could've dropped it in the cave?" Their afternoon spelunking excursion had been mostly fun, except for one snafu. Mel's knees still smarted from when she'd skinned them.

"I guess so." Pam shook her head. "Man, we are not having good luck on this trip."

"And it's about to rain. What if I dropped it outside, somewhere on the trail? I can't leave it out here overnight. It'll get totally ruined—soaked, stepped on, or stolen."

Pam bit her lip. "We'll have to look for it."

"I'm sorry, Pam," Mel said ruefully. "It's getting late, and we need to get back, but I don't want to leave my phone out here."

"I understand; I'd be worried sick about mine. Okay, I'll keep calling your phone. You listen for your ring."

Melanie followed her roommate back the way they'd come; they weren't far from the cave. Pam kept dialing Mel's number, and they listened and listened.

An electric tingle filled the air, heralding the coming storm. The atmosphere set Melanie's nerves on edge and addled her brain. Mugginess clung to her skin, and she longed to be somewhere warm, dry, safe, and familiar.

They had almost reached the entrance to the cave when they heard something, but it wasn't a phone ringing. Footsteps crunched toward them.

Who else was out here this late? The girls shone their flashlights in the direction of the sound.

Soon a figure appeared—a short and stocky figure that looked more and more familiar as it came closer. *Oh, dear God, no!*

Their classmate Timmy Simmons stood there, blinking at them like a possum caught in headlights and pushing his glasses farther up his pimply pug nose.

"What are *you* doing here?" Pam said in a suspicious tone.

Groaning inwardly, Mel thought, *Of all the people.* All *the guys from Van Zeelen it could have been. It had to be* him.

"Nice to see you, too, Pat, and Melody." Sarcasm and sweat oozed from Timmy's pores.

"It's *Pam* and *Melanie*," retorted the tall girl, bristling.

Timmy waved a hand dismissively, and the haughty look remained as he said, "Yeah, whatever. And why shouldn't I be here? What are you two doing here?"

"We happen to be camping, obviously," Pam shot back. "And I

realize that's what you're doing too, but why aren't you with the rest of the guys? Playing hide-and-go-seek?"

"No." He sniffed. "That game's for kids. We're playing our own version of *The Hunger Games*."

Which, if I recall, was also played by kids. Biting back the comment, Mel said, "Sounds like fun. Now, if you'll excuse us, we have a lost phone to hunt down."

But as she and Pam made to move around Timmy, he followed.

"Is there something else you wanted to say?" snapped Pam.

He shifted his feet and ran a hand through his mousy-brown mullet, but somehow he managed to keep the arrogance on his face as he said, "I thought you might need some, uh, help with finding your phone. I'm very good at finding things."

Melanie forcibly restrained herself from snorting in disbelief. *The only things he's good at finding are the best ways to tick me off.* Like hovering over her shoulder when she was proofreading articles and "correcting" her incorrectly. "I think we can manage by ourselves, thanks. Pam's been calling it so we can listen for the ringtone."

"Yeah, and I'll try again now," her roommate said, making a show for Timmy of speed-dialing Mel's number for the umpteenth time.

Timmy ignored his cue. Instead, he gestured toward the cave mouth. "Do you think it could be in there? Did you go exploring?"

"As a matter of fact, we did," Mel said, "but as you can see, that sign says the cave is off limits after dark." She pointed her flashlight beam at it.

"So what? No one's going to know if you go in there now—I don't see any guards standing around. . . . Oh, wait, I get it: You're just scared because it's a dark, spooky cave, aren't you?" Timmy laughed. "Typical girls."

"Hey, if you want to get in trouble, be my guest," Melanie shot back. Her temper was slowly heating up; if she'd had hackles and fangs, they would have been raised and bared by now.

Since she did not, Timmy pressed on, clueless, boasting that *he* wouldn't be afraid to go into the cave at night. "If I had a flashlight. It'd be plain stupid to go in without one, of course, 'cause you'd get lost. Although I'm sure that if I somehow managed to find myself in that situation, I could find my way out pretty easily, since I've got such an excellent sense of direction."

"Then why don't you find your way back to your own group and leave us alone?" Pam said through gritted teeth.

Timmy fidgeted and glanced around in several directions. "I—I was going to," he said, "but I thought it would be fun to, uh, let them worry about me for a little longer. Play a bit of a joke on them. Ha, ha. . . ."

He's definitely lost out here, Mel thought with a sigh. *No flashlight, abandoned by his friends (or so-called "friends"), and he's got to be scared, even if he won't admit it. We can't leave him here like this.* She didn't want to have to bring him back to her campsite, but if he wasn't sure how to get back to his, then what else could she do? She had no idea where the guys were staying.

"Look, Timmy," she said, "I know that you're lost, and you might as well admit it. You need us to help you get out of here, and we will. We have a map back at our site, and if you remember the number of the site you're staying at, I can drive you there."

Before Timmy could reply, another rumble of thunder split the air, louder this time, and raindrops splattered down. The trees were growing more and more agitated by the wind; the older ones creaked and moaned.

"Weather's starting to get bad," said Pam, shivering. She zipped up the front of her hoodie.

"All right, all right, so I am a little . . . disoriented," Timmy admitted. "The guys must have swiped my flashlight as a prank or something. If I just had that—"

"Yeah, sure, whatever." *I've heard enough of your lame excuses,* thought Mel. Glancing up at the sky again, she frowned at the thick cloud cover and was rewarded with a fat raindrop splattering into her eye. "Ow!" she said, rubbing it.

"It's going to start pouring at any moment," Pam said. "And I, for one, would prefer not to have to hike back to our tent in the rain. Why don't we duck inside the cave for a while and see if the storm passes? We can stay in the entrance."

Melanie frowned again. She wasn't too fond of the prospect, but neither was she keen on trudging a very long way through cold rain and mud. "Okay," she said as more droplets splashed onto her head. She led the way into the cave.

2

The Beast

They ended up staying in the cave much longer than they'd expected. As Pam had guessed, buckets of rain began to fall soon after they'd sought shelter. A quarter hour passed, and the trio grew restless enough to consider exploring the cave a bit further.

"We do have flashlights," Pam said, "and I didn't see any cameras earlier. We should be all right. Your phone could be in here somewhere, Mel. I'm going to try calling it again."

She did so as they delved into the cavern's depths. They trudged for quite a while without hearing a sound other than their own whispery footfalls and the *drip-drip* of rain through the occasional crack in the ceiling. Melanie checked the ceiling for bats but didn't see any. She wasn't about to admit that the gloomy cave did spook her, like Timmy had taunted. As long as she had companions—undesirable though one of them was—she felt reasonably safe.

They followed the red arrows on the walls, the girls scanning every inch of the ground for Melanie's phone. Timmy glanced around in a preoccupied manner, and sometimes he winced at shifting shadows. *Ha—he's guilty of his own accusation,* Melanie thought. *But at least he's not running his mouth, for once.* A frightened Timmy was apparently a quiet Timmy.

Half an hour went by, and they didn't see or hear any traces of the lost phone. "Did we come this far earlier?" Pam asked as they entered an enormous, open cavern with tunnels forking off in several directions.

"Yes, I remember this room—the beehive," Melanie replied. "And I believe we went ... that way." She pointed at the tunnel directly opposite.

"We might as well go look," Pam said. "I'll dial your number again."

The tunnel they'd chosen had a low ceiling, low enough that Pam had to duck her head. The ground was uneven, and each of them stumbled once or twice. The passageway grew narrower and narrower as they trekked along, but eventually it opened to form a room, rough but uncluttered by stalagmites. The only other exit was a tunnel in the wall through which a fairly thin person might crawl.

Opposite the crawlspace was a niche in which someone had stashed a pile of clothing: shoes, socks, even a belt.

"Okay, that's weird," Pam said. "Either there's a streaking hermit who lives in here, or—"

"Hey, look, it's my phone!" said Melanie, shining her flashlight into the waist-high crawlspace. A small silver object glinted at the far end, near where the crawlspace joined another room.

She wormed her way into the tunnel. The others turned to watch her, Pam aiming her light at Mel's retreating feet.

"You okay getting it?" Pam said.

"Yeah," Mel called back.

After crawling a dozen claustrophobic feet, she grabbed the phone. Sure enough, it was hers—the screen bore an image of Pam and Melanie making goofy faces in front of their dorm, Hartman Cottage. Mel grinned with relief and began to scoot backward.

Timmy better not be staring at my butt, she thought. "Ow!" she cried as her knee scraped a sharp rock. She hoped her cuts hadn't started bleeding again.

"You all right in there, Mel?" Pam called. "You got your phone?"

"Yes and yes. I bumped my knee; that's all."

Maybe I should climb out of this end and turn around so I can see where I'm going, Melanie thought. She scooted forward once more and was about to drop into the large cavern beyond when a low, throaty growl froze her in place.

What the—?

They appeared, at the far end of the dark cavern: two glowing yellow circles with deepest black at their centers.

The fiery eyes swiveled and fixed straight on her.

Sweat broke out on Melanie's forehead. Fingers of dread traced a glissando down her spine. A scream caught in her dry throat.

The eyes narrowed, and an earsplitting howl echoed through the cavern. The creature advanced, its bulk emerging from the shadows and into her flashlight beam: a huge canine form. Its hackles were raised, and its fur stood on end. The skin of its muzzle bunched above its nose as its lips peeled back, revealing gleaming white fangs dripping drool.

She scrambled backward, ignoring the pain of her knees scraping against rock. *Please don't let it fit in here!*

The beast bounded across the cavern, massive paws propelling it with astounding speed. Snarling and foaming with rage, it lunged at the narrow tunnel opening. Its head and front paws surged inside, and it wriggled and writhed, trying to squeeze its shoulders in. Its slavering jaws snapped wildly.

Then it suddenly stopped thrashing. Its furious, eerie golden eyes caught Melanie's wide brown ones.

She tried but failed to tear her gaze away from the beast's. Those ghastly, hypnotic orbs stared *into* her. Her muscles slackened, and her breath caught.

A sharp, searing pain shot through her hand, and consciousness returned to her, sending her backward once more.

"What's going on in there, Mel?" Pam screamed. "What's happening?!"

Fierce growls, frightened whimpers, and scraping sounds emanated from the crawlspace. Startled, Pam dashed to the edge of the tunnel and shined her flashlight in. Feet and legs motored toward her. A moment later, Pam caught Melanie as she fell.

Mel trembled violently, eyes stretched wide with terror, nostrils flared. Tears streamed down her cheeks; blood coated her knees and palms. "Run!" she croaked.

Timmy yelped and took off. Mel grabbed Pam's hand, and the girls dashed after him.

Pam threw a glance over her shoulder and saw two yellowish points of light gleaming in the dark tunnel. The hairs on the back of her neck prickled. "What the—hell is—that thing?"

Her friend was sobbing too hard to reply.

"Is it following us?" Timmy squeaked.

"It will be, as soon as it gets out of that hole!" Pam swerved sharply to avoid the stalagmites in her path.

A minute later they arrived back at the enormous "beehive" cavern.

They dashed straight across it, into the passageway by which they'd entered. Pam kept listening for signs of pursuit. The animal's growls had died away, but Pam held no hope that the beast would give up. She figured it could track them by scent, and Melanie was bleeding.

Thinking of bleeding ... "Did it hurt you?" she asked her roommate. "Did it bite you anywhere?"

"I—I don't know," said Mel. "It all—happened so fast. ..." She sounded like she was growing tired already.

How much longer can we keep going? Pam wondered. What if the beast caught up to them? *Just keep running. Just keep running.*

They pressed on, dodging between rock formations and keeping watch for the red arrows that pointed the way out. After what seemed like an eternity, they heard the pattering of rain. *Almost there!* The ground's uphill slant leveled out, and suddenly the cave mouth yawned before them.

They burst out into the rain, now only a light drizzle. Timmy took an abrupt spill in the slick mud, landing hard on his rear end.

The girls stopped running and tried to help him, but he slapped away their hands. "I can get up by myself!" he snapped.

"Who's there?" called a voice from the surrounding darkness.

Pam nearly jumped out of her skin. Melanie let out a small shriek, and Timmy whimpered. A man wielding a long-barreled gun stepped into view from behind a tree.

"Sir! You've got to help us!" said Pam, thinking he was a park ranger although he wasn't wearing a uniform. "There's a, a monster in there, and it's coming after us!"

The man's eyes widened. "Is it huge, with glowing yellow eyes?"

"Yeah. How did you kn—?"

"Get out of here *now!*"

He believes us! "Aren't you going to run, too?"

The man raised his gun, aiming it at the cave mouth. "No. I will deal with the beast. That's why I'm here."

He acts like he knows all about it! thought Pam, astonished.

"Wait a second," said the gunman, holding up a hand. "Before you leave, tell me: Did it bite any of you?" His voice was grave, and he scrutinized each of them from head to toe. His eyes lingered on Melanie's knee abrasions and blood smears.

As she turned to give Melanie a questioning glance, Pam saw that there was quite a bit of blood on her roommate's left hand. But Mel shook her head. "W-why?" she asked. "Does it have rabies or something?"

Before the gunman could say or do anything else, an enraged howl echoed from inside the cave. The girls jumped, Timmy yelped, and the stranger tensed. "All right," he said, "you kids get out of here and leave the beast to me. I've been tracking it, and I know how to bring it down. Go!"

They followed his orders without hesitation. As they tore off down the trail, they heard the gunman call after them: "If you can't find your way out of the forest, climb a tree! It can't follow you. You'll be safe after sunrise."

The trio ran farther and farther, slipping in muddy patches and praying that they were going the right way each time they reached a fork. Rain had washed away the girls' marks.

Pam's legs and lungs screamed at her, but she wouldn't stop. She couldn't. Even though a man with a gun now stood between her group and the monstrous creature, she didn't dare let down her guard. She didn't want to tempt fate.

Beside Pam, Melanie lurched and pitched forward, barely catching her balance by grabbing hold of the nearest tree trunk. Timmy, a few paces behind, almost slammed into the girls. He cursed. "C'mon, we gotta keep going!"

Ignoring him, Pam reached out and grabbed her best friend's arm to help support her. "Are you okay, Mel?"

The smaller girl nodded, but her panting and wheezing and the way she leaned heavily on Pam told a different story.

"Are you sure?" Pam shone her flashlight next to—not in— Melanie's face and saw that there were dark circles under her eyes. "Maybe we should stop and rest."

"No! We can't! We have to get out of these woods!" Timmy insisted. He stomped a foot in impatience, eyes darting around in fear.

Melanie groaned and swayed. Pam steadied her and frowned at Timmy. "Help me out, then," she said, hoisting Mel's left arm over her shoulders. Timmy grumbled but slung Mel's right arm across his shoulders.

The trio hobbled along, their height differences increasing the discomfort of their strange six-legged race. Pam's back ached from hunching at an awkward angle. Mel stumbled, and her feet dragged in the mud. Her slack wrenched Pam's right side further downward, pinching her shoulder blade. Pam screwed up her face, bit her lip, and bore the pain.

Just when she thought she'd have to switch sides with Timmy or risk dropping her friend, Mel's knees buckled.

"Hey!" Timmy protested as her weight dragged him down. He let her go and jumped back to avoid falling himself.

Mel slid out of Pam's grasp and sprawled, unconscious, on the muddy path.

"Why'd you do that?!" Pam screamed at Timmy.

"Why d'you think?" he shot back.

Pam dropped down next to Melanie and shook her awake. Hoisting her up again, she said, "C'mon, dear, we have to keep moving. We're still in danger."

With a small moan, Mel stood, legs trembling like the strings of a plucked cello. She staggered and clutched at Pam. "Just leave me here," she rasped.

"You really *are* out of it!" Pam retorted, feeling Mel's forehead— which was burning up.

Timmy kicked at a bush and cursed.

Pam sighed. She felt his urgency. What if the beast got past the gunman? She hadn't heard any howls or gunshots, though. *Melanie's in no shape to keep going, and I don't want to worsen her condition. If only I could carry her!*

"Here, Mel, why don't you sit down against this tree?" she said at last. She helped her friend to the ground. "I don't hear that thing coming. We may be in the clear."

"Are you crazy?" said Timmy. "It could be stealth-tracking us, moving silently like a ninja. It could be seconds away from pouncing!"

What a drama queen, thought Pam. She was about to retort that the creature hadn't demonstrated that it was the epitome of subtlety, but Melanie spoke first.

"I'm sorry, guys." Her voice was a soft moan.

"Don't be," said Pam. "It's not your fault."

Timmy growled and paced around until Pam thought he was going to carve a rut into the dirt trail. "Here," she said when she couldn't stand watching him anymore, "take my flashlight." She thrust it at him.

"Go on—find your own way out of the woods."

He took it but didn't move. "I, uh . . . well, the trail just . . . goes in too many directions. I don't know if I can . . ."

Pam remembered that he'd been very lost when she and Mel had run into him at the cave mouth. *Oh, great,* she thought. *There's no way he can make it back by himself. We're stuck with him.*

Then her ears caught Melanie's quiet suggestion: "Why don't we try to climb a tree? Remember what that hunter guy told us?"

"Oh yeah," said Pam. "Good thinking, Mel. Are you feeling okay enough to do it?"

Her roommate nodded.

Pam retrieved her light from Timmy and started inspecting the forest around them. "Let's see, which one of these trees would be easiest to climb?"

Half of the trees here were evergreens with skinny branches, sticky sap, and prickly needles; she eschewed those as poor options. Among the deciduous trees, many were too young and frail. She walked farther and finally spotted a sprawling oak a dozen yards off the trail. Its thick branches looked sturdy and reached low enough for the trio to catch. "I found a good one," Pam said, returning and helping Melanie to her feet.

Timmy grumbled about the plan, but he scrambled up first and climbed the highest. Pam gave Mel a boost and then followed her up.

Please, please let us be safe now, Pam thought as she hugged one of the oak's broad limbs and forced herself not to look down. They'd climbed frighteningly high.

As the night wore on, she listened for gunshots, howls, or human screams, but none of those echoed through the silent forest. Eventually the light drizzle of rain petered out, to her relief. She'd been shivering in her damp clothes since they'd escaped the cave, and she prayed that she and the others wouldn't catch pneumonia.

A few branches above Pam, Melanie Caldwell alternated between shivering and roasting; a high fever held her in its grip. The world blurred and swam in front of her eyes, and she clung to her perch as tightly as she could, fearing that she'd become dizzy and fall.

Melanie's left hand throbbed in time with her heart, needles of pain shooting through her arm whenever she moved it or for no reason at all. Her fingers were half numb, half tingling. During the flight to safety, she'd been so panic-stricken that she'd barely noticed the pain. But now that they were resting here, her hurting hand hollered for attention.

She lifted it toward her eyes, squinted, and shook her head to try and clear away the mental haze. It dispersed a bit, and she noticed a torn spot along her hand's outer edge, halfway between her pinky finger and wrist. Blood seeped from the wound despite its diminutive size.

Why did it hurt, while the abrasions on her palms no longer did?

Mel examined the wound more closely. It was triangular and rather deep—a puncture mark. Something had pierced the skin, something thinner and more knifelike than the rocks in the cave. There was a whitish substance crusted around the edges of the mysterious wound.

What ... what happened back there? She struggled to recall the terrifying moments after the beast had appeared.

Images flashed through her mental fog: hypnotic, hellish eyes—a low, menacing growl—the beast lunging at her—bone-white fangs gleaming—

Stop, stop! Tremors of fear racked her all over again, and her gut heaved and threatened. Melanie clung to the tree and fought to calm her body and mind. *Deep breaths. In and out. In and out.*

The controlled breathing slowly relaxed her. Then the haze began to creep back across her consciousness, lulling her into drowsy tranquility. *No—stay awake,* she told herself. *Think of where you are.*

But tendrils of mist kept reaching out to her; the fog roiled and gathered strength. It sapped her resistance and tugged her toward oblivion.

The clouds above trundled eastward, pushed along by a strong wind. They broke rank and tore where the cloud cover had been stretched thinnest. The moon leered down, round and full, a great eye searching through the foliage, searching for *her*. ...

Her eyes drooped, and she slumped back against the trunk of the oak.

3

Complications

He resurfaced into consciousness in the usual manner, post-transformation: trembling with fear, exhaustion, and pain. As always, it took several moments before he became fully aware of himself and his surroundings. But this morning, the process of reawakening reached its end much more abruptly when he realized—

He wasn't in the cave anymore. He was in the woods.

Shit. What the hell happened last night?

A groan escaped his lips as he struggled to pull himself up to a seated position. His head swam, and he gulped in deep, steadying breaths. As soon as he was able to focus his eyes, he inspected the area around him for signs of a fight—of a kill.

If he *had* attacked someone last night, there would be trails and puddles of blood close by, with a mangled corpse at the center of the mess. His hellish alter ego liked to stay near its fallen prey, gnawing at and shredding the lifeless body. Unless, of course, there was other prey to bring down.

He shuddered in terrified anticipation. However, as he looked around at the towering, stately pines and scanned the ferny underbrush and the damp forest floor, he could find no signs that anything dangerous had happened here. No splash of red marred the calm greenness.

Before he allowed relief to flood him, he inspected his hands. Splotches of dried mud mingled with plant debris across his palms and under his fingernails. More mud and pine needles clung to the rest of his pale, naked body, along with a fleeing spider ... but there was no blood. Nor was anything crusted around his mouth except the usual saliva.

17

Maybe . . . maybe nothing bad had happened.

But it still wasn't good that he'd escaped from those caverns.

Erickson, you idiot, he berated himself. *How did the wolf get out of there? You squeezed through spots it was too big to get through.*

He had figured out that his wolfish form was bigger when, years ago, he'd awoken post-transformation to find himself stretched through a hole in a sturdy chain-link fence, his back and shoulders striped with lacerations. The wolf must have been struggling there, but as a human he could crawl through without a scratch.

From that time on, he'd used this knowledge to his advantage. If he couldn't find a safe room with a heavy-duty and lockable door, he transformed in a location from which the monster could not escape due to its size. When he'd moved here, he'd hoped the forest cave would calm the wolf. Until now, it had seemed to be a positive change of scenery.

After climbing carefully to his feet, Erickson stumbled over to the nearest tree and grabbed it for support. Blood whooshed in his ears, and the world spun once more. He waited for the black edges to leave his vision before taking a few steps. This area of woods looked familiar, and he realized he was quite close to the clearing outside the cavern's entrance. Sure enough, he soon reached it—and then halted abruptly.

A man with a gun loitered in front of the cave.

Dammit. Erickson retreated behind a waist-high bush. He didn't relish the idea of confronting a stranger when he only had some mud and pine needles protecting his most vulnerable areas.

A twig snapped under his foot, and the gunman swiveled and met Erickson's startled gaze. "Hello," the man said calmly, as if it were the most natural thing to meet a naked stranger in the forest.

Lips tightly clamped, Erickson studied the man warily. He guessed he was in his mid-thirties. His features were plain, forgettable, his height and build average. He was dressed in jeans and a flannel shirt— not a flak jacket or army fatigues—and didn't strike Erickson as menacing . . . until he looked more closely at the man's eyes. Something burned in them. Determination. Fanaticism, even. This man had a goal, and he was going to do whatever it took to achieve it.

Erickson's first instinct was to turn tail and flee. But before he could, the stranger took a step toward him, held up an open hand, and said, "Please, I mean you no harm. I've been waiting for you but didn't want to scare you when you first woke up. I want to talk to you."

Although the man's weapon had been lowered this whole time, Erickson asked gruffly, "What's with the gun? Aren't those prohibited? And who the hell are you?"

"My name is Gary Saddler," the stranger replied. "And yes, it is illegal to carry firearms here, but they don't search your vehicle thoroughly when you check into the campgrounds. This is only a Pneu-Dart—a tranquilizer—anyway." Making no sudden moves, he propped the long-barreled rifle against a rock.

More questions sprang into Erickson's mind: *What's he doing out here with a thing like that? And how did he know to wait for me here? When, where, and in what state did he first find me? How long ago* was *moonset?* The back of his neck was prickling, but he waited in silence. He'd let this Saddler do the talking for now, and he would choose whether to answer or not.

After a moment Saddler continued, "I'm sorry to say that I had to use my weapon on you last night." A knowing gleam flashed through the man's eyes as he fished two bent darts from his pocket and held them up.

Erickson fought to keep his expression from altering and his knees from buckling. *Shit—he knows.*

Surging with nausea, Erickson struggled to choose his next words carefully. Should he act like he had no idea what Saddler was talking about, tell him he was nuts? Or should he just run away? That probably wouldn't work, given his current state. Every joint and muscle had been raw with pain since he'd regained consciousness, and it was amazing he was still standing.

Saddler shrugged his shoulders and said, "I understand you must be surprised and probably upset right now, Mr. Erickson. Or can I call you Nicholas? I apologize for pouncing on you like this, especially when you are obviously not feeling well."

"What do you want with me?" Erickson snarled. He resented being spied upon, especially when he was in this defenseless state. The fact that he was unclothed didn't bother him as much as the weakness did.

"Just to talk about a few things," said the man called Saddler in what he seemed to believe was a reassuring tone of voice. "I think you will find that I am on your side, sympathetic to your . . . condition."

"Oh, yeah?" Erickson said. "Well, right now my *condition* is that I am tired, pissed off, and would very much like to retrieve my clothes from that cave before it's crawling with campers." He glanced pointedly toward the dark entrance.

Saddler nodded. "I can understand that. Here, take my flashlight. Go ahead, find your stuff and get dressed, and then we can talk. I'd invite you back to my camper, but the wife and kids are with me, and they can't know what I've been up to. In fact"—he glanced at his watch—"I had better get back there soon before they wake up. I'll find a way to ditch them for a while and meet you at your RV."

"You know about my RV?" Erickson said. "How long have you been following me?"

"This is the second month I have observed your visits to the cave. We haven't known about you for much longer than that."

"What do you mean, 'we'? Are there *more* of you gun-toting psycho wolf chasers on my trail?"

A wry grin formed on the gun toter's face. "Not that I know of. I was referring to an organization comprising mostly werewolves—with a few exceptions, such as me. A brotherhood. A pack, you might call it."

Erickson didn't know how many more surprises he could handle in one morning. "Ah, so this is about recruiting new members, then, is it?"

"Correct," said Saddler.

"Well, sorry, but I'm not interested." Free hand assuming the fig-leaf position, Erickson emerged from behind the bush and started to head back into the cave.

Saddler blocked his path, frowning. "Wait a minute," he said. "That was an awfully hasty dismissal. Think about this for a moment: Wouldn't it be an asset to you, and give you a sense of belonging, to gain companions who understand what you have to deal with every full moon? Or, I'm guessing, every day of your life? The guilt, the secrecy—"

"Like I said, not interested. I've been dealing with things perfectly fine for the last fourteen years."

Saddler's eyebrows went up. "Is that how long you've been living like this?"

Erickson shrugged. "Something like that. But I don't see how it's any of your business."

"Just seems like a terribly long time to be cut off and alone."

"Yeah? I've gotten used to it, and I'd prefer to stay a lone wolf than join your wussy Werewolves Anonymous group." He shouldered his way past Saddler and into the cave.

A strange look crept into Saddler's eyes as he watched Erickson's retreating form, which was pale against the dark stone. "You're wrong about us," Saddler called after the other man. "I'll be waiting at your RV to tell you more."

)) ● ((

A mile away, Pam Grazziano groaned in her sleep and suddenly jerked awake. "What the . . . yikes!" She looked down and then clutched at the trunk of the oak, feeling dizzy. The forest floor was still several yards below her.

Crap. We stayed up here all freakin' night! Are the others okay? She turned her gaze upward, saw that Melanie and Timmy rested safely above her, and sighed in relief.

Pam's limbs ached and felt as inflexible as the thick branch on which she perched. At least she'd managed not to plummet to her death!

She hadn't meant to doze off. She'd intended to keep a watchful eye on the ground and to monitor her feverish roommate, who'd passed out soon after they'd climbed up. However, as the hours had crept along and no monsters had prowled beneath their hiding spot, Pam had found it increasingly difficult to keep her eyelids from drooping. She couldn't recall drifting off, but it must have been several hours ago, because the sky had been dark then and was bright now.

"Safe after sunrise" echoed in her memory. *Okay. Time to get down from here and back to camp*—and *to get rid of Timmy.* She wondered if anyone from his group had bothered to search for him. *Ha, doubt they stayed out in that weather for very long.*

Pam shivered. Her damp clothes clung to her, and she felt disgustingly clammy. *I'm going to need about five showers when we get back to the dorm.* She hoped bugs hadn't crawled into her mouth while she'd slept. "Ugh," she said, and squirmed upright.

Now she was almost at Melanie's eye level. She put a gentle hand on her roommate's shoulder, praying she wouldn't startle her too much.

"Hey, Mel. It's morning. Wake up. Careful—we're in a tree, remember?"

Fortunately, Melanie didn't jerk awake like Pam had. She gave a small grunt and muttered something incomprehensible. Her eyelids fluttered and slowly lifted.

Pam gasped. She wobbled and nearly lost her footing.

For a brief moment, Melanie Caldwell's dark brown eyes had shone with an eerie golden light.

)) ● ((

Nick Erickson had plenty of time to mull over Saddler's words while trekking back for his clothing: "You're wrong about us."

This Organization is not some stupid support group?

He shuffled along wearily through room after room and passageway after passageway, grabbing on to the rock formations and walls for support. He was in no hurry. Each minute he spent in here was one minute longer that Saddler had to wait for him. Erickson figured he had no chance of getting out of Pine Groves without the gunman bothering him again. Saddler would surely be at the RV. *That meddling son of a—*

How did he catch me off guard? How does he know about me? How on earth did I end up outside this cave?

He clenched his teeth. *I'll wring some answers out of him. Before I listen to any more crap about the Organization, I'll make him tell me what happened last night, whether I hurt anyone.* Then Saddler could take his turn and blather on about his werewolf club.

What exactly is the group's purpose? Couldn't be as innocent as Friday night bowling and pizza, could it?

Despite Erickson's determination to remain self-reliant, he felt a pull toward this group. He'd never thought too much about the fact that there could be many other werewolves out there, scattered across the country—maybe even living nearby.

Why *hadn't* he given it more thought? Next June would mark a decade and a half since the cursed event that had destroyed his normal human life.

He'd been bitten (had almost lost his right foot) back in 2002 during a hunting trip to Eastern Europe with a couple of his best friends.

Actually, the trip was half business—they'd spent the first several days hammering out contracts with their company's new Romanian clients. Afterward, the three American businessmen had rented a cabin in the rugged Southern Carpathians and donned their wilderness gear, cross-bows and all, for a week of pleasure.

How quickly that pleasure had turned into pain, peril, and perni-cious problems. Sometimes he wished he *hadn't* been able to escape that damned creature. It would have saved other lives, later on, if he'd lost his own then.

Erickson's melancholic musings faded as he stepped into a huge, open cavern that was crisscrossed by many other passageways. This was the room he had come to think of as Grand Central Station. It wouldn't be long before he reached his sartorial stash and regained a bit of his humanity by covering up certain important parts of it.

Crossing to the narrowest of the passages, Erickson ducked his head and entered the roughly formed, low-ceilinged conduit. After staggering a hundred more yards, he reached the room with the tight crawl space from which his wolf form shouldn't have been able to escape.

His outfit from the night before was tucked in the niche where he'd left it. He grabbed the clothes and stuck Saddler's flashlight in the nook. The beam bisected the room and illuminated the crawl space.

Erickson drew in a sharp breath when he noticed a dark reddish-brown substance crusted along the lower edge of its opening. As soon as he was fully dressed, he grabbed the light and went over to examine the stains.

Their taste and smell confirmed what he'd feared: blood. Streaks of it stretched farther back along the floor of the crawl space, nearly to its other end.

Erickson's gut lurched, and his heart pounded. That blood hadn't been here last night. *Is it mine? Please let it be mine.*

It could be his. The wolf had managed to squeeze through here, and most likely it had scraped itself up in the process. There was no evi-dence of abrasions left on Erickson's body—but there wouldn't be, given the rate at which he healed around full moons. Running through rain-soaked underbrush would have washed away the bloodstains.

You didn't find any corpses, remember? Or blood anywhere else.

Relax.

His thoughts returned to Saddler. *He'll know something about what happened. He can tell me if any other people were involved. This can't be his blood, and he might not have even entered the cave. But he could've seen others coming out of it.*

With a sigh, Erickson turned and headed back toward the mouth of the cave. It was time to face his stalker. And Saddler had better give Erickson some concrete, truthful answers.

4

Return

Is this what it's like to be plastered? wondered Melanie Caldwell, who had never been under the influence of anything except a Catholic upbringing and a loving family.

Leaning heavily on Pam's arm, Mel stumbled along the trail that led back to camp. The air oozed around her, and the scenery reeled by in slow motion: Trees bent at odd angles, convex and concave, like in funhouse mirrors.

She closed her eyes for a moment, nauseated. *Please let my head clear up.*

She longed to go back to sleep, but she feared the nightmares. All night, hungry, hypnotic golden eyes had stalked her through shadowy worlds. She'd tried to escape, to wake up, but the nightmares had held her in their grip.

She whimpered at the memory of the eyes—and of the gleaming fangs.

"Are you okay?" asked Pam, halting on the trail. In Melanie's vision, sparks of light flowed around Pam, pulsating and over-focused—but then she blinked, and there was only ordinary sunshine limning her friend.

"Yeah," said Melanie. "Don' worry, 'm fine. Jus' wanna get back."

"What the heck is wrong with her?" whined a voice from behind the girls. "Sounds like my old man getting home late from a bar."

"Shut up!" Pam snapped. "Mind your own business, Timmy."

Timmy? Oh, yeah. Crap, thought Mel. This weekend sucked, big time.

Sucked? No. Getting a bad grade sucked. Tripping and skinning your knee sucked. This weekend had turned into a full-blown carnival of creepy clowns juggling butcher's knives.

At last, the trio reached the edge of the woods and emerged into the grassy outskirts of a cul-de-sac. Most of its campsites were empty. A weathered black-and-tan RV loomed just to the left of the trailhead. Three spaces in the other direction, Mel's rusty Honda waited patiently next to the tent she and Pam should have slept in last night.

"A bit farther," Pam said as she guided Melanie over to the car and propped her against the hood. It felt like a rocking boat. "Can I have your keys?"

Melanie furrowed her brow.

"In your pocket?" her best friend prompted.

"Oh, yeah."

Pam opened the passenger side door and eased Melanie down onto the seat, legs dangling out the side. "I think I'm going to drive today, since you're not in much of a state to—" Pam gasped. "Melanie . . . didn't you have some pretty big scrapes on your knees last night? There's blood there, but it looks like the skin . . . it looks like you never even got hurt!" She knelt for a closer look.

Before Melanie could reply, Timmy came over and said, "Are you two planning on driving me back to my campsite now or what?"

"Yeah, yeah, keep your pants on." Pam huffed. "You haven't told us what site you guys are staying at."

"Uhh, number 78—one of the large group ones."

Reaching over Melanie, Pam pulled their Pine Groves map out of the glove box. She spread the map open on the side of the car, running her finger across the paper. "Here we go. It's on the other side of the park, maybe a five-minute drive away. Go on and get in the car, Timmy."

While he climbed in the back seat, Pam helped Melanie swing her legs inside the Honda. "We going home soon?" Mel asked, flopping back. She struggled to keep her eyes open and focused.

"Right after we drop Timmy off." With a frown, Pam placed a hand on Melanie's forehead. "You're burning up, sweetie. I should take you to the nurse's office when we get back to campus. You know what? I'm going to tear down the tent and pack up the car so we can leave straight from the guys' campsite."

"Oh, great. How long is that going to take?" Timmy griped.

"It'll go quicker if you help me."

He climbed back out of the car, grumbling.

Melanie started to drift off while she waited for Pam and Timmy to disassemble the camp. After a few minutes, she opened her eyes to see if they were almost finished. That was when she noticed that two other people had joined them.

Mel immediately recognized one of the newcomers, a young man with short-cropped dark hair and a build like a basketball player's—tall and lanky, yet muscled. *Luis is here. Wait—why is he so wet and muddy?*

She squinted at the man standing next to Luis and realized he was the gunman from last night (now *sans* weapon). *Strange,* she thought, but fell back into a doze before she could think much more.

A knock on her window startled her awake. "Hey, Melanie. How are you feeling?"

Hmm? Oh. She gave Luis as much of a smile as she could muster. He pulled her door open and knelt in the gravel beside the car. "Been better," she answered, finding it strange to be looking down into his eyes instead of up.

"Pam told me you were getting sick." The concern in his voice was clear. "I hope it's nothing serious, like pneumonia."

"Me too."

"I heard you guys were stuck in the woods overnight."

Mel nodded.

"That sucks. So was I. Not stuck, I mean—just out looking. Anyway. It was really cold and wet."

"You stayed out *all night* looking for *Timmy*?"

He shrugged sheepishly. "Yep."

Wow. That was sure nice of him. And crazy.

"You're gonna go see the nurse when you get back, right?" he asked.

"Yeah."

"Good. Hope you get well soon." He hesitated and then gave her a pat on the arm before looking away and blushing.

Melanie's cheeks felt hot too, but that might have been from the fever. "Thanks," she said, feeling comforted and awkward at the same time.

A moment later she heard the trunk spring open. There were a few small *thumps* as someone tossed gear into it, and then the trunk slammed shut. Luis stood up, gently closed Mel's door, and climbed into the seat behind her. Pam and Timmy also piled into the car. "Ready at last," said Pam with a sigh.

She drove them across the park and dropped off the two guys. Timmy left without saying a word, but Luis thanked the girls and waved goodbye, flashing Mel a kind smile.

Melanie slept during most of the ride back to Wellsboro University. Before she knew it, Pam was leading her through the door to the health center and signing her in. Then they were in the exam room and the nurse was sticking a thermometer under her tongue, squeezing her arm too tightly with the blood pressure cuff, and shining a stupid light into her eyes and throat.

Mel endured the exam, but she longed for her bed and for unconsciousness. She answered the nurse's questions without paying too much attention—until the woman grabbed her left hand to get a better look at the wound, which still burned mildly.

"Did something try to bite you?" the nurse asked. "It looks like an animal's fang nicked you. It's red and might be infected."

Mel fidgeted, stared at the floor, and muttered, "Big raccoon was hiding in the trash." To her relief, Pam didn't call her out on the lie.

"You need to get vaccinated for rabies," said the nurse, pulling out a disinfectant swab to clean the wound. It stung, and Mel flinched. "I assume you haven't been already?"

Actually, Mel had—in high school, she'd volunteered at an animal shelter to round out her college application . . . although she almost hadn't done it because of her fear of needles. She explained to the nurse, who smiled. "Excellent. Then you'll only need the three boosters instead of ten."

Ten?! Mel had never been so grateful in all her life for the initial shot.

"I can't give you those here," the nurse was saying, "so I'm going to send you to the emergency room in town. I'll call them and let them know you're coming."

Groaning inwardly, Melanie thought, *How much longer till I can get back to sleep?* But she complied, and Pam drove her into town.

The hospital wasn't far from the university, and an ER nurse ushered the girls back to a room right away. Melanie cringed at the sight of the needle and shed a few tears during the administration of the vaccine—straight into the wound, which made its throbbing intensify. She endured a more thorough examination than at the school health center. Pam sat near her patiently and quietly, murmuring words of support and helping answer questions (based on Mel's raccoon story).

"Typically, we'd keep you overnight for observation," said the ER nurse. "But since you were inoculated five years ago, you should still have plenty of those antibodies in your system. They can last up to ten years. Plus, your fever is low, it's been more than half a day, and there's no sign of spreading infection, so I feel justified in releasing you. But come back immediately if you experience any of these symptoms." She handed Melanie printed instructions on post-visit care and when to come back for her other two shots. Finally, after three hours, the ordeal was over, and Mel and Pam headed back to campus.

When they reached their dorm, Hartman Cottage, Pam pulled the Honda right up to the front door. "I'll help you inside before I go and park," she told Melanie.

"Thanks, but I'm fine," said Mel. "I can walk by myself." She already felt like a big baby for crying at the hospital.

"You sure?" said Pam. "Well, at least let me unlock the house. Wait a minute till I get the door open, 'kay?"

Melanie nodded and waited. Then she stepped shakily out of the car and tottered through Hartman's front door. She made it all the way across the living room to the foot of the stairs before plopping down on the third step from the bottom.

"Getting upstairs might be a challenge," she admitted.

Pam smiled. "Let me park the car between some yellow lines so we don't get a ticket, and I'll help you up."

)) ● ((

It was nearly pitch black in the room when Melanie woke again, disoriented. But then her head cleared and she realized that the weird, drugged sensation from earlier had gone away. *Thank goodness.*

Slowly she sat up and reached for her alarm clock, its crimson glow the only source of light around. The large red digits informed her it was just after 2:00 a.m.

Grumbling quietly about losing her whole Sunday, Melanie got up. Careful experimentation showed her she could walk steadily across the floor. Pam's deep, even breathing continued undisturbed as she tiptoed past her roommate's bed.

Mel eased the door open and stepped out into the hallway, where emergency lights cast a soft glow. She made her way to the dingy white bathroom she and Pam shared with their suitemates.

Have I always been this pale? she wondered, gazing into the mirror. The sprinkling of freckles across her cheekbones stood out more than ever, but otherwise, she looked the same.

Then her stomach growled. *Holy crap, I haven't eaten anything in over twenty-four hours! ... Shouldn't I feel weaker and shakier than this?* Where her strength was coming from, she didn't know, but thoughts of food overwhelmed this curiosity. She padded downstairs to the kitchen, hoping to find something left in the fridge with her name on it.

A girl with long, curly black hair sat at the kitchen table. Books and papers covered half the table in front of her, and she was poring over a thick textbook by candlelight.

Melanie was unsurprised to find this particular housemate of hers awake so late into the night. "Trying to conserve electricity, Jos?" she asked her friend, gesturing at the assortment of votives and tapers.

Jocelyn Beaumont grinned and looked up, catlike green eyes glimmering. "I find this kind of light to be soothing and conducive to studying."

"Well, I suppose it's fine for eating, too," said Melanie with a shrug. She walked over to the fridge and perused its contents. A large red-and-yellow apple was perched atop a blueberry bagel on the middle shelf, with a note in Pam's handwriting tucked under them. "Mel—I swiped these from the cafeteria in case you woke up starving. Love, P."

A smile stretched across Melanie's face; the bagel was her favorite kind, and the apple looked like a honeycrisp—another favorite. She grabbed the food and a bottle of water and settled into a chair opposite Jocelyn.

Her suitemate watched her as she chowed down. "When was the last time you ate, girl?" Jos asked. Melanie mimed her mouth being full, so Jos continued, "Pam told me a little about your trip. Can't say I regret not tagging along. Were you guys really up in a tree the whole night, or is she just being dramatic as usual?"

Melanie winced and reflexively swallowed a large hunk of bagel. Too soon. It stuck in her throat, and she coughed and struggled to get it down.

"Careful," said Jocelyn, her eyebrows going up in alarm. She started to rise from her seat. "You okay, Mel?"

"Yeah," Melanie said when she was able to speak again. She finished the rest of her food more slowly while Jos tried to pry details out of her about the Pine Groves excursion. Jocelyn's shrewd gaze unsettled Melanie, and thoughts of the dark cave and the wolfish monster worsened her discomfort. She refused to divulge much information.

At last Jocelyn said, "All right, if you won't tell me, then I'll have to ask: Is it true that you guys got chased by some kind of wild animal?"

Melanie sucked in a sharp breath. Fortunately, no food was in her mouth this time, but it felt like something else had caught in her throat—a lump of anxiety and fear. *Pam! Why would you tell anyone about that?!* She squirmed in her chair and couldn't meet Jocelyn's eyes. Instead, she looked down at her hands in her lap and traced around the puncture mark on her left hand with her right index finger. The wound remained raw and tender.

Then her knees caught her attention. Feeling a strange flutter in her stomach, she remembered that she had scraped them badly in the narrow tunnel. How had the abrasions healed so freakishly quickly? Even Pam had noticed. And if she'd suddenly developed super healing powers, then why hadn't the tooth mark healed also?

Jocelyn's soft, smooth voice cut through her thoughts. "Sorry for asking about that, Mel. I can see it bothers you. You don't have to talk about it if you don't want to."

Melanie looked up at her friend once more and nodded, then stood up from the table. Throwing her empty bottle into the recycle bin, she said, "I'm dying for a shower, and I should get back to sleep since I have an early class." She also longed to brush her teeth and change into pajamas—she still wore Saturday's jean shorts and t-shirt. *Ugh, I'm a mess.* "G'night, Jos."

"G'night."

꜀ ꜀ ◉ ꜀ ꜀

The following day after lunch, Melanie arrived at her European history class early. The lecture hall was already half filled; about eighty students sat or stood, heads buried in books, pizza slices flopping in their hands, or feet up as they swapped lies about finishing the reading assignment. Pam sat near the center of the room, chatting with a girl behind her, and Melanie headed their way.

The air hummed and vibrated with a cacophonous tangle of conversation. Mel focused, and individual voices separated from the mass. She picked out a girl's voice and listened harder—

"—and I was like, seriously? I'm a Capricorn. You don't expect—"

The girl's breath stank of onion rings. Mel looked around, but the crowd blocked her view. People bumped and jostled her, but she might have been standing alone. Unreality blinked with her eyelids.

Another scent caught her attention: a weird, sickly sweet aroma she'd never smelled before. It resembled rotting fruit, and it came from off to her right. Ten desks away in that direction sat Timmy Simmons, surrounded by half a dozen other students. A smug look was plastered on his face, and theatrical hand gestures underscored whatever story he was telling. Concentrating, Mel picked up:

"...biggest one I'd ever seen! Now, I've gone hunting plenty of times with my dad, and I've taken down lots of large animals, including a full-grown grizzly bear last summer. But this thing—well, I admit, I was a touch nervous. But I knew and he knew that he was the one lower on the food chain. I stood my ground and stared him down while the girls screamed and ran away...."

That numbskull! Mel fumed. If she listened any longer, she might throw up. She finished weaving her way to Pam and plopped down next to her.

"And here she is now," crooned a delighted-sounding voice. "I'm dying to hear your side of the story, Melanie."

Mel had been so preoccupied with not bumping into people, and with Timmy and all the smells, that she'd failed to notice whom Pam was talking with—her friend Alexis, who had a reputation as the school's gossip queen.

Crap, Mel thought, twisting around to face the grinning redhead. Alexis also reeked of something resembling rotten fruit. *What* is *that?*

Eyes gleaming like those of a snake stalking mice, Alexis leaned forward and said, "So. Melanie. Were you and Pam really out in the woods all night with Timmy?"

"Not by choice." Mel wrinkled her nose. "He was lost, ran into us, and then we ended up all being lost. The rain washed away the arrows we drew on the trail."

"Sure, sure." But Alexis's grin broadened, and Mel's heart sped up. *What is she thinking now?*

"So it wasn't a *ménage à trois* then?" Alexis trilled, before erupting into giggles along with the girl sitting next to her.

"That's disgusting!" Pam cried, loudly enough to turn several heads in her direction. But soon enough, she joined in the giggling.

Mel winced at the attention and at how lightly Pam was taking the teasing. After drawing in a deep, calming breath, Mel said, "I can't believe your major isn't journalism, Alexis. It seems like you're aiming to become a gossip columnist. Better yet—you'd do great work for a tabloid."

"Aw, c'mon, Mel—" started Pam, sobering.

"Or maybe it was a foursome," Alexis continued, undeterred. "I heard Luis was out all night in the woods too. You guys drove him and Timmy back to their site, didn't you?"

"Because we're decent human beings, yes," said Mel.

The gossip queen persisted: "You and Luis tutor Spanish together, don't you?"

"That's not a secret or anything." Mel shifted in her seat, more than ready for this conversation to end. She glanced around, but there was no sign of the professor. Mel prayed that he would hurry up and arrive and start class.

Especially after Alexis said, "Well, *I* bet you do more than tutor together." That hungry, reptilian smile was back on her face.

"Mind your own business!" Melanie snapped, flushing beet red. "We're just friends."

"Really? So it *wasn't* a lovers' quarrel? It wasn't Luis who caused your injuries? Someone said you had some pretty bad cuts and scrapes." Alexis craned her neck, scanning Melanie for wounds. Mel was glad she'd worn long pants. She crossed her arms defensively over her chest, careful to tuck her left hand under her right arm.

Pam came to her aid. "You know Luis is a great guy. Not a violent bone in his body."

Oh, no . . . Mel wanted to face-palm. *She did* not *just use the word "bone"!* That was throwing Alexis one for sure.

But before the gossip queen could make any sexual innuendoes, the door near the front of the lecture hall clicked open, and the professor walked in. Mel breathed a sigh of relief as she and Pam swiveled around to face the stage. "Let's not sit by her again," Mel muttered under her breath.

Pam frowned. "Chill out, Mel. You know she was just hasslin' ya. No one actually thinks you and I had a threesome with Timmy."

"Timmy might!"

"Geez, well, Timmy also thinks professional wrestling is real."

"Good afternoon, everyone," Dr. Ayers greeted them from the podium. He reminded the students of the chapter they were on, gave them a moment to open their books, and began his lecture on the Romanov dynasty.

It took several minutes for Melanie's mind to calm down and focus on the lesson.

I'm glad Alexis didn't bring up the cave and the . . . thing in it, she thought, suppressing a shudder. Absently, she stroked the wound on her left hand. The fang mark showed no signs of healing: It hadn't scabbed over, and every once in a while it would leak a few drops of blood, unprovoked. She'd covered it with a Band-Aid close to her skin color and had been trying to keep that hand out of sight of everyone, including Pam. That was tricky, since Melanie normally held silverware and writing utensils with her left hand.

What in the world is going on with my body?

5

The Game

After a couple of weeks, the gossip concerning Pine Groves—and regarding Melanie's love life—guttered and flickered like a dying fire. Mel avoided Timmy as much as possible, giving him only brief, icy glances at *Sentinel* meetings and refusing to speak a word to him. As for Luis, she'd never hung out with him outside of tutoring hours, so she kept up that pattern, although she felt bad about it. He was a nice guy. If the circumstances had been different . . .

Neither she nor he brought up the rumors about their alleged tryst, and Mel figured Luis was also lying low and waiting for the forked tongues to stop wagging. It worked: Deprived of fuel, the rumor-mongers soon slithered along to the next hot piece of hearsay.

Melanie wished she could move on as easily and forget about the terrifying beast in the cave. But the small puncture wound it had given her healed at a languid pace, its fiery red resisting extinguishment and continually leaking blood. *How much longer am I going to have to keep wearing Band-Aids and writing with my right hand?* she wondered. *How long until Pam, Jocelyn, or someone else notices and asks, "Aren't you a leftie? Why'd you switch?"*

Worse, the pair of golden eyes kept intruding into her thoughts and dreams. This morning she had jerked awake, hyperventilating and drenched in sweat, from a particularly disturbing nightmare:

She walked through the woods bordering Wellsboro. Rustling nearby made her freeze and listen. A bone-chilling howl split the air.

She ran.

The trail stretched on, endless. Branches slapped at her face and arms. One sliced her neck.

Hartman loomed ahead. She threw open the front door, leaped over the threshold, and slammed the door shut.

The dorm was dark and quiet, but she was not alone. Other lungs respired and other hearts pumped blood. Slowly, she turned to face the living room.

All seven of her housemates waited for her, hands on hips or arms crossed. They were staring at her—staring with seven pairs of golden eyes.

A shriek tore from her throat. She bolted past the group and up the stairs, then locked herself inside her bedroom. What am I going to do?

A flash of golden light glinted from one of the walls, from the mirror hanging above her dresser.

From the reflection of her own golden eyes.

Melanie had woken up whimpering in fear. Thank goodness Pam had been in the shower already and hadn't heard. Mel didn't want her friend worrying about her. She was fine. This PTSD, or whatever it was, would go away soon enough.

It had better.

At least her classmates were no longer teasing her. And most of the taunts and snide remarks had been aimed at Timmy anyway. Once people had found out he'd been ditched by his camping buddies and had gotten terribly lost in the forest, Timmy had become a laughingstock.

Serves him right for blabbing, Mel had thought at first. *It totally backfired on him. Ha! What did he expect?*

But her anger toward him had cooled with the mid-October weather and had turned into pity. She swelled with gratitude that he'd toned down his loud-mouthed boasting—the last few *Sentinel* meetings had been a lot quieter and calmer.

The newsroom's layout table was where Melanie sat on this sunny but chilly Thursday afternoon. Editions of the *Sentinel* came out biweekly, and articles were due every other Wednesday. Since many of the writers habitually failed to turn in their assignments until midnight, Mel usually didn't start looking over the articles until Thursday.

This issue's batch is a bit sloppy, she thought as her eyes and pencil roved across a printed-out article. *It looks like I'm going to be here for a couple of hours again.* Eating a late dinner had become an every-other-Thursday tradition for her.

No one else was in the room, which Melanie preferred. The temperature, lighting, ambient noises, and comfort level of her chair were perfect for promoting concentration. But she couldn't focus. She shifted in her chair, moved it an inch closer to the table, and then an inch back. Random images flew into her head. Then the words began to swim before her eyes, undulating like a desert mirage.

What the heck is going on? Setting down her pencil, she shook her head rapidly, trying to clear it. She read another paragraph, and then the random images pushed back into her mind. The muscles in her lower legs spasmed like a tap-dancing routine.

Melanie dropped the pencil. *Am I developing ADHD? Is that possible when you're past your teenage years? Whatever this is, it's not good. If it keeps up and prevents me from finishing my work on time . . .*

It was probably just stress; a timeout should help calm her nerves. Standing up, she stretched her arms, legs, neck, and back, then strolled around the room. Her circuit brought her to the office's computers. Absently, she moved their mice to clear away the screensavers. *Sentinel* folders had been left open on two of the screens. A schedule of upcoming volleyball games greeted her from the third monitor.

Tomorrow night there was a big game against Wellsboro's rival. It was a home game, the first of two matches that the Wellsboro Lady Knights would play against the Lady Eagles of Brookside College. "Lady Eagles Soar up to Challenge the Lady Knights on their Royal Court," the headline would read. Mel grinned to herself, and then her thoughts turned to Shari Quinlan.

Shari was Melanie's other suitemate and Jocelyn's roommate. Mel had no idea why Shari and Jos had decided to room together, since Shari was a perky, bubbly blonde—a type that usually annoyed Jos. They'd decorated their room in an odd mishmash of pinks, pastels, pictures of kittens, and boy-band posters on one side and black, crimson, deep purple, and posters of dragons and dark fairies on the other.

Shari was also Wellsboro's star volleyball player. This entire week, she'd been chattering about nothing but Friday's game, begging the girls to come and cheer her on. Mel and Pam had assured Shari that they'd be there and drag Jocelyn along.

Melanie unconsciously drummed her fingers on the back of a chair. *Thump, thump, thump-thump, thump.* Faster and faster she tapped out a rhythm. Little throbs of pain pulsed above and between her eyes, and her heart kept time with her fingers' manic beat. Images of volleyball players, nets, and a cheering crowd swirled through her mind along with other, more frightening images—glowing yellow eyes in a dark cave, white fangs gleaming, jaws foaming and stretching open—

She whimpered and then jumped as a click and a loud creak sounded behind her. Panting and clutching at her chest, Melanie spun and saw that it was only her "boss" entering the room. The ancient door of this office never opened quietly. *Sheesh, calm down,* Mel told herself.

The *Sentinel's* editor-in-chief, Dawn Fincher, was a stocky college senior with a no-nonsense air. She strode in confidently. Her typical expression of mild annoyance was on her face, and a load of papers and books was in her arms. When she saw Melanie, she said, "Hey, Caldwell. You fed up with those articles already?" She grinned and dumped her stack of stuff onto the layout table near Melanie's papers.

"Not exactly," said Mel, smiling faintly. Twinges and prickles shot through her arms and legs, begging her to pace, but she gritted her teeth and kept as still as she could. "I seem to be distracted today. Thought I'd walk around and clear my head."

Dawn narrowed her eyes at Mel, but said, "You should try sticking your head out the window in the cold air. That's what I do, this time of year."

"Hmm, good idea," said Melanie. She walked over to the nearest window and cranked its rusty, recalcitrant handle, slowly pushing the lower pane outward and letting a chill breeze rush in. She stuck her nose through the gap, like a canine on a car ride, took several deep breaths, and began to feel refreshed.

"That worked pretty well," she said to Dawn—and then she noticed the wind had scattered her papers everywhere. "Oh, crap."

Dawn chuckled. "Don't get all flustered on me. You look kind of jittery today, Melanie. Did you switch from decaf to regular or something?"

Mel shook her head. "No," she muttered. "I honestly don't know what's going on with me." *But whatever it is, it had better not stick around much longer.* She had important things to do—and there were people, like Dawn, counting on her to do them well.

)) ● ((

"Go, Lady Knights! Wooooo!" Pam cried as she bounced through the door to their bedroom the next evening.

Melanie looked up from her computer and grinned. "I see you're pumped up and ready to head over there. Game doesn't start for half an hour."

"I know. Gives me plenty of time to put on some red-and-gold face paint. You want any?"

"No, thanks. That stuff makes me break out."

"Yikes," said Pam. "Okay, no paint for you. By the way," she continued casually, rummaging in her dresser drawer, "I didn't see you at dinner tonight. Did you skip out?"

Mel bit her lower lip. "Yeah. I wasn't hungry; my stomach's been feeling kind of weird today."

"Oh, no. I hope you're not getting sick again."

"Took the words right out of my mouth," said Mel.

What she didn't tell Pam was that she'd felt antsy and fidgety all day, just like yesterday afternoon in the *Sentinel* office. She'd had to force herself to sit still during classes and not jump up and pace around like she'd wanted to. *What the heck is wrong with me?* she thought. *If this doesn't stop soon . . .*

I need to finish my freakin' homework and editing! To her annoyance, she was only halfway done with both.

Pam left the room carrying tubes of face paint, and Melanie heard her bustle into the bathroom. She returned her eyes to her computer screen, but the library e-book open on it wavered and danced before her eyes. Was the monitor acting up?

She leaned in closer and squinted at the text. The sentences were long and complex, and she hadn't clicked to the next page in what seemed like hours. *What an obnoxious thing to have to read,* she thought, and yawned. Blood rushed in her ears, and it felt like someone was pinching her forehead. Massaging it, she made another attempt to read the onscreen textbook. The words had stopped undulating, but now they looked like Latin.

"Dammit," she said, and pushed back her chair. "I can't take it anymore!"

"Can't take what anymore?" said a smooth voice from the doorway.

"Oh! Jos, hi." Melanie blushed as she stood up and her suitemate walked in. "Um, just stupid homework. Y'know. They've been giving out a ton of it lately."

Jocelyn Beaumont nodded, twirling one of her black curls around a long white finger. "My profs aren't going easy, either."

I have to persuade her to come to the game, Mel remembered, groaning inwardly. It would be easier to take a cat for a walk around the block. She racked her brain, trying to find the right words to say, but then Pam pranced back into the room.

"How do I look?" she crowed, striking poses like a model and framing her face with her hands. The left half of it was scarlet, the right half gold.

"Whoa," said Jocelyn, raising an eyebrow. "Um ... yeah. Pretty awesome, Pam."

Melanie grinned broadly. "Shari will love it."

"Are we ready to go?" Pam beamed, obviously delighted with her appearance. "Are you coming along too, Jos? Please say you will, this time. Please!"

Jocelyn gave a loud sigh. "I suppose. Otherwise, I'll have to endure my roommate's reprimands for the rest of the semester. Let me get my shoes and coat." She drifted out of the room.

"That was surprisingly easy," Mel whispered to Pam, pulling on her own jacket.

Minutes later, the three girls climbed into Melanie's car, and Mel drove them across campus toward the athletic center. The large, square brick building was visible from quite a distance away, its floor-length windows blazing with light against the backdrop of inky sky. Clusters of people sifted in through the main doors, and the parking lot was already packed. "Wow," said Mel. "What a turnout. Looks like a lot of Brooksiders are here too."

"They're here to watch their team get *crushed!*" said Pam. She giggled. "Besides, what else is there to do on a Friday night around here?"

A line of pedestrians crossed in front of the Honda, which had only been moving at five miles per hour. "I'm gonna drop you guys off at the door and then try to find a place to park," said Mel. "Maybe we should have walked."

"Okay. We'll save you a seat," said Pam.

She and Jocelyn scooted out when they got close to the front of the building. An impatient honk sounded from the car behind them. Mel gritted her teeth and kept her fingers—including the middle ones—clamped around the steering wheel.

After she finally found a parking spot, she hiked back across the lot, threaded her way between a dozen groups of milling people, and strode into the gymnasium.

It felt like someone had shoved a basket full of old, sweaty gym socks right under her nose. Melanie staggered. A tidal wave of rubber, face paint, and perspiring bodies rushed over her. It took her a moment to recover. *Geez,* she thought, holding her breath. *Did everyone pick today to skip their shower?*

The bleachers on the right-hand side were quickly filling up with the home-team crowd. Mel scanned the sea of faces for Pam and Jocelyn. She spotted them about ten rows up, sitting with several music-major friends of Pam's. Jocelyn saw Melanie and waved, and Mel climbed up to join the group.

"Whew," she said as she plopped down next to Jos. "Sure is crazy out there—and in here." *Ugh, someone nearby is wearing about a gallon of musky cologne.* She wrinkled her nose and tried not to breathe through it.

Jocelyn nodded, immune or oblivious to the malodorous atmosphere. Her smartphone was out on her lap, and Melanie could see that she had already been texting someone. Mel grinned. *Typical, crowd-phobic Jos,* she thought.

The Wellsboro and Brookside teams jogged onto the court, and thunderous applause erupted from the crowds on both sides of the gym. Ostentatious, hyped-up announcements boomed from the commentators, and the first of three fifteen-point matches began.

Shari was one of the starters. She played fiercely, diving and making a spectacular save only four plays into the game. Melanie enjoyed watching her friend, but after Shari rotated out, she grew restless and found herself itching to stand up and walk around. The air had grown even riper and hotter, and she thought she might puke or pass out if she stayed there much longer. "I'm gonna get a drink at the water fountain," she told Jocelyn. "Be back soon."

"Mmm-hmm," said Jos, and returned her attention to her phone.

As Melanie squeezed her way to the aisle and started climbing down the bleachers, she glanced across to the other side of the gym. Her steps slowed, her attention drawn to a young man at the edge of the Brookside crowd.

Leaning against the wall by the lobby doors, he had a distinct air of separation from the other students. Dishwater-blond hair fell nearly into his dark eyes; he was rather thin and pale but very attractive. Mel stared for a moment, then blushed as he suddenly looked up and met her gaze. His eyes widened.

Flashing an embarrassed smile, Melanie looked away. She reached the gym floor and pushed through the nearest door to the lobby. Relief rushed over her with the cooler, fresher air. She sucked in deep breaths, wiping sweat from her forehead.

A door clicked open at the far end, the away crowd's side. Of course, it was *him*. Mel ducked her head and veered toward the water fountain. After taking a long drink, she turned and almost bumped into him. "Excuse me," she said, at the same time he said, "Sorry—hey, have I seen you somewhere before?"

Heat crept back into her cheeks. "Um, I don't think so."

The way he studied her face put her ever so slightly on edge. "I'm Gavin," he said after a pause.

"Melanie."

"Nice to meet you," they chorused.

"May I?" Gavin gestured at the fountain, and Mel scooted out of the way. He took a couple of big gulps, then wiped his mouth on his sleeve. "That hit the spot. It was getting really hot in there."

"Yeah. Feels much better out here." *And smells better too.*

Mel shuffled her feet, mind racing but failing to come up with clever conversation. *Why do I always freeze up with cute guys? Pam would know how to break the ice.*

Mel was about to say that she should get back to her friends— although she'd much prefer to leave the stuffy building instead—but Gavin spoke first. "I just feel like we've met before, or . . ."

She raised her eyes to his; they were almost as rich of a dark brown as hers were. At the connection, his body tensed and jerked. His eyes grew wide, glassy, and unfocused.

"Hey, are you all right?" Mel's hand automatically lifted to steady him, but he came out of it after only a moment.

The color drained from his face. An expression of pain replaced the blank one. "Impossible," he whispered.

What the heck? thought Mel. *This is getting a little freaky.* She took a step backward, definitely ready to return to her friends.

"Wait, Melanie," Gavin said, and held out a hand as if to stop her from leaving. "I'm sorry. I'm sure you think I'm weird, but I have to ask you an important question. Have you gone camping recently?"

How is that important? "Yeah, about a month ago. Why?"

He gave a long sigh. His shoulders drooped, and his eyes looked haunted. "I need to tell you something, something absolutely crucial."

Mel raised an eyebrow. A snarky comment popped into her head, but she stifled it and said, "What do you mean?"

Gavin glanced around the lobby. A dozen other students stood in groups, chatting and laughing together. "Do you mind if we go and talk somewhere more private?" he said in a low voice.

Alarm bells rang inside her at the word "private." *Fat chance, Captain Creepy.* "Why do we need to do that?"

"Shoot," he said, "that didn't sound quite right. I don't mean we should go find a dark alley. Just outside the building is fine; there are benches by the front doors, aren't there?"

"Yeah." Night had fallen, but plenty of bright lamps illuminated the perimeter of the athletic center. The building had a lot of windows too, and most of the benches could be seen from the lobby. "Okay."

She and Gavin headed for the front doors. Melanie unwrapped her jacket from around her waist and pulled it on, expecting the October air to bite her like an ice puppy. Instead, she found it to be more like a calm, lazy old dog. *I thought it was supposed to get down into the forties tonight.*

She walked over and sat on the best-lit, most visible bench. Gavin joined her, leaving a couple of feet between them. Stars twinkled overhead, and the large, round moon hung above the eastern foothills. The quiet night was broken only by the sound of distant cheers and tennis shoe squeaks filtering from the building as if muffled by cloth.

For a long time, Gavin stared down at his hands. He wore a light jacket and no gloves, and she noticed that there was a fragile quality about those hands, although not a feminine one.

"I don't know where to start," he murmured. "You're not . . . going to like hearing this at all."

"Hearing *what*?" Her voice came out more harshly than she'd intended. The suspense was killing her. A million unlikely possibilities raced through her mind, and she found it difficult to sit still.

Gavin apologized again before she could. Then he looked straight into her eyes and asked, "Did you go camping at a national park called Pine Groves?"

She blinked. A cricket chirped. The wind rustled the branches of a nearby tree.

"How—?" she faltered. "How did you . . . ?"

"Did you go inside a cave at night?" he pressed.

Ice trickled down her spine. "How could you possibly—"

"There was something in there, right? It bit you."

Golden eyes flashed in her memory. Melanie flinched, recalling her most recent nightmare. She opened her mouth to demand that he stop messing around and freaking her out, but her throat constricted, choking off her voice.

Gavin's expression softened, and his hand twitched as if he wanted to reach out and grip hers but had thought better of it.

She couldn't meet his eyes any longer. The festive sounds emanating from the gymnasium called to her, and she stood up. "I gotta go."

"Wait! Melanie!" He jumped up and followed as she strode away. "This is very important. Please! Listen to me."

"What are you doing? Leave me alone!" she said. "Your dumb joke isn't funny."

"I'm not joking," he said, and his voice sounded sad and resigned. "I wish I were, believe me."

"Do you have friends at Wellsboro? Catch the latest gossip? Did Timmy put you up to this? If he thinks he can—"

"Who's Timmy? No, I'm telling the truth. Nobody put me up to this."

"Oh, yeah? What are you, some kind of psychic then? Did you read my tea leaves?"

"No, I . . ." Gavin trailed off, knit his brows together, and stamped a foot in impatience. "I can't tell you how I know, but . . . I can show you some evidence of what I know about you."

"Huh?"

He held out his upturned, open palms. "Can I see your hand, please?"

"Oh, I get it," she said. "You're a palm reader."

"No, Melanie." He rolled his eyes.

"Tarot cards?"

"Just give me your hand."

She resisted for a few more moments, but eventually she placed her right hand on top of his left one. It felt as warm as hers did; at least it wasn't clammy. She huffed and put on her most cynical face.

Instead of turning her hand over to examine it, as Mel had anticipated, Gavin gripped it lightly and reached into the back pocket of his jeans. *What's he going to bring out? An astral map?*

Before she could react or feel afraid, he whipped out a Swiss Army knife with practiced ease. He sliced a shallow line along the back of her hand, and blood beaded there.

"Ow!" Melanie shrieked, yanking her wounded appendage from his slackened grip. She jumped backward. "Are you insane?! What the *hell* did you do that for?!"

Gavin closed the knife, put it away, and didn't answer immediately. Too shocked to run away, Mel stood there nursing the stinging cut and glaring at him. She was about to flee to the girls' bathroom to run cold water over the cut when he spoke in a tone that was surprisingly full of authority. "Watch your hand."

"What?!"

"Take a look at your hand and tell me if anything's happening."

"You're unhinged, aren't you?" Melanie spat.

He bit his lip. "I'm sorry for cutting you. It was the only thing I could think of to do. I have a handkerchief you can use to wipe away the blood." Slowly, cautiously, he reached into the front pocket of his jeans. "It's okay; I haven't used it. Here." He proffered a white piece of cloth.

She narrowed her eyes but accepted it reluctantly, checking that it smelled clean before dabbing at the blood dripping from her hand.

When she lifted the hanky and peeked underneath, she expected to see more blood welling up, but a different sight met her eyes.

A scab had already formed.

The wound had stopped throbbing, too. The pain vanished, leaving a warm, tingling sensation in its place. Melanie's jaw dropped, and she watched as the red line shrank and the scab fell off. The wound faded to her skin color, smoothed out, and disappeared, all in under a minute.

"What—why—how did you do that?" she whispered fearfully.

"It wasn't *my* doing, Melanie," said Gavin. "Your body healed itself. I think you should sit back down now. I need to tell you what really happened to you last month at Pine Groves."

6

Captive

"You're out of your mind," Melanie snapped, after hearing his explanation. But her eyes were wide with churning fear.

Gavin shook his head. "No, I'm not," he said, his voice level and calm. "Think back, Melanie. You were crawling through a narrow passageway in the cave that night, and a beast with glowing yellow eyes came. It bit your hand and passed its curse on to you—turned you into a werewolf."

"How could you possibly know what happened?" A tremor passed through her small frame. She clutched her left hand protectively, hunching over the bandaged appendage, ready to bolt.

"It doesn't matter how I know," he said. "What matters is that you believe me, because I'm telling the truth. Think of what's at stake if I'm right. It's too risky not to prepare for the worst outcome."

In a tone more confident than she felt, Mel said, "Risky? Yeah, it's so risky that something that *isn't real* might be real."

"How about if I offer you some more evidence?" Gavin countered. "If that wound healing so quickly wasn't enough ... Have you felt strangely restless for the past few days? Has your sense of hearing or smell grown stronger?"

She bit her lower lip and shifted on the bench. "That doesn't prove anything."

"But isn't it a bit too weird to ignore?"

"No. My IQ is way too high to believe in stupid scary stories about ghosts, vampires, or werewolves. I never even believed in Santa as a kid." *Why is he spouting this nonsense?*

Why haven't I left yet?

"Can't you consider—for a tiny window of time—that something

47

you believe, or don't believe, might be wrong? Science and logic aren't absolute authorities. There are plenty of things in the world that no one can explain."

Melanie shook her head. She didn't want to hear this.

"You have to admit that you don't and can't know everything," Gavin continued. "You can't prove I'm wrong about werewolves, but tomorrow, I can prove that I'm right."

No.

"Have a little faith, and trust me. I'm warning you: You'll deeply regret it if you don't."

Stop. Please stop.

"If you don't leave campus tomorrow afternoon and find a safe place to lock yourself up before moonrise—"

"Shut up!" Melanie clapped her hands to the sides of her head.

"You know the danger. That beast would have killed you if it could've. What do you think you'll do when you transform? I'll tell you what: You'll rip everyone around you to pieces. And then you'll *eat* them."

"I said, shut *up!*" Her eyes were tearing up. Why were her eyes tearing up?

"If you don't know of anywhere safe to go, I can help you." Gavin's voice was rising in pitch. "Melanie, please, you can come with me—"

"No!" She sprang from the bench. "I've had enough of this crap. I'm out of here!"

As she ran back into the gymnasium, she heard Gavin growl, angry and low.

Melanie burst through the door to the ladies' bathroom and locked herself inside a stall. The room reeked, and her stomach churned, but she clamped her fingers over her nostrils and stayed put. She needed some time to calm down and regain her composure before joining her friends again in the bleachers.

Werewolf . . . curse . . . danger . . .

Eerie golden eyes glowing in the dark cave . . . white fangs gleaming, darting toward her—

Stop it! she screamed inside her head. *There's no way he's right! It was a wild dog—it had to be. Dogs' eyes glow like that in pictures. It was a trick of the light. I got a rabies shot. I'll be fine.*

What about the cut?

A magic trick. It had to be.

But how on earth did Gavin know about what had happened? Pam wouldn't have told him.

Was he there? Her brow furrowed in concentration as she tried to remember. . . . *Wait a minute—maybe that RV was* his.

Only a few other people had been camping in the same cul-de-sac as Mel and Pam: a couple with two young children directly across from them, and an RV whose occupant(s) they'd never once seen during the entire weekend three spaces to the left. Pam, in hopes of meeting an attractive young male or two, had knocked on its door to say hi on the first evening, but no one had answered. The RV had remained a silent, mysterious monolith, dark against the darker woods edging the cul-de-sac.

It was a longshot, but the RV could have been Gavin's. But why would he either never be in it, or be sitting inside in the dark not answering his door? Both options had "creepy" written all over them.

Suppose he was there, but not in the RV. He might have been camping in a different part of the park.

He couldn't have been in the cave with us, and certainly not the room that thing was in—it would have killed him. Or severely injured him. He doesn't have a scratch on him. He must've been in the area somewhere, *though. I didn't see him, and I don't think Pam or Timmy did either. But it was dark. . . .*

How else could he possibly know if he wasn't around?

Melanie took deep, shaky breaths. In and out, in and out. She didn't know any meditation techniques, but if life kept throwing this much stress at her, she should probably learn some.

Everything's fine, she told herself. *It's most likely the gossip chain's fault that he knows.*

But a little voice at the back of her mind said, *Really? Someone else knows that much detail? You're the only one who saw that creature, and you never told anyone that much about it, not even Pam.*

Well, maybe Gavin heard a couple of details Timmy leaked, then made up the rest and happened to get it right.

That explanation didn't satisfy, but she could come up with no other.

A few minutes later, Melanie felt composed enough to venture back out to the gymnasium. If she didn't return to her friends soon, they'd worry about her. She was surprised Jos hadn't texted her already.

Peeking out of the bathroom, she scanned the lobby for Gavin, but he was nowhere to be seen. She let out a relieved sigh and reentered the smelly gym.

"There you are," said Jocelyn, looking up as Mel plopped down next to her. "You were gone for quite a while."

Melanie shrugged and avoided eye contact. She craned her neck to watch the action on the volleyball court. "What round is this?" she asked Jos. "Two or three?"

"Three. We won the first match and lost the second."

"Huh."

Mel was aware that her suitemate was watching her with narrowed eyes, but she pretended to be oblivious and feigned keen interest in the game.

Then Jos said, "I saw some guy watching you and following you, earlier. Looked pretty cute from here. Were you talking to him?"

Argh, thought Melanie. *She notices everything.* Adopting a casual attitude, she shrugged again and said, "Just some Brookside guy. Yeah, he approached me in the lobby; he thought I looked familiar and asked me if we'd met before. I said no, and we chatted a bit, but then I thought I should get back."

"Ooh." Jocelyn's green eyes lit up like traffic lights. "If a guy opens with a line like that, it means he's into you. He thinks you're cute, Mel! What's his name? C'mon, I want all the juicy details!"

Melanie groaned inwardly. She knew avoiding the interrogation would only make things worse. "His name's Gavin," she said. "And I'm pretty sure he wasn't flirting with me. I'm not as naïve as you think, Jos; I believe he genuinely thought he'd seen me somewhere before. Guess I've got a doppelganger out there."

"He could just be a good actor."

"He didn't steer the conversation in any sort of romantic direction.

The bragging, stupid grin, and poser body language weren't there either."

"His loss." Jocelyn's face showed mild disappointment. "He's probably gay or something."

He's something, thought Mel.

Jos returned her attention to her smartphone, and Melanie watched the volleyball game. When Wellsboro scored the winning point, she jumped up and cheered with the rest of the home crowd.

Forget about Gavin, she told herself. *Enjoy being here with your friends, having fun. Living a normal life, free of psychos.*

Thank goodness, that handsome lunatic remained out of sight. She hoped he'd gone home and would never set foot on her campus again.

)) ● ((

Moon's almost full again already, thought Nicholas Erickson, frowning as he peered out the window at the loathsome satellite.

It leered down, unhindered by clouds, on the RV park where he was staying. *I control your life,* it said. *My power is almost renewed, and tomorrow night I will reclaim your body.*

Erickson's hands clenched into fists, but he might as well be fighting against time, gravity, or entropy—his curse was equally insurmountable.

That blasted Gary Saddler was proving another formidable foe. During the past few weeks, the gunman had left several messages on Erickson's voicemail and had even mailed him a letter! *Damned, meddlesome bastard. I've made it crystal clear that I'm not interested in his dumb group. Why won't he leave me alone?*

Why am I still here, anyway? I should've moved on—and I ought to dump my phone and get a new one. Erickson knew how to disappear; he had done it plenty of times. Now, though, so close to the full moon, it was too late to find another hideout. He had no choice but to return to the cave this month.

And he harbored no doubts that Saddler would be there waiting for him.

Erickson cursed himself. *Nothing but a fool, my whole life. Every time I've got a good thing going, I can't hold on to it.* The cave and the tranquil national park had served as a pleasant refuge, one he wouldn't have minded using indefinitely. But its appeal had expired much sooner than he'd wished.

So why hadn't he skedaddled? He knew the answer, deep down, but was afraid to admit it to himself, to acknowledge his weakness:

He was clinging to memories from his old life. Memories he should have suppressed long ago. Recollections of better times in this region of the United States. He'd grown up and spent a significant portion of his life in the Appalachian foothills.

He was also something of a stalker, himself. Not a pushy one like Saddler—just a silent, hidden observer. Although he knew their relationship could never be restored, at least he could catch glimpses from a distance and imagine his loved one's heart was healing with him out of the picture.

Erickson sighed and stirred the coffee he hadn't been drinking. It had stopped steaming, and its bitter smell had soured with cold. The clink of the metal spoon against the ceramic mug broke the stillness. His reverie had pushed away the familiar evening sounds of the RV park, but now they returned: insects chirping and humming, a man and a woman arguing in the next trailer over, cars whizzing past on the freeway, and (on occasion) semi trucks' engine brakes growling.

He stood abruptly and dumped the coffee down the sink. He had no taste for food or drink tonight; his stomach twisted, and his limbs were practically quivering with nervous energy. Self-medicating failed to alleviate these lunar symptoms, so he didn't bother taking sedatives. Their effects never lasted long, due to his metabolism's monthly elevation.

Besides, he disliked feeling out of control. The next three nights, he would have no choice; but tonight, he did.

Losing control...

Dark memories plagued him. Leaning against the counter to steady himself, Erickson drew in a sharp breath that turned into a sob. Images flashed through his mind: the torn, blood-soaked bodies of his victims lying still and lifeless. Some were barely recognizable as human.

Jamie...

NO. Don't go there.

He slammed his fist on the mottled Formica surface. More sobs shook his frame. Although years had passed since he'd killed anyone, the memories remained as strong as jabs to the gut. No matter how he tried to drown them, bury them, or fight them off, the ghosts of his past clung to him and surrounded him like dense fog.

Whether he lost or kept his consciousness, there was no escape. No peace.

Why haven't I killed myself yet? he pondered for the millionth time. What was it that had kept him—so far—from driving his RV off a cliff or from spiking his coffee with rat poison?

Simple: fear of what lay on the other side. Erickson had never pretended to have a clue about what happened to a person after death; he fervently hoped it was nothing, oblivion.

If there is a hell, I'm more than qualified to go to it. I might even be in it right now. Is that the price a werewolf has to pay?

A knock at the door jerked him out of his thoughts. *What—who . . . ?*

Then he had an unpleasant suspicion. Gritting his teeth and scowling, he padded to the door and looked through the peephole.

He'd been half right, half wrong. Two people stood waiting outside.

Saddler had brought a friend.

〉 〉 ● 〈 〈

Melanie Caldwell tossed and turned in her bed for hours that night, but sleep evaded her. As the evening progressed, so did her agitation. Every little noise—the creaking of the old house, the ticking of the wall clock—rang so loudly in her ears, she thought she was going crazy.

Worse, she couldn't suppress her memory of the cave. Glowing yellow eyes narrowing as they met hers . . . white fangs gleaming and dripping with spittle . . .

Stop, stop! she begged her hyperactive brain. *It's over now. I'm safe. Please,* please *calm down and let me get some rest.*

"Can't you even consider that something you believe might be wrong? There are plenty of things in the world that no one can explain."

The wind howled mournfully through the trees outside her window, and Melanie wanted to moan too. She curled into the fetal position and hugged her knees tightly to her chest.

Hours later, she awoke, having no idea when she'd drifted off. The sun shone brightly through the crack between the curtains, and she squinted and shielded her eyes.

It was Saturday, thank goodness; but instead of calm and relaxed, she felt the tug of unaccomplished work. Due to her restlessness during the past few days, she'd failed to finish editing the *Sentinel* articles. Groaning, she made her way to the deserted *Sentinel* office.

She tried to sit still and concentrate on her work, but within minutes her newfound ADHD resurfaced. Her limbs tingled, her mind raced, and her frustration grew. The sunlight streaming through the windows was awfully bright. The clock's ticking punctuated the silence like shots from a BB gun. The room reeked of lemon cleaner.

It took Melanie three hours to edit a dozen short articles. By the time she finished wrestling with them and herself, she'd developed a raging headache, and she longed for a nap.

She left the office and headed back down the empty hallway toward the exit. As she reached for the push bar, her ears caught the sound of soft footsteps behind her. She stiffened. *I thought I was alone. Is it Dawn?*

Before she could turn to look, an arm wrapped around her waist like an iron band, clamping her arms to her sides.

Lightning shot down Mel's spine. *What the—?* She balked and kicked, her fight instinct tempered by disbelief. Was this some kind of joke?

"Let me go!" she screamed. It wasn't Dawn, for sure. Had to be a guy. Too tall and strong to be Timmy. Luis would never do such a thing to her—this was no hug.

The arm pulled her closer against a hard body. Warm breath rushed over her neck. Damp, pungent cloth pressed over her nose and mouth.

"Mmmph!" Mel protested. The hand held the cloth firmly in place. Its astringent smell made her nauseous. Her lungs fought to suck in air.

She thrashed and wriggled, kicking backward at her assailant's shins. He jerked when she landed a blow, but lifted that leg and clamped it around both of hers. With his body coiled around her like a caduceus snake, she could barely move.

Who are you!? she wanted to yell. *What the hell—!*

But the world began to spin and turn black. She realized, as her consciousness faded, that the cloth had been soaked in a soporific drug.

Her body went limp in his arms.

Melanie woke in a dark, cramped space. She couldn't see anything, but walls pressed in all around her. Everywhere she touched, she felt coarse fabric. She lay on it, and it was just above her and to the sides.

A deep, throaty humming noise filled the air, accompanied by a higher-pitched whizzing sound. The floor was vibrating. Abruptly, it lurched and bumped. *Wait a minute,* she thought. *This must be . . .*

The trunk of a car.

I've been abducted!

7

Changes

She could barely breathe. Something pressed tightly against her mouth and grazed her nostrils. Eyes wide, panic surging, she clawed at her face.

A strip of plastic-like material across softer fabric: He'd taped the drugged cloth in place. The astringent smell was gone, the sedative evaporated.

Ripping off the tape stung. Melanie threw the gag away in disgust, then massaged her sore cheeks. Gulping deep lungfuls, she tried to calm her rapid heartbeat.

How long had she been here? How far away from campus was she?

The crunch of gravel was not a good sign. She didn't know of anywhere in the Wellsboro area that had gravel. Not this much.

It made no sense. Who would kidnap her? She didn't have any enemies—any real ones. Certainly no dangerous ones. Timmy came closest to what Mel would consider an enemy, but she'd already determined it couldn't be him. Not the one who'd grabbed her, anyway.

Is some other classmate pulling a sick prank on me?

It didn't feel like a prank.

Melanie tried to push away thoughts of serial killers and rapists and of being some pervert's "type"—petite brunette—but the possibilities were many and terrifying. She tucked her knees to her chest, wrapped her arms around them, and sobbed.

As her tears subsided, she looked around. The trunk was empty apart from her. No tool of any kind to help her escape. Her purse was gone, her phone with it. She lifted the carpet from the floor to check for a tire iron underneath, a spare, or even a jack, but the space where they should have been was empty. *He's removed every last thing?*

She shuddered. He was smart and well prepared.

She couldn't focus on that now. She needed to think. Strategize.

Her clothes were still on, thank goodness. She didn't feel injured. He hadn't even tied her up! Probably expected her to stay unconscious. She was a bit queasy, and her stomach growled; it had been hours since she'd eaten. But generally, she was fit to fight.

The urge to kick and scream and pound on all the surfaces around her washed over Melanie, but she resisted. She would only hurt herself and wear herself out. *Don't make noise. Don't attract his attention. He'll stop somewhere secluded and come back here and . . .*

Make sure she didn't make any more noise.

So she curled up in a ball again, waiting. Trying to think helpful thoughts, tactical thoughts, not ones that would increase her fear.

The car decelerated, then came to a stop. The engine's purr cut off, jolting her into a still, ominous silence. Melanie froze. She heard a door opening, felt the car shifting as the driver climbed out. The door slammed shut. Footsteps crunched, slowly coming her way.

I won't let him kill me without putting up a fight! She shifted into a better position to leap out at him, her hands poised to use as weapons. But they trembled.

Keys jingled, and one slid into the lock. With a pop, the trunk door lifted. Mellow light and fresh, cool air rushed in.

Then he came into view—jeans, t-shirt, neck, chin, face . . .

Rage replaced Melanie's fear.

"You!? What the *hell!"*

Gavin held up his empty hands in a gesture of peace, but a determined look was on his face. "I'm sorry, Melanie," he said. "I didn't want to do things this way, but I had to. You wouldn't listen to me."

"I'll get you thrown in jail for kidnapping!" she yelled. "You should be locked away in a mental hospital!" Her fingers twitched with the desire to claw his eyes out, but caution kept her from attacking. He was strong and could be dangerous.

"I'm protecting you. Saving you," he said, his voice and his gaze calm and level.

"Ha!" Melanie scrambled out of the trunk, still glaring at him, and then looked around. They were deep within a forest, as she'd suspected. Trees—mostly evergreens—stretched as far as she could see. A large, nice-looking log cabin stood a few yards away. The daylight was fading.

"Where are we? Take me back to Wellsboro right now," she demanded. "Or else—"

"Can't do that yet." Gavin reached back to pull something out of his jeans pocket. Melanie tensed, expecting the knife again; but instead, he brought out a small mirror and held it in front of her face.

She almost screamed when she saw her eyes.

"No. No!" Her protest turned into a moan as she slapped her hands over her face, hiding her eyes. "Enough stupid tricks! Think you're some kind of magician? First pretending to cut me with that knife, and now this?"

"It happens when your emotions are especially strong during the days before, during, and after a full moon," he said.

This can't be real. This can't be happening. But she remembered the nightmare she'd had about her eyes glowing yellow. Her heart pounded in her chest, and nausea threatened to overwhelm her. She sucked in deep breaths of pine-scented air.

Gavin glanced at the sky, which was streaked with ribbons of gold and pearl. "We need to get inside," he said. "The moon rises in twenty minutes. There are safe rooms in the cabin."

"I'm not going anywhere with you!" Mel managed to squeak, but her legs were trembling. She felt them growing weaker, the world rocking like a raft. The edges of her vision were darkening.

He caught her as she fell. She tried to talk, to hit or kick him, but her limbs and voice wouldn't cooperate.

When she came to, she was lying on a hardwood floor in a dimly lit room. The only source of illumination was a skylight high above her that showed a patch of deepening blue. There was nothing but empty space surrounded by dark wood on all six sides—no furniture, no decoration, and no possibility of escape except a single closed door.

Locked? Melanie wondered. Probably, but she had to check. She stood up shakily, tiny pricks of light dancing before her eyes, and leaned against a wall. When the dizziness passed, she walked to the door. Now that she was closer, she could see that there was no keyhole, only solid, smooth brass. The knob was cool to the touch and wouldn't turn. Wrapping both hands around it, she threw her weight backward and forward, but the door was solid and didn't budge. *What the heck? ... Must be locks on the outside frame. What kind of crazy house is this?*

It was the trunk all over again. No tools, no release levers or cables to pull—

She roared and banged on the door. "Let me out! Gavin! I know you're there, dammit! Please!" *No, don't cry!*

Pressing her ear against the door, she quieted down, waited, and listened. Footsteps padded toward her. They stopped right outside. There was a pause.

"I would advise you to undress," came Gavin's voice. "Otherwise, the changes will tear your clothes to shreds."

Melanie jerked in fear. Remove her clothes? Did he have a camera in here somewhere? Was that his game? Feeling naked at the thought, she scanned the corners of the ceiling but saw no lenses watching her. It was dark, though. A knothole in the wood could easily disguise a camera lens.

I won't give him that satisfaction. She crossed her arms and backed away from the door. He said nothing more, and after a moment, his footsteps retreated.

Melanie paced the room. What should she do? If only she had a flashlight. Her eyes had adjusted pretty well to the gloom, but soon it would be full-fledged night.

She searched the walls with her fingers, feeling for cracks or weak spots. She knocked on the wood paneling to check for hollow areas. No such luck. The floor seemed solid and impenetrable as well, and free of trap doors. The high, angled ceiling was far out of reach.

At last she flopped down in a corner, tired and frustrated. Her anger was rising, her fear waxing, and her hope waning. She curled her legs up to her chest, shoved her hands into her hair, and shook as her thoughts raced in miserable, terrified circles.

And then the pain began.

It started with a jolt, surging through her belly and up her spine. She gasped. Had that been an electric shock? How? There were no wires, no power in here.

A sharp tingling rushed over her but then pulled back. A whimper escaped her lips, and tears welled up in her eyes. She tried to stand, to move somewhere else, to get into a more comfortable position—but her arms and legs were suddenly weak. She struggled to lift herself from the floor.

Another wave of pain hit her, sending her back onto her rump. This time, the discomfort didn't subside completely. The tension it left behind in her muscles, and the ache remaining in her bones, foreshadowed another round of agony.

It came within moments. Her muscles clenched and then felt as if they were going to rip apart. Her bones creaked like twigs about to snap. Melanie screamed, and she kept screaming as dark auburn fur sprouted on her hands and arms and shot, needlelike, from her legs. Bones shifted and ground together. Her spine elongated, and her knee joints crunched into reverse. Her skin stretched as tightly as an over-filled water balloon. A painful, squishy feeling deep within her suggested organs moving around and reshaping.

Her lungs were on fire, and when she tried to clutch her chest, claws broke through her fingernails and tore her skin. Thick black padding blossomed on her palms. Her skin split apart, and her thumb ground down through bone and twisted, sharpening into a dew claw.

Her body was tearing itself apart and reforming into something new and strange. Completely without anesthetization.

When nothing human remained, darkness spread like a blanket.

)) ● ((

Jocelyn's phone chimed five times in quick succession. That'd be Pam, then; she didn't know anyone else with the habit of sending a series of short text messages rather than one long one. Sure enough, the messages were from Pam, and they read:

"Is Mel there with you?

"She's not answering her phone.

"Haven't seen her since breakfast.

"Left her several voicemails and texts.

"This isn't like her. :/"

But it's just like you, Jos thought with a wry grin. She shifted positions on her bed and stuck a bookmark in *Candide*. The house was empty and silent—Shari out partying and Pam presumably at the music building. A whiff of sandalwood incense drifted pleasantly under Jos's nose as she responded: "No, she's not here. I haven't seen her all day either. Are you sure she didn't have a hot date?"

"With who?

"Luis?"

"No, I saw him heading to the gym on my way back from dinner."

"Is there another guy interested in her?

"Do you know something I don't?"

Jos frowned, thinking back to yesterday.

"Well, not really. There was this guy at the volleyball game, but she swears it's not like that. They just talked for a little while."

Instead of chiming with another text, Jocelyn's phone played "Lacrymosa" by Evanescence. Pam's voice came over the line, higher than usual, strung with tension. "Tell me everything," she demanded.

After Jos related what she knew, Pam sighed. "That's anticlimactic. Mel never mentioned Gavin to me, so she must not be into him. Which brings us back to—where the heck is she?"

Mother hen, Jos wanted to say, *they all eventually leave the nest.* "I'm sure she's fine, Pam. There's not much trouble you can get into around here, and Mel's a good girl; she's smart and sensible. She'll probably be back any time now. I'll let you know the minute she is— unless you get back first, of course."

Pam gave a dissatisfied grunt but said, "Okay, I guess you're right."

Hours later, as midnight approached, Melanie's continued absence and lack of communication began to worry Jos, too. She and Pam lounged on the couch downstairs, waiting and listening for Mel's car to pull up. Their other housemates trickled in one by one, except for Shari, who frequently spent weekends at her boyfriend's apartment. *Mel sleeps here every single night and would've told us if she were doing otherwise.*

Eventually, Pam's eyelids drooped and she drifted off, still clutching her phone. Jocelyn, a night owl, tried to distract herself by reading. But her imagination took her dark places.

Mel's car broken down, stranding her in the middle of nowhere, her phone battery dead. A stranger driving up, offering help—and abducting her.

Or the same scenario with her car broken down, but Mel deciding to hike through woods at night and getting mauled by a bear. (Did bears live around here?)

Enough, Jos ordered herself. She dialed Melanie's number again.

The call went straight to voicemail. Jos didn't bother to leave another one.

)) ● ((

It was cold.

Everything hurt.

She couldn't move.

She dreaded opening her eyes.

Was she awake or dreaming?

She was scarcely conscious of her surroundings, except for the feeling of a hard, flat surface underneath her. It was smooth and chilly against her bare skin. She became aware that she was shivering.

Even that small movement was painful. Every inch of her body was so sore that it felt like she'd run a marathon in the desert and had fallen onto a cactus every few feet.

Hesitantly, blearily, Melanie opened her eyes. She blinked until the room came into focus.

Oh. Crap.

Sprawled belly-down, head angled to one side, she could see mostly floor but also partway up a wall. Early morning sunbeams filtering in through the skylight illuminated scores of deep gouges, many of them smeared with dark red stains. Her nose caught the coppery tang of blood.

What . . . ?

And then her stomach lurched as she realized how those bloody scratches had gotten there—and why blood covered her hands.

A hoarse groan sandpapered her parched throat. She shut her eyes. Tears streamed down her face. She dry heaved a couple of times.

After sobbing for long minutes, she quieted enough to hear footsteps approaching her door. She tensed up, her sore muscles protesting. Was Gavin going to come in here? Her clothes were across the room, shredded to ribbons, and she felt too weak to get up and retrieve them anyway.

But a gentle knock sounded, and a woman spoke. "Melanie? Are you awake, dear?" Five clicks followed, deadbolts unlocking, but the door remained shut. "I've brought you some clothes. I'll leave them right outside your door—unless you want me to bring them in?"

Melanie was so confused, she didn't know what to think or how to respond. Finally, she rasped, "I'll get them myself."

"All right," replied the woman. Her voice was kind and had a trace of an accent Mel couldn't place. "You'll be more comfortable in a guest bedroom, if you want to sleep for a while. There's one two doors to your right. . . . Oh, I'm sorry. I'm Cara Doyle. Gavin's mom."

His mom is here? That took a moment to process.

His mom. Weird thing for a serial killer to—

Except he wasn't a serial killer, was he? He'd been telling the truth. Mel was a—a—

Although she couldn't figure out how Gavin knew about her being bitten, she realized she owed him a huge debt. Not that that made her want to see him again.

Maybe he knew *that*, too, which was why he'd sent his mother to the door.

Cara Doyle's footsteps had retreated, and the coast was probably clear to grab those clothes. But Melanie felt reluctant—and not just because she was exhausted and sore.

If she got up, opened that door, got dressed, accepted the offered bed and hospitality, it would mean acceptance of her new situation. Her new life.

A miserable, cursed existence.

Gavin's voice in her mind: "You'll rip everyone around you to pieces. And then you'll *eat* them."

No. No, this couldn't be real. Whatever had happened—

She couldn't remember what had happened. Only the pain. The twisting, wrenching, popping, screeching pain.

And then another mind, devouring hers. And then—

Not oblivion. Something worse.

Go back to sleep, a voice told her. *When you wake up, you'll be in your room with Pam. This is all a bad dream.*

She wished that were true. She wished this felt like something her unconscious mind had conjured. It did, in a way, but not to her five senses. Dream walls and dream floors didn't feel like anything; she never touched or noticed them. These wooden ones that surrounded her were hard, cold, full of texture and knotholes—and covered in deep gouges screaming for her attention.

I would've been better off if Gavin had *killed me.*

She was stuck. Stuck bearing this awful burden alone.

She wanted to cry again, but tears wouldn't come. Her body was desperate for water and food, but she refused to move.

When drowsiness came, she didn't fight it.

Light blazed through the room and warmed her skin, coaxing her awake. The soreness from the transformation had abated, but now her muscles were as stiff as the floor beneath her.

And her mind was as numb as her body. Mechanically, she lurched upright and over to the door. Automatically, she put her ear against it and strained to hear any noises. Nothing. She opened the door a crack and looked down. A pair of drawstring pants and a purple sweatshirt sat neatly folded at the threshold, along with some purple-and-pink-striped socks and fluffy yellow slippers. The clothes smelled freshly laundered. She brought them inside. *Whose are these—Gavin's mom's?* She must be tall, because the pants were too long on Melanie, who had to cuff them up.

Before venturing out of the room, Mel collected the scattered scraps of the outfit she'd worn yesterday. None of it was salvageable. Even her shoes had been mangled by teeth and claws. She wished her underwear and bra had survived; it was awkward and uncomfortable not wearing them. It would be weird wearing someone else's, though. Unsure of what to do with her ruined clothes, she left them in a pile in a corner.

Outside the room was a long hallway with half a dozen doors. Most of them were closed, but she could see that the room next door was a bathroom.

At least it was me.

Melanie gripped the hand towel holder and leaned against the wall, not sure whether she wanted to puke or faint.

It could have been Pam.

Or Timmy, she supposed. But she didn't want it to be Timmy either. She didn't want it to be anyone. She didn't want it to be herself, but if it had to be someone, *Let it be me.*

I can be strong.

I can deal with this.

What next?

She scrubbed the dried blood off her hands at the sink, then splashed her face and gulped water from the faucet.

I should also thank Gavin. If he hadn't kidnapped me—

You'll rip everyone around you to pieces. And then you'll *eat* them.

Or bite them. Make them what I am.

She wanted to snoop in the other rooms but restrained herself, fearing getting caught. She was a guest here. She should be polite, go introduce herself to Mrs. Doyle, and thank her for her hospitality, if she was still around.

Let it be me. Not Pam.

She ran her fingers through her tangled hair as she approached the end of the hall that opened into a sizeable kitchen. The décor was a blend of rustic and modern, the appliances new and shiny. Buttery sunlight poured in through large windows.

If not for Gavin, it wouldn't have been just me. It would also be Pam. And Jocelyn, and Shari, and the others.

A wide archway to the left led into the living room. Its walls resembled a log cabin's, and there was a grand stone fireplace complete with antlers mounted above the mantle. The plaid couches and matching overstuffed chairs looked cozy.

It could still be Pam and the others.

It took a moment for Melanie to notice the woman sitting in a rocking chair in a far corner, reading a book. She had glossy black hair, the beginnings of laugh lines, and Asiatic features. She looked up and smiled. "Ah, you're awake."

Confused, Melanie stammered, "Oh, hi, um . . ."

"Cara," the woman reminded her.

Gavin's mom is Asian? Must be his stepmother.

Cara Doyle stood up and approached her guest, holding out a hand. Melanie shook it. It was as warm as Cara's eyes and smile. "Nice to meet you."

After thanking her hostess for the change of clothes, Melanie looked around and asked, "Is, um, is Gavin here?"

"Last I checked, he was still napping."

That was when they heard a door opening down the hallway. Footsteps approached. "I'm up," said Gavin, entering the room. His voice was scratchy, and dark circles hollowed his eye sockets.

Melanie glanced at him but then shifted her gaze to her feet. She studied the fluffiness of her slippers—they reminded her of baby chicks.

Silence stretched.

Why is he *so worn out?* she wondered. *Was he up all night? Doing what? Keeping watch?*

Before she or Gavin could think of anything to say, Cara put in, "I bet you two want lunch."

"Yes, please," chorused Melanie and Gavin. Startled, they looked at each other and then away again.

They followed Cara into the kitchen, where she pulled out bread, lunch meat, lettuce, and mayonnaise. "Sit down," she told them. "I've got this."

While Cara whipped up sandwiches with practiced ease, Melanie sank gratefully onto a cushioned chair at the marble-topped kitchen table. There was a bowl of fruit on it, and she grabbed a banana. Her hands shook so much it was embarrassing.

Gavin took a seat at the opposite end of the table. He leaned forward and rested an elbow on it, cupping his chin in his hand. Melanie sneaked glances at him and noticed he looked pensive. But there was something else. Something was different about his appearance, aside from the exhaustion. What was it?

Cara set the sandwiches in front of them and poured glasses of ice water. Melanie thanked her and tried to eat like a lady, not a Labrador retriever.

When she was almost done, she shot another glance at Gavin, and her eyes locked with his. She was about to look away but suddenly realized what the slight discrepancy in his appearance was. Unable to stop the words from tumbling out, she asked, "Are you wearing contacts? I thought you had brown eyes."

They were a light hazel today.

Gavin's face took on a guilty expression. He swallowed and said, "Um, no, I'm not wearing them right now. But I do wear brown ones."

"Why?"

He exchanged glances with Cara. "You haven't told her yet," she murmured.

Gavin shook his head.

"Told me what?" Melanie was squirming with curiosity.

"I'll show you," he said quietly. Closing his eyes, he screwed up his face in concentration.

What . . . ? This is too weird, thought Mel.

But then he opened his eyes again, and hers grew wide as she understood.

Gavin's irises had ignited into fiery wheels of gold.

8

Cabin

OCTOBER 16–17, FULL MOON (SECOND NIGHT)
"You—you're a w-werewolf too," Melanie stammered. Her jaw had dropped, and her mind was reeling.

The gold dimmed and then left Gavin's eyes, only to be replaced by a sheen of sorrow. "Yeah," he said, "since I was a little kid."

Holy crap. She couldn't imagine what his life must have been like.

"My parents built this place for me," he continued. "This is where I go every full moon. We're near DuBois, a couple hours southwest of Wellsboro. My parents live an hour east of here in Pleasant Gap. Yesterday morning, my dad came and made sure the backup safe room was ready, which is where I put you."

She nodded, processing.

"I'm truly sorry for what I did to you, Melanie. For scaring you so much."

"Oh." The apology took her by surprise. Chewing her lower lip, she considered his words and his expression. They seemed genuine, contrite, and hadn't included "I told you so" or "It was for your own good."

Cara Doyle cleared her throat. "I can see there's a lot that you two need to discuss. I'll be down the hall doing some cleaning." She stood up and left the room.

"Apology accepted," Melanie said quietly. "And . . . thank you for saving me. And my friends."

A hint of a smile played on Gavin's face. "Welcome."

Now that the air had been cleared, Melanie felt muscles relax that she hadn't noticed were tense. She wasn't in enemy territory; she was safe and among allies. She had so many questions, though.

"Why don't we go talk in the living room, where it's more comfortable?" Gavin suggested, seeming to read her mind.

He settled onto an armchair near the fireplace, and she sat on its twin, facing him across the hearth. Immediately, she voiced the concern weighing most urgently on her mind: "My friends are probably freaking out, wondering where I am. Can you drive me back soon?"

Frowning, Gavin said, "I'll take you back to Wellsboro, but not today."

"What? Why not?!" Mel demanded.

"Because it's too far of a drive. We wouldn't make it back before moonrise."

"Huh?"

Sorrow crept into his eyes again. "We have two more transformations this month, Melanie—tonight and tomorrow night. Tonight is the true full moon."

She gasped. "Are you serious? *Three* times every month?"

"Afraid so."

Memories of last night flooded back, and tightness gripped Mel's chest. Her mouth was dry, her tongue like a roll of blank, crumbling parchment. She knew that a maelstrom of anger should be howling inside her, but instead she felt empty. Silence pressed down on the room, thick and suffocating.

"I'm sorry," said Gavin. His words fell hollowly to the cold stone hearth.

Abruptly, she stood and walked to a window, turning her face so he couldn't see it. Deep green pines and orange-brushed maples and elms stood outside, their branches dancing lightly in the wind. Birds flitted about, squirrels chattered and chased each other, and the sun beamed down from a brilliant blue sky dotted with fluffy clouds. How could the world be so peaceful yet so messed-up at the same time?

She heard Gavin say, "I'll go get your purse and phone so you can call your friends." His footsteps creaked on the hardwood floor.

Taking a bracing breath, Melanie sat back down. When Gavin returned with her belongings, she fished her phone out of her handbag and saw that she'd missed seven calls from Pam and Jos. Pam had also sent her a string of text messages. "Mel, where are you? . . . Are you okay? . . . Please call me soon!"

Melanie had to scroll to see them all.

"Oh, boy. I'm in deep doo-doo," she said.

Pulling up her contact list, she found Pam's number, but her finger hovered above it, hesitant to dial. *Let it be me.*

If she told Pam the truth, what would Pam do?

She'd want to come with me. Protect me.

You'll rip apart—

It could still be Pam.

"Are you going to tell them the truth?" Gavin asked neutrally.

I can be strong.

"No." She was sure about that. "But whatever I say, it's going to be hard for my friends to believe. I've never done anything like this before—disappearing and not telling anyone."

The two of them brainstormed excuses, but Mel didn't like anything they came up with. She was growing tired again, and she didn't want to speak to Pam right now. At last she reopened the text-messaging app and typed: "I'm okay. Don't worry. Be back in a couple days. Emergency came up." Then she turned off her phone in case Pam tried to call.

Gavin yawned, and Melanie involuntarily copied him. He smiled at her and said, "We both need naps."

Mel agreed, but there were so many important questions, and she was itching for answers. Just then, however, Cara Doyle entered the room and said, "I agree. You two should get some rest while you can. Melanie, let me show you to the guest room."

"All right," Mel relented. They'd be here for a couple more days—plenty of time to interrogate Gavin. She stood and followed Cara to the hallway, Gavin at their heels.

Cara pushed open a door and flicked a light switch. "This might be my favorite room in the cabin," she said, dimple and laugh lines appearing. "I call it the Butterfly Room."

Melanie didn't need to ask why. Pictures of the winged insects, and brightly colored mounted specimens, decorated the walls—which were a warm light beige. Lavender and mossy green were the other dominant tones, patterned together with touches of ivory on the curtains and bedspread. The quilt and pillow shams looked homemade. Mel wondered if Cara had sewn them, but she was too exhausted to think to ask. The scent of lavender from the candles on the dresser lulled and relaxed her.

She said "thank you" and "goodnight" to her hosts, and Cara promised to wake the two young werewolves shortly before moonrise.

Moonrise.

Before moonrise.

When she'd—she'd—

Melanie screamed as her skin split, as her bones cracked and her joints twisted. She screamed and she kept screaming until the wolf came, and then—

Melanie rolled over and pressed her face into her pillow.

She screamed and she kept—

Stop it! Stop thinking about this! Go to sleep!

And when you wake up, the wolf will come.

Crushing feet into paws. Crushing her mind into—

Stop it!

But she couldn't stop it. Her body tightened around her pillow and shook. Tears streamed uncontrollably, and her throat ripped itself rawer with silent screams.

I can't do this again. I can't. I can't. I have to get out of here—

It could still be Pam.

When Cara came back hours later, it was to a seemingly calm Melanie. The girl sat cross-legged on the floor, breathing out, in, out. Mel felt weak and pale, the strength wrung out of her like the tears.

"It's time," Cara said, and Mel climbed stiffly to her feet, a puppeteer's plaything. Her legs jerked out one in front of the other.

In the hallway, she crossed paths with a groggy Gavin. He gave her a friendly nod, and she responded with a half-hearted smile. She watched as he entered the room across from her safe room, and she caught her first glimpse of his. Scratches covered its walls, and the wood paneling was torn off in places, revealing brick underneath. There were no deadbolts on the outside of Gavin's doorframe. It must lock from the inside. Well, that made sense—he had never been held hostage here. He'd known what was coming, the first time he'd used this place. Right? She wondered about his early life and what it was like to be a child werewolf. Later, she'd ask him more about his past—and to reverse the locks on her room.

"Ten minutes to moonrise," Cara said from behind Mel, startling her. "If you set your clothes outside in the hallway this time, I'll replace them with a fresh outfit for tomorrow."

"Okay." Reluctantly, Melanie trudged to her safe room and stopped at the door. The stench of bleach assaulted her moon-sensitized nostrils. The bloodied walls had been scrubbed clean, but no bleach could remove the blood from her memory.

Fingers, scratched down to the bone.

Melanie shook like a leaf, staring and staring as she clenched the doorframe with white knuckles.

"Go on in," Cara said. "I'll lock it behind you."

Yes. What Cara said made sense. Go in. Just one foot in front of the other.

Mel didn't move. Her fingernails bent against the doorframe.

"Melanie?" Cara asked, touching the girl's shoulder. "You only have five minutes. If you need help—"

The pain was already approaching, the same ache as yesterday. And next—next—

"Melanie, I know it's tough," Cara said gently, "but you need to go in now."

Mel looked at her with empty eyes. "I know," she said.

Cara put one hand over hers. "Let go of the doorframe."

No! No, no, no! She wouldn't do it. She wouldn't go in that room again. She couldn't—

It could still be Pam.

Or Cara.

I can be strong.

With her opposite hand, Mel peeled her fingers from the doorframe and toppled into the room beyond. She heard Cara lock the deadbolts one by one.

And she waited for the moon to rise.

)) ● ((

The temperature was dropping more drastically at night, this time of year. Erickson knew he'd have to find an indoor hideout before next full moon. Even though his imminent transformation elevated his body temperature, the cold got uncomfortable as soon as he disrobed. The cave's stone floor was frigid under his bare feet. The rock surfaces of the narrow tunnel were even chillier against his knees, legs, and hands. Occasionally, his shoulders or back grazed the tunnel's roof, and he flinched at its icy touch.

Definitely not coming here in November.

After hoisting himself out the other end, relieved, he paced the perimeter of the spacious cavern beyond. His thoughts turned to Gary Saddler.

He'd left the man sitting on a boulder outside the cave's entrance, sipping from a thermos. Erickson could have kicked himself for not bringing a hot drink of his own. Saddler had offered to let him take the coffee, but he'd declined. Being in anyone's debt left a much bitterer taste in his mouth than coffee would.

Can't believe I allowed him to come along . . . not that I could stop him. When Saddler had shown up at his door a couple of nights ago, Erickson had worked up his most intimidating face, golden eyes glowing, and had been about to ream Saddler out—until he'd caught a closer glimpse of *her.*

Her name was Chandra Kapoor, and Saddler had introduced her as another member of the Organization. A werewolf. She couldn't have been older than thirty—a bit young for Erickson, almost young enough to be his daughter—and she was gorgeous. Curves in all the right places, but still slender. Doe eyes and a pair of gams to die for.

In a daze, he'd invited them inside, and he'd listened, mostly to Chandra. Saddler was wise to let her do the majority of the talking. *Dammit, he sure knows what cards to play.*

So here they were: Saddler guarding Erickson like a loyal dog. "Don't you have a job? What about your family? Do they know about your extracurricular activities?"

"I'm a police detective," Saddler had explained, flashing his badge. "I take a personal day, my wife thinks I'm at work . . . or, in this case, camping with some buddies for the weekend."

Chandra had offered to come along and change in the cave with Erickson, but he'd drawn the line there. Two wolves trapped together couldn't be a good idea. Would they rip each other apart? Would his wolf . . . try anything?

"It'll be okay," she'd said, a mysterious glint in her eye.

"How do you know?" he challenged.

A coy smile blossomed on her full lips. "Come to a meeting, and I'll tell you."

A meeting? Erickson thought now, memories of her long lashes tantalizing him. Luring him.

His wife had had lashes like Chandra's. Dark, silky, lustrous hair like hers. There wasn't much of a resemblance beyond those features, but the way he and Glynnis used to look at each other . . .

A sharp pang jabbed his chest, and at first he thought it was from the tragic memories. Then he realized his transformation was starting.

Soon, all memories and all humanity were gone.

)) ● ((

Melanie awoke in more pain than the previous morning. Groaning, she blinked until her vision cleared. The safe room was still pretty dark, but she could make out the scratches and smears of blood on the nearby wall. It looked like almost every square inch of paneling had been gouged.

Suddenly, the raw pain didn't matter—nothing mattered as much as getting out. Mel grabbed the door and hurriedly snatched the clothes outside. She hardly noticed the new undergarments in the pile, hardly noticed anything as she pulled the material rapidly on, leaving the door open a crack so as to never lose sight of the way out—

Out! Out!

Out to the safety of the Butterfly Room, to fall into dark dreams so much kinder than the mind of the wolf.

She was running through the Pine Groves forest. Everything was dim and blurry, shifting and shadowed. Was it night or day? She couldn't tell; a thick mesh of branches overhead obscured the sky. The woods enveloped, closing in, pressing down, roots rising to trip her. Fear clutched at her heart, but her legs dragged her along.

The entrance to the cave appeared in front of her. No, stop! *she told herself.* Don't go in there! *But her feet wouldn't obey, and she plunged into the deeper darkness.*

She navigated the twists and turns, caverns and passages, as if they were a puzzle she'd long ago solved, until her rogue feet brought her to the last place she ever wanted to see again—the room with the crawl space.

Crouching down, she peered inside the tiny tunnel. Two yellow dots gleamed at its far end, and angry growls commenced. They turned into shrieks, howls, and snarls as the beast advanced toward her.

Why wasn't she running away?!

You are destined for this, a familiar male voice rang in her ears. With shock, she realized the words had echoed out from the tunnel. She could only kneel, rooted to the spot, and watch the beast struggle closer. At last it was near enough for her to catch a glimpse of its face.

Gavin?!

Melanie jerked awake, shivering and shaking. The sheets were tangled around her, and she felt cold and hot and sweaty.

It was him. He bit me! That's how he knew about me!

Bright sunlight made her curtains glow, and the clock on the wall said it was almost noon. She'd gotten several hours of rest, and after that nightmare, she didn't want to go back to sleep.

The bathroom was empty, so Mel stripped and stepped into the shower. She spent a long time under the hot, soothing stream of water, trying to calm her mind and wash away the strong emotions the dream had stirred up—anger, fear, betrayal, confusion, mistrust.

A dream isn't proof, she lectured herself. *Don't attack him when you see him. That won't help you get answers.*

But fingers of dread still poked at the base of her spine. What if her subconscious *had* deduced the truth?

Half an hour later, she reluctantly turned off the water, then dried off, dressed, and made her way to the kitchen. Cara smiled at her. "Hungry for lunch?"

"Yes. And, uh, thank you for the . . ."

Gavin walked in, and Melanie's mind screeched to a halt. *You bit me! It was you!*

His mother's mouth twitched into a grin, and she nodded. "You're welcome. Figured you were pretty uncomfortable without them."

You did this to me!

Cara served them grilled cheese sandwiches and tomato soup, and after lunch, she disappeared down the hall again.

Gavin just kept sitting across from her casually, no big deal. *Doesn't he feel any remorse at all?*

Taking a deep breath, trying to keep her voice calm and even, she said, "I know it was you."

Gavin looked up at the break in her voice. "What?"

"I know it was *you!*" Melanie repeated, voice rising against her control. "You were the one who bit me! That's how you knew what happened to me!"

Gavin jerked back, but he'd evidently expected something like this, because he said, "No, Melanie. It's—"

"You BIT me!" Melanie interrupted, her voice rising to a shriek without her meaning to. "You DID this to me!"

"Melanie—"

"Don't LIE to me." When had she gotten to her feet? "I SAW you. DON'T LIE TO ME!"

"I'm psychic," Gavin said.

Melanie blinked and gasped, momentum lost. Of all the things she'd expected to hear, this wasn't one of them.

"I was here last full moon," Gavin said. "You can ask my mom; she came with me."

"Of course she'd stand up for you ..." Melanie said, but the wind had left her sails, and she found herself collapsing back into her seat. "But I saw ... I ..."

Had a dream.

Melanie, you idiot. It was just a dream.

But I saw ...

Melanie buried her face in her hands, hiding the tears streaming down her face. Hadn't she run out of tears yet?

"Sometimes," Gavin hurried to explain, as if explanations would calm her, "I see the future. I get these visions. My grandma had them too. She said it's the 'second sight' from our Welsh blood. Anyway. The night before that volleyball game, I was brushing my teeth and I looked in the mirror and saw myself at the game. I'm not really into sports, and I wasn't planning on going. But then I knew I had to.

"See, the visions are always important. They're never wrong, either. I thought there would be something I was supposed to learn or some-one I was supposed to help." He looked down at the floor and mut-tered, "But I was too late to keep you from getting bitten in the first place." Scowling, he slammed his fist on the arm of his chair.

The heat of his sudden anger dried Melanie's tears, and she stared wordlessly at him.

"Why didn't it warn me a month earlier?" Gavin whispered. Gold flashed in his eyes. "I would've gone to Pine Groves and done something to make you leave." Melanie had to lean forward to hear, "No one deserves *this*."

Silence stretched, save for the birds twittering outside. Clouds shifted; light played across Gavin's face and revealed blond highlights in his hair.

Mel struggled to believe his unlikely story. She'd learned of werewolves' existence less than forty-eight hours ago. Now psychic powers were real too?

Recalling his brief seizure-like episode in the gym lobby helped, and she asked him about it. "Was that another vision?"

"Yeah. That's the one that showed you in the cave getting bitten."

"Oh."

Even if he's lying and he did bite me, he sure seems to regret it. And it wouldn't have been on purpose. His mind was gone; the monster had taken over. He couldn't help what he did.

Besides, he saved me. He didn't have to do that.

The hollow, empty feeling was back, consuming her chest.

"I always kind of assumed I was the only one with this curse," she heard Gavin whisper. There was loneliness in his voice and weary defeat in his slumped shoulders.

"But what about the wolf who bit you?" she asked gently. "Don't you think he or she is still out there somewhere?"

"Oh. I guess you're right," he said. "I was so young when it happened, though, not really aware of what was going on. The memory has faded so much. All I know is, I don't have a clue who the person was because I never saw their human form. They're probably long gone— probably don't even know what they did to me. So they left me alone in this, and I never had anyone who truly understood."

Melanie felt the urge to lean forward and put her hand over his, but she restrained herself.

"Not that I wanted there to be others suffering this way," Gavin went on. "I would never wish this curse on anyone, Melanie. Believe me. I wouldn't do a dumb, reckless thing like transforming in a cave with no guarantee I wouldn't get out and hurt people. That's why I have this place."

She nodded. After a long moment, she said, "I believe you." It was true for now, at least.

"Thank you," he said softly.

The room was warm and filled with the scent of cinnamon. The whistle of wind through the trees outside was low and soothing. Clouds moved back over the sun, and the resultant dimness lulled Melanie. She thought of returning to the Butterfly Room and taking a nap, but didn't care to have any more nightmares. She sat up straighter and tried to dispel her drowsiness.

"One more night here," she murmured to herself. Then she asked Gavin, "Today's Monday, isn't it?"

"Yeah," he said. "We missed our classes today."

"And we'll miss them tomorrow too. Crap." She tried to remember what assignments were on her syllabuses for this week. *It'll probably be okay. I'm caught up on my homework, but I need to finish a couple of reading assignments. I won't let myself get behind.*

An image of Pam's worried face floated into her mind. Her best friend was probably going crazy in her absence, chewing her manicured nails or pulling out her carefully coifed hair.

It could still be Pam.

Melanie couldn't tell her.

9

Warning

The next morning, Melanie tried to flee her safe room as quickly as she had the previous day; but her scratches were deeper, hurt even worse— and they bled on the outfit Cara had left her. Guilt- and pain-ridden, she finally collapsed on the Butterfly Room's soft bed. She slept until Cara woke her at two p.m.

"Melanie," said the woman, gently nudging her shoulder, "you and Gavin should get ready to go. If you leave soon, you can be back at school in time for dinner."

"Huh? Oh. Right," Mel rasped. Lethargic limbs protesting, she dragged herself out from under the warm comforter. She longed to sleep the rest of the day away, but her throat was parched and her stomach growling, and she remembered that Pam and her other friends were probably racked with anxiety. Mel hadn't turned her phone back on since she'd sent Pam those text messages two days ago, and she wondered how many return messages awaited her. She'd check later.

After washing up in the bathroom, she entered the kitchen and saw that Gavin was at the table chowing down on a couple of thick, meat-loaded subs. Cara had just set out a plate of food for Mel, and she smiled at Mel before disappearing down the hallway.

"You have a great mom," Mel commented as she and Gavin ate, pretending that everything was normal. "Is she your stepmom?"

"No, she and my dad, Jeff, adopted me when I was eleven."

"Oh," said Mel. "What does your dad look like? Do you have a picture of him?" She glanced around, noticing the room's décor lacked the personal touch of family photos.

"Yeah, hang on," Gavin said, and strode down the hallway to his

79

room. He returned with his wallet, flipping it open and showing Mel a three-by-five of a beaming couple. A muscular African American man with a graying goatee had his arm around the willowy Cara, who leaned contentedly against his shoulder.

"They seem happy and loving."

"Yeah, they're great." Gavin smiled. "Mom's a counselor, and Dad's an anesthesiologist."

Melanie grinned wanly. "So both of their jobs involve taking away pain."

Her comment elicited a chuckle from him. "Guess so."

Then Mel thought, *Oh! That's how Gavin got hold of whatever drug he used to knock me out. And with a doctor's salary—and Cara might have a PhD, too—building a nice place like this probably didn't set them back much.*

"I packed you some snacks for the road too," said Cara, reentering the kitchen, smelling like bleach.

"Thank you so much. For everything," Melanie said.

Cara put a hand on Mel's shoulder and once again flashed her gentle, genuine smile. "You're welcome." She paused, then added in a contemplative voice, "I've been doing this monthly routine with Gavin for more than ten years now."

Glancing at him, Melanie thought, *That's far too long. I'll do my best to end it, for him and for me. There's got to be a cure.*

The two young werewolves finished eating and then gathered their few belongings. Melanie pulled on the brand-new tennis shoes Cara had bought for her. They resembled the ones Mel's wolf form had destroyed, and her hostess had refused to let her pay her back for them.

"Goodbye," said Cara, hugging her son and then Melanie. "Take care of yourselves. You're welcome here any time, Melanie. Let me give you my phone number before you go."

The two women exchanged contact information, and Gavin took Mel's phone and used it to call his.

Heading out the front door and into the sunny afternoon, Mel shielded her eyes and drew in deep, invigorating breaths of crisp autumn air. She felt like a prisoner who'd just been released. Slowly, she followed Gavin to his tan Ford sedan, enjoying the smells of pine, moss, and soil still damp from last night's rain.

One month before I'll have to think about this again.

One month to learn how to be strong.

For Pam.

Gavin slid behind the wheel, and Melanie climbed in the passenger's side. The car crunched down the long gravel driveway.

Several minutes passed in silence. Gavin was concentrating on staying alert and awake. He'd downed an energy drink right before they'd left, but his metabolism would remain heightened for a couple of days, and the caffeine's effects would wear off within an hour. Another drink waited in his cup holder.

Fortunately, traffic was light and no lanes were closed due to construction—a near miracle in Pennsylvania. The weather was perfect, the bright cerulean sky mostly clear of clouds. Tall trees lined the highway on both sides, their leaves dancing on a breeze and blushing scarlet, burnt orange, and gold.

Gavin's thoughts drifted to Melanie. Observing her out of the corner of his eye, he noticed that her hair glinted with highlights the color of the autumn leaves. She was leaning against the headrest, dozing, so he risked a more direct glimpse. Dark circles under her eyes stood out starkly against her pale skin. She looked worn out and somehow childlike. The urge to protect her welled up inside him.

Her long-lashed eyes fluttered open, and he quickly turned his attention back to the road. She yawned and stretched, and after a while, they fell to talking. Gavin told her about the computer-science degree he was pursuing, and Melanie talked animatedly about working for the school newspaper. Eventually, however, as they both knew it would, the talk turned to werewolves.

"I've been one for fourteen years," Gavin said. "Ever since I was eight."

"Haven't you tried to research a cure?" Melanie asked.

"Of course," he replied. "I looked through tons of websites and books, especially when I was a teenager. But there's a lot more advice out there on how to kill us than on how to help us. Some say death is our only cure. And many of the other suggestions are violent too, like killing the wolf that bit you or having a close friend stab you with a silver knife."

Melanie winced.

"Aside from those, I found a lot of weird mystical stuff, instructions for ceremonies and rituals. Then there are the religious suggestions: splashing a werewolf with holy water, having a priest perform an exorcism. Or there's the aconite plant, also known as—"

"Wolfsbane," said Melanie. "Isn't that poisonous?"

"Yes, it's highly toxic. Even a tiny dose can be lethal to normal humans. As for its effect on werewolves, sources don't agree about whether it helps us or harms us. Some say wolfsbane merely repels a werewolf, some say it's deadly, and some say that in the right dosage it can be used to make a potion that will cure us. I found a few recipes, but they have awful ingredients and are based on legend, not scientific research. Melanie, there's no way I'm messing around with wolfsbane. It's a nasty, painful way to die."

"I see." Her voice was very small. Letting out a dejected sigh, she turned and gazed out her window.

I wish I could've given her better news, thought Gavin as he stared ahead at the long stretch of dark gray highway. His hands gripped the steering wheel more tightly. It was one thing to give up and accept his own fate; it was another to tell someone else, someone who was starting to feel like—*Like what? A friend? Family?*—to resign herself to her fate.

"Hey," said Melanie, breaking him out of his thoughts, "your dad's an anesthesiologist, right? Hasn't he ever tried to give you drugs for the pain?"

"Sure," said Gavin. "They didn't help much, and they wore off quickly. Even when he gave me as high of a dose as he dared."

She frowned. "Has he tried testing your blood or DNA, doing a CT scan on you—anything like that?"

"He's done a lot of lab tests and some scans, but he couldn't find any abnormalities or any clues for a treatment or cure."

"What about alternative healing?" Melanie pressed. "Have you tried meditation, hypnosis, acupuncture?" Desperation was creeping into her voice.

Gavin shook his head. "Never gave it much thought. Nobody I know is into that kind of stuff, not even my mom. She grew up in

Hawaii, and her auntie had an acupuncture studio, but Mom's always been more modern than traditional."

"Wow, Hawaii," said Melanie, perking up. "Cool. *That's* the bit of an accent I heard in her voice. I've always wanted to go to Hawaii. Have you been there?"

"A few times."

"Aw, I'm jealous."

Gavin grinned, happy that he'd unwittingly steered the conversation toward a more upbeat topic. He described the islands to Melanie, and she asked questions.

As they drew closer to her campus, though, he brought the topic back around to werewolves. He wanted to give her an important reminder before they parted. "Don't forget to be especially careful to control your emotions during the few days before and after a full moon. It's lucky that your eyes are already brown, so you can start wearing dark contacts like I do and no one will notice." He told her which brand was the best to buy and recommended a good optometrist.

Melanie thanked him and then asked, "By the way, do we have a silver allergy? Because I've got mostly silver jewelry."

"No, we don't. You can still wear it. And crosses don't repel us, either, so you can wear a silver cross necklace if you have one."

"I thought crosses were a vampire thing."

"Some legends attribute the fear of them to werewolves too," he replied. "I've also had holy water sprinkled on me, and nothing happened—good or bad."

"Has your shadow ever taken the form of a wolf?" she asked.

"Only when I *was* a wolf."

"What about animals getting skittish around you?"

"Not that I've ever noticed."

Half a minute later, Melanie shifted in her seat and said, "We're almost there." They'd reached the Wellsboro city limits and were only a mile from her campus. Detecting a hint of nervousness in her voice, Gavin glanced at her and saw that she was frowning slightly, twirling a strand of hair between her fingers. He could understand the apprehension—she'd left campus as one person and was returning as a different person. She had secrets now.

They passed through the university's front gate. Melanie waved at the guard, who nodded back. "Take a left, please," she told Gavin when they came to a fork in the road. "Gotta get my car from behind the com building."

He recognized the route he'd taken a few days ago—the road that curved around the edge of campus like an arm holding back the thick woods. The sun rested below the treetops, throwing long shadows everywhere. Students, some alone but most in groups, trekked across the hilly campus toward a large building at its center. Probably the cafeteria, Gavin guessed, since the dinner hour was beginning.

As they rounded the side of the three-story brick building where Gavin had kidnapped Melanie last Saturday, he saw that her small blue Honda was waiting patiently right where she'd left it. He parked his car next to hers and cut the engine. "Well, here we are," he said.

"Yep," Melanie murmured. "Thanks for bringing me back." She made no move to unbuckle her seatbelt or to open her door.

"No problem."

They glanced at each other and then looked away. Melanie opened her mouth to speak but, hesitating, shut it again. At last she drew in a deep breath and let herself out of the car.

Longing to stretch his weary, aching limbs, Gavin climbed out too. A spasm of pain shot through his lower back, and he failed to stifle a groan. "Are you all right?" Melanie asked, walking over to him.

"Yeah. Don't worry," he said, meeting her concerned gaze.

And then it happened again. He was pulled into her eyes as a vision overtook him.

A man in dark sunglasses was driving up to the Wellsboro gate and flashing a police badge at the guard. The guard waved him through, and he cruised around campus in his unmarked car, scanning groups of students. He parked in a central location, exited the vehicle, and meandered around the sunlit university on foot. It appeared he was searching for someone. . . .

Gavin emerged from the vision feeling puzzled and worried. His eyes refocused on Melanie's face. "What did you see?" she asked quietly.

He told her, and her eyes grew wide. "This guy could be looking for you," Gavin warned, "since what I see usually pertains to the person

I'm with. And he's giving me dark, ominous vibes. Be careful, Melanie. He's not dressed like a cop or driving a police cruiser, but you should avoid men wearing dark sunglasses. He's average height, average build, no distinctive features. Brown hair, possibly in his mid-thirties."

"Okay. I'll try to stay indoors on sunny days for a while. I assume you don't know exactly when he's going to come around?"

"No. Didn't see a calendar. Or his license plate number." Gavin frowned. He described the man's car to her, but it was a fairly common American-made sedan with no modifications or bumper stickers. Plus, it was black, one of the three most popular color choices. Several students here might drive an identical model.

When he felt like he'd given Melanie all the information he could, Gavin checked his watch and said, "I'd better get going. Don't want to make you miss your dinner, and I'm ready for mine."

"Yeah. Okay. Better let you go." Fiddling with the hem of her shirt, Melanie shifted her weight to her other foot and added, "I'll be sure to bookmark the NASA moon phases website. So, um, I can come to the cabin with you next month, too, right?"

"Of course." He gave her a reassuring smile. "I'll call you a day or so before I pick you up."

"All right. Have a safe trip home."

"Thanks." Gavin slid behind the wheel of his car again, watched her climb into hers, and then drove back to Brookside.

Melanie glanced around warily as she parked next to Hartman Cottage. Nobody was in sight, and the dorm's windows were dark. *Good. Hopefully Pam and the others are all at the cafeteria.* Mel needed a bit of time alone before she faced her friends.

Letting herself into the cottage, she tiptoed upstairs. Her door was closed and locked, to her relief. It felt strange walking back into her room, like she was returning from a months-long journey in a distant land. But she'd only been gone for three days.

Melanie flopped down onto the bed, a wave of exhaustion overtaking her. She yearned for sleep, but her stomach growled. Groaning, she sat back up. She wondered if Pam was at dinner or if she'd finished and headed to the music building to practice. Mel hoped for the latter.

As she stepped back out into the hall and padded toward the bathroom, Mel heard her suitemates' door opening. She froze. Jocelyn appeared and immediately spotted Melanie. "You're back," she said, her tone a mixture of surprise and relief.

"Yeah," was all that Melanie could think of to say.

"You sure scared us, Mel."

"I . . . I'm sorry." A lump of guilt tightened her throat.

Jocelyn's shrewd green eyes narrowed, studying Melanie curiously, and Mel worried that her friend would start asking probing questions. But after a moment, Jos said, "I'm heading down to dinner. You coming?"

"I was just going to freshen up. I'll be ready in a minute."

"I'll wait."

To make sure I don't disappear again?

At the sink, Mel splashed her face and patted it dry, then peered closely at herself in the mirror. *Those stupid dark circles.* She hadn't showered today, and her hair was limp and disheveled. The phrase "hot mess" sprang to mind, causing her to wrinkle her nose—both at the overused expression and at the truth of it. Quickly, she combed her hair, pinched her cheeks to put some color in them, and returned to the hallway. Jocelyn was leaning against the wall, arms crossed, a serene and meditative look on her face—like she could have stood there for hours.

"Does Pam know you're back?" she asked Melanie as they left their dorm. The evening air was brisk, and the first faint stars were appearing in the darkening sky.

"No," said Mel. "I've only been here for fifteen minutes and haven't seen her."

Jos pulled her phone out and began to type a text message. When she was done, she said, "There. I told her. Now she can have some peace of mind."

"Is she . . . mad at me?" Mel asked hesitantly.

Pursing her lips, Jocelyn considered the question. "More like worried. To death. Like a mother whose child has vanished."

"Oh, great," said Melanie. She wasn't surprised, though, after hearing and reading the messages Pam had left her.

"Are you going to tell us where you were and what you were

doing?"

Melanie stumbled and stopped walking. They had almost reached the student center, and half a dozen other people were standing around within earshot. "Not here," said Mel in a low voice, stalling. She strode ahead of her friend into the building and led the way to the cafeteria.

After loading up trays, she and Jos scanned the seating area. Several tables in their usual corner were empty, and they headed that way. The most direct route took them past a table full of guys who had been at Pine Groves—Timmy among them. *Ugh.*

She prayed he wouldn't look her way, but to her chagrin she heard his nasal voice call out, "Cutting classes lately, huh, Melody? What's the matter? Can't handle the pressure?"

Melanie fumed, clenching her teeth and her tray tightly. Nasty words boiled up in her mind, along with the urge to throw her baked potato at Timmy's smug face. Then she thought of her eyes glowing yellow and of Gavin's warning. *Crap. I've got to be careful.* Taking a deep, steadying breath, she walked away without saying a word.

Jocelyn delivered a swift riposte in Mel's stead: "I'm surprised you can even find your way to your classes, *Tommy.*"

Timmy's ears went red, and his tablemates roared with laughter. Jos beamed at them, then flounced away looking delighted with herself.

"That was awesome!" said Mel, snickering as she sat down.

"Well," said Jos modestly, "I do have four older brothers. Had to learn how to hold my own."

They talked about family and other safe topics while they ate. To Mel's great relief, Jos didn't bug her again about where she'd been.

Back in the dorm twenty minutes later, Mel crawled into bed, achy and unable to fight off her exhaustion any longer. She was asleep in seconds.

When Pam returned from choir practice, she found the room dark and could hear soft, even breathing coming from her roommate's bed. *Thank goodness.* Even though Jocelyn had told her that Melanie was back safe and sound, she'd needed to see her for herself.

What's going on with you, Mel? Pam thought for the thousandth time, tiptoeing over to her best friend's bedside in the dim light from the open door. *Turning off your phone, missing classes. And Tuesday is one of your tutoring nights. You're supposed to be in the library with Luis.*

Pam leaned down for a closer look at Melanie's face. It was wan and pinched, as if she were in pain or having nightmares. Sympathy swept through Pam, dispelling her frustration and the desire to wake Mel and demand answers. *Poor thing. Let her rest.* They could talk in the morning.

Gathering some books and papers from her desk, Pam went downstairs to do her homework. Fortunately, her housemates didn't have the TV on tonight. The only distraction she had to fight off was curiosity.

Later, as Pam lay in bed on the brink of slumber, she heard Melanie whimpering and mumbling in her sleep. The words were quiet and slurred, but Pam caught "wolf" and "Gavin" and "gotta be a cure." *Strange,* she thought before drifting off.

At 6:30 a.m., Pam's alarm woke both girls. Melanie greeted her roommate in subdued tones, her voice hoarse and a guilty expression creeping onto her face.

"I'm so relieved you're okay," said Pam, trying not to sound too stern or too chipper. "So, what was the emergency you said came up?"

The blood drained out of Melanie's face, and she looked away. "I—I can't..."

"Can't tell me? Why not?" demanded Pam. "After what you put me through—"

"I'm really sorry, Pam. I didn't mean to scare you."

"Why did you wait so long before letting me know you were all right? I was about to call the cops! I thought you got kidnapped!"

At those words, a shadow passed over Mel's face. "I wasn't able to use my phone for a while," she said.

"Where were you, some place with no reception?"

"Something like that," Melanie mumbled.

Letting out an agitated huff, Pam said, "Mel, I don't know why you feel you have to be so secretive about whatever this is. I'm your best friend; you know you can tell me anything. I won't judge."

Her roommate nodded.

"You looked awful last night," Pam continued. "You went to bed so early, like you were sick or something. I was worried about you."

"I'm sorry," Melanie repeated meekly. "I was tired, but I'm fine now."

Pam had had enough of the apologies. "Okay. I'm glad you feel better. You're back, you're safe, and that's what matters. I can't make you tell me where you went, but I wish you'd trust me. Just promise me you won't run off like that again, please."

"I . . ."

Pam wanted to punch her pillow. *Why is that a hard thing to promise?* Her hands balled into fists. "Melanie—"

"I promise I'll tell you if I'm going to leave for a while," Mel interrupted.

"Are you *planning* on being gone for days again?" Pam felt shocked. "Why—"

Abruptly, her roommate stood up and walked to her closet. "We need to get ready for class. You want to shower first, or can I?"

"Whatever. Go ahead," Pam muttered.

Melanie gathered a change of clothes and her towel, then exited the room. Pam sat there on her bed for several minutes, processing the conversation. *It's like she came back as someone else.*

10

Search and Research

That afternoon in the *Sentinel* office, Melanie struggled to focus during the staff's biweekly news huddle. Instead of contributing to the brainstorm, she sat in a corner intermittently staring into space and snapping back to the meeting. Editor-in-chief Dawn Fincher's stubby piece of chalk assaulted the board with a furious *clack-clack-clack* as she scribbled the ideas that students called out. Occasionally a heated debate erupted. But despite the noisy, stimulating atmosphere, Mel's thoughts kept floating away to her argument with Pam, her impressions of Gavin, and his warning about the man in dark sunglasses.

She felt awful about being so secretive and upsetting her roommate. But what was the alternative? Tell Pam the truth? The truth was crazy and unbelievable—not to mention horrifying—and her best friend would almost certainly think it a lie. If Melanie proved she was a werewolf, Pam might react with fear and revulsion and end their friendship. Or she'd try to come with Mel next full moon and get hurt.

Which is more likely? she wondered. *Pam's not a fair-weather friend. She's trustworthy, accepting, and kind. Then again, she's never had to deal with anything like* this *before. There's no precedent to—*

"Hey, Caldwell," said Dawn, waving a hand to get Mel's attention. "Would you mind writing an opinion piece for this issue? The topic's up to you."

"S-sure," stammered Melanie. Heat rushed into her cheeks. The editor-in-chief looked like she was about to comment on her daydreaming, but then turned back to the chalkboard and scrawled Melanie's name under Editorials.

Timmy Simmons, who sat across the room from Mel, caught her eye and smirked. Wrinkling her nose, she directed her gaze elsewhere.

Before long, the people and sounds in the *Sentinel* office faded into the background once more.

Images and memories floated into her mind: dust motes dancing in the bright sunlight streaming through the office windows. The restlessness and fatigue she'd felt as she'd worked here alone on Saturday afternoon. The smell of lemon cleaner and the loud, incessant ticking of the clock. The startling scuff of quiet footfalls behind her in the hallway.

When was that man in dark sunglasses going to come prowling around? Mel had checked the weather report, and the forecast showed several rainy and overcast days in a row, starting tomorrow. Already, clouds were rolling in from the north to blanket a good portion of the sky. It looked like it would be a while before her unwanted visitor showed up.

Gavin said he was a cop, Melanie remembered. That was rather unnerving. She couldn't possibly be in trouble with the law, and she had no plans to do anything that would cause the police to come after her. She wondered if Gavin had misinterpreted the vision, or if it could be wrong, or if it could change depending on her actions. Maybe it was a warning to be cautious and the cop was symbolic.

"Okay, people, I like what we've got here," said Dawn, pulling Mel back to reality. "Everything's due a week from today, but if you need an extension for some reason—a *good* reason—ask me. Meeting adjourned."

The other students in the room stood up and filed out. Mel followed them, making sure to avoid Timmy. She headed back to Hartman Cottage to work on homework until dinner.

When Pam returned from her classes, she greeted Melanie cheerfully, as if there hadn't been tension between them that morning. They chatted and studied for midterms.

After dinner, Pam went to the music building to practice. Back in their room, Melanie closed and locked the door. Gavin had said there was no cure, but in Mel's opinion, he'd given up ridiculously easily. By his own admission, he hadn't even tried anything.

She wasn't going to give up. Ever.

She sat down at her computer, opened her web browser to a search engine, and typed "werewolf cure." Half a million results popped up.

She spent the next hour clicking on links and skimming pages. To her annoyance, she found the same kind of drivel that Gavin had mentioned on the way back from the cabin. "Wolfsbane ... exorcism ..." she muttered.

Would exorcism work? Gavin had tried holy water, but he hadn't said anything about exorcism—and, unlike wolfsbane, it wouldn't kill her if it failed to work.

Did she believe in the power of exorcism?

"I believe in werewolves," Melanie muttered, and made a mental note to come back to the idea.

"Exhaustion?" she exclaimed in disgust, sometime later. "Wearing out the were? Seriously? Nobody'd be one after their first transformation."

Perusing a different web page, she shuddered as she read its suggestion to pierce a werewolf's hands with nails. She instinctively clutched her hands, thumbs rubbing the opposite palms as if trying to wipe away the pressure of cold iron. Further down that page it said, "Rub opium in the werewolf's nostrils before bed."

Nothing but gruesome, illegal, and ridiculous ideas.

But it might still be better than—

Even if I had to try all of them—

But maybe try the safe ones first.

Melanie let out a heavy sigh. *What does the internet know, anyway?*

Practically nobody believed in werewolves these days. All the websites she'd checked out treated them as legendary. She needed to find a site created by people who did believe and who knew what they were talking about. *Other werewolves have to be out there, and some of them might have web pages.*

Typing "werewolves are real" into the search box, Mel began looking at another set of results. She became so absorbed in her research that she failed to hear the doorknob jiggling and a key turning in it. She jumped as the door creaked open and Pam's voice said, "You *are* here. Why'd you lock the door, roomie?"

Melanie quickly closed the browser window and swiveled in her chair. "Hi. Um, sorry—I must've locked it out of habit."

"Oh. That's cool." Pam smiled and plopped down onto her bed. She was soon chattering about Aaron, who'd smiled at her a lot tonight, and the girl talk made Melanie grin and relax.

Later, when they were climbing into bed, Pam said, "I heard you talking in your sleep last night. Sounded like you were having a nightmare, but you also said 'Gavin.' Were you dreaming about Gavin Rossdale, or the Gavin from the volleyball game?"

Mel's stomach lurched. She hadn't mentioned him to Pam, had she? *Don't think so.* "H-how'd you know about him?"

"Jos told me."

Of course.

"She also said he's pretty cute." Pam gave Mel a mischievous, knowing wink.

Melanie sighed. "Yeah," she said at last, "I think he did pop up in one of my dreams. I forget what it was about, though."

"So what'd you guys talk about? At the game, I mean."

"I dunno. Just stuff. How hot it was in the gym—boring things like that. You know I'm socially inept, especially with guys."

Raising an eyebrow, Pam said, "C'mon, Mel, I still think you're holding out on me. You're not that bad at talking to guys. If you're dreaming about him, he must've made *some* impression on you."

Argh, you and Jos are incorrigible! But maybe their prying could work to Mel's advantage. If her friends ever spotted Gavin picking her up at full moons, they'd think nothing of it except that he and Mel were dating—might as well establish that impression now. "All right," she said. "He might have asked for my phone number."

"I knew it!" crowed Pam, bolting upright and bouncing in her bed. Its aged springs creaked in protest. "Mel, why didn't you tell me earlier? This is exciting! Has he called you yet?"

"No."

"Aww. Well, I bet he will soon."

It was Melanie's turn to shrug, although she knew he would—but not for the reason Pam was thinking.

Closing her eyes, Mel tried to fall asleep, but her mind took forever to settle down. Pam's words had inspired tantalizing thoughts of Gavin and then of her future in general—marriage, kids, being happy together and free of her curse. A warm, golden glow tinged these imaginings. Then doubt cropped up. *What if we never find a cure? Kids—can I even have them now? Wouldn't my transformations squeeze them to death, wrap the umbilical cord around the baby's throat, or cause the cord to break loose? Even if a baby survived, it might inherit this cursed condition.*

Becoming a mother had never topped Mel's unwritten list of life goals, but feeling her ability to have children slipping away was unpleasant. Even if she adopted, she wouldn't be able to take care of a baby at certain times. If she was ever going to be a parent, she would have to get rid of her stupid curse first, and that only increased her determination to find a cure.

No matter what it takes, she thought before drifting off, *I will find one.*

)) ● ((

NOVEMBER 7, FIRST-QUARTER MOON

The knock on his door tonight wasn't unexpected. Nervously, Erickson ran a hand through his graying hair before opening the door and greeting Chandra. He apologized for the neighbors' loud bickering as he stepped aside for her to enter. A sweet cloud of lilac perfume accompanied her in. "Coffee?"

"Yes, please."

He'd also picked up a cherry pie from the local diner he frequented, and Chandra accepted a small slice. "Sorry I don't have ice cream," he said. He hadn't been thinking of à la mode until just now.

"That's all right." Chandra gave him a reassuring smile, which set his stomach aflutter.

After dessert and the obligatory small talk, Erickson cleared the plates and refilled the mugs. "So," he said, resuming his seat, "you said you know a good place for me to use next full moon?"

Chandra nodded. "The Organization has a couple of different safe houses—a main one and a smaller one." She must have seen the hesitation on his face, for she continued, "If you're not ready to take that step yet, there's another place I used to use before joining up with them."

"Where is it?"

She pulled out her phone and showed him on the map app. "Not too far from here, actually. Secluded. I can take you there, say, tomorrow, if you want to check it out in advance."

"I'll think about it," said Erickson, fiddling with his mug and studying the table's wood grain.

Truth be told, he hadn't had much luck finding a new hideout on his own. *Maybe that's another sign I should move on.*

Later, when Chandra was gone, he lay in bed unable to sleep. It wasn't the full-moon restlessness yet, but his mind and heart were torn.

Forget all this nonsense. Run while you can. Any attachments you make are bound to complicate things. What kind of tangled web might he find himself in, getting involved with a group of werewolves? Or any people in general? There were always the politics, the hierarchies, the façades put up, the sycophants, the power plays, the insincerity....

On the other hand, these people could prove to be good companions. Provide support, protection, and help stave off loneliness. It might be nice to see the same faces around on a regular basis. To get to know someone again. He realized he didn't really *know* anyone anymore. *Maybe not even myself.*

He certainly wasn't the young, naïve, ambitious businessman from a decade and a half ago.

Was there any of that man left inside, or had he been completely devoured by the monster?

)) ● ((

NOVEMBER 10, WAXING GIBBOUS MOON

Melanie couldn't believe how time had flown. Like an eye blinking languidly, the moon had squinted, shut, and then reopened, swelling larger and larger in the sky. Mel's restlessness had grown with it. She sat in her afternoon class, tapping her toes under her desk and trying to take careful notes on *Beowulf,* but her obsession over finding a cure kept intruding, the contradictory, useless advice circling round and round, the tens of hours she's spent online and in the library branded into her vision. And whenever she banished them, mental images of a lush forest intruded, along with the urge to run through it. The room was full of so many noises and smells—*Blasted fly, I'm gonna rip you ... Does that guy have beef jerky in his pocket?*—competing for her attention.

Focus, Melanie, focus.

Her periods of concentration never lasted long.

Two days from now, she'd have to disappear again—which, of course, Pam wasn't going to be happy about. But there was no choice in the matter. Mel sighed inwardly. *I will find a cure. I will!*

The professor's lecture turned to the sacrificial death of the Anglo-Saxon hero, and that lured Melanie's attention back. Fighting the dragon to save his people had cost Beowulf his life and the faithfulness of most of his friends.

Death. Abandonment. A bloody, warlike existence. Those concepts swirled around in Melanie's head. They didn't seem so remote or unrelated to her anymore. Deep inside her lurked a beast that craved violence and blood, and she could feel it pacing around its prison, yearning for its approaching release.

Kill the wolf that bit you. How many times had she read that suggestion for a cure? More death, more bloodshed.

Let me out. Let me kill, said the wolf.

No! I could never do that! She couldn't strike down whomever had inflicted the cursed bite upon her.

Most likely, she'd never find out the person's identity. Returning to Pine Groves and waiting near the cave entrance just before moonrise was far too dangerous. And the person might have moved on to a different hideout.

Did she *want* to know who had bitten her? Knowing wouldn't reverse the past, wouldn't fix her situation. Possibly, this faceless person had friends and family who'd grieve his or her loss. Or maybe he or she was tormented, miserable, and alone. Either way —

The bell rang so deafeningly that Melanie flinched. Grabbing her book and notes, she slid from her seat and hurried out of the building. She moved as if to flee her recent thoughts but slowed when she emerged onto the sunlit campus grounds. Shading her eyes, she thought, *It's awfully bright today. Are my sunglasses in my bag?*

Dark sunglasses. The prowling policeman. She stopped in her tracks, and a chattering pair of girls had to swerve around her to avoid a collision. One of them wrinkled her nose and huffed, but Mel didn't notice; she was busy glancing in every direction and preparing to duck for cover if she spotted a man wearing shades.

By the time she got back to her dorm, she'd relaxed. Nearly a month had passed since Gavin's vision, and she hadn't seen a single stranger on campus who fit the description he'd given her. Perhaps the cop *was* merely symbolic.

11

Tail

I owe you one, Aaron, thought Melanie as the front door clicked shut behind her roommate. Pam's newest beau had asked her out this rainy Saturday, providing Melanie a perfect window for escape. Now she could sneak out without lying about where she was going or worrying that Pam would try to stop her—or to come along. *It won't be Pam.*

Mel waited to let Aaron's car get a decent distance away and then slung her packed bag over her shoulder. On her way out of the room, she placed a note on Pam's desk: "I have to go again. Back on Tuesday. Please don't worry. – M." Then she made her way down to her car and drove off.

It was noon, but she was skipping lunch; her stomach had been twisting in knots since breakfast, like it had done right before the last full moon. Gavin was meeting her at a twenty-four-hour supermarket with a gigantic parking lot, where Melanie would leave her car for the next few days. She'd insisted on this arrangement because of the gossip factor. If people saw her leaving with a boy on Friday and returning on Sunday, they wouldn't think too much of it—sure, they'd spread rumors about the pair shacking up, but they wouldn't pry further. But Mel and Gavin were going to be gone on strange days— Saturday through Tuesday. What would her classmates make of that? Best not tempt them.

Mel had offered to drive Gavin to the cabin, but he had politely refused, and she'd thought with a wry grin, *I bet he's one of those guys who is so attached to his car, he has to drive himself everywhere.* It didn't matter. She'd give him some gas money.

Gavin had called her a couple of times, but she hadn't seen him. The main purpose of his calls had been to make sure she was taking care to avoid the prowling cop. She'd promised him she was.

Reaching their rendezvous point, Melanie scanned the rows of cars for Gavin's tan Ford, but she didn't see it. She pulled her Honda into a spot some distance from the other vehicles, then sat watching fat droplets of rain splatter on her windshield.

I should've come to Wellsboro to check on her instead of only calling, Gavin thought as he drove. *She said everything was okay and the coast was clear, but maybe she just didn't see the guy. My visions have never been wrong. This one couldn't be, could it?*

Doubt filled him, but he tried to suppress it. It was pre-transformation jitters—that was all.

He saw that Melanie had beaten him to the meet-up location and parked alongside her. She smiled at him, climbed out of her car, and jumped into his front passenger seat, letting in a chilly, wet gust of air. "Whew," she said, tossing her bag on the back seat and finger-combing her windblown hair. "Lovely weather we're having, huh?"

Gavin chuckled. "Yeah."

"Hi," Melanie added. "Good to see you."

"You too," he said with a grin. Her presence had warmed the atmosphere in the car, and he could feel the tension easing from his shoulders and back.

Pulling the Ford out of the huge parking lot, he turned south onto the highway. "Did you have any trouble getting away from Pam?"

"No, thank goodness," Melanie said, and explained about Pam's date. "How about you? You got a roommate to escape from every month?"

"No, I have my own apartment off campus."

"Nice."

Their conversation drifted from one topic to another as they sped along. The rain pounded on the roof and windshield, the wipers squeaked, the wind moaned, and the tires whizzed and whooshed on wet pavement. The world was a gray blur, the few other cars around them muted and ghostlike in the gathering mist.

Half an hour into the trip, the downpour finally tapered to a drizzle, and the fog dissipated somewhat—enough for Gavin to tell that they were alone on the highway. That wasn't surprising, since they'd left the busy areas behind and entered open countryside. Glancing in his rearview mirror a minute later, though, Gavin caught movement. Two blurred lights.

For the next ten miles, every time his eye strayed up to the mirror, Gavin could see the two lights in the same position. No closer, no farther.

He'd put the car on cruise control, and they weren't much behind schedule, so there was no need to speed up, but he accelerated anyway. Another couple of miles, another few glances in the mirror. The lights remained.

"Hey, Melanie, can you see the car behind us?" he asked casually.

She turned and looked. "No, but I see headlights. Why?"

He shrugged.

Fifteen more minutes passed, and the lights behind them failed to budge or vanish. They'd grown slightly larger, in fact. Gavin's hand twitched on the steering wheel. He eased up on the gas to see if the lights would come closer, allowing him to glimpse the vehicle, but they stayed back. He could detect only a shadow, a smudge in the rain. Headlights and darkness.

Noticing the deceleration, Melanie joked, "Lead foot turn to feathers?"

The corner of Gavin's mouth lifted, and he brought the car back up to seventy. "Sorry, I just . . . those lights following us . . ."

Melanie frowned and then unbuckled her seatbelt. She swiveled and knelt on her seat, squinting at the road behind them. "The rain's making it hard to see."

"There's a gas station ahead. Let's pull off and wait a few minutes for them to pass," Gavin said. "Don't worry; we're nowhere near late."

They approached an exit ramp and merged onto it. The fog was a bit thicker at the top, tattered ribbons of mist clinging like spider webs to the trees beyond the service station. They parked in the station's empty lot, and Gavin turned the car off so its lights went out. He kept an eye on the freeway below but saw no headlights pass through the murky strip of road. After five minutes, he said, "Well, guess we're all right. Let's not waste any more time." He started up the Ford again, and they headed back down to the highway.

Nearly half their journey had passed, and the dashboard clock read

1:25. Two hours and thirty-five minutes till moonrise. That left them a spare hour. At 1:30, they came to the outskirts of a city, and traffic picked up. Dozens of lights appeared ahead and in the rearview mirror. Five minutes later, the lights had all dropped away ... all except for one pair.

Something cold slithered in Gavin's stomach. The two white lights had assumed the same position as the ones before. Automatically, his foot pressed harder on the gas. Three mile markers ticked past. Instead of fading away, the lights came closer, but still stayed far enough back that the vehicle remained nothing more than a dark spot in the rain.

Stupid weather. If only I could see better. He knew it would be pointless to slow down again, though—the other driver would, too. Gavin's grip slipped on the steering wheel, his palms slick. Less than two-and-a-half hours to moonrise. He tried to swallow a growing lump in his throat. "M-Melanie," he said as calmly as he could, cursing the slight stutter and the crack in his voice.

"Yeah?"

"We might have a problem."

"What?" she asked, forehead creasing.

"I think the car behind us is tailing us. I think it's the one we tried to let pass."

For the third time, Melanie turned to peer at the lights. "How can you tell?"

He explained about the distance the vehicle was keeping and how it matched his speed. The concern on her face grew, and she said, "Why would anyone ... What should we do?"

"That's what I'm trying to figure—wait." Gavin stiffened in realization. "It's him. It has to be," he growled, fingers tightening on the wheel as if around someone's throat.

"Who?"

"That cop I saw in my vision, prowling your campus. He must've found you after all."

Melanie made a noise halfway between a whimper and a groan, then spat out a couple of unladylike words. Taking a deep breath, she calmed herself and apologized. "If it *is* him, he's going to be hard to lose."

"You're right. We can't just pull off at a gas station again."

"So what do we do?"

They lapsed into silence. *We can't under any circumstances lead him to the cabin,* Gavin thought grimly. *But where . . . how . . . ?*

"We probably can't use speed to get away from him," he said aloud. "Aside from the obvious risk of getting pulled over, this car only has a four-cylinder engine, while his might have a V6. He's most likely driving the black Chevy Impala he had in the vision. It may be outfitted with a six-cylinder. Could be his undercover vehicle."

"Fantastic." Melanie chewed her lower lip and wrung her hands. "You don't think this is about . . . you know . . ."

I sure hope it isn't about her—our—condition, thought Gavin. But what else could it be? Dread rose within him, mingled with confusion. Whoever this guy was, how the heck did he know or suspect Melanie's secret? And he'd soon discover Gavin's, if they didn't lose him.

"And he's a cop, too," Melanie said angrily. "It's not fair."

Gavin shuddered in agreement and checked the dashboard clock: 1:50. One hour and ten minutes till they reached the cabin. He thought about their route and about their extra hour, and an idea came to him. "I'm going to call my mom. I think I've got a plan. But it'll involve backtracking; we've already passed where I want to go."

"Do we have enough time to do that?"

"Barely. It's half an hour behind us, so it would use up all our spare time. But it's the only way I can see to lose him."

Her eyes grew wide, and for a moment she looked like she would protest, but she simply said, "Okay."

Grabbing his phone, Gavin dialed Cara and explained the situation. "Dad's at work, right?"

"Yeah," Cara said.

"We're about to head that way—should be there in thirty minutes. Can you meet us there and park around back? We'll come in the front by the ER."

"Got it."

When they came to the next exit, they took it and reentered the freeway going in the opposite direction. *This had better work,* Gavin thought, jaw set.

Twenty-five minutes later, they neared the city of Lock Haven. The cop's headlights had followed them but were now lost in a sea of other lights. Gavin steered the car off the freeway. A couple of turns brought him to a bigger intersection with a stoplight, beyond which were Lock Haven Hospital's front driveway and main parking lot. The lot was crowded. Approaching the green light, he prayed, *Turn yellow. Turn yellow to buy us some time.*

It turned yellow. Gavin zoomed under it before the signal changed to red, but the car behind him had to stop. He pulled into the black asphalt lot and drove past half a dozen packed rows, then parked his compact Ford between a hulking Transit van and an SUV.

"Come on—we don't have much time." He and Melanie threw off their seatbelts and sprinted toward the brick building.

Cara was waiting for them. She jammed baseball caps in Gavin and Melanie's hands and swapped Gavin car keys. "This should work," she said. "I'll stick around and keep an eye out for shady characters."

"Thanks." Gavin shot a glance at the entrance, gave Cara a peck on the cheek, and pulled Melanie into the maze of corridors. As they hurried through the sterile-smelling white hallways, they wedged on their hats. Two minutes later, they reached a back door and slipped out through it.

Gavin spotted Cara's car and hit the unlock button on the key fob. The slate-gray Nissan hybrid's headlights blinked, welcoming its new passengers in. "Our pursuer could be patrolling the parking lot," Gavin realized. "He might've guessed what we're up to. Hurry—duck down in the back seat and keep low to the floor. He'll be looking for a car with two people in it, not one."

She gave a brisk military nod and obeyed.

Within seconds, Gavin was easing the Nissan out of its space, scanning in every direction for a black Impala, twitching at anything that moved. He took the nearest exit and drove down back streets toward the interstate, checking in his mirrors the entire way.

Five miles down the freeway, the number of headlights following them had dwindled to zero. "I think we've lost him," he said. Melanie breathed a grateful sigh and unfolded herself from the floor.

Gavin consulted the dashboard clock. It was 2:35. "Don't relax yet. We only have an hour and twenty-five minutes till moonrise."

"How long does it take to get to the cabin from here?"

"Hour and thirty."

"Well, gun it!"

Gavin pressed a bit harder on the gas pedal but said, "Getting pulled over for speeding will make things worse, you know."

"I know." She crossed her arms and slumped back. Her eyes closed, her expression pained. He barely heard the second "I know."

He could smell her fear, although it didn't show on her face. *She's putting up a brave front,* he thought, and admired her for it. He'd never been anywhere near late to the cabin before. What if they didn't make it by moonrise and transformed in the car? *Don't think about that. Just drive.*

For the next ten minutes, they rode in tense silence. Then Gavin's phone rang. It was Cara, reporting that she hadn't seen any shifty men walk in.

"We seem to have lost him," he told her.

"That's wonderful," she said. "In case he's still lurking around the parking lot, I'll leave your car here for the next few days and ride home with your father. Do you want one of us to come over tonight and keep watch?"

Gavin shot a quick glance at Mel. "Thanks, but better not."

"All right," Cara replied. "Call me if anything—if you need anything. Love you."

"Love you too, Mom."

After he hung up, Gavin glanced in the rearview mirror again and saw that Melanie was grinning. "What?" he asked.

"Oh, nothing." She turned away and covered her smile with a hand.

Girls, he thought.

He was glad Cara hadn't seemed to realize how late he and Melanie were. *I've already given Mom and Dad plenty to worry about over the years.* Guilt stirred memories, and he became lost in reverie for a long stretch of glistening gray highway. It was hypnotizing—the endless yellow double line; the feel of smooth, constant motion beneath his comfortable, cushioned seat; trees and cars and signs whizzing past.

The late afternoon sky brightened, and the storm clouds dissipated. Nearing the end of its westward course, the sun slanted in through the windshield. Gavin squinted and lowered his visor, but it didn't reach down far enough. He hated driving west this time of day.

On top of the poor visibility, his insides were churning and his joints aching. His body remembered previous full moons all too well; it knew what was about to happen. *Stop complaining,* he told it, gritting his teeth. *There's nothing I can do.*

He couldn't wait for the next few days to be over.

Lying down on the back seat, Mel tried to keep her eyes shut and her breathing steady and slow. Panic wouldn't get them there any sooner. But she couldn't keep her stomach from writhing. It must be due to the full moon, not nerves, she decided. A headache was building, and she massaged her temples. Also mounting was the temptation to ask, "Are we there yet?" She clamped her lips shut. *Trust Gavin and be patient. We'll make it in time. We have to.*

Feeling the car slow and hearing the tick of the turn signal, Melanie sat up and saw that they were merging onto an exit ramp. Out of sudden fear, she checked behind them, but there were no other cars in view. "Almost there," Gavin said.

She nodded. Last time she'd come this way, she'd glimpsed none of the route. But there wasn't much to look at here—more forest; gas station signs sticking up above the tree line in the distance; a dilapidated car parts store that was clearly abandoned, the cracked pavement of its parking lot dotted with clumps of tall grass.

A couple of turns, and they hit the narrow, bumpy gravel driveway that ended at the cabin. *What time is it?* Her watch said 3:57. *Three minutes!*

Gavin accelerated. The car bounced and juddered, and Mel clung to the seat back in front of her, praying they wouldn't swerve and crash into a tree. On and on they sped through the darkening forest. When would it end? Trees, trees, trees, trees, trees—*Come on!* ...

There! The woods broke, and they were in the clearing. Gavin didn't stop in front of the cabin but drove around behind it and parked in the grass.

Melanie grabbed their bags and flew out of the car. Gavin was right beside her, fumbling with his keys while he ran. He looked sweaty, and his eyes shone with a feverish light. Hands shaking, he struggled to fit the key into the back door. The key ring slipped from his fingers as he doubled over, clutching at his midsection and letting out an agonized moan.

Mel dropped the bags. "Crap!" She snatched the key off the ground and slid it into the lock—right before the first jolt of pain ran down her spine. She and Gavin tumbled over the threshold and staggered down the hallway to their safe rooms.

Once inside hers, Mel shut the door and leaned against it, panting, another wave of pain washing over her. Fur spread over her hands and up her arms as she clicked the deadbolts into place, starting at the top, working her way down to the bottom.

Then the twisting and grinding began.

12

Communiqué

Pam's alarm buzzed at 8:00 the next morning, since it was Sunday. She groaned, hit snooze, and rolled over, exhausted from an anxiety-filled night. After tossing and turning for hours, she'd finally drifted off well past midnight.

The sound of running water loosened sleep's grip on her. For a moment, her heart leapt. *Is she back?* Pam dragged herself out of bed and stumbled into the hallway. Knocking lightly on the bathroom door, she called, "Mel? Is that you?"

"No—sorry," came Jocelyn's muffled voice.

Disappointment like boulders sank in Pam's stomach.

At breakfast, she pushed her eggs and bacon listlessly around her plate. Between bites of pancake, Jos tried to engage her in conversation. "How's Aaron? What movie did you guys see? Was it any good?"

Pam mumbled succinct answers, barely making eye contact.

"Okay," said Jos with a sigh, "I know you're freaked out again about Mel. But at least she left a note this time, right?"

"Yeah. Said she'll be back Tuesday." Pam scowled.

"So that's, what, about three days' absence? Isn't that how long she was gone last time?"

Pam thought for a moment. "That seems right."

Jos put down her fork, a familiar analytical gleam entering her eyes. "Last time she didn't give us any warning, and later she said an emergency had come up. This time it's different; it's scheduled. She knew ahead of time. But both absences are the same length. Hmmm ..."

While her suitemate muttered to herself, trying to establish a pattern or connection, all Pam could muster from her own brain was fear and growing resentment. *Doesn't Mel value our friendship? We*

106

don't have to hide anything from each other. She should know I won't judge her. Why'd she suddenly put up this wall?

Pam's brooding thoughts drowned out the chatter, laughter, and clanking silverware around her. She stabbed her eggs, as if they were the source of her irritation.

A voice nearly made her jump: "Hi, Pam. Hi, Jocelyn. Is Melanie around?"

It was Luis. He stood holding an empty tray, a smile on his face but mild concern in his eyes.

While Pam debated replying truthfully or not, Jos answered, "Hey, Luis. Um, no, Mel's back at the dorm. Not feeling well—stomachache or something."

"Oh. Well, tell her I said 'get well soon.'"

"Gotcha." Jocelyn saluted.

Watching his tall, lean form walk away, Pam said, "You know he's totally into her."

Jos grinned. "That's pretty obvious."

"If they get closer and she keeps disappearing like this, I wonder—"

"Who keeps disappearing?" a nasal voice cut in.

Ugh! Pam twisted completely around in her seat; she hadn't realized Timmy was sitting back to back with her. *Why didn't Jos notice and warn me?* Now his leering face was much closer to hers than she ever wanted it to be. His breath stank of pepper-and-mushroom omelet. "None of your business," she said sharply, scooting backward.

"It's Melanie, isn't it?"

Pam was so floored that he'd gotten Mel's name right that words eluded her.

"No, Mel's around," said Jos. "In her room, sick, like I just told Luis."

Timmy's owlish eyes narrowed behind his glasses. "Really." He didn't sound convinced. "Dawn Fincher, the *Sentinel* editor, was trying to get ahold of her yesterday—said she hadn't turned in the last few articles she was supposed to proofread."

Pam frowned, but Jos shrugged and said, "We don't know anything about that. I'm sure Mel's on top of things and will turn them in soon."

"She better, because the issue goes to press tomorrow morning." With a condescending smirk, Timmy turned back to his breakfast.

Jocelyn had finished her pancakes, and Pam quickly crunched down the last of her bacon. She rose from her seat, Jos following. When they were safely away from Timmy's prying ears, hiking back to Hartman, Pam said, "I can't believe she'd miss a deadline."

"Mm-hmm." Jos kicked a pebble a few times, seemingly concentrating on the simple game. But Pam could sense the wheels turning.

Dead leaves skittered across the pavement. The sky was overcast, the wind cold. Pam wrapped her arms around herself, casting a doleful eye at the mostly skeletal trees edging the campus. *So dreary with the fall colors gone.*

Abruptly, Jocelyn said, "Let's try and catch her before she can leave next time—assuming there *is* a next time."

"Okay," said Pam, perking up.

She'd already been planning to watch Melanie like a hawk.

)) ● ((

Erickson swam back up into awareness, every joint and muscle throbbing. He groaned and shifted on the cold floor—and even that slight movement sent piercing pangs through his rib cage. He stilled. Waited. The pain ebbed, slowly. Seemed like it was taking longer to go away with each passing month.

He opened his eyes a crack and remembered where he was: an upstairs room of an abandoned house. Chandra's pre-Organization hideout.

The boarded-up windows hardly let in a single ray from the rising sun, but it was bright enough to make out the tattered and shredded floral paper sloughing off the walls. The hardwood floor was faded to a dull ochre and was crisscrossed by jagged scratches. Erickson's eye wandered up to the extensive water damage on the ceiling, and his nose wrinkled at the smell of rot and mold. A sticky dampness hung in the air and clung to his bare skin. This place was still better than the cave, though.

Hearing footsteps and creaking boards on the ground floor, he tensed up. Fear shot through him. Was it burglars? Or worse—wolf hunters?

Moments later, he heard water running and then beeps that sounded like those from a microwave. He was paranoid; it must be only Chandra, who'd stayed in another room. Then again—*She's up already?*

Well, she's young. More resilient. Might not have been doing this for as long as I have.

He lay there a few more minutes before dragging himself to his feet, grabbing the waist-high wainscoting for support. When the blackness left his vision, he retrieved his clothes and dressed himself. Every joint protested.

Downstairs in the kitchen, Chandra had made tea and was toasting rye bread. Erickson's mouth watered. He sank into a chair with only a slight wince and rasped, "Good morning."

She smiled as she greeted him, sounding energetic. Was it an act, or did she really feel as well as she looked and sounded? She wasn't wearing makeup, but her hair was clean and combed, her breath minty, and her clothes freshly laundered (he could smell the detergent).

"Here you go." Chandra set a plate of piping-hot toast in front of him. Butter was already on the table. "Four to start, but I can make more."

"Four's fine. Thanks."

As they ate together, Erickson couldn't help but feel strange. *It's like we're playing house without sleeping together or any sort of romance at all.*

Bummer.

Later, he went back upstairs to nap and, out of curiosity, peeked into Chandra's safe room. It sported similar wallpaper and flooring to his, but something wasn't right.

There were no scratches. No gouges or marks of any kind. Anywhere.

)) ● ((

"Honey, wake up so you can go to bed" flitted through Melanie's mind as she faded back in. The words were a memory of her mom's voice, talking to her dad while gently shaking him awake. Growing up, Mel had heard this line on countless evenings—her dad frequently fell asleep on the couch watching primetime TV, and her mom roused him around ten so he could sleep in his own room.

(It helped to think about mundane things like that.)

Waking up after a full moon only to climb into bed reminded Mel of that . . . except this hard, wooden floor wasn't the comfy couch. And she wasn't warm and cozy under an old quilt.

Teeth chattering, she forced herself up. "Augh," she groaned, clutching her side and stumbling as red-hot pain shot through her. She grabbed the mangled doorframe and panted. The agony dulled. Slowly, she undid the bolts and listened for sounds of Gavin getting up.

Her ears caught halting footsteps. They were so muffled, they must have been coming from his safe room, not the hall. She peeked out. The hallway was clear. She grabbed her bag and brought it inside, then dug out a pair of pajamas. Since the weather had grown colder, she'd switched to her winter sleepwear, a thick flannel pants-and-top set. Frumpy but worth it.

The bed in the Butterfly Room was as soft and inviting as the pajamas. Cocooned within its cotton sheets, she drifted off almost instantly . . .

. . . and entered a shadowy world. An even darker shadow was stalking her, its eyes two pinpricks of yellow against black. It chased her down empty streets, through narrow alleys, between tall buildings like the legs of giants.

The pinpricks broadened into a pair of headlights. The shadow took on the shape of a police cruiser and gained speed. She ran from it, gasping and stumbling, searching for a place to hide.

All the doors were locked. She pounded on them and yelled. Nobody came.

The shadows dispersed, and a world of brilliant light burst in upon her. The radiance had no source; it sparkled everywhere like multifaceted gems casting rainbows. She stood before huge, gleaming gates wrought of gold and pearl. A man with a long white beard sat on a gilded chair. A book lay open on a table in front of him.

"S-St. Peter," tumbled from her mouth. Her jaw had dropped. "How did I get here? How'd I die?" Had the cop run her over?

The bearded figure gazed sternly at her but didn't utter a word. Her apprehension grew. Come on—say something! Tell me it's all right, and you're letting me in!

When she couldn't stand the silence any longer, she asked meekly, "Y-you're going to let me into heaven, right? I got baptized. I did my confirmation."

St. Peter's eyes filled with sadness. He lifted a hand and pointed at her chest. She looked down and saw a sludgy black substance oozing through her shirt, above her heart. The stain spread, and thick droplets splattered onto her feet—which were morphing into paws with sharp claws.

"You are unclean and unfit to enter," the saint said in a deep, resonant voice.

"No!" she cried, watching in horror as her legs sprouted fur. The transformation worked its way up her body.

"You are damned, werewolf ..." echoed in her mind as she fell, spiraling down into a bottomless black pit.

Bright daylight streamed in through the translucent curtains. Melanie jerked awake, a scream tearing from her throat. Her breath was quick and ragged, her heart thumping crazily. *Only a dream. Only a dream,* she told herself. *Calm down. You're safe. You're alive.*

She heard footsteps, and Gavin poked his head in, eyes wide with alarm. "Are you okay?"

"Yeah," she said, sitting up and letting out a long sigh. "I had a nightmare."

"Oh. That sucks."

"You can say that again."

He stood there in the doorway, looking unsure about whether he should enter or not. She wished he would, but the right words eluded her, and she didn't want to pat the bed in invitation and make things awkward. So she swung her legs over the side of the bed and stood up. "Guess it's time for lunch." The clock on the nightstand said it was getting close to 1:00.

Gavin nodded and moved back into the hall. Melanie grabbed a change of clothes and went to the bathroom to freshen up. By the time she emerged, she could hear him opening and closing cabinet doors in the kitchen.

The dream preoccupied her, and she couldn't shake off the unsettling questions it raised: *Is there a spiritual element to this? Are we under a curse? Are werewolves ... damned?*

She wanted to ask Gavin what he thought, but she felt self-conscious about it. What if he was an atheist and scoffed at her concerns?

Entering the kitchen, Mel found him spreading peanut butter on slices of bread. "Sometimes you just want a PBJ," he said, and grinned. He was making four sandwiches.

She gave him a smile back, but it soon faded.

"You sure you're all right?" he asked.

"What? Oh. Yeah. Fine."

"Still thinking about the nightmare?"

"Uh-huh."

A pause. "You want to talk about it?"

Yes. Maybe. "Um . . . if you want to hear about it."

"Go ahead."

She sat down at the table and grabbed an apple from the fruit bowl. *Cara must stock this place right before full moons,* she thought, absently twirling the crimson fruit between her fingers.

Gavin set two sandwiches in front of her. Before he began eating, he bowed his head briefly. *Did he just pray?* That gave Melanie the courage she'd needed. "Do you believe in heaven and hell?"

"Yes," he said simply. "Do you?"

"I think so. I'm Catholic, but I don't really go to church anymore," she admitted. "Too busy with school and everything, you know?"

He nodded and waited.

"Anyway, my dream. I dreamed that . . ." It was hard to say aloud. "That I died and was at the gates of heaven. And St. Peter, he wouldn't let me in. He said werewolves are damned."

"Ah," said Gavin as if unsurprised. He took another bite and chewed thoughtfully.

At last, she said in a small voice, "Do *you* think we are?"

His eyes looked clouded, his expression uncertain. Hesitant. "I honestly don't know," he said. "If you believe the legends . . . but they don't all agree on details. No holy book mentions our kind, as far as I know."

"Hmm." She didn't know any better than he did.

They continued their meal in silence. *Well, what did you expect?* Mel thought. *A miraculous revelation? Indisputable evidence?*

She tried to push the disquiet from her mind and think about other things, but that was difficult.

Gavin brought up a new topic—but it wasn't a cheerful one. "I keep wondering about that car that was tailing us."

Crap. Yeah. Although they'd lost the guy, Melanie didn't feel a hundred percent safe. Maybe it was just paranoia stemming from her dreams. Or maybe the paranoia had *caused* her dreams. Whatever the case, it seemed like their stalker could have found them, could be lurking in this forest somewhere, spying on them.

The hairs on the back of Mel's neck prickled. Her eyes went to the window, half expecting a face to be pressed against it. She saw only trees and blue sky.

"Did you go outside and take a look around?" she asked Gavin.

"Not yet, but I'm going to."

"I'll come too."

They threw away their empty paper plates and put on shoes and jackets. Stepping out the back door, they scanned the calm green forest. They studied the trees, the underbrush, the grass in the clearing around the cabin. No figures perched in the treetops. No binocular lenses were visible in the scraggly bushes. No footprints or tire tracks marred the earth. Not even their own; they had been washed away by the night's rain. A few muddy puddles lingered in the shadows of the towering pines. Except for the usual birdsong, all was still and quiet.

Heading around to check the front of the cabin, they passed Cara's car. The passenger side faced them, and Melanie's gaze strayed in the window . . . and then became riveted on the driver's seat.

Something white sat on it. A folded piece of paper.

Her stomach lurched. "G-Gavin, did you leave a piece of paper on the seat of your mom's car?"

"No," he said, moving closer to look inside the Nissan. His eyes grew wide.

They turned in slow motion and met each other's frightened stare. "How . . . ?" Mel's voice withered away in a surge of panic.

"This is . . . not good." Gavin's tone was level, but his hands trembled. He swallowed and said, "I know I locked it."

Melanie stood, rooted to the spot, but Gavin tried the passenger door. Locked. The other three were, too. No evidence that the car had been tampered with. Gavin let himself in with the key, grabbed the paper, and held it as gingerly as if it were covered in thorns.

Once back in the kitchen, Gavin unfolded the paper and smoothed it on the tabletop. Mel scooted close to him—so close she could feel his body heat and smell his Old Spice—and they scanned the message at the same time.

Melanie and Gavin,

We know what you are. We know all about you. You're like us.

Strength lies in numbers, and people like us should protect one another. Welcome to our Organization.

We will be in touch.

P.S. We take our privacy very seriously and will take steps if you divulge any information about our Organization to humans.

There was no signature. It was written in cramped, angular hand-writing—not sloppy, but not immaculate either. Most likely masculine.

When Mel and Gavin finished reading, they stared at each other again, slack-jawed. Melanie moved a foot or two away, embarrassed at how close they'd been. Her heart was pounding, and not only from the letter's contents. But the warm tingle quickly faded. Confusion, lingering fear, and astonishment jockeyed for position in her mind.

Gavin spoke first, his voice husky. "They know quite a bit about us."

She nodded. "It has to be from whoever followed us."

"Shit. Didn't matter that we lost him at the hospital. I should've known he'd find us another way. If he is that cop from my vision, he might've run plates—"

"Yeah. I didn't think of that either. Don't beat yourself up over it."

Gavin sighed. "You're right. No sense dwelling on what-ifs. We need to focus on how to deal with this."

"Exactly."

After a thoughtful pause, he said, "So, he's not working alone. This is . . . much more than I expected."

"Me too. Do you think they're trustworthy?"

"That's not the impression I got from my vision."

Oh, yeah. The vision, Mel recalled. *How do those work, anyway?*

"What about it—I mean, what details gave you that feeling?"

"I . . . can't really say. Just intuition. A sense of wrongness, of warning."

"You didn't see him doing anything bad?"

"No. But I've learned to trust my instinct, Melanie. It hasn't been wrong yet."

"Okay." *He was right about me, and he saved me. Saved Pam and Jocelyn and everyone in my dorm. That's a good track record. I guess I should trust him on this too. Not blindly, though.* "So we know the cop in your vision was bad. But what if that wasn't him tracking us? Maybe the Organization's his enemy."

Frowning at the note, Gavin said, "Maybe, but . . . no, it doesn't feel right. Look, the Organization's made up of werewolves. But this guy who tracked us down can't be one. If he is, he took a big risk chasing us so close to moonrise. Maybe he's crazy and didn't care? No, he seems too calculating for that. And he may have needed all night to track us down. And he *did* track us down. An ordinary person couldn't have done that, but a cop could. It fits."

Melanie agreed. *Why's he working with, well, monsters?* she wondered. She hated the sound of the "M" word; it was more accurate than she cared to admit. *Gavin and I aren't dangerous most of the time. In human form, we're not much of a threat to anyone. But who's to say that about* them*?* What if the Organization's human personalities and goals were not so different from their wolfish ones?

A prickle formed at the base of her scalp.

But the note mentioned protecting one another. *Protecting from what, or whom? Is there another enemy—and these guys are actually allies? Someone* else *could be after us?* That was an unnerving thought.

"'Strength in numbers,'" Gavin was saying. "I wonder how many werewolves are in the group. A handful? A couple dozen?"

The possibility that there were that many local werewolves sent a jolt of lightning down Mel's spine.

I've been living in a bubble, she thought. *Sheltered and naïve, wearing rose-tinted glasses.* How many other clichés could she use to describe her life before the past month—or until the last few minutes?

She picked up the note and studied it more closely to see if anything else popped out at her—about the words, the handwriting, the ink, the paper itself. Nothing did. No new clues surfaced, even after she sniffed the page. (The mix of coffee, leather, and aftershave was hardly incriminating.)

Gavin's focus had returned to their stalker. "How'd that cop I saw get tangled up with these people? They sound like a gang, and why would any good cop help a gang? Either they're threatening him and forcing him to work with them, or he's crooked and he's getting something from them—money, perks, whatever."

Melanie frowned. "There's a third option, y'know: He's just a good guy helping other good guys. Maybe he's related to one of them, and his job has nothing to do with his involvement."

"I'm not convinced," said Gavin, crossing his arms. "There's something fishy about this whole situation."

There was. *But what happened to you to make you so suspicious of everyone?* Mel wanted to ask, but she bit her lip. An adopted werewolf must have plenty of trauma, and this wasn't the time to pry.

"I still think they're a gang and they're up to no good," he continued. "But I do concede that they're not as aggressive as a typical gang would be. Why'd they only leave us a note? Why not break in here and confront us? Why are they hanging back?"

"See—evidence for option three," said Mel, bobbing her head vigorously. She wanted these people to be good; she wanted *everyone* to be good.

"Maybe," Gavin said doubtfully, and left it at that.

Mind still churning, Melanie shifted in her seat. The refrigerator hummed; the wind sighed; clouds shifted over the sun, dimming the room. Fatigue washed over Mel, and the chair's spindle back pressed against her spine like iron bars. Her body urged her to lie down and get some rest, but she resisted. What if she had another nightmare?

She could at least sit in a more comfortable place. She headed to the living room, settled on the couch, and hugged a pillow.

Gavin followed and sat on the chair nearest to her. Slumping back with a sigh, he massaged his temples. His face was pinched, forehead creased in pain. But before long, his brow smoothed and his eyelids drooped. Then they closed.

Melanie couldn't help but study his face—the thin, angular features;

straight, perfectly proportioned nose; pale, clear, almost luminescent skin; hint of dark blond stubble on his chin; tousled bangs reaching nearly to his eyes.

His lips moved, and his voice came out softly, words half-slurred: "Whoever these people are, I don't want anything to do with them. How do we know they're even werewolves? They could be humans planning to use us as weapons or play Dr. Frankenstein."

Those were two possibilities Mel hadn't considered. But that kind of stuff only happened in books and movies—right? Grip tightening on the pillow, she said, "Maybe."

The mantle clock ticked away the passing seconds and minutes. Gavin's eyes stayed shut, and his breathing became deep and even. *He must be really worn out. Ten years of full moons taking a toll on his body . . . How long can we live like this?*

She thought of death again, and of St. Peter. His stern face, his sad eyes, his words.

Damned.

Her eyes jerked down to her chest, where she'd seen the black ooze in her dream. Moving the pillow, she saw that her sapphire-colored sweater was clean, unstained. But that wasn't much reassurance.

Whether the Organization was good or bad, trustworthy or not, paled in comparison with a much greater uncertainty: that of her eternal destiny.

13

Confrontation

It took longer for her to move today, on the third morning. Though she was cold and longing to climb into bed, sheer exhaustion and pain pinned her down like a wrestler three weight classes above hers. When she finally crawled to the door, she shivered and shook so much that it took her a couple of minutes to undo the five deadbolts.

"Gavin," she croaked around the edge of her door. "You all right?"

There was no response. She cleared her throat and called his name again.

Nothing. Fear flashed through her. *What if—?*

Pulling on her clothes as quickly as her stiff limbs would allow, Mel staggered into the hallway. She tried opening Gavin's safe-room door, but it wouldn't budge. She pounded on the door, wincing at the pain that shot through her hand. "Gavin! Please answer me!"

The faint groan and rasping voice that responded were the most welcome, reassuring sounds she'd heard in a long time. "Thank goodness," she breathed.

She trudged to the Butterfly Room, craving but dreading sleep. *Please no nightmares,* she prayed as she pulled the covers up to her chin.

Melanie awoke hours later to a quiet, peaceful house—almost *too* quiet and peaceful. Not much light filtered through her window. It was overcast outside, and she couldn't tell the time of day without referencing the clock.

Nearly two p.m. *Whoa. We gotta get back.*

Gavin wasn't in the hall, bathroom, kitchen, or living room. The door to his bedroom was shut. She didn't want to barge in, but they needed to go soon to avoid driving after dark.

An idea occurred to her, and a grin blossomed on her face. She went back to the kitchen and hunted through the cupboards and fridge. She selected a box of macaroni and cheese, then grabbed a package of hot dogs for protein.

When the food was cooked, Mel chopped the hot dogs into small chunks and mixed them into the mac and cheese. It looked fancier. She breathed in the savory smells of the steaming food, and her stomach growled.

"Gavin," she called, knocking on his door, "I made lunch. It's late. We need to get going."

Hearing him stir, she padded back to the kitchen and spooned their meal into two bowls. She set them on the table and sat down to wait for him. She had to restrain herself from digging in before he arrived.

"Oh," he said upon entering the room. His hair and shirt were rumpled, and he rubbed grit out of his eyes. "Cool. That looks pretty good. Thanks."

They inhaled their food and then packed up to leave. It was almost three o'clock, and Mel knew the sun would be setting by the time she got back to Wellsboro.

As Gavin locked the cabin, Mel scanned the clearing and the woods once more. They seemed tranquil and unoccupied. But the note kept echoing in her mind. She'd studied the ominous words during the past couple of days.

People like us should protect one another.

What might she and Gavin need protection from? Themselves, definitely. And—others? Government experiments or—or something worse.

But if that was the case, why weren't they approaching more directly, showing their faces? Why use stealth? Didn't they realize how shady and off-putting that was? Not the best recruiting technique.

Once she and Gavin were on the road, she remembered to turn her phone back on. Unsurprisingly, she'd missed a slew of calls from Pam. Mel gritted her teeth. *Why can't she just let me be my own person?*

I'll never let it be Pam. This curse is mine to bear, and mine alone.

There was also a voicemail from Dawn. "Caldwell, I need those last three articles by this evening," it began.

Mel's stomach flipped. *What last three articles?* Had more been emailed to her after she'd left campus? Why couldn't people just turn in their assignments on time?

"... If I don't receive them by then, we're gonna have to print them with possible errors." Mel knew how Dawn felt about *that.* "I can glance at them myself, but I don't have the eye you do. Anyway, I don't know where you went or why you're not answering my emails. I hope you're doing okay and this doesn't become a habit. Talk to you later."

Mel deleted the message and hung up. Sticking her phone back in her purse, she muttered, "Great."

"Everything all right?" asked Gavin.

She sighed. "Well, I missed a deadline."

"For the newspaper?"

"Yeah."

"How bad is that? Like, stubbing your toe bad or breaking your leg bad?"

Mel thought about it. She'd never failed to meet a deadline before. "Somewhere in between, I guess—maybe a Charlie horse. It's only a first offense."

"Oh. That's good."

Yawning, Mel slumped back in her seat. *It'll be okay; my track record is still better than everyone else's. Dawn will forgive me.*

The scenery blurred as it whizzed by. The trees were mostly bare now, and the beautiful, bright colors of fall had faded into drabber greens and grays. An occasional red barn drew her eye, and once a yellow Corvette zoomed past, but there wasn't much else to see.

Cozy heat poured from the vent. Mel wanted to nap but knew she ought to keep Gavin company and help him stay alert. Sitting up straighter, she racked her brain. Inevitably, her thoughts returned to the Organization.

"Are you going to tell your parents about the note?" she asked.

He nodded. "Of course. How is the group going to find out I did?"

An unsettling thought entered her mind: "Do you think they bugged this car?"

Gavin's eyes widened, and he was silent for a long moment. Then his voice came back harsher. "They'd better not have—but Dad and I will search the car. Either way, I *am* going to tell my parents," he said in a whisper so low she had to read his lips. "We shouldn't face this problem alone. I don't keep secrets from my mom and dad."

Guilt stirred inside Mel. *I'm keeping secrets from mine.* No way was she going to tell her parents about what she'd become. Or about this Organization. She envied Gavin—Cara and Jeff had always been aware of his problem, had accepted and adopted him knowing. They'd chosen to raise a high-risk kid. Mel's situation was the opposite; she felt like her parents didn't know her anymore. There was an "old her" and a "new her," and they were separated by a deep, rocky, frightening chasm. Her parents were used to and comfortable with the old Melanie, the daughter they'd raised, the promising young woman they thought she was. If they found out what had happened, how would they react? Cross the rickety rope bridge? Burn it?

It had been several days since she'd talked with her mother. Mel called her mom every week, but she hadn't been home to visit this semester because her parents lived ten hours away, in Indiana.

Her thoughts jumped forward to Christmas break. *Crap—what will I do at that full moon? What days is it on? Will I have to spend* two *full moons at home?* The blood drained from her face, and she gnawed her lower lip as she checked her phone calendar. The moon would wax full again on December thirteenth, she discovered, meaning she'd transform on the twelfth and fourteenth too. *You gotta be kidding me— that's during finals week!* She was going to have to beg her professors to let her take the exams early. *Fantastic. More lies to spin. And less time to study.*

All in exchange for misery.

As for the January full moon nights, they would fall on the tenth to the twelfth. Mel's calendar said Wellsboro's spring semester didn't begin until the sixteenth. She would have to find a hideout back home. Crud. There didn't seem to be a way of getting around that; leaving a week early for school would present complications. First, her parents wouldn't be thrilled. They'd want to enjoy her company for as long as they could. Second, the dorms wouldn't be open yet. Where would she stay if she returned here early? The Doyles' cabin? For a whole week? She didn't want to impose on their hospitality.

I can't let it be my family, though.

Maybe she could ask Gavin, but not right now. Her forehead was throbbing, right between her eyes, and she didn't want to think about anything. Slouching back in her seat, she rubbed at the ache and prayed it would fade soon.

Melanie and Gavin rode in silence for miles and miles, afraid to say much lest their conversation was indeed being listened to. The sun sank lower and lower behind them, and in the pearlescent sky, glowing threads of coral and goldenrod wove through murky violet and cobalt.

Headlights blinked on around them. The freeway had become an artery pulsing with red and white sparks. Normal people heading home from work to their ordinary families and horror-free lives.

It was fully dark—except for the glow from the streetlamps—when they reached the huge lot where Mel had parked her car. Relief washed over her to see the Honda sitting there, apparently untouched. *What if the Organization bugged it?* She didn't have a clue how to search for a bug or what one looked like, but she could have Gavin and his dad help her.

She and Gavin stepped out of Cara's car to say goodbye, and once again, he urged her to be vigilant. "Call me if you notice anything or if they contact you. I'll do the same."

Mel agreed and tossed her bag into her back seat.

Gavin started to climb back into the Nissan but added, "Don't go walking around alone after dark, either. Please ... be as careful as possible."

"Yes, sir." She saluted smartly.

The corner of Gavin's mouth twitched. "Gotta look out for each other."

It was hard to tell in the dark—was he blushing? Her own cheeks blazed like a bonfire in the crisp autumn air. "I appreciate your concern. You be careful, too."

He nodded seriously and said, "I am. I will be."

)) ● ((

Pulling up at the campus guard shack, Melanie saw Luis Vargas sitting inside the tiny building. *When did he become a guard?* She lowered her window a few inches to greet him.

Luis flashed her a charming white smile. "Hi, Melanie. How's it going?" His smile vanished as he studied her face. "You okay? You look really tired."

His polite way of saying "You look like hell." Which I do. "I'm all right."

I'm not all right.

"You gonna be in the library tonight?"

Crap. Tuesday. Tutoring. Melanie had a job and responsibilities, though they hardly seemed real at the moment. Or not as real as the wolf. She held back a sigh. "Yeah, I'll be there. Will you?"

"Yep. My shift's almost over. See you there." With another friendly grin and a wave, Luis activated the gate, and it rose to let her pass.

She drove to her dorm first to drop off her bag. Hartman was dark and empty, a gloomy silhouette against the black forest. In the bathroom, Mel combed her hair, scrubbed at her face to put color in it, and dabbed concealer under her eyes. Then she trudged down to the cafeteria.

Dinner dragged dismally. Mel hardly tasted her food. She spent the half hour avoiding Jocelyn's piercing green gaze, and Pam spent the time avoiding eye contact and conversation with Melanie.

Tutoring hours didn't start until 7:30, and it wasn't even 6:00, but Mel fled to the sanctuary of a far, deserted corner of the library. A musty tan armchair sat by itself, hidden behind a bank of tall, solid oak bookshelves. Curling up in the chair with one of her textbooks, she tried to read the assigned chapter. Before long, though, her eyelids grew heavy and slipped shut.

The sound of laughter woke her an hour later. She couldn't see the people on the other side of the shelves, but her ears immediately registered that Timmy was among the coed group. *Great.* Mel attempted to resume her reading despite the distracting voices. Turning pages noiselessly, she prayed that no one from the group would need a book from back here.

At 7:25, she could still hear the girls and guys gossiping and giggling. Why wasn't the librarian scolding them? It was time for Melanie to go downstairs and sit at the central bank of tables, where students could approach her for help with their Spanish homework. But there was no way out of this corner except to walk past Timmy and the others.

Mel grumbled to herself but stood up. *Ignore them. Don't look at them. Pretend they don't exist.* She clutched her book tightly to her chest, straightened her back, and held her head high. She strode around the corner of the shelves as if she owned the library, as if she hadn't been cowering in the corner—

She froze when she heard Pam's voice. "Hi, Aaron." Mel recognized the flirtatious tone and pictured her best friend batting her eyes. Rolling hers, Mel decided to wait and listen. She didn't relish seeing Pam right now, although better her than Timmy. Mel prayed one or both of them would leave soon.

"Is it true your roommate disappeared for the past few days?" said a male voice Mel assumed was Aaron's.

"Where'd you hear that?"

"Alexis. Timmy. Bunch of people."

Pam sighed. "Yes, it's true," she admitted, her voice heavier than a stack of dictionaries.

"I knew it!" That was definitely Timmy. Melanie imagined him leaning forward, triumph gleaming in his eyes.

She fumed. *Mind your own business, you little—*

"I thought you guys told each other everything," said Aaron.

"I thought we did too. Guess I was wrong." Pam sounded forlorn.

Snidely, Timmy put in, "She also missed a deadline—didn't proofread all the articles she was supposed to. I wonder if she's getting sloppy in her other classes, too."

Mel clenched her fists and ground her teeth. *You stupid, arrogant, misogynistic—*

A female voice asked, "Where do *you* think she went, Pam?"

"Damned if I know."

"She get a boyfriend or something?" the girl continued. "Luis hasn't been missing. Some guy from off campus?"

Oh, God. Melanie squeezed her book even more tightly, the blood draining from her face. Her knees threatened to buckle, and she leaned against the sturdy bookcase. *Please stop talking about me. Please, Pam, don't mention—*

"Not that I'm aware of," Pam answered slowly.

Good. Forget that conversation. Forget his name.

"I think she'd go out with Luis if he asked her. I think he'd like to ask her, too."

Shit. Pam!

"Wait, I forgot," said her roommate. "There's another guy. Gavin.

Yeah, I wonder if she's been with him."

I am going to kill *you, Pamela Jane Grazziano! What the hell do you think you're doing?!*

"OoOOoo." Melanie could hear, smell, *and* taste the intrigue radiating off the girl and whoever else was listening. "Tell me about him."

"He goes to Brookside. She met him at a volleyball game a couple months ago...."

Blood rushed in Mel's ears, drowning out Pam's words. Rage burned in her gut and surged upward through her chest like lava. Her body shook with it, the warning tremors before a violent eruption. The air seemed to compress and then ignite around her.

She stomped around the corner of the bookshelves, eyes flashing.

Her footsteps faltered. Pam, Timmy, and the others weren't right on the other side of the shelves. They sat at a table about thirty feet away.

It didn't matter. She knew what she had heard. She marched on, a vengeful storm goddess.

They noticed her when she was about ten feet away. Timmy's smirk broadened. Pam stopped in the middle of a sentence, her face turning bright red. "M-Mel. Hi. I didn't know you were—"

"Some best friend *you* are!" Melanie growled.

"I—I'm sor—"

"What I do in my free time is nobody's business! My relationships are nobody's business! My *life* is nobody's business! You nasty, backbiting vipers had better get that straight!"

Some of the people at the table had the grace to look ashamed, casting their gazes down at their laps. Tears welled up in Pam's eyes. But Timmy kept grinning as if Melanie were the most entertaining spectacle he'd seen all week. "Good speech," he said mockingly. "Maybe it'll win you an Emmy."

"Shut up, dumbass! Your vapid, egotistical, poisonous personality is a disgrace to humanity!" Mel spun on her heel and stalked away, huffing like a bull, ignoring the gawking from everyone she passed. She stamped down the stairs to the ground floor and headed for the table where Luis sat, but she couldn't bring herself to face him. She couldn't stay in this building. Correcting her course, she skirted around the bank of computers and hurried toward the front doors.

Luis spotted her and called to her across the lobby. "Melanie, where are you going? What's wrong?"

She didn't answer. She didn't look back. Outside, she sprinted through the freezing air toward her dorm. The wind bit her face, and she stumbled on uneven pavement, but she kept running. Tears burned in her eyes; sobs built in her chest.

Can't go back to Hartman, she realized halfway there. *Pam will come eventually.* Mel dreaded facing her roommate again. *How could she do that to me?!*

Where on earth am I going to go?

The *Sentinel* office had a couch. She didn't have her key, but the room might be unlocked; Dawn frequently worked there late into the evening. Mel didn't want her "boss" to see her this upset or ask what had happened, so when she slipped inside the communication building, she headed directly to the bathroom.

The tears burst from her eyes as she stood in front of the mirror, gripping the cold porcelain edges of a pedestal sink. Her shoulders shook and her knees wobbled. The truckload of her exhaustion, pain, and fear crashed down.

Why is all this happening to me? Why did Pam have to gossip about me? Why did that stupid Organization have to bother me and Gavin? Why can't everybody just leave me alone?! Why ... why did I have to get bitten?! Everything's gone to hell.

Her knees gave way at the remembrance of her dream about St. Peter. She slumped to the floor and bawled harder. Her chest felt ready to squeeze out black ooze at any moment.

Minutes passed like hours. Cold from the hard tile floor seeped through Mel's jeans. Her emotional torrent ebbed into sniffles and long, shaky breaths like rippling waves. Embarrassment swam to the surface, but it was accompanied by relief. *Good thing I came in here. That meltdown could've happened in front of Dawn.*

Slowly, she picked herself off the floor. Puffy red eyes gazed mournfully back at her in the mirror, and she looked away. *Oh. It's a good thing I'm wearing my contacts.* No doubt there would have been a golden blaze in her eyes, and what if Pam or Timmy or anyone had seen that?

My ears, she thought, realizing—her sense of hearing was still amplified. That had to be how she'd overheard the group's conversation from thirty feet away through a solid wood barrier. Maybe they *had* been talking quietly, since the librarian hadn't shushed them.

Now that she was thinking more clearly, Melanie became aware of the putrid stench emanating from the stalls behind her. She wrinkled her nose, and her stomach churned. *Got to get out of here.*

She composed her features into a neutral expression. She had to keep up the mask. No one could know about her anguish and fear, and no one could help her if they did know. Not even Pam.

Mel clenched her fists as she walked to the newspaper office. Pam didn't deserve the truth. She'd forfeited her right to it.

The *Sentinel* room's light was on, and Dawn Fincher sat at one of the computers, clicking away with the mouse, arranging files in folders. "Hey, Caldwell," she said, taking in Mel's appearance without comment. "When'd you get back?"

Melanie blushed. "This afternoon." She scuffed her toe and stared down at the floor. "Look, Dawn, I'm really sorry—"

The editor waved a hand dismissively. "Ah, don't sweat it. Everyone slips up every now and then. Didn't expect it from you, but I'm sure it won't happen again."

Finally meeting Dawn's gaze, Mel wondered if her words contained a mild, veiled threat. "It won't," she said.

"Good!" Dawn gave a rare smile, but her businesslike expression quickly returned. "Speaking of good, you arrived at a good time. I got this idea for the next issue. Let me run it by you."

"Okay." Mel sank onto the couch, welcoming the distraction.

Around 8:30, she started to yawn.

"Sorry to bore you to death," Dawn said wryly.

"Nah, you didn't. I needed to get my mind off some stuff."

"You sure you haven't switched from decaf?"

Mel chuckled. "Nope. I mean, yeah; I'm sure I haven't."

"Well, hey, I'm not your mom, but you should probably go to bed."

The thought of returning to her room made Mel stiffen. "Um, I kind of had a fight with Pam," she admitted. "I'd like to avoid her for a while."

"I see. I won't tell anyone if you crash on the couch tonight. You're already on the verge of zonking out. No blankets around here, though, and it's gonna get cold."

Melanie figured the chill would wake her up after a couple of hours and she'd sneak back into her dorm once she was sure Pam had gone to sleep. She lay back and got comfortable, crossing her arms over her chest vampire style.

Bright light glowed through her eyelids, rousing her. What—it was morning and she was still here on the couch? *Crap.*

"Uugghh." Mel's limbs complained as she sat up and stretched. Her hair felt matted, and a trail of drool had dried on her cheek. She licked a finger and rubbed the crusted saliva off.

The clock said 7:00. Nobody came in here that early. Thank God. She grabbed her backpack and hurried out of the office. *Dammit,* she thought on her hike back up to Hartman. *I missed the entire window of time that Pam was sleeping. I'm an idiot!*

She'd have to face the music major.

Pam was in the shower when she arrived, which Melanie counted as a blessing. She considered hiding in the tiny hall closet while Pam transitioned back to their bedroom, then darting into the bathroom and hoping Pam would think she was Shari or Jocelyn.

You'd only be postponing the inevitable.

Before she could make up her mind, Jos poked her curly head through the doorway. "You're back. Were you gone all night?"

"Uh . . ." The running water stopped with a loud squeak, and Melanie scuffed her toe on the carpet. "Accidentally fell asleep at the *Sentinel* office," she confessed, then wondered why she'd done it. *Well, unlike* some *people, Jos can keep secrets.*

Jocelyn gave a small "Hmm." Her eyebrows knit together, and she opened her mouth as if to say more but shut it instead. She disappeared, leaving Mel to speculate nervously about what wheels were turning in her mind.

A minute later, a floral scent filled the air, and Pam walked in, her hair up in a towel. She stopped short when she saw Melanie. The two stared awkwardly at each other for a few seconds before looking away. "Hi," Pam said in a timid, strained voice.

"Hey," Mel replied shortly, her eyes fixed on the toiletries and fresh clothes she was gathering up.

She tried to leave the room, but Pam caught her arm and said, "I am so, so, so, so, so, so sorry, Mel! Please forgive me! I'll never gossip about you again. It was a huge mistake." Her pleading gray eyes showed earnest sincerity.

Nevertheless, Melanie wanted to scream in her face: *How could you in the first place?!* She set her jaw and leveled a steely gaze at Pam. Her roommate's hand fell away, and her lower lip trembled.

Phrases like "Too little, too late" and "You cut me too deeply" floated through Mel's head. Resentment tightened like a fist around her heart. But then she recalled how kindly Pam had cared for her after the Pine Groves fiasco—taking her to the nurse and the hospital for a rabies shot, helping her up the stairs, leaving food for her in the fridge.

Mel's posture relaxed and her features softened. She let out a long sigh. "All right. I forgive you."

Her friend's face lit up, and she bounced on her toes and hugged Mel. "You're the best!"

A grin slid onto Melanie's face. "I know."

But as she stood under the hot shower water shortly later, she thought, *I'm still not telling you my secret.*

Pam wasn't earning her complete trust back any time soon.

14

Consequences

Friday evening, the diner was packed and noisy. Erickson didn't care; he sat tucked away in a corner, blending into the background, and no one bothered him. It was easy to be alone in a crowd. His mind was far away from here, anyway.

These days, his thoughts frequently wandered back to Chandra.

Her unscratched room. Her strength and energy on post-transformation mornings. What could they mean?

Erickson had asked her, but in typical fashion, Chandra had teased him. "I'll tell you if you come to a meeting. There's one next Monday at seven."

Sticking to his part in the routine, he'd balked and said he'd answer later.

Most of a week had gone by, and he was still mulling. And trying to work out the mystery surrounding Chandra.

One theory that floated through his head tonight was: *Maybe she isn't actually a werewolf.*

But she had to be one. She'd smelled like one. His wolf had been hyper aware of the pheromones she'd given off—it had clawed deep gouges into his door and the wall beside it, no doubt trying to get to her.

Could she reek of wolf but not be one?

Erickson tried to conjure up her sweet, slightly spicy scent. That was hard to do in a place saturated with greasy food and steaming coffee. What kind of perfume did she wear?

He caught a whiff of something floral, mingled with sweat. It was familiar, but it wasn't right. Not Chandra. Reemerging from his reverie as if from deep underwater, he blinked up at his favorite waitress,

130

Joelle.

The large, middle-aged woman stood beside his table, gesturing at his mug with a pot of decaf. "Another refill, honey?" she drawled in her pleasant, motherly voice.

"Yes, please." Erickson smiled his thanks as she poured.

Joelle gave him her own gap-toothed grin, set her free hand on her ample hip, and said, "You look like you's deeper in thought than old Socrates—like I could walk past you wearin' nothin' but an apron and you wouldn't notice."

Erickson could have done without *that* mental imagery, but his lips quirked, and he shrugged. "Just trying to figure out whether I can trust a certain person or not."

"Man or woman?"

"Woman."

"Young and pretty, or more like me?"

"What's the difference?"

Joelle blushed, then waggled a scolding finger. "You're just tryna get free dessert off me."

"Is it working?"

She leaned forward conspiratorially, mirth in her protuberant dark eyes. "The pie or the brownie?"

"Brownie, please."

A grin split Erickson's face as Joelle ambled away across the black-and-white-checked tiles, her generous backside undulating like a waterbed.

When she returned with his dessert, he said, "She's considerably younger than me, and very, very pretty."

"Hmm." A sly look crossed Joelle's face. "Is this a datin' type of situation?"

"No. It's more than just her involved. I should've said I'm trying to figure out whether I can trust a certain group of people."

Joelle pursed her lips. "Hard to say, not knowin' 'em. I'm guessin' they ain't a charity organization or a local softball team?"

Erickson shook his head wryly.

Resting a hand on his shoulder, the waitress said, "Nick, you always here alone. You eat, you tip well, you's polite, you leave quietly. I never seen you with family, friends, girlfriend, nothin'. You seem like you mus' be a lonely man." Compassion crinkled her eyes.

He looked away, down at his brownie, feeling the sad truth of her words sink in.

"Long 's these folks ain't a crime syndicate or nothin', I say you go for it. Take a chance on 'em. Nobody wants to die alone. Nobody should live like that, neither."

That night as he tried to fall asleep, Joelle's words haunted him. Next door, the neighbors were at it again. He couldn't remember their names (they usually called each other "Dumbass" and "Slut") but he sure knew their voices. *They're always at each other's throats, yet they've stayed together for who knows how long.*

However turbid their relationship, they had one. That was more than he had.

Resolve crystalized inside him. He sat up and reached for his phone.

"What time is the meeting?" he texted Chandra.

)) ● ((

The Monday before Thanksgiving, Gavin called Melanie to check up on her.

"All quiet on the northern front," Mel joked. Stretched out on her bed, books and notebooks scattered around her, she shifted to a more comfortable position. Pam was in the music building and the door was shut, so Mel could talk freely as long as she kept her voice low. "How did your parents take the news about our new 'friends'?"

He sighed. "They're worried and scared. Jeff really wants to come guard the cabin next month, and he's mad that I told him it's not a good idea. I mean, he knows it's not, but he hates that."

"It does suck. But it's nice that you have such a protective dad."

"Yeah. My parents both are. They'd do anything for me. But I want to protect them, too."

Mel smiled wistfully. Her envy of his family resurfaced, but not in a resentful way. Rather, she yearned to be a part of it.

She and Gavin talked about their home life growing up, and then about school and the upcoming holiday. Mel admitted she was staying on campus (despite Pam's invitation to come with her to Virginia) and would most likely eat Thanksgiving dinner in the cafeteria.

"No, you can't do that—that's awful," said Gavin. "You have to come to my house."

A warm tingle spread through Mel. Her mind raced with images of spending happy evenings with the Doyles, eating and chatting and laughing together, sitting on the sofa snuggled up against Gavin, his arm around her, her head leaning on his shoulder. . . .

"So, do you want to come?" he asked.

"Oh. I, um—yeah," she blurted out. *What am I doing? My homework will never get done!* "Is it okay with Jeff and Cara, though?"

"Of course."

"You asked them?" She raised an eyebrow.

"No. But they'll say yes."

"Can you please ask them officially and then get back to me?"

He snickered. "All right, but I already told you what they're going to say."

"Did you have a vision about it?"

More snickering. "I'll call them and then call you right back."

"Okay. 'Bye." Mel hung up and waited, twirling a strand of her shoulder-length hair and staring into space, too distracted by daydreams to study.

Five minutes later, the phone rang again. She snatched it up and said a breathless "Hello?"

"Pick you up at eleven on Thursday," said Gavin.

"Cool." She kept her voice casual but squealed on the inside.

Great, she thought after they said goodbye for the second time. *I'm definitely not going to finish this blasted homework.*

And I can't tell Pam about going to the Doyles'. She might be upset that I chose them over her.

)) ◕ ((

NOVEMBER 24, WANING CRESCENT MOON

"Gavin—dinner's almost ready! Get your brother out of that tree, would you?"

"Yes, Mom!" As fast as his little legs could carry him, he ran to the far end of their sprawling back yard, where his younger brother perched in the big crabapple tree. Gavin craned his neck and called up, "Mom says you gotta get down. It's time to eat."

"I don't wanna!" the tiny boy protested.

Hands on hips, Gavin said, "You have to. Mom says so."

"You're not the boss of me! I want Daddy!"

Gavin's face fell. He scuffed his foot in the grass, crumbling a dead leaf to smithereens. "Dad's not back yet. But he will be soon." I hope.

"Daddy has to come get me down," his brother insisted.

Gavin said nothing but hoisted himself into the tree. I wish Dad wouldn't work so much. If he doesn't get home soon, he'll miss Thanksgiving dinner, and Mom won't be happy. *Reaching his brother, he put his hand on the small boy's arm. "I really wish Dad was here too. I hate how he always stays so late at the office and goes in on holidays. But Mom is here, and she's been cooking all day for us. We need to help her have a good Thanksgiving. Can you come down so she's not eating alone?"*

His brother sighed, and then his lower lip quivered. Sniffling, he allowed Gavin to help him to the ground. Gavin slung an arm around his shoulders, and the two brothers trudged back to the house together.

Their father failed to show up until their mother was rinsing plates and loading the dishwasher.

Gavin realized his own lip was trembling, and he felt a stray tear course down his cheek. He slowed the car as he approached Wells- boro's front gate. *What's with me, getting worked up over those ancient memories? That was a different lifetime.*

It was gone now. His birth family.

Embarrassed, he wiped the tear away and composed himself. Melanie was standing at the curb outside the gate. He leaned over and popped the passenger door open, returning her smile as she climbed in. Her face was flushed prettily from the chill air. "I hope you haven't been waiting long," he said.

"Nah, only a minute or so." She grinned. "The guy in the guard shack offered me hot cocoa."

"That was nice of him." Gavin released the brake and started the car back down the road, a strange twist in his stomach.

"It's nice of *you* to pick me up," Melanie said. "And I'm making you take some gas money this time." Pulling a twenty-dollar bill from her purse, she shoved it in his face.

"No, keep it," he protested, swatting her hand away.

She laughed and tossed the bill in the back seat. "It's yours now. I probably owe you more than that." Her voice grew quiet. "I owe you a *lot* more than that."

Gavin threw a sidelong glance at her. A shadow had passed over her face, but she soon brightened up again. "So, does your family have any unusual Thanksgiving traditions I should be prepared for?"

The drive passed quickly with lighthearted talk. Just before noon, they arrived at the Doyle home, a large yellow Cape Cod with white trim and a wraparound porch. Flower boxes adorned the windows, although at this time of year, they were barren.

"It's lovely," said Melanie.

"They take good care of it," Gavin said, pushing open the hunter-green front door, which was decorated with a festive autumn wreath. Tantalizing smells greeted the pair. "Hi, Mom! We're here!"

Cara called a cheery welcome from the kitchen. Gavin led Melanie to the aromatic epicenter of the house, where his mom was checking on the turkey. Closing the oven, Cara straightened up, tucked a stray strand of blue-black hair behind her ear, and beamed. "Good to see you again, Melanie." She wrapped the girl in a warm hug. "Can I take your coat?"

"I got it," said Gavin, taking his turn embracing his mom while Melanie removed her teal pea coat. She handed it to him, and he noticed how nice she looked in her lavender blouse and dark brown dress pants. Her glossy hair was partially pulled back, her makeup understated but becoming.

There went his stomach again. What was its problem today? He paused in the hallway until the fluttering feeling subsided.

"Can I help with anything?" Melanie asked Cara.

"You can put the mashed potatoes in that bowl and set it on the table. Everything else is almost ready."

"Where's Dad?" said Gavin, rejoining the women.

"He should be back from the shelter any time now."

Confusion crossed Melanie's face, so Gavin explained, "He's help-ing serve dinner at the local homeless shelter."

"That's awesome." She smiled.

More flutters. Shyly, he turned his gaze away.

Fifteen minutes crawled by. Melanie and Cara chatted while Gavin paced the kitchen and the dining room. The cloud of sweet and savory scents filling his nose was driving him crazy, and his stomach struck up a yearning monologue. He nibbled on crescent rolls and olives and picked at the turkey until Cara playfully swatted his hand and shooed him away from the cooling feast. "What could be taking your father so long?" she said, frown lines appearing. "I'd better give him a call."

Gavin could hear the rings on the other end. Three, four, five of them and no answer. Memories of his birth father missing Thanksgiving dinner resurfaced, and the food he'd just eaten turned to lead. A swirl of unpleasant emotions kicked up, but he told himself, *It's not for the same reason. I'm sure he's got a good one. He's not at some bar. He's probably talking with Pastor Bill or praying with somebody.*

Cara left a message on Jeff's voicemail. She tucked the turkey back into the oven and put the potatoes, green bean casserole, and other side dishes under a warmer. Time passed. Cara busily circumnavigated the dining room, straightening place settings and chairs and picture frames. Gavin caught a faint whiff of fear.

Cara called again and again, but no answer. Gavin parted the curtains of the front window. The street was filled with parked cars, but his dad's was nowhere in sight. "Something's not right," he said.

Melanie joined him, forcing a smile. "I'm sure he'll be here any minute. Maybe he's caught in traffic and his phone died."

"Even if that were the case, it's been so long. . . . This isn't like him. He knows we're waiting, and he—"

Frenetic techno music cut off Gavin's words. He snatched his phone from his pocket. *Blocked call.* "Hello?"

A deep, silky voice: "Gavin Doyle. We told you that we take our privacy seriously."

The Organization. Had to be. *They* did *bug the car.* "Where's my dad?" Gavin demanded, trying to keep his tone firm. "What'd you do to him?"

"Jeff is perfectly fine, for now. But you need to learn that there are consequences for disobeying us."

Gavin gnashed his teeth, and his fingers twitched with anger. If he could get his hands around this man's throat . . . Catching his eye, Melanie gave Gavin a worried, questioning look. She could probably hear the voice on the other end.

Cara had walked over to join them, eyes wide, hand fluttering to her heart. "Gavin, is that—?"

He held up a hand. The man on the phone was speaking again: "If you want to see him, there is a favor you can do for us."

"Like what?" Gavin snarled.

"We'll tell you later."

"How do I know he's really there with you?"

"His wristwatch has an engraving. 'Yours for all time. CAD.' It's a gold-and-blue Invicta diver's watch. Very nice."

"That's not proof. I want to talk to him."

"You're in no position to be giving me orders, kid."

Gavin growled. "He'd better come back, unharmed, with that watch, and *soon.*"

The man *tsk*ed. "You take us for killers or thieves? We're not after a ransom. We don't want your money—we want you. And Melanie Caldwell."

The temperature in the room dropped ten degrees. The knots that had formed in Gavin's midsection tightened as if he were about to transform. He wrapped his free arm protectively around his stomach and glanced at Cara and Melanie. They stared at him, frozen in shock. Swallowing back the lump in his throat, Gavin tried to focus his jumbled, racing thoughts, to form another coherent sentence.

"This is not the way we would have preferred to do things," the man continued. "We would rather cooperate and enjoy a mutually beneficial relationship."

"I'm having a hard time believing that."

A longsuffering sigh. "Mr. Doyle. I admire your caution and your resolve. I urge you to reconsider your stance. When your father comes back to you safe and sound, perhaps you will realize our good will toward you and—"

"When will he be back?"

"That is up to my superior."

Gavin snarled in frustration. "Well, put *him* on, would you?"

"I'm afraid that isn't possible at this time."

"For someone who's been talking about cooperating, you sure aren't doing much of it yourself."

"Quick to make accusations, hmm?" The voice now had a sharper edge. "If you're feeling self-righteous, remember that it was you who transgressed our conditions and set this unfortunate scenario in motion."

"I never agreed to—"

"Nonetheless, consequences remain. Good day, Mr. Doyle."

Beep. The call ended.

For a long minute, Gavin and Melanie and Cara stared at each other, openmouthed and speechless. Then Cara clutched at Melanie's arm, and the two women sank to the couch. Melanie put a comforting hand over Cara's.

"Please . . . explain," said Cara, looking up at her son with wet eyes. "Who was that? Jeff—is he okay?"

"Yes, I think so." Gavin related what the man had said, surprised at how calmly he was able to speak. Rage and fear were duking it out inside him, but guilt pushed up between them like tree roots cracking pavement open. When he was finished explaining, he found that he was having trouble staying on his feet, so he lowered himself onto a chair. He put his face in his hands. "This is all my fault."

"Honey," said Cara, wiping her eyes, "you know it isn't."

"If I hadn't told Melanie in the car that I was going to tell you—"

"There's no guarantee they wouldn't have done something like this sooner or later."

Gavin let out a muffled noise halfway between a groan and a snarl, furiously calculating his next move. *Should we go to the police about this? The cops can't all be working with the Organization. Or would that make things worse?*

I need a vision showing me what to do.

"I'm so sorry," said Melanie, timidly drawing him out of his miserable thoughts. "But I wonder what that favor is."

Dread settled like a heavy cloak over Gavin's shoulders at the reminder. Whatever the Organization was going to order them to do, he figured it wouldn't be something he'd want to do. "Who knows." He imagined himself refusing flat out, but that might mean not seeing his dad again. He clenched his fists and seethed. *Damn them. Damn them.*

Looking at Cara, he saw that her head was bowed, her eyes closed, her lips moving in inaudible prayer.

Oh. He should probably give that a try, too. He threw up a quick, silent cry for help in case it might make any difference.

He had his doubts.

15

Task

Well, that's the first time I've felt guilty for eating Thanksgiving dinner, reflected Melanie as she returned to her dorm that evening.

After the Organization's phone call, she and Gavin and Cara had sat around numbly. Then Cara had stood up and strode to the kitchen. "He wouldn't want us to waste all this food," she'd said simply, carrying the loaded platters back to the dining table. Mel had rushed to help, but Gavin had taken a while to stand up and follow.

Hours later, under tenebrous twilight clouds, Gavin had dropped her off at Hartman Cottage and then headed back to his parents' house to wait for another phone call. A call telling Gavin and Melanie what the Organization wanted them to do.

Mel closed the front door behind her, turned to head upstairs, and felt her foot squash something thin and papery into the living room carpet. She bent down and picked up a plain white envelope—now crinkled—marked with her name.

She didn't open it until she'd gotten up to her room, removed her coat and shoes, and settled comfortably on her bed.

Dear Melanie:

Safety relies on security. Members of our organization are vulnerable, just as you are. Imagine how you would feel if you knew we were telling strangers about you, about your secret.

We reached out to you and Gavin in good faith, risking our lives and freedom to help you, and Gavin betrayed us. We understand that it is tempting to tell things to our families, but people talk. Even well-intentioned people slip up and make mistakes... and a mistake on the part of Gavin's parents would hurt more than him: It would hurt all of us, too.

Holding Gavin's father is an extreme measure, but we haven't hurt him and we won't. We just need Gavin to understand that this is serious. He has betrayed us and risked our lives for purely selfish reasons when we were only trying to help! Realize that, if you are part of our organization, we'll protect your secrecy and security as zealously as we're now protecting ours.

We're afraid that Gavin didn't react well to our call and may have given you a false impression of our intentions. That's why we decided to write to you. We hope this letter clears things up.

It was unsigned. The handwriting appeared to be the same masculine scrawl as the note Mel and Gavin had received at the cabin. Mel folded the letter closed with a sigh that turned into a groan. *Now what am I supposed to think?* This was all so confusing.

While she understood Gavin's fear, mistrust, and concern for his father's safety—she worried about Jeff, too, of course—the letter opened a different set of eyes inside her. The view through them was strange and uncomfortable, like trying on someone else's glasses, but she was adjusting, and some blurry shapes were coming into focus.

I believe them, she realized. The Organization might have acted forcefully, and its members clearly wouldn't tolerate disrespect, but she believed they'd do what they said and return Jeff unharmed if she and Gavin cooperated.

Still, she knew next to nothing about the Organization, which kept her wary. What was its goal? What would their task be? When would they receive it? Mel was dying to find out, although apprehension niggled.

What if the Organization asked them to do something bad, and she and Gavin refused? What would become of Jeff Doyle?

Images flashed through her mind: Jeff sprawled broken in a ditch, blood pooling black under the moonlight. Jeff on his knees, begging for mercy. Jeff thrashing as they—

She shuddered. *Stop it!* she told her overactive imagination. *They said they wouldn't hurt him.*

A scraping noise punctuated the silence and made her jump. Her heart pounded, and her eyes darted around the room. Then she recognized the semi-familiar sound. It was a tree branch, whipped by the wind, scratching against her window like a cat asking to come in.

Melanie flopped backward on her bed, then stared up at the ceiling. The light fixture gave off a wan, yellowish glow, jaundicing her spirits. She was alone in an empty house at night, and—she'd locked the door, right?

Yes. She remembered doing so after waving goodbye to Gavin, right before stepping on the letter. She'd also locked her bedroom door.

She sat up and tucked the letter back into its envelope, then buried it under old socks at the back of her underwear drawer. *Stop thinking about it,* she ordered herself. *I need a distraction. This place is gonna creep me out otherwise.*

Might as well do some more werewolf-cure research since there was no chance of being caught right now. Because looking at gruesome images of werewolves mauling people or being skinned alive was sure to lift her spirits.

A little research, and then funny videos on YouTube, she compromised, scooting into her desk chair.

As she moved the mouse to wake the computer, her phone blasted "Mama Said Knock You Out." Grinning, Mel answered the call. Her mother was a better distraction than anything.

>)) ● ((

NOVEMBER 25, WANING CRESCENT MOON

Erickson didn't get out of bed until two o'clock the next afternoon, his head splitting and his bladder threatening to burst. Yesterday was a blur—he'd spent it drunk, as he did with all major holidays since his family had broken up.

After vomiting copiously, he downed coffee and aspirin, then nibbled on a piece of toast. He managed to keep that down, so he ate another before climbing back into bed.

He might not remember yesterday, but he clearly recalled Monday night—the Organization's meeting. It had been held in the smoky back room of a raucous pub called McCullough's Tavern. Chandra had driven him there and introduced him to a dozen other werewolves (that many!) including the McCulloughs: Roy and Simon, middle-aged brothers from Ireland and the head honchos.

For an awkward twenty minutes, Erickson had sat and listened to a spiel about helping and protecting your fellow wolves, blah blah, nearly identical to the malarkey that Saddler had spouted at Pine Groves.

But *after* the meeting... his conversation with Chandra was what really stuck in his mind. It was the crux, the lynchpin, the only thing drawing him back.

He'd finally found out her secret. And it had opened up a whole new world of possibilities for him.

She *was* a werewolf—but a different breed, or whatever you wanted to call it. One that possessed a distinct advantage.

And if Erickson joined the Organization, there was a good chance that someday he might gain that advantage for himself.

ꜱ ꜱ ● ꜱ ꜱ

NOVEMBER 29, NEW MOON

The weekend limped past in a dreary haze. Mel's housemates returned Sunday afternoon and evening, chattering about their delightful holiday and all the amazing food they'd eaten. When Pam questioned Mel about how the cafeteria's Thanksgiving dinner had tasted, Mel shrugged and said, "Not much different from the rest of their gourmet cuisine."

"That bad, huh? Did you at least get to talk to your family?"

"Yes." Melanie didn't have to lie there. Her mom had passed the phone around. She'd also chatted with Gavin on Sunday; he'd called to report no news from the Organization and no Jeff. She hadn't told him of the Organization's letter.

"How's Cara holding up?" she'd asked him.

"Amazingly well. Never met a more peaceful woman in my life."

"She's quite something."

"Don't I know it."

Tuesday morning, Melanie woke feeling particularly rested because the moon was new—her favorite of its phases. No lingering headaches or joint pain; no violent urges, restlessness, or hypersensitivity to smells and sounds. She almost felt like a normal person again. Almost.

On her way to breakfast, she stopped and checked her post office box. In it she found a parcel delivery slip. *Hmm, another care package from Mom?* She'd eat first and then pick it up. She headed into the cafeteria and wolfed down eggs and toast, anticipating a large box full of homemade baked goods or other treats—maybe a crisp twenty-dollar bill—although her mom hadn't mentioned putting anything in the mail.

The middle-aged woman who ran the package center had a witch's lock that was starting to blend into her graying hair. She apathetically eyed Mel's slip over thick tortoiseshell glasses and produced a plain brown box the size of a dozen stacked magazines. Nodding gruffly, she handed the parcel to Mel, who lifted it easily; it was lighter than she'd expected. Much lighter than magazines. Probably a pound or less.

It was also not postmarked from her mom. In fact, there was no return address at all.

Hiking back to her dorm, Mel grew more apprehensive with each step. She cradled the package gingerly, as though it would explode from too much pressure. *What the heck is this? Who sent it?*

She shut the door of her room behind her and sat down on her bed, then examined all six sides of the mysterious box. Aside from her name and address and postage, there were no other markings—no Fragile, no This Side Up.

She dredged the depths of her purse and found her pocket knife. Carefully, she slit the tape across the top of the parcel and lifted the four flaps. Inside, under some packing peanuts, was another plain brown box. A note was folded on top of it: "Do not open, for Jeff's sake. Wait for further instructions. Destroy this paper."

Her heart rate sped up. The Organization. The task.

Omigosh, what if there's a top-secret document in here that they want us to deliver?

But surely the Organization wouldn't trust them with anything too important. What would the Organization think an appropriate test—or punishment? Maybe this was even a trap, a test within a test designed to check whether they could be trusted with something as simple as delivering a package.

She pulled out her phone and texted Gavin about the box.

"They haven't called me back yet," he replied. "I would just hide it for now."

Great. Another lovely delivery from the Organization hidden in my room. Sighing, Mel closed the parcel back up. She stashed it deep beneath her bed, sandwiched between storage bins.

Out of sight, but far from out of mind.

During dinner that evening, Mel's phone chimed with another text from Gavin: "They called."

Mel scarfed down the rest of her food and then hurried out into the frigid night air.

"What do they want us to do?" she typed, hiking back to her dorm.

"Take it to this address: 3545 Cedarwood Rd."

"When?"

"Tomorrow after classes."

All through tutoring hours, she couldn't focus on anything but the package and what might be in it. It was even more distracting than Luis's white teeth and dimples, which kept flashing at her as he talked about the holiday weekend and his family. When he asked about Mel's Thanksgiving, she shrugged and said, "It was fine." Her eyes darted around, hoping for someone to approach them for tutoring so she didn't have to keep lying.

"You okay? You seem kind of *preocupada*," said Luis.

"Oh. *Lo siento.* I just . . ."

"*No hay problema.* I understand. The end of semester's getting close, and you've probably got a lot of homework and papers like I do."

"*Exactamente.*" Melanie smiled in relief and gratitude, but guilt lurked underneath.

Luis opened the book he'd brought and flipped to a section near the end. Mel returned to reading her European history textbook. *The Cold War was a state of military and political tension following World War II. . . . "Living in the shadow of a threat" . . . espionage and many secrets . . . I know a thing or two about secrets—and secret errands—now.*

"Hey, um," Luis broke into her thoughts.

"Huh?" Mel looked up and saw that his cheeks were flushed.

"Do you want to . . . well, uh, sometime, maybe—"

"Excuse me," said a young-sounding female voice before Luis could stammer another word. "Are you guys the Spanish tutors?"

Melanie turned and saw a thin-faced girl with spiky blonde hair and a diamond stud in her nose; she looked older and tougher than she sounded. "*Si.* What level are you taking?"

"Two."

Glancing at Luis, Mel raised her eyebrows in a silent question: *You or me?*

"I got this," he said with a smile that didn't meet his eyes.

He and the level-two student moved to a separate table, and Mel watched them with fresh guilt. It was nice of Luis to give her more study time. She hoped she wasn't treating him coldly. What had he been about to ask?

）） ● （ （

NOVEMBER 30, WAXING CRESCENT MOON

The next day, as soon as her last class was over, Melanie drove off campus and turned south onto the main highway. She'd arranged to meet Gavin at the same rendezvous point they'd used for this month's full moon, since the huge parking lot was on their way to 3545 Cedarwood.

"Hey," said Gavin when she slid into his passenger seat. "I looked up this place, and it's a unit in a strip mall. It's supposed to be vacant and for rent."

"Fantastic," said Melanie. "That's not shady at all." Shifting the box on her lap, she remarked, "Feels like this could be full of cotton."

"I doubt it is."

An icy feeling washed over Melanie although the car's heat was cranked up. *Don't let him get to you.*

The drive took twenty-seven minutes. Mel had never ventured down these roads before. They wove like a needle and thread in and out of small towns—buttons dotting a patchwork quilt of fields and woods.

The green turned to gray, and they entered a drab concrete jungle. Graffiti was scrawled across crumbling brick buildings and rotting clapboard fences. Litter blew past like tumbleweeds. The clouds hung low and leaden. A few more turns, and the strip mall came into view. It had been stripped, all right—of half its tenants. The few that remained, huddling together like cattle in a storm, sold deli sandwiches, cell phones, cigarettes, alcoholic beverages, manicures, tanning services, and tattoos. *All you need in life, right here,* Mel thought wryly.

They cruised through the sparsely populated parking lot, scanning numbers on the building's front façade until they found 3545. The fading digits were displayed above a glass door covered by brown paper on the inside. The windows were blocked in the same manner, allowing no glimpse of the interior. Signs declared "For Lease" in large hunter-green letters, with a phone number underneath.

Melanie and Gavin threw each other nervous looks before getting out of the car. Hugging the box to her side, Mel started toward the apparently vacant unit but tripped on uneven pavement. She stumbled forward, and the box nearly slipped from her grip. Gavin caught her elbow and steadied her. "Thanks," she said breathlessly.

He nodded in response, because at that moment, a rusty white Cadillac drove past blasting hip-hop music. The bass was cranked up so high that it rattled Mel's ribcage. She winced.

She and Gavin reached the door of unit 3545, paused in front of it, and glanced around. A couple of men were just leaving the tattoo parlor four doors down, admiring the newly inked, raw red patches of skin on their bare arms. *No jackets? Aren't they cold?* The deli, two doors in the other direction, broadcast the savory smells of ham and pickles and yeasty bread. Mel's stomach growled for dinner. The food also reminded her of Thanksgiving and Jeff's kidnapping, which was why they were on this strange errand. *Is he here? Is anyone here?*

She fingered the canister of pepper spray in her pocket. Her dad had sent it to her last semester after viewing some particularly grim news stories about the epidemic of rapes on college campuses. Wellsboro was small, and nothing ever happened there; Mel had stashed the pepper spray in the bottom of her purse and forgotten about it until today.

Meeting eyes with Gavin again, she tried to gather courage from him. He looked as reluctant as she felt, but he reached out and tried the door—which was unlocked. It swung silently open, and he and Mel entered the unit's front room: white tiles, gray wallpaper, unfurnished. The lighting was dim, but a sliver of bluish light beckoned them from underneath a closed door at the back. It, too, was unlocked, and they stepped into a room several times larger than the empty foyer.

Mel's first thought was of a doctor's office waiting room: carpet patterned in heather gray and navy blue. A rather sterile smell. A few chairs lining one wall. No coffee table with magazines, though. *As if I'd want to sit around reading in a place like this.*

Melanie became aware of a faint, low humming noise that sounded like it was coming from behind a third door. Before she and Gavin could cross the carpeted room and knock or try the handle, the door opened and a man stepped through.

He looked to be in his sixties and wore a clean white lab coat over a brown plaid shirt and red bowtie. His stooped shoulders reduced him to slightly below average height, and his salt-and-pepper hair was mostly salt. Wire-rimmed glasses rested beneath bushy eyebrows and over the heavy purplish bags under his eyes. *Eastern European,* Mel speculated. His dark eyes seemed intelligent and wary but not unkind.

"Hello," he said in an accent that confirmed Mel's guess. "You have a delivery for me?"

"Yes." Mel craned her neck to see the room behind the man as she and Gavin approached. Stark white walls and cabinets. A glimpse of polished black countertop. A kitchen? No other people were in sight, and the old man appeared unarmed. *Thank God.* The guy didn't strike her as dangerous, but looks could be deceiving.

She proffered the package, and the man accepted it with liver-spotted hands. "Excellent. Thank you for bringing this." A momentary smile deepened the lines on his craggy face.

"Is my dad here?" Gavin asked. "When are we going to get him back?"

"He is not," said the man, "but I was told that he will be returned safely after you bring me this."

Gavin nodded, and some of the tension drained from his shoulders. Mel grinned at him and put a hand on his arm.

". . . And after you do one other thing," said the old man.

"Like what?" Her grin faded.

The man turned to go back into the white room, and he gestured for Melanie and Gavin to follow. Exchanging uneasy looks, they trailed after him and stepped into what Mel realized was a laboratory. The acrid stench of chemicals greeted her—if it had been near the full moon, the odor would have overwhelmed her. A trio of computers huddled on an L-shaped desk, one whirring quietly. Beakers, glass vials, and other equipment waited along the obsidian countertop. The man deposited his package among them.

In another corner Mel saw a couple of gray padded chairs and a white supply cart. A red box was mounted on the wall near it. Memories of her trip to the hospital rushed back. *Oh no, don't tell me—*

"Please sit down and roll up your sleeves," said the old man, indicating the chairs. "I need a sample of your blood."

"What?!" said Melanie and Gavin in unison. Gavin stepped protectively in front of Mel, and she clutched at the pepper spray in her pocket.

The old man regarded them calmly.

"Why?" challenged Gavin.

"I am not at liberty to tell you."

"Oh, that's gonna convince us to cooperate."

"You did want to see your father again, correct?"

Gavin pulled out his phone. "I'll get the police involved. Something tells me you're not using this place legally."

"Do you mean the police in town here, or the officer positioned outside your parents' house, waiting to escort Cara off the premises?"

The blood drained from Gavin's face. He swallowed and choked out, "The—the guy who tailed us?"

"The detective working with our organization. This room is under surveillance, and he will know if you resist. The men holding your father will also know, and I cannot guarantee they will keep their promise to do no harm."

Dammit! thought Mel. They'd left Cara wide open like an unprotected king. Checkmate.

Muttering curses under his breath, Gavin put his phone away. "Fine," he growled, and removed his jacket with angry, jerky movements. "I get to sterilize the needle myself."

"Fair enough," said the doctor. He retrieved a Bunsen burner from a cabinet and lit the flame.

"D-do we both have to do this?" stammered Mel, taking a step backward.

"Yes," said the doctor.

"But . . . I . . . can't. . . ." Another step.

"Melanie, just do it—there's no choice."

Hot tears brimmed in her eyes. *Hold them back!* The canister in her pocket felt cool and smooth in contrast. Her grip on it tightened. But if she whipped it out and used it, what then?

Snatches of the letter from the Organization replayed in her mind: *Members of our organization are vulnerable, just as you are. ... We reached out to you and Gavin in good faith.*

She was disinclined, under these circumstances, to believe that. But Gavin was right: There was no choice.

Her hand slipped from her pocket. "I ... hate n-needles," she admitted, feeling foolish.

"Would you like me to give you a sedative, something to relax you?" said the doctor, his face softening.

"No!" It was bad enough he wanted to take something out of her veins—no way was she letting him put something into them!

Gavin had already seated himself in one of the chairs. The doctor opened a drawer in the cart and pulled out a needle and syringe, both encased in plastic, new and sterile looking. He handed the needle to Gavin, who unwrapped it and passed it through the open flame. The doctor tied a tourniquet around Gavin's now bare upper arm and flicked a finger at the inside of his elbow. "Got a nice one," the old man murmured, swiping at the skin there with a sterilizing wipe.

Mel cringed and turned away as the doctor slipped the needle into Gavin's vein. "Good, good flow," she heard, and felt nauseous.

It was over in less than two minutes. The doctor whisked four vials with bright red blood to a nearby fridge. Gavin tugged his sleeve down over his bandaged arm, stood up, and walked to Mel. "Please," he said, looking into her eyes. "For me. For my family."

Lower lip quivering, Melanie blinked back her tears and nodded. She took deep breaths, in and out. Gavin helped her out of her coat and guided her over to the chair he'd sat in. It was still warm. He sat next to her and held her right hand after she'd rolled up her left sleeve. The scent of his Old Spice filled her nostrils, and that and the feel of his strong hand encasing hers soothed her to a small degree.

The doctor pulled out a fresh needle and syringe. Gavin held the needle in the fire. Mel closed her eyes and felt the rubber tourniquet squeezing, pinching. The muscles in her face screwed up just as tightly.

Flick, flick. *Ouch.* Pause. Another few flicks at a different spot on her arm. "Ah, found one." A cold, wet feeling. The crackle of plastic. A longer pause.

Mel tried to go to her happy place—a tranquil beach in a tropical paradise she'd only ever visited in her imagination—but the pleasant picture was overpowered by a vision of the old man stabbing her in the neck with the needle. She stifled a whimper. *Please get this over with already!*

The pinch in her elbow didn't hurt as much as she'd anticipated. She gasped and then released the breath she'd been holding. "It's okay," Gavin said gently.

"It's working, right?" she said through clenched teeth.

"Yep. Coming out almost as fast as mine did."

A long moment later, she felt the needle slide out and the doctor's hand holding a piece of cotton tightly over the wound. She opened her eyes when he asked her to take over the job so he could unwrap a bandage. After he'd stuck it on, she hurried to roll her sleeve back down and throw on her coat.

"We all good now?" she said in clipped tones. "Jeff will be returned safely?"

"Yes. You may go. Thank you."

Gavin gave the man one last scowl and then followed Melanie from the room. She stalked to the front door without looking back and burst out into the frigid late-autumn air. It was dark now, with only half the streetlamps lit. Cigarette smoke drifted by, but the air felt fresher than inside that awful lab. A tiny sob escaped Mel's throat. She hoped Gavin hadn't heard.

Silently, they walked to his car and climbed in. He turned the key in the ignition, but before he took the car out of park, he turned to her with eyes full of gratitude and apology. "Thank you, Melanie. I really owe you one."

"No," she whispered. "We're even now."

16

Strike Two

DECEMBER 1, WAXING CRESCENT MOON

The building was completely white inside. Everywhere she looked— walls, floor, ceiling—was stark, clinical white. Whiter than bones.

As she sprinted through never-ending hallways, shadows grew and deepened, turning everything gray. Fluorescent bulbs flickered and threatened to die. Locked doors and dead ends blocked her way.

Footsteps echoed behind her. They were slow and shuffling but somehow kept pace with her. She hadn't seen her pursuer, but she knew what he looked like: white lab coat. Ebony eyes behind glinting glasses. Liver-spotted hands clutching a long silver needle.

Pain stabbed her neck. She howled, hand flying up. A cold, thin spike: deep, tenacious. She yanked at it with all her might, and at last it popped out.

Blood gushed down her back and over her shoulders. She screamed and tried to staunch the flow.

Red, red. Her hands—everything was red.

Rasping laughter rang in her ears.

Panting and sweaty, Melanie awoke from the nightmare. "Oh God," she breathed, heart pounding, eyes darting around. She was in her own warm bed. The room was dark, but the glowing digits on her bedside clock showed 7:29. She deactivated her alarm before it could screech at her.

Her hand touched her face. There was something crusted there. And on the pillow, a dark, wet spot. Sweat? Tears?

Blood.

She yelped, and her hand flew to her neck. Blood there, too. Her fingers came away crimson.

She jumped out of bed and ran to the mirror. Blood ran in rivulets from her nose, down her cheek and neck. There was no puncture wound. Just a regular old nosebleed.

Mel closed her eyes and tipped her head back in silent gratitude. Thank goodness. Also thank goodness Pam wasn't in the room.

What's that old doctor guy going to do with the blood he took from us? she wondered as she showered and dressed. *Clone us and make a werewolf army?*

Star Wars-esque images flashed through her mind: rows upon rows of empty-eyed Melanies and Gavins standing at attention inside a huge bunker, dressed in white armor, claws extended instead of blasters. It was so ridiculous she almost giggled—but only almost.

And what had been in the box? *We should've asked the doctor his name. . . . Probably wouldn't have told us.*

The police, medical personnel. Did the Organization have government influence? Just how far did its reach extend?

Gavin texted her at lunchtime, telling her Jeff had returned late that morning.

"Yay! ☺" she typed. The Organization had kept its word. *Maybe they did reach out to us in good faith.*

Gavin's next messages made her think again: "He woke up at a bus station, alone. He had to buy a ticket home. No one saw who brought him in. His wallet was still in his pocket, not missing anything.

"He doesn't remember much about the time they held him. Must've been really drugged up. A few vague memories of being fed and taken to a bathroom. No memories of faces. He was in a small room with a bed and a desk. The window was boarded shut. No idea where he was."

She swallowed around a lump in her throat.

"These people are not good guys, Melanie."

She really hoped he was wrong.

)) ● ((

December had blasted its way in with strong winds and a scattering of rain. The penultimate *Sentinel* issue of the semester blew out from the Wellsboro press that afternoon. Surreptitiously, Mel watched people reading it in the cafeteria and the library. She hoped no one noticed how sloppy her editorial was. Dawn probably had, and Mel prayed she wouldn't harangue her about it. With finals to study for, not to mention homework and reading assignments to catch up on, Mel's time was stretched precariously thin. Cramming till two a.m. was taking its toll.

But she couldn't get another C on a test, like she had in medieval lit last week.

Tonight, Thursday, was a tutoring night. She sat at a library table with Luis, neither speaking after their initial greetings, both with noses buried in books. *If I look busy enough, maybe no one will bother me,* Mel hoped.

Two out of three professors had granted her permission to take their exams early; the other had pushed his to the end of exam week. Melanie didn't have to reschedule her Monday final, since it was first thing in the morning, and she wouldn't need to leave for the cabin until that afternoon. The Tuesday and Wednesday tests were the ones she'd had to move. Thursday morning—two weeks from today—she and Gavin would be done transforming for the month and could return, but Mel was sure she'd be exempted from her Spanish final that afternoon. Señor Miller waived his exam for students making an A. *At least I'm sure to get one in that class.*

Around a quarter after eight, she stood up, stretched, and took a long drink at the water fountain. On her way back, she noticed Timmy Simmons seating himself at a table near hers. He pulled two books from his bag but opened a copy of the *Sentinel* instead. Mel wrinkled her nose and returned to pore over several heavily highlighted pages of a textbook.

Pricks ran along the back of her neck, like someone's eyes were on her. She glanced up. Timmy had been squinting at her over the top of his newspaper, but he hid behind it when she frowned at him.

Eww, why was he watching me?

Was something spilled on her shirt? Was her hair messed up? She didn't think so. Thrice more she looked over at Timmy, only to catch him averting his eyes.

Irritation rose within her, but she told herself firmly: *Ignore the little punk. Don't let him get to you. He's trying to mess with your head or something.* Was he out for revenge because of the sentences she'd rearranged in his latest articles? His quartet of comma splices had been nauseating.

At last, nine o'clock rolled around, and Mel could escape from the library and her peeping Tim. She packed up her schoolbag, then saw Timmy copying her actions. *What the heck?* She fumed as they pulled on coats and gloves in tandem.

Hurrying toward her dorm through frigid darkness, she wished she'd driven herself to the library. She almost wished she also had the feverish feeling that meant the moon was a few days from full—but only almost.

In the silence between the wind's howls, her footfalls echoed tersely off the buildings around her. Then she registered another set of footsteps shuffling a short distance behind her. *You've got to be kidding me.*

Melanie whirled around and caught Timmy spinning on his heels and heading back toward the library. Angry words welled up, but she restrained them.

Since when had that pest been interested in her?

A chill ran down Mel's spine that had nothing to do with the weather. Another stalker popped into her memory: the cop.

He remained a specter—a blank, featureless face and form swathed in mystery. How had he found her? If neither she nor Gavin knew him, how had he caught wind that they were werewolves? Who'd tipped him off?

Thoughts of the Organization, the package, and the needle-wielding doctor made her wrap her arms more tightly around herself. She realized she was breaking her promise to Gavin. She'd told him she wouldn't go walking around alone after dark. *Crap.* But the library wasn't far from the cafeteria, and she'd traveled to dinner with a group of her friends. She hadn't thought to bring the car, hadn't planned this far ahead.

Nervously peering around, Melanie saw only a couple of other people scurrying across campus, both of whom she recognized. She passed a clump of bushes and jumped as they rustled. *Stupid—it's just wind.*

Would the Organization send her any more letters? Would one of its members come here to talk to her in person?

Wait. She stopped. *Is* Wellsboro *the connection?*

What if one of her fellow students was a member of the Organization, or had ties to it?

Nah, that's crazy.

Was it, though? It would explain how quickly the cop had discovered her.

Mel shuddered and picked up her pace, her mind outdistancing her feet. So far, it seemed the only people to take note of her disappearances were Pam and Jos. And Timmy. Anyone else? What about faculty? Mel's professors hadn't commented on her absences from class, but their attendance charts would show a monthly pattern.

This is nuts. I can't go suspecting and mistrusting everyone. She'd been living in fear, and it was exhausting. She didn't want to crank it up to total paranoia.

Taking deep breaths, she admonished herself to mellow out and keep a rational mindset. Analyze. Reason. Who could know about her, and how? Go back to the beginning. Back to Pine Groves. Who had been around during that awful weekend? Pam, Timmy, and Luis. The rest of the group of guys, too, but they weren't as close to the situation.

Pam. Timmy. Luis.

There was no way the traitor was Pam. She obviously hadn't a clue about Mel's secret, and she was Mel's best friend—she wouldn't betray her.

What about Luis? He was a kind, honest, respectable guy, as far as Mel was aware. She doubted the rat could be him—didn't want it to be—but she wasn't well enough acquainted with him to say for sure. She put him on the back burner.

That brought her to the final member of her mental lineup—an obnoxious, contrary, favored contender for culprit. Timmy.

He didn't see the beast chasing us, but he heard its howls. He could've realized the moon was full and figured things out. I've been absent from Sentinel *meetings, and distracted during them. Dawn has noticed a change in my behavior. Timmy also has motive—he's never liked me—and he's no model citizen.*

Right now, Timmy seemed the most likely spy. He wasn't a werewolf, but the Organization had human accomplices.

Melanie clenched her fists and seethed. *If he* is *the one who betrayed me, I'm gonna pulverize him. Eviscerate him.* A low growl escaped her throat.

But how could she find out for sure?

> > ● ⟨ ⟨

"Psst." *Thunk.*

A moment later: "Psssst." *Thunk, thunk.*

Melanie grunted softly, then jerked awake. Crap. She'd nodded off in history class. Someone behind her had roused her, kicking her chair and hissing. She checked and saw, to her distaste, that it was Timmy.

"What's got you so tired, Melody?" he taunted in a low voice she could barely hear over the professor's lecture. "Or should I call you Moody?"

Posture stiffening, Mel ignored him and resumed scribbling notes. *How much did I miss?* Dr. Ayers had been talking about Stalin, last she remembered, but now he was on to Mussolini.

When Timmy kicked her chair again, fury rose within Mel. She shot him a death glare that dared him to try it again. He smirked back.

Several minutes passed, more or less peacefully—although Melanie's mind was anything but peaceful these days. But then: *Thunk!*

Mel whirled and growled, "Stop!"

A wave of giggles passed over her classmates. Dr. Ayers paused his lecture and raised a stern eyebrow. "Is there a problem?"

Blushing deeply, Melanie said, "No, sir. I'm so sorry." But she gathered her books and moved three rows up.

Next period, she arrived at the *Sentinel* office and found just Dawn, fortunately not Timmy. The editor-in-chief greeted Mel and rose from the computer she'd been sitting at. "Come talk with me on the couch, Caldwell."

Uh-oh. Mel didn't like the seriousness in her tone, not one bit. Gingerly, she sat on the opposite end of the creaky old sofa from Dawn. Mel's palms felt clammy as her hands clasped and unclasped in her lap.

"I've been hearing rumors," Dawn began. "You and Timmy are having some problems, huh?"

"His fault," Melanie muttered, feeling childish but, in her exhaustion, starting not to care.

Dawn frowned and said, "I trust you'll work those out and not let them affect your work. Frankly, I expected more from your last op-ed assignment, Melanie. I thought you'd take a much more creative approach to that topic. And I found a couple of blatant errors you missed in other articles."

Mel hung her head. Anxiety churned in her gut, but anger toward Dawn grew as well. She gritted her teeth. *If she had any idea what kind of crap I'm going through . . .*

"The first time, when you didn't finish proofreading articles, I let that slide. We all get too busy sometimes. But now I'm going to have to give you a second strike, which really surprises me. You're the last one I thought I'd be having this conversation with. . . .

"Don't make it to three, Melanie. I know Timmy's a pest, but he's not worth it. You have to learn how to deal, how to block him out. Think how badly he'll bug you if you get suspended."

Throat tightening, Mel nodded. "I—I understand," she forced out, embarrassed at how choked her voice sounded.

"Good." Dawn flashed a brief smile, then returned to her computer.

Later, as Melanie left the com building, she passed Timmy on his way in. "How'd Dawn feel about your latest article?" he said, giving her an infuriating grin.

Mel glowered and pushed past him. They jostled shoulders in the process. "Watch it," she snapped, though it hadn't been clearly Timmy's fault.

"*You* watch it. You did that on purpose."

"As if I'd want to touch you!"

"No—high-and-mighty Melanie never associates with lesser folk," Timmy mocked. "Think you're better than everyone else? Well, here's some news for you—you're not."

Hands balling into fists, face flushing with anger, Melanie growled, "I never said I was!"

"Really? Spreading all those rumors about me after the camping trip. Laughing with your friends over how I got lost."

"I didn't spread any rumors—I've got better things to do, and there were a lot of other people on that trip. Did you forget about *that?*"

Timmy scowled. "There you go, acting all high and mighty again." In a high-pitched voice, he mimicked her: "I've got *better* things to do."

He stuck his nose in the air and pretended like he was primping long hair.

Without thinking, Mel lunged forward and shoved him. Timmy staggered backward and then wobbled, arms flailing as he slipped on a patch of ice. He lost his balance completely and fell to the hard cement. "Augh," he moaned, clutching at his backside.

Crap! Mel whirled around to see if anyone had witnessed the altercation. Nobody was in sight; she'd gone out the back door, which was closest to the *Sentinel* office. The office was four classrooms down from here, so Mel guessed that Dawn couldn't see her and Timmy from the window.

Still, she high-tailed it back to Hartman and flopped onto her bed, heart hammering in her chest. It took several minutes for her to catch her breath and calm down.

Would Timmy tell Dawn what she'd done? Would Dawn believe him?

And right after she told me to learn how to block him out.

Mel's anger turned inward. *I have* got *to get control of myself!*

Full moon wasn't for another week and a half. This couldn't be her wolf, could it?

） ） ● ((

DECEMBER 9, WAXING GIBBOUS MOON

The Friday before exam week arrived with egregious speed. Melanie took her two early rescheduled tests and then headed back to her dorm, anxious about how she'd done. She'd studied copiously, but the empty classrooms had been hot and full of distracting scents and sounds, and concentrating had been difficult. Wiping her slick palms on her jeans, she mentally cursed the moon.

Please help me maintain my 3.9 GPA!

That didn't seem too likely.

Her bedroom was locked, Pam undoubtedly off practicing at her second home, the music building. *I should write my monthly note to her now so I don't forget last-minute.* Mel scribbled a few lines on a piece of paper, which she tucked away in her purse.

With not much else to do before dinner, she studied—or tried to. She wriggled around in bed, her back against the headboard, legs drawn up in an easel shape to support a book. After a while, she switched to a cross-legged position, balancing a textbook on one knee and a notebook on the other. Soon she tired of that and flipped onto her stomach. Her feet tapped against the headboard, and she got more rhythm practice done than reading. *Maybe I should go accompany Pam on the drums.* Sighing, Mel slapped her book closed. *This is pointless.*

There was a knock at the door, and Jocelyn stuck her head in. "Hey, Mel, do you have any aspirin? I'm out, and I can feel a headache coming on."

"Sure. It's in my purse," said Melanie without thinking. But as Jos strode to her dresser and grabbed her handbag off it, Mel remembered the note to Pam and blanched. "Wait, don't—"

But Jos's hands were already inside her bag, lifting its topmost item: the note. *Please don't read it,* Mel prayed. She yearned to snatch it from her friend, but that would be suspicious, and maybe Jos wouldn't pay attention to the words on the paper.

Jos set the note aside, but then her eyes narrowed and she picked it back up to scan it. She leveled a stern gaze at Mel. "You're taking off again. When?"

"None of your business!" Mel shot back, boiling mad. "What are you doing looking at my personal stuff?" She jumped from her bed and tried to seize the note, but Jos held it high and out of her reach. "Give it *back*!"

"Not until you're willing to talk about this and tell me what's going on!"

Mel took a lunging leap, swiping at the note, fingertips brushing a corner of it. At that moment, Jos moved her arm, and Mel's nails caught Jos's forearm, gouging four parallel red lines right through her sleeve. "Ow!" Jos shrieked, recoiling.

What the—? Melanie gasped when Jos rolled up her sleeve, revealing the damage her nails had done. Nails? More like claws: thick, yellowish, and curved. How had they grown that long and sharp so quickly? She'd made Jos bleed.

"I—I'm sorry!" Mel cried, panic seizing her. She stared at her hands as if they were someone else's, or part of a Halloween costume. *Go away!* But the claws remained. Tucking them out of sight under her arms, she ran blindly from the room. Her feet pounded down the steps;

her pulse pounded in her ears.

"Wait!" she heard, but didn't stop. She grabbed at the front door handle, flung the door wide open—

—and smacked into a tall, lean, but well-muscled person standing on the front patio. Luis. "Whoa there!" he said, regaining his balance and steadying her. Mel took in his startled expression, the long-stemmed red rose in his hand. "Where you going in such a hurry, *bella*?"

"Sorry!" She plunged past him, toward the parking lot, toward her car.

She heard another cry to wait, this time in Luis's deep baritone, but didn't heed his plea either. *What have I done? What an idiot! I hurt my friend! Why do I have claws? Did she see them?* Mel glanced at them again in horror, not breaking stride.

Is it possible to infect someone by scratching them?

As Melanie jumped into her Honda and sped from the lot, Luis Vargas stood gaping, bewildered. Should he go after her? Before he could sprint to his car, he heard feet thumping down the stairs inside Hartman and Jocelyn Beaumont appeared, black curls askew. Her pale face was screwed up in frustration or pain, and her right sleeve was rolled up to her elbow. She held a washcloth to her bare forearm.

"Jocelyn, are you okay? What happened?" Luis asked. "Why was Melanie so upset?"

Leaning against the doorframe, Jocelyn pursed her lips. "I'm not entirely sure."

"Is your arm all right?" A red circle was blooming in the blue wash-cloth.

"Oh, this? Nothing serious." She pressed the cloth down more tightly.

"Are you sure? Let me drive you to the nurse's office."

"No, thanks. It's not that deep. I'll be fine." Her eyes fell on the rose he held, and her expression softened. "Is that for Mel?"

"Yeah," Luis admitted, blushing.

Jocelyn grinned wryly. "Your timing didn't work out so well."

"Story of my life." He threw a glance in the direction Melanie had gone. "Do you know what's been troubling her lately? She's been acting strange. Different. Distant."

With a frustrated sigh, Jocelyn said, "No, but I wish I did. I tried to ask her, and she . . . reacted badly and ran off."

Reacted badly? The arm wound—could *Mel* have done that? *No way.* Luis shook his head in disbelief. She wasn't a violent girl.

"I still think you should let the nurse take a look at that," he told Jocelyn. "Could there be broken glass inside?"

"It's not from glass."

"Then what—"

"Look, Luis, just drop it. Please." Jocelyn backed up a step and put her hand on the door as if to close it.

Luis felt an urge to smack the doorframe. He glared at her, nostrils flaring. "What's with you girls being so secretive?"

"I don't know why or what Mel's hiding, but as for me, I'm not one for sharing details before I know what they mean—or if they mean anything."

Huh? What the heck's that *supposed to mean?* Luis opened his mouth to reply but turned and stalked away without a word. Passing the bushes that edged the cottage, he threw the rose into them. *Mujeres locas.*

Mel got halfway through town before she remembered she didn't have her purse—or her driver's license. Crap. Better drive carefully. Or stop driving. No one had pursued her.

She pulled into the busy lot of a Burger King and parked. It was dinnertime, evidenced by the long drive-thru line, and she'd grown quite hungry. The greasy smell of sizzling meat was tantalizing. *But I don't have my wallet. This sucks.*

She contemplated going back for it and her coat, but her mind replayed the scene with Jos, and she cringed. *I can't go back there and face her yet. What if . . . ?* Her forehead hit the cool, hard leather of the steering wheel. Tears tried to squeeze out through her closed eyelids. *I didn't turn her, did I?*

Screaming as her skin split open—

Jocelyn screaming as her *bones cracked and* her *joints twisted—*

No! Don't let it be Jocelyn!

Several tears, and one ragged sob, escaped.

Sniffling, Mel felt a large drop of liquid descend through her nose. Expecting only snot, she swiped at it with her hand and saw a trail of red. Another nosebleed? *Stupid dry winter air!*

She reached in her glove box and pulled out a wad of tissues. She stuffed one in her nostrils and tilted her head back, pinching the bridge of her nose.

A knock on her window startled her.

A woman, maybe in her late twenties, with copper skin and jet-black hair, had approached, unseen. She was attractive, well groomed, and well dressed, so Mel figured she hadn't come to ask for money. *Good, because I've got nothing right now. What's this about? Do I have a flat tire?*

Slowly, she cranked down the window, and frigid air rushed in. Mel could see the woman's breath and her own breath. "Hello. I'm sorry to bother you," said the woman. "I just wondered if you were all right."

"Huh? Oh. Uh, yeah, I'b fide," Mel said nasally, adding, "Thang you. My tire's not flat or someding, is it?"

"No, no." The woman gave a reassuring smile. "You just looked a bit . . . lost. Distressed."

Religious nut come to show me the way? Mel's stomach sank.

"Not trying to sell you any religion," the woman said, as if reading her thoughts. "Just an ordinary citizen trying to do her random act of kindness for the day." She stuck out her hand. "My name's Chandra. Can I buy you dinner?"

17

Discovery

Over the weekend, Melanie watched Jocelyn carefully. Jos didn't exhibit any signs of illness, though Mel caught her rubbing her bandaged arm and wincing. *Do people always get as sick as I did after they're infected?*

She called Gavin to ask, and he said yes—at least, in his personal experience. "But I don't know if scratching someone is enough to turn them. I've punched guys and given them bruises and black eyes since becoming a werewolf, but I've never drawn blood."

It was hard for Mel to imagine Gavin brawling or picking fights, and she said so.

"The other kids started them … usually," he replied, meaning the kids at the home for troubled children where he'd lived before the Doyles had adopted him. "I wouldn't worry about Jos. I seriously doubt you can pass the curse when you're not in wolf form."

Not completely reassured, Mel checked at least a dozen online sources as well. Most of them agreed with Gavin, which brought her some comfort.

Monday arrived hazy and gloomy, matching Mel's mood. She muddled through her exam, then grabbed lunch and prepared to leave campus.

Jocelyn stopped her in the living room just before she left Hartman. Face pinched and pallid, she folded her arms—slowly, gingerly—and planted her feet. Her eyes were hard, glinting emeralds, boring into Mel's.

Melanie bit her lip and looked away. Half-consciously, her thumb traced over her fingertips, checking the nails: normal. "Hey," she began. "I—"

163

Jos cut her off. "Dialogue," she said, voice rich with disappointment. "Tell me the truth, Mel. You're not in any trouble or doing anything dangerous or illegal, are you?"

It would be dangerous to stay here, Melanie thought. "It's nothing like that," she said. "Don't worry."

But worry *and* doubt cropped up inside her. *What if . . . ?*

Maybe she should tell Jos everything. She could drag her along to the cabin, lock her up until after the moon rose. The internet had said Jos would be fine, but the internet hadn't exactly been a reliable source before. Was there any other way she could be completely sure Jos hadn't been turned? Some kind of quick test?

Like what? Gavin had cut Mel with a knife. *Yeah, that'd go over really well. . . . Or I could make her angry and see if her eyes turn yellow.* But Mel didn't want to do that either, if there was another option. She was so sick of all the tension around here. She'd been certain she'd made Jos boiling mad on Friday, but when she'd returned that night, Jos had been calm and cool and had accepted her apology.

"How's your arm?" Mel asked.

Jos shrugged. "Fine." But her stiff posture suggested otherwise.

Still in pain after three days? Mel's gut twisted. "Can I see it?"

"Um, sure." Reluctantly, Jos unwound the ACE bandage.

Mel sucked in a sharp breath. The four scratch lines were puffy and red. They didn't look like they'd had a weekend to heal. They looked fresh. Infected.

A fist squeezed Melanie's heart, and sweat broke out on her forehead. As Jocelyn wrapped her arm back up, she thought, *I have to tell her. If I don't, and she* was *turned—*

The dorm's front door swung open, dousing them in a cold breeze. Brianna, one of the girls who lived on the first floor, sauntered in, boyfriend in tow. Giggling together, the pair skirted Mel and Jos and headed to the back of the house. A pungent blend of perfume, cologne, and pheromones trailed after them.

Wait—scent! Why didn't I think of it before? If Jos were a werewolf, she'd smell like one. Especially right before the full moon. Melanie didn't think her friend's scent had changed, but she had to be sure before she left. She tried to wave away the hormonal fog, but it persisted. *Geez.* "Can we step outside for a second, please, Jos?"

"Oookay." Jos raised an eyebrow but followed.

The crisp air brushed refreshingly against Mel's feverish skin. She drew in a deep, invigorating breath. Beneath the odor of moldering autumn leaves, she detected lemons and honey, minty shampoo. *No trace of wolf—same old eau de Jos.* Mel released the breath in a sigh of relief.

Shivering without a jacket on, Jos wrapped her arms around her svelte frame. "Why exactly are we out here?" she asked.

She's not burning up like I am, either. A huge grin spread across Mel's face. "Oh, uh, I just thought the fresh air would make both of us feel better."

"Well, it's making me uncomfortably cold. You do look like you feel better, though. 'Course, you've got the advantage of a coat."

"Yeah. Sorry, you can go back inside. I gotta leave. I'll see you in a few days. No worries. Oh, and please get that wound checked out."

Jos watched Mel stride to her car, overnight bag slung over her shoulder. She shook her head and rubbed her arm before going back inside Hartman.

〉 〉 ● 〈 〈

"You were right," Mel told Gavin as he drove them to the cabin. "Jos wasn't turned. She smells human. Her arm looks awful, though."

The familiar sights of the highway streamed past: patches of deep-green pine trees, the occasional silo, Holstein cows dotting whitening fields. The asphalt hummed quietly beneath the Ford's tires. There wasn't enough snow to warrant using the squeaky wipers, and Gavin hadn't turned the radio on, so relative silence reigned . . . a thick, warm, and pungent silence, the balsam-and-fir air freshener on the dashboard failing to disguise the scent of wolf.

"Maybe we can't *turn* people when we're human," Gavin said slowly, "but maybe we can hurt them more than usual. Did you notice our super strength around full moons?"

Mel's eyes widened. "No. Can we, like, lift cars or something?"

He chuckled. "That'd be cool, but no. We *can* punch through walls or mattresses easily, splinter doors—stuff like that."

"More escapades from your violent past?"

"Ha, ha."

Miles whizzed by. Snow speckled the windshield. Mel's thoughts meandered to another concern: "Do you think the Organization will show up and bother us?"

"That did cross my mind," Gavin said darkly.

"What d'you think they're doing with our blood?"

His fingers tightened around the steering wheel. "Nothing good."

She opened her mouth to joke about the clone army but changed her mind. He wouldn't laugh—not with the mood he was in.

Mel and Gavin had talked about transforming in his parents' basement this time around; Jeff and Cara had one safe room down there and could set up another. But two wolves would make a lot of noise, which the Doyles' neighbors might hear despite the soundproofing measures. Gavin's dad had said he'd further insulate the basement walls, but Gavin had stubbornly refused. "I don't want to tempt the Organization to skulk around the neighborhood," he'd explained. "And I don't want attention drawn to the house—especially not with innocents around."

Exasperated, Jeff had installed an alarm system on the cabin. He'd also booked a room at a nearby inn. "Call me if *anything* odd happens," he'd said.

Snow swirled around them, gloomy gray clouds hovering low. The large, fluffy flakes began to stick. The grass alongside the freeway resembled a green tablecloth with a white lace overlay, but its beauty was little comfort.

Halfway to the cabin, Gavin took an unfamiliar exit. "Checking for tails," he explained. "I know they don't have to follow us anymore, but . . ."

No headlights pursued them this time, and they arrived with nearly an hour to spare. They stashed their bags and then wandered into the living room, Gavin taking his usual chair, Mel across from him. She smelled cedar, pine, and ashes from the cold hearth, although it was clean. The empty fireplace made the room bleak and lonely.

"I think we're going to get a few inches of snow tonight," Gavin remarked.

"Mmm."

"I'm always a bit worried that someone will spot our tire tracks and follow them here. Even if it's only curious kids."

Mel's eyes widened. "No one's ever come poking around before, have they?"

"No."

"There's a security system now, so they'd probably hesitate to try and break in."

"I doubt kids would try too hard."

"Yeah," said Melanie. She felt somewhat safe, but not completely. Never completely—not anymore.

Ten minutes to moonrise, the two young werewolves locked themselves in their rooms and hunkered down to wait. Mel hugged her legs to her chest, naked, pale, and shivering. She rested her forehead on her knees to avoid the ugly sight of mangled walls.

)) ● ((

5:00 P.M.

Normally, Jocelyn Beaumont found it easy to concentrate on homework, chores, and other projects. This afternoon, she settled down at her desk to cram for her remaining finals, but her thoughts raced and her arm throbbed. The words in her philosophy book spun and swayed like drunken ballerinas. Spikes of pain stabbed her under the ACE bandage, which felt strangely warm. *What the heck?*

Each tick of the wall clock cracked like a whip. *Hurry up! Read this page! Move on to the next!*

Fed up with the distractions, Jos stood and paced. She rubbed her arm and gritted her teeth. Time for more aspirin.

Footsteps creaked on the stairs. Jos heard Pam humming an aria while she unlocked her door. Jos had just swallowed the aspirin when the humming trailed off, and Pam wailed, "Not again!"

Must've found the note.

Jos gulped her water, then stuck her head in her suitemates' room. "What again?"

Pam scowled and thrust a small piece of paper at her. "This."

"Ah," said Jos, scanning it although she didn't need to. "Your elusive roommate, the Vanishing Woman."

"Did you know she was about to leave again?" Pam demanded, eyes narrowing.

Reflexively, Jos rubbed her injured arm. She kept her face impassive. *Should I tell her everything?* So far, Pam hadn't noticed the bandage under Jos's sweater sleeves, or at least hadn't commented on it. But the girls had been busy studying. *Aw, why not? She's the one who's closest to Mel; I guess she has the right to know.*

Pulling up her sleeve, Jos displayed her bandaged forearm. Pam gasped. "What happened?"

"Your roommate."

"*What?!* Melanie hurt you?"

"Not on purpose." Jos recounted Friday's incident, not mentioning what Mel had been trying to grab out of Jos's hand or why. "Her nails were ... different. Longer and sharper, like talons." When Pam gave a dubious frown, she insisted, "I saw them—I'm not making it up! It was super weird."

She unwound the bandage, wincing at another stab of pain. The scratch marks glared up at her: angry, red, and inflamed. "Holy cow!" said Pam. "That looks awful! Have you gone to the nurse?"

"No," Jos said, shocked at how much worse the wound had gotten. "I didn't think I needed to. It wasn't this bad before."

"Come on, I'll take you."

The two girls bundled up and trudged to the campus health center through lightly falling snow. Jos turned her face up toward the black sky. Patches of stars twinkled icily. The cloud cover shifted, and an edge of the moon appeared. More and more of the moon revealed itself; it was a day away from full, bright and ringed by a halo against the clouds.

Pain sawed through Jos's arm. She clutched at it and stumbled along, concentrating on putting one foot in front of the other.

Pam murmured, "Could be infected. What kind of infection, though? Mel's not sick."

"Mel doesn't *appear* sick," said Jos. "Doesn't mean she isn't."

A cold breeze whistled along the ground, carrying the scents of pine and soil. The girls rounded the corner of the science building, and their destination came into view: a squat brick structure with narrow windows, most of which were lit.

They reached the health center and signed Jos in. No one else was in the waiting room. After a minute, the nurse called the girls back to the exam room. One look at Jos's scratches, and the woman's corn-flower-blue eyes darkened with concern. "You should go to the ER. You may need a rabies shot. Have you had any fever, headaches, nausea, or vomiting?"

"No."

"What kind of animal did this?"

"Um, a dog. A big one."

"I see," said the nurse, frown lines creasing her broad forehead. "Well, let me clean that before you go."

She swabbed the wound gently, but Jos sucked air through her teeth as searing pain shot up her arm. When the nurse smeared on antibiotic cream, Jos half expected it to sizzle like grease on a hot skillet, but it was like ice.

"Get to the ER," the nurse advised when she'd finished. "Do you have a ride?"

"I'll call my boyfriend," Pam offered, and did just that.

While they waited for Aaron to show up, the girls stepped outside. Jos stared up at the sky, her thoughts hazy. *Where's Melanie right now, and what's she doing?*

If Mel had some weird infection, did that have anything to do with her disappearances?

"This is like déjà vu," said Pam.

"Huh?"

"Taking a friend to the nurse's office and then to get a rabies shot. It was Mel the first time."

"Really? When?"

"Right after the Pine Groves trip. I brought her to the health center because I thought she was coming down with pneumonia. She had a nick on her hand. It was tiny, but the nurse said it looked infected."

"But if Mel got the shot, she can't have rabies. That means I can't either."

"We should still have a doctor look at your arm. What if it's, like, staph or meningitis?"

"We had to get vaccinated for meningitis when we started here."

Pam shrugged. "That's good."

Both girls fell into silence. Jos replayed Pam's words. Could the nick on Mel's hand have any significance? "Tell me about the incident in the cave again," she said. "I want to know every detail."

⁂

The next afternoon, Melanie woke from her post-transformation nap and headed for the kitchen. She noticed Gavin in the living room, perched backward on the couch, staring out the front window. "Hungry?" she called.

He failed to answer or even turn toward her. Rigid and immobile, he looked as if he'd frozen in place. "Hey, what's wrong?"

Wordlessly, Gavin pointed out the window. Mel followed the trajectory of his finger, her eyes sweeping over the snow-covered ground. There wasn't much to see: a smooth white expanse, black trees frosted white below gray sky ...

... and, scattered across a patch of yard below their window, tracks. Paw prints.

Large paw prints.

Mel gasped. "Those look like—"

"They're spelling out a message," Gavin said grimly.

She picked it out, assembling meaning from the chaos:

JOIN US
BE FREE

There were no human footprints to be seen.

"How in the world ... ? That's not possible." Heart pounding and breath quickening, Mel met Gavin's gaze. They stared at each other, hazel irises into brown, brimming with burgeoning questions.

A tiny seed of—what? Warmth? Excitement? Hope?—released its first green tendrils within Melanie. The implications of a sentient animal with paws that size, so near to the size and shape of *her own* ...

"They've done it," she whispered, awe filling her voice. "They found a way to keep their minds."

Gavin gave a stiff nod, his mouth a thin line, features pinched and cold. "So it would appear."

Here we go again with the skepticism and mistrust. Frowning, Mel racked her brain for how to help him see things her way. Her whole worldview was changing, expanding. A slow smile blossomed on her face, pushing the frown upward like soil; the hopeful tendrils grew and sprouted leaf buds. *Think of the possibilities. ...*

The Organization's private letter to her had mentioned reaching out in good faith and trying to help. This must be the help they could offer. Although it wasn't a total cure, it would benefit her and Gavin immensely. Mel wondered if the old doctor was conducting research that had led to their ability to keep their minds. That could be why he'd drawn their blood. *Maybe one day he'll find a way to stop the transformations! Or at least the pain.* Was that too much to hope for?

Perhaps it was time to tell Gavin about the letter.

Collecting courage and careful words, she seated herself next to him. "I know you had a vision that made the Organization seem untrustworthy," she began, "but I have some evidence that suggests the opposite."

"Like what?" he asked, skeptical.

"Well, um, I got a private letter from them."

"*What?*" His eyebrows shot up, and Mel caught the scent of anger. "When?"

"Thanksgiving night. I know, I know; I should've told you sooner. I'm sorry." She highlighted the letter's main points, emphasizing the tone of comradeship and helpfulness, then relating her theory about the doctor's research. "If that isn't the help they meant ... well, come on, it has to be."

Gavin crossed his arms and shook his head. "That doesn't convince me to trust them."

"Why not?"

"Why not? They spied on us, Mel. They kidnapped my dad!"

With a sigh, Mel glanced out the window again. A doe peered back at her from the edge of the woods. "I know. But they kept their word and returned him unharmed."

"Only after threats and coercion."

"But if drawing our blood was for our benefit—"

"The ends don't justify the means," he said flatly, arms tightening.

"Okay, so they don't have a squeaky-clean record, and they made us do something scary. But I honestly think they're trying to help us the only way they know how. Would you have given your blood if you didn't feel you had to?"

"You can't just say 'sorry' and shake hands and make up after the kind of stuff they did!"

Don't forget what you *did—blabbing to your parents when they asked you not to,* Melanie wanted to say. Instead, she asked: "Don't you want to keep your mind when you transform? Not to have to worry about hurting anyone?"

"I don't worry," Gavin said. "Not anymore. I have this place."

"Yeah, but what if . . . you might not always." *I might not always.*

"Why wouldn't I?"

She changed her tack. "Wouldn't it be fun not to have to coop ourselves up at full moons? To run through the woods, explore? Be free?" She gestured toward the words printed outside in the snow.

"Don't tell me you're falling for that propaganda."

"But there's proof! The paw prints are proof. The Organization has figured out how to stay sane, and they can teach us or give us their medicine, or whatever."

"One of them knows how to stay sane. That doesn't mean anything for us."

"Ugh!" Mel threw up her hands and sprang from the sofa. *I can't talk to him right now.* Striding to the kitchen, she opened the fridge. "I'm starving."

Gavin joined her as she spread mayonnaise on slices of bread. "Melanie, I'm trying to protect you. They could be trying to trick us."

"How? There's no way a regular animal—or human—spelled out those words."

"Even if they have a way to keep their minds, it doesn't mean they'll share it with us for free." He emphasized the last word, his eyes piercing hers.

Her hand stilled. He had a point.

"Please don't do anything rash like contacting them. We need more time, more evidence. We can't trust them this quickly."

Mel slapped lettuce and turkey onto the bread, then silently handed Gavin a sandwich.

"This is good," Gavin said between bites, giving her a small smile.

She returned it reluctantly. "So, are we going to stay here or go to your parents' house?"

"I was thinking of leaving. But the Organization's holding back, and I don't want to risk my parents' neighbors hearing us. I wish my mom and dad lived out in the country."

"Your dad's never researched a way to help you stay yourself as a wolf?"

"A little. But he's an anesthesiologist, not a geneticist or whatever. He's mostly tried to help with the pain."

"I know I asked you this kind of question my first time here, but what if we were able to find a way to keep our minds without the Organization?"

"I'd love that. It'd be wonderful. I just don't see how. I gave up my search years ago."

And mine has failed dismally so far, thought Mel. She'd pored over websites every few days, whenever she got spare time and was alone. Nothing.

But I can't quit. I won't.

The next morning, Melanie woke to find the deepest, most prolific gouges her wolf had ever put in the walls. Did it know who was outside, or at least who had been the other night?

Agony hit her body full force, paralyzing her with a thousand stinging wasps. Blurrily, Mel saw that her arms were as scratched as the walls. Blood filled her hair and stained her flesh. Hints of white bone gaped sickeningly between the ravaged remains of skin.

This felt a lot more like a third full-moon morning than a second full-moon morning.

Or maybe like a seventh.

This had to stop. She couldn't keep doing this. How on earth had Gavin put up with this for more than a decade?

Unconsciousness beckoned her, and she willingly succumbed.

The sun was higher when she woke again. Her wounds had healed, light pink lines all that remained under crusted blood, and the pain had dulled to stiffness. She dragged herself into the Butterfly Room, fully intending to nap for another few hours. Then she thought of the paw prints and the offer of freedom. *Could* she ever be free of this curse? Not just her mind but her body too?

She had to talk to others. She and Gavin were only two people, and young ones at that. They needed access to a broader range of knowledge and experience. The Organization had a doctor researching a cure.

Doesn't mean they'll share it with us for free, echoed Gavin's words from yesterday.

It would be worth the price.

I have to leave them a message.

Mind made up, Mel sank onto the bed. How would she do it? Leave her own prints in the snow, or write in it with a finger? The snow could melt or the message get buried in further snowfall. Gavin might see it and trample it out. *He's so stubborn,* she thought, her hands balling into fists.

Pen and paper were much safer. But where could she put the note?

The Butterfly Room had a small desk, and Melanie opened its drawer. A steno pad lay inside under an assortment of other office supplies. Perfect. She sat down at the desk, thinking. Her hand shook a little as it gripped a pen, more from fatigue than fear.

"I'm interested," she wrote. "Let's keep in touch. – Melanie". She'd almost written "Let's meet" but decided against it for now.

There were no envelopes in the drawer. She folded the note several times and then considered where to hide it. It couldn't be fully hidden, or the Organization wouldn't find it. Did the cabin have a doormat?

Opening her door as quietly as possible, Mel padded into the hallway and listened for Gavin. She peeked in the kitchen and the living room—no sign of him. Most likely, he was fast asleep. She put her ear to his bedroom door and thought she heard a soft snore.

Mel tiptoed to the back door and cracked it. Wind gusted in, and she shivered. Looking down, she saw a fuzzy brown mat half buried in snow. *All right, here goes,* she thought, heart fluttering. She crouched down and lifted a corner of the mat, then slid the note under and made sure a corner of it was sticking out. What if more snow fell and covered it? What if the note became soaked and unreadable?

The kitchen had Ziploc sandwich baggies. Mel retrieved one, sealed the note inside, and slipped it back under the mat. She'd check closer to moonrise this evening and brush the note off, if need be.

Satisfied, she returned to her room and snuggled under the covers for a nap.

Her alarm woke her at three p.m. Stomach growling, Mel went to the kitchen and fixed herself a sandwich, munching on an apple as she did so.

"There you are, sleepyhead," Gavin called from the living room.

She started, feeling somewhat guilty, but suppressed the feeling. "Rough night," she said, glancing at her hands—the pink lines were all gone now. *That's a darn good thing. If I had to return to school covered in scratches . . .*

"You mean rougher than usual, right?" said Gavin with a sardonic smile.

"Well, yeah." She grinned wryly back at him, though resentment lay underneath.

They passed the afternoon studying. When moonrise drew near, they retreated to their safe rooms. Mel waited until she heard the sound of Gavin's five deadbolts, let a few more moments pass, and then eased her door open as silently as she could. A floorboard creaked as she padded down the hallway, and Mel froze. She glanced back at Gavin's door. It remained shut.

Hand on the knob of the back door, Mel knew the wind was going to gust in again and Gavin would probably hear it. She had to risk it.

Sure enough, the wind howled as it blew in. *Don't hear it. Don't hear it.*

She could still see the corner of the note; it hadn't snowed further. Mel prayed the weather would stay clear overnight.

She closed the door and heard another one groan open. *Crap!*

"What are you doing?" Gavin asked, poking his head into the hall-way.

"Oh, um, just . . . making sure that . . . Well, I thought I heard—"

"Is someone out there?" His tone was sharp, fearful.

"No." Mel flushed and looked away.

Gavin's hand reached down and grabbed his clothes, which he'd left outside his door. After dressing, he joined Mel at the back door. He sniffed, frowned, and narrowed his eyes at her. *Can he smell my guilt?*

Most likely.

Gavin opened the door. Despite the chill and his bare feet, he stepped outside and peered around. Darkness had fallen; the snow lit the forest with a ghostly gleam. He cocked his head, listening. "I don't hear anything."

"Yeah, guess it was the wind," Mel said weakly. Her eyes strayed down to the mat.

Unfortunately, Gavin chose that moment to turn and look at her. He followed her gaze. "What's that?" Bending, he picked up the note.

Melanie cringed as he read it, anger spreading across his face.

His eyes were golden when he turned their fierce gaze on her. "You're sneaking around behind my back *again*?! I told you to *wait*!" he growled. "What part of that didn't you understand?"

Indignation rose. "Who put *you* in charge of my life?!"

"Maybe if *you* were a little more careful and sensible—"

"Ex*cuse* me?" Mel jammed her hands on her hips. "*I* am one of the most cautious, reasonable, and intelligent pe—what are you doing?!"

Before she could snatch it away, he'd ripped the note into pieces.

"You have *no right*!" she screamed. She wanted to cry. She wanted to claw his eyes out. She wanted to—

"I'm just trying to help—augh!" Gavin groaned, doubling over and clutching the doorframe.

Shit. Moonrise. "This conversation isn't over," Mel growled, as sparks of pain shot up her own spine.

But it was for the time being. She and Gavin raced back to their safe rooms and shut themselves in. *That jerk!* thought Mel as she collapsed, panting, in a corner. A few tears fell, leaving hot, wet streaks down her face.

18

Impasse

The silence on the return drive felt less than companionable. Melanie spent most of the trip staring out at the snow-dusted pine trees and fields—not really seeing them, instead focusing on how to persuade Gavin to give the Organization a chance. He'd apologized this morning, but Melanie still felt upset. *I hope he's not always that controlling.*

She could understand Gavin's anger toward the Organization; it sucked that they had felt they had to resort to kidnapping. She herself had been plenty steamed about the doctor invading their veins. But it was all for a good reason, right?

The ends don't justify the means, Gavin had said. Mel had thought she believed that too, but nothing in her life was clear or easy anymore.

Why oh why won't Gavin listen to me? I've got to find some way to thaw him out.

Covertly, she studied his profile. Dark smudges underscored his tired hazel eyes. His shoulders slumped. Light-brown stubble lined his tensely set jaw. He seemed to be held together by fraying string, animated by sheer willpower.

He's had a difficult life, Mel thought, softening. *Can't wash away that kind of hurt quickly or easily.*

That was the trouble. She couldn't heal his heart; no one could. Words couldn't. Time, maybe, but they didn't have that. What else?

Experience. Gavin needed to have some positive experiences with the Organization. How could she contact them now, though? If only he hadn't ripped up her note, or she'd had time to write another. *Jerk,* she fumed again. It was too bad the paw prints hadn't spelled out an address or phone number.

Briefly, she considered returning to 3545 Cedarwood—but no, that neighborhood was too dangerous.

Maybe someone will approach me on campus. That was the only possibility she could hope for. She prayed that someone from the Organization would confront her face to face.

As they drew nearer to Melanie's car, she thought ahead to the next full moon: January tenth to twelfth. She and Gavin planned to use the cabin, even though winter break wouldn't be over yet. She'd have to devise an excuse to drive back early.

Gavin dropped her off, and they said a terse goodbye. A frigid wind shoved Mel, bullying her into her Honda. The engine coughed and wheezed but rumbled to life. *This old rust bucket needs a tune-up when I get home.*

The car had better make it to Indiana.

It made it to her dorm at least, and she slogged upstairs, backpack feeling much heavier than it had on Monday. Without even unpacking, she climbed into bed and fell fast asleep.

Hours later, Pam shook her awake. "You're missing dinner," she said flatly before walking away. Her shoulders were as rigid as steel girders, her back a brick wall.

Groggily, Mel grunted her thanks. She shifted, stretched, and stumbled out of bed. Blood rushed to her head and pounded in her ears; pain stabbed her forehead. Closing her eyes, she leaned against the bed frame.

Pam left for dinner without offering to wait. Mel preferred that to an interrogation. She was dressed but took her time freshening up in the bathroom. A trickle of blood issued from her nose, splattering a red bouquet across the white sink.

As she cleaned up, she remembered the rose Luis had been holding the evening she'd hurt Jos. *I think I may have hurt him too.* Guilt swelled, and she scowled, fed up with the feeling. If only she could wash *it* down the sink.

Fortunately, she didn't encounter Luis outside or in the cafeteria. Jos, Shari, and a few other friends were at the table with Pam, and Shari steered the conversation down a cheerful avenue. If she noticed the tension between her roommate and suitemates, she didn't let on.

Pam headed off to the music building, and Mel trudged back to

Hartman, shivering with every blast of wind. Her joints ached from both her recent transformation and the glacial air. She climbed into bed with her European history textbook, intending to cram but knowing the inevitable. Soon she was fast asleep, drooling on an illustration of Lenin leading the Bolshevik Revolution.

)) ● ((

When Pam returned to her room, the door was unlocked and the light on, but Melanie was out cold. *Why's she always so tired when she gets back?* She frowned at Mel, then crept closer and leaned over her, listening to her deep, even breathing. *Okay, I'm acting like a creepy stalker here.* She backed away but continued watching Mel's pale face.

Mel, do you have cancer? HIV? Hepatitis? Are you going away to get treatments? Why won't you tell me? She doubted Mel was getting chemotherapy, because her hair wasn't falling out. It looked like the same silky auburn hair—same length, same style—that Melanie had always had, not a wig. Pam resisted the urge to tug at it.

Something small and silver caught her eye: Mel's phone, which rested on her nightstand.

No. Don't even think about it, Pamela Jane. That's just wrong.

But Mel could be in some kind of trouble, and I might find out something that could allow me to help her.

Pam's fingers twitched, and she battled with her conscience for several minutes. The phone was right there, easily accessible, and Pam guessed Melanie would sleep soundly and long . . . like she always did when she came back from who-knew-where.

One step closer. Two steps. Three soft steps brought her within reach of the phone and whatever secrets it might hold. Her hand hovered . . . retreated . . . returned . . . grabbed. Her eyes darted to Mel. No sign of waking. Pam tiptoed to her bed and turned the phone's volume off to prevent it from making any unexpected noises. She opened the text-messaging app and perused the list of conversations.

Gavin Doyle's name was near the top of the list. Pam opened that thread and began to read.

Whoa, whoa, whoa. They've been meeting up? They go away together? A cabin?

Were Mel and Gavin shacking up? Strange days for romantic rendezvouses, since some of them interfered with school. The timing didn't make sense, especially since Mel had always been such a serious student. She wouldn't jeopardize her grades for a boy.

More baffled than ever, Pam scrolled to earlier messages. There was something about a package . . . and about a "them." "What do they want us to do?" Mel had asked (meaning with the package). Gavin had texted her an address, which Pam committed to memory before continuing to read about Jeff (whoever he was) being held hostage.

This can't be good. Melanie, what the heck have you gotten yourself into?

A quiet knock at the door made Pam jump and nearly drop the phone. She whisked it behind her back as her gaze flew to Mel. Her roommate didn't stir. Pam replaced the phone on the nightstand, padded to the door, and cracked it. Jocelyn stood on the other side.

Putting a finger over her lips, Pam slipped out into the hallway and shut the door behind her. "What's up?" she whispered.

Jos's green eyes narrowed. "What's up with you? You look like you've got a secret."

"Shhh. Let's talk downstairs. I just found out some stuff that I *have* to tell you."

)) ● ((

The next day, after her history exam itself became history, Melanie grabbed lunch and began the ten-hour drive home. With the help of four cans of Red Bull, she reached the eastern suburbs of Indianapolis before midnight (and without falling asleep at the wheel).

Her parents' weathered white bungalow looked the same as ever in the streetlamp's pool of soft yellow light. Well, maybe a bit more paint than before was flaking off the front porch's round columns; her dad worked long hours at a lumberyard to keep up with the bills and had little energy left for home improvements. Mel wondered how her current exhaustion compared to his day-to-day fatigue.

She climbed the creaky, uneven wooden steps and pushed open the door to fall into her mom's warm embrace. Her dad was next in line, and then her brother, Matt, who emerged from his dark cave of a room to give her a sloppy teenage side-hug. Mel noticed with surprise that his voice had changed and his height had surpassed hers. After the hug, he loped back to his room to resume whatever RPG he was currently obsessed with.

Fortunately, her mom only fussed over her for five minutes—though a long five minutes. That was what you got when your mom was a former nurse. "Sit down. You're so pale." She felt Mel's forehead and frowned. "You're running a slight fever. Did you stay up too late studying for exams?"

"Not really. No all-nighters," she half-lied.

"Hmmm. Well, chop-chop! Off to bed. We can catch up in the morning."

"Yes, Mom." Mel didn't need to be told twice. She bade her family goodnight and hurried off to brush her teeth. Minutes later, she was climbing the stairs to her room and snuggling under her covers. Inhaling deeply, she sighed with pleasure. The sheets were fresh and fragrant, smelling of ocean breeze laundry detergent.

It was good to be back with her family. Home. Surrounded by walls that, though a bit aged and cracked, were saturated with love.

A dense forest shrouded in the gloom of night. She was running, being chased. Branches slashed at her face—

No, her muzzle.

She looked down and saw large paws pounding along a dirt path. Powerful front and hind leg muscles propelled her at inhuman speed. A thrill rushed through her, but fear soon returned. Who—or what— pursued her?

After bursting into a clearing, she slowed and spun around. A few heartbeats later, another wolf bounded into the clearing. He was a male—she could tell by scent. Lean, light brown, and a bit larger than she was. He stared at her, hackles raised, but made no move to attack.

She squinted and took a step toward him. Hazel eyes burned with an eerie golden glow.

Gavin.

She knew him, but did he know her? She searched for intelligence, for humanity, in the eyes.

They narrowed. The skin bunched on his muzzle. Fangs bared, a low growl rumbling in his chest.

It's me! *she tried to tell him, but he lunged at her, claws extended.*

The impact knocked the wind out of her. She panted and fought for breath as they rolled in dewy grass. Snarling, biting, kicking, clawing.

Stop! she screamed.

He didn't stop. Scratches opened and bled on her front legs. More thick, warm blood oozed down her neck and flanks. She stayed on the defensive, blocking blows, trying not to inflict serious injuries. But how long could she hold back? If he didn't let up soon, she'd have to strike back hard or be killed.

Gavin, please! It's me! It's Mel!

His teeth flashed toward her jugular. She twisted away just in time, and he bit deeply into her shoulder. She howled in pain. Kicked and thrashed wildly until she shook him off. He leaped backward, all four paws braced against the soft grass. Before she could react, he came at her again, snarling and foaming.

There was no glint of recognition in his eyes.

Despair sank its fangs into her heart. She couldn't do it, couldn't kill him.

But maybe she could slash him up enough to send him running away.

She bit and clawed furiously, drawing blood, slicing deep wounds. His ferocity increased in turn. Jagged lacerations marred both their pelts. Red spread through their fur like conquered territory across a map.

He kept aiming for the throat, and she kept dodging and striking nonlethal blows. The fight seemed to go on forever. They were trapped in a Möbius loop. Doomed to a Sisyphean fate. Older wounds healed, but fresh ones opened. Her strength ebbed and flowed, ebbed and flowed . . .

She jerked awake. Felt a soft, strong hand on her sweaty brow and another squeezing her shoulder. "Melanie, Melanie. It's okay, sweetie." Her mom knelt next to the bed, speaking soothingly. "You were having a nightmare. It was only a dream, honey."

"Oh . . . oh." Mel released a shuddering breath. She focused on her mom's clear blue eyes and relaxed. "Was I screaming?"

"No—more like grunts and whimpers."

"Did I, um, say anything?"

"Nothing intelligible."

"Okay."

A pause. "You want to talk about it?"

"Uh, I mean, there's nothing to ... I dreamed that I flunked all my exams."

"I'm sure you didn't fail any of them."

"Totally unrealistic, yes." *I hope!* "But it didn't seem that way in the dream."

Her mom nodded and patted her arm. "You'll find out your grades in a few days, and I'm certain you did as well as always."

Melanie was far from confident about that, but she kept her doubts to herself. Academics were a big concern, but not the biggest anymore. Nor were her increasingly frequent nosebleeds.

Gavin was.

The nightmare had burrowed far beneath her skin. She *had* to convince him to cooperate with the Organization.

19

Guardian Angel

LAST WEEK OF WINTER BREAK, JANUARY 9, WAXING GIBBOUS MOON
Geez, the wind must be on steroids. It battered Melanie's car and
threatened to push it into the next lane. Worse was the lack of visibility: a near-total whiteout. She could see maybe ten feet ahead.
Creeping along the freeway at twenty miles per hour, she felt trapped
inside a cocoon—or a shroud.

*So thoughtful of this blizzard to schedule itself for the day before
full moon.*

She hoped her frenzied windshield wipers wouldn't fly off into the
blank beyond.

A voice in her head (which sounded an awful lot like her mom's)
nagged her to stop and wait out the storm, but stubbornness kept her
from pulling over. She was a Northerner—she'd driven through worse
before, and for less important reasons.

Besides, she wanted to be back already. Back with Gavin. Back in
the Organization's territory. Where they could contact her in person.
Hopefully soon.

Halfway through Ohio, the snowstorm let up, and she could finally
see her surroundings. There wasn't much to look at—frozen fields, a
couple of other cars ahead of her on the inadequately plowed road—
but the improved view calmed her. Her fingers were sore from gripping the wheel so tightly. She flexed them and shook out her hands.

The vent exhaled warm air. The radio crooned oldies; Mel wasn't in
much of a punk-rock mood today. Sure, the moon had her amped up,
but the solitary, insular journey had an otherworldly feel. Like she was
in a ship sailing for days through dense fog in uncharted waters.

Near the Pennsylvania border, the divided highway grew icier. She
reduced her speed, fingers tightening and cramping once more. If only

she had snow tires. After the recent repairs, though, that luxury hadn't fit in her budget.

Two cars followed at a safe distance, and a pair of taillights shone a hundred yards ahead. Snow swirled again. Sundown approached.

Then the concrete barriers appeared—inches away from the edge lines. On both sides. Her heartbeat sped up, and her foot pumped the brake. Cursing, she drifted toward the middle of the road and straddled the two lanes. She doubted anyone would try to pass her.

There was no warning. The road grew clearer of snow and slush, and Mel sped up, eager to reach her destination.

One moment, she was gliding smoothly along at forty miles per hour; the next, the Honda was spinning out of control.

Crunch! The passenger-side corner of her front bumper hit a concrete barrier. Her body slammed into the ballooning airbag. Blood gushed from her nose. Her breath was torn from her chest, so she couldn't even scream.

The car spun and bounced off the opposite barrier with another sickening crunch. The back bumper screeched as it hit. Screaming metal twisted in on itself and clanged off the car.

Hyperventilating, tears and blood streaming down her face, Melanie clung to the wheel. The car fishtailed and bounced, taking a brutal beating.

At long last, the Honda lost momentum. It came to a stop against the slow lane's barrier. Mel shook, chest heaving, erupting into a full-on ugly cry. She barely noticed the two vehicles that had been behind her drive cautiously past.

But the car she'd been following stopped. A figure climbed out and headed Mel's way. The person wore a fur-lined white parka with the hood pulled closely around his or her face, but the boots looked feminine and the legs shapely in tight jeans. Sure enough, it was a woman who strode through swirling snowflakes and tapped at Melanie's window. "Hey, are you okay?"

As soon as Mel's eyes locked onto the woman's face, another shock ran through her. *Chandra?*

Was this really the same woman who'd approached her in the Burger King parking lot last month and bought her dinner? What was she doing *here*?

Hand trembling, Mel cranked her window down. She swiped at the blood on and around her mouth, its taste metallic on her tongue. "Ch-Chandra?"

"Yeah, how . . . wait, it's Melanie, right?"

Mel nodded.

"Small world! Oh my God, you poor thing, you must be so scared. Are you injured?"

Mel pushed away the deflating airbag to examine herself. Her shoulders and neck were sore, but her torso and legs felt fine. She detected no cuts or scrapes. "Don't think so." She clutched her throbbing nose. The pain was already subsiding. *Shoot, the quick healing.* Would Chandra notice?

She had to see if her nose was broken. She pulled down her mirror and took a fearful look. Her face was a ghastly sight, and she couldn't help but wince. Pale with bruises forming under the eyes, blood everywhere. And her cute, round, button nose . . . now looked even more like a button—a crooked, reddish-purple one—since buttons were generally flat.

More tears erupted. "Ohh nooo," she moaned.

"It's okay, honey. You're going to be all right. Just stay calm." Chandra reached in and put a leather-gloved hand on her shoulder.

Mel buried her face in her hands, unable to control the racking sobs. Some of them turned into hiccups.

Chandra gripped her shoulder more tightly and shook it. "Melanie. You're all right. You should get checked out at an ER, though, okay? I saw signs for a hospital. Let me take you there. See if your car will drive."

The car. What kind of shape was *it* in? Mel took deep breaths, and slowly the hiccup-sobs abated. She unbuckled and stepped out of the Honda to assess the damage.

Half the back bumper was gone. Dents marred all four sides. And she'd *just* had the dumb jalopy repaired. Now she'd have to deal with an auto body shop and the insurance company too. Fantastic. She'd never made an accident claim before. Would her rate go up? Was it worth keeping the car, or would it be cheaper to get another one than to report and repair this one? *I do* not *need this right now!* Fresh tears welled up.

She climbed back in and tried the engine, which she'd turned off. It growled to life. "Yeah, you better," she told it through clenched teeth.

"Good, she still drives. Follow me," said Chandra. "I grew up not far from here. I'll get you to that ER."

While Chandra walked back to her own car, Mel peeked in the mirror again. Her nose remained purplish and tender. And bent a little to the right. She nudged it leftward carefully, whimpering at the spike of pain and pop of cartilage. She didn't want it to heal badly. And it was healing—quickly.

Will the doctors notice? Should I really go? Another bill ... she thought with chagrin. Her parents were going to freak out.

The dusky sky deepened to indigo as she tailed Chandra. They took the first exit they came to and made several turns through a business district. The hospital sat between an office park and a pair of high-rise apartment buildings. More of a medical center, it wasn't as large as the hospital where Jeff Doyle worked, serving a small-town area rather than a big city. Three stories held a couple dozen windows, all glowing a friendly yellow. The moon hung large, low, and golden above the building. *Tomorrow night,* it taunted.

Mel parked next to Chandra in the front lot. The two walked together through the main glass doors and down a short corridor to the ER entrance. "Thank you so much," Mel said. "You didn't have to do all this."

Chandra shrugged and smiled. "Happy to."

"Seriously, you must be my guardian angel or something."

A glint came into Chandra's deep brown eyes. She leaned in conspiratorially and said quietly, "Honey, I'm no angel, but do you want to know what I *am*?"

Mel's stomach did a tiny flip. "Um, what do you mean?"

Chandra paused—but not in a hesitant way. She made full eye contact and seemed to relish the suspense. "I'm like you," she whispered at last.

Another flip, and a step backward. "I-I don't know what you—"

"Sure you do, Melanie. Haven't you noticed my scent? It should be obvious, with your senses heightened right now." Her grin was broad and white, pointed canines gleaming.

Blood rushed in Mel's ears and sang through her veins. *I've been so stupid!* Sure, the sterile hospital smell was overpowering, but wolfish undertones asserted themselves. Wide-eyed, she gaped like a fish, then stammered, "Y-you're a . . . Wait, are you part of the . . . ?"

"Organization? Yes."

"So that wasn't a chance encounter at Burger King."

"No. Neither was today. I apologize for that, but they told me to make sure you got back safely."

"How'd they know I was driving back today?"

"We're looking out for you; we have sophisticated means at our disposal."

So they did *put a tracking device on my car.* Mel knew she should be angry and creeped out, but she'd wanted this: in-person contact. She still wanted it. "I understand," she said. Considering the Organization's need for secrecy and security, she couldn't blame them for going to such lengths to vet her. And Chandra *had* been helpful and kind. Mel would ask them to remove the tracker later.

"You must have many more questions for me," said Chandra. "But you probably want to see a doctor first."

"Well . . ."

A sly grin. "Except you've already healed." Chandra motioned toward a nearby bathroom, and Mel followed her into it. Fortunately, it was unoccupied. Unfortunately, its pungent aroma made her almost wish the airbag had broken her nose clean off.

She took a look in the mirror and gasped. Her nose had straightened (mostly) and returned to its normal color. A gentle, hesitant prod. No pain. "Holy cow!" she exclaimed. Chandra chuckled. The bruises were gone from under Mel's eyes, too. She soaked some paper towels and scrubbed the blood from her face and neck.

"Like it never even happened," said Chandra, arms crossed smugly.

"Tell that to my car."

"You've been given a gift, Melanie."

"Sure doesn't feel like one."

"You've yet to tap into its full potential."

Mel's face lit up. "Oh, right—the cure!"

Pursing her lips, Chandra said, "About that—"

The door swung open, and a woman dragged in a bawling toddler. "It's okay now, it's okay," the mother soothed her daughter. The little girl's face was beet red, snot trailing from her nose to her mouth. With an apologetic look, the woman led the child into a stall. The ceramic tile amplified the girl's piercing wails, and Mel couldn't help but cringe.

"Shall we continue this discussion elsewhere?" said Chandra.

Mel was more than happy to escape the overpowering smells and sounds. She and Chandra exited the bathroom and the hospital. Full darkness had descended, though the parking lot was well lit. A few flakes fluttered, glinting gold in the lamp light, but the storm had moved on.

Back at their cars, Mel asked, "If you knew about my fast healing, why'd you bring me to a hospital?"

"I figured we should talk in a public place where you felt safe, in case what I had to say made you uncomfortable."

"Ah." Made sense. "I . . . was uncomfortable at first," she admitted. "I mean, being contacted by the Organization. But I think I've come to understand you guys. And I'm very interested in that, um, thing you have that lets you keep your mind. What were you going to say about it?"

An elderly man and woman shuffled past, hunched against the wind (or maybe just bent with age). Chandra waited until the couple was out of earshot. She opened her mouth, but then closed it. "Hmm, it's getting late," she said with a glance at her watch. "Let's talk about that some other time. You've still got a long drive ahead."

Mel frowned but didn't argue. She *was* dying to be done with this stupid trip and to fall into a warm, soft bed. She and Chandra exchanged phone numbers and climbed into their cars.

Before Mel could start the ignition, her phone chimed. Gavin had messaged her: "Are you almost here?"

"No. Got in a little accident. Don't worry, I'm fine. About to get back on the road. Be there in two hours."

She wanted to mention Chandra helping her but figured it was a bad idea. For now.

"Oh no. Glad you're okay. Stay safe."
Wait till he sees my car.

The dashboard clock read 11:00 when Melanie steered her battered Honda onto the cabin's long gravel driveway. Clouds obscured the moon and stars, and there wasn't much snow to reflect light under the thick forest canopy. She turned on her high beams—thank goodness they were intact.

The lights of the cabin winked like fireflies between the trees. She crunched down the final stretch and parked in front of the familiar, welcoming sight of her monthly refuge, its porch light on to greet her.

)) ● ((

JANUARY 10, FULL MOON (FIRST NIGHT)

Jocelyn Beaumont let out a quiet moan and rubbed her throbbing arm. Was this wound ever going to completely heal? It had been, what, a month? Last week the scratches had been pink and mild and calm, but yesterday they'd started reddening. Today the pain had decided to return. *What is going on?*

And why hadn't her most recent dose of aspirin kicked in yet? She'd taken it more than half an hour ago.

Jos squirmed in bed, restless despite her fatigue. She tried to focus on the late-night movie special playing on TV, but the B horror flick was a yawn fest. The film wasn't that funny, and it certainly wasn't scary.

Turning her gaze to her window, she caught a glimpse of the fully round moon. The first one of the year—the Wolf Moon, the weather man had called it. Each month's full moon had a name, but Jos only knew a couple of them. Her birth month, October, had the Hunter's Moon. She'd entered the world beneath its watchful eye.

A neighbor's dog howled in the distance. Ominous organ music emanated from the TV. A woman walked alone through a dark, misty cemetery. *Why do people in movies do such stupid things?* Jos knew there was a vampire stalking the woman and figured she was about to die or be turned. *Surprise me for once, would ya?*

She plumped up the pillows behind her and checked the time. Nine p.m. Since it was break, she could probably text Pam and get a response.

One arrived within a minute. After initial greetings, Jos complained: "My arm is killing me. The scratches are inflamed again."

Pam sent a shocked-looking emoji.

"Talked to Mel lately?"

"No, have you?"

"Nope."

Jos left the conversation with Pam and messaged Melanie. Pam didn't say anything more for almost an hour, and Jocelyn guessed she'd called or texted Mel, too. At nearly ten p.m., Jos's phone chimed again.

"Can't get ahold of Mel."

"Me neither."

"Well, it is kind of late. Maybe she's sleeping."

Maybe . . .

20

Caleb Connor

Dead of night. She stood in the center of a round, grassy field. Crickets chirped; a cool wind blew across her skin. A dirt road encircled the field, campsites radiating outward like sunrays. Forest fenced in the cul-de-sac.

I'm back at Pine Groves.

Thick clouds obscured the moon and stars, but a swift wind ushered the clouds along, like an invisible stagehand clearing away one backdrop to replace it with another. What new scene was being set?

When the moon came into view, she gasped. It was full—and here she stood, human! Examining her left hand, she found no trace of a bite scar. Had she traveled back in time?

Her Honda was here, its back bumper intact, all damage gone.

Pam was nowhere to be seen. Neither was anyone else.

Off to Mel's left, the RV waited stoically, a boxy figure against the dark trees.

Her eyes and feet were drawn to the door. She gave in, approached, and knocked.

A minute passed. No answer. Her hand reached out of its own accord to try the handle. It turned, and the door popped open.

Stillness, silence, and shadow. As her eyes adjusted to the gloom, she saw a kitchenette (pots and pans piled high in the sink; sticky stains covering the countertop), a dining area (table littered with dirty dishes and abandoned mugs), and a sleeping area (messy blankets trailing down to the floor). A short hallway led to a bathroom. She didn't care to see what state that room was in.

Then she became aware of a smell. Not from the bathroom; all around her. It saturated the RV.

192

Wolf. Male wolf. Familiar. Gavin?

No, but close. Something was slightly off.

Overwhelming sorrow tainted the scent. Deep-seated grief, tinged with regret.

What had this person done?

The hairs on the back of her neck prickled. She had to get out of here. She closed the door, hopped down the step, and headed for her car. The prickling intensified.

He was here. He was watching.

Her gaze turned to the woods, and she squeaked in fear.

Two yellow pinpricks gleamed in the underbrush.

He emerged: a scrawny tan wolf. He had the same hazel eyes as Gavin, but he was thinner, more grizzled, and his muzzle was graying.

Was this Gavin, a decade or two older?

Heart pounding, mind spinning in confusion, she backed away slowly. The wolf watched her but stayed put. Those eyes captivated her; they held such pain and despair. They alarmed her ... and they drew her in.

Melanie woke, nestled safely in the Butterfly Room's warm bed. Dust motes danced in a sunbeam above her. The sweet fragrance of lavender candles welcomed her back to reality.

She sighed, scrubbed a hand over her face, and reluctantly got up. What was with these dreams? Gavin had visions during waking hours. Was she working the night shift in the prophecy department?

The bathroom was empty, hers to claim. As hot shower water cascaded over her shoulders, she debated telling Gavin about this latest dream. She knew his family didn't own the RV, and she believed his assertion that he hadn't bitten her. Apparently, though, her subconscious had doubts. *Don't mention that to him. He doesn't need to know about any of these dreams.* They didn't cast him in the most favorable light.

And they probably weren't prophetic. Just jumbled concoctions thrown together by a brain unfettered from rational control. Some part of her was trying to make sense out of the chaos—if that were possible.

Gavin seemed so sure that what he saw was going to come true, but her dreams didn't engender that kind of confidence. They left her with more questions than answers. She'd never believed in psychics or dream interpretation, but since werewolves were real . . .

Thinking of werewolves—the Organization. Eyes widening, she gasped. *Wait! What if they know who owns the RV?*

Why hadn't she thought of that before?

She finished her shower and toweled off quickly. Grabbing her phone, she texted Chandra: "Is there a member of the Organization who drives an RV and uses a cave in Pine Groves National Park at the full moon?"

The response didn't come until halfway through breakfast.

"Why? Do you know something?"

"No, but I hoped you would."

"We have a couple of safe houses members can use. They're nowhere near that park. We don't recommend places like caves that aren't secure."

Mel frowned and jabbed her eggs.

"Somefing wrong?" Gavin asked through a mouthful of sausage. He swallowed. "Bad news?"

"No, not really. Just . . . it's nothing."

"I'm not thrilled about going back to school either," he said, smiling.

Mel nodded absently and stared out the kitchen window. Frosted pine trees sparkled in the morning sun. A bright red cardinal sang and hopped from branch to branch. There was almost no wind. An ideal winter day. Too bad they had to leave in an hour. With classes resuming tomorrow, the dorms opened at eleven a.m. today.

It had been strange spending a whole week at the cabin with Gavin. He and Melanie had slept a lot, and she was glad they'd had time to recover before the new semester began.

After cleaning up their dishes, they finished packing and prepared to leave. As Mel checked around her room to make sure she didn't leave anything behind, her phone chimed. Chandra again.

"Meeting on the 19th at 7 p.m. Location will be given that morning. Bring your friend if you can."

Like Gavin would come. Mel replied: "I'll see what I can do."

She wasn't even going to ask him. She knew what his answer would be.

Mel couldn't stop thinking about the meeting during her drive back to Wellsboro, and while she unpacked and settled in. She'd arrived before Pam and was glad to have time alone to ruminate.

The meeting is Thursday, but tutoring doesn't start up till next week. Hope the meeting doesn't go too late. Why can't they have it on the weekend? I wonder if anyone in the Organization is a student like me. They're probably all adults. Is there anybody close to my age? How many of them are there? How many werewolves could possibly live around here? Is that doctor going to be there? Maybe he'll tell me about the cure.

She wouldn't be thrilled to see him; she wasn't letting go of her grudge yet. But she needed information, and as a physician, he probably knew a lot more about the cure than Chandra did. Mel wanted technical details. Those were safer than vague explanations.

"Girl, what the heck happened to your car?!"

Melanie jumped; she'd been so deep in thought, she hadn't heard Pam's footsteps on the stairs.

"I slid on black ice and crashed into some barriers."

"Holy crap! Were you hurt?" Pam dropped her bulging bags, dashed to Mel, and hugged her. Stepping back, she looked her over and smiled. "You look fine."

"I was going pretty slowly, so I wasn't injured. Just a bit of whiplash."

"Thank goodness. Did you know Aaron was in a terrible car accident three years ago? He still has a scar on his . . ." Pam chattered away as she began to unpack.

Half an hour later, the girls reunited with Jos and Shari, and they walked down to the cafeteria for lunch. "The four musketeers are back together!" Pam crowed, slinging her arms over her suitemates' shoulders.

Mel followed a step behind, smiling faintly but feeling like a rejected D'Artagnan.

Inevitably, their lunch-table talk revolved around winter break. Mel gave enough details to satisfy her friends' curiosity. Of course she had to relate the story of her crash, but she left out the parts about her broken nose and Chandra. "My dad says I should get my car fixed rather than buy a new one. Do you guys know of a good body shop around here?"

None of the girls did. Melanie would have to ask other people or find one online.

As the four of them finished their meal, a pair of guys walked by, chatting. Mel's fork froze in midair above the last bite of her mac and cheese—she thought she'd heard one of the guys say "werewolf." *Nah, I must be mistaken.* But she listened carefully.

"Do you think that video was doctored, or could it be real?" asked the shorter guy, blue eyes wide. Mel recognized him as a gullible freshman on the *Sentinel* staff who wrote mediocre sports articles.

"It has to be fake," his taller companion said in a know-it-all voice. "Technology can do amazing things. Vampires, werewolves, Bigfoot . . . I stopped believing in monsters when I was, like, eight."

The shorter guy bobbed his head in agreement, and they exited the cafeteria.

Mel swallowed around a lump in her throat. Her mouth had gone dry and she'd lost her appetite, but she forced down her last gooey, cheesy bite. She didn't want her friends to notice any more strange behavior.

Mel was even quieter on the return hike than on the way to the cafeteria. Soft snowflakes fell as they walked, slowly obscuring the grass. The sidewalk, trees, cars, and buildings were whitening too. The weak sun fought futilely to break through the cloud cover.

Wrapping her arms tightly around herself, as if to keep her curiosity from bursting out, Mel trudged onward. She couldn't stop thinking about the video the guys had discussed. *I've got to find it and watch it ASAP.*

Mel couldn't get any time alone until after dinner, when Pam went out to a movie with Aaron. As soon as the door closed behind her roommate, Mel jumped up and locked it. Then she slid into her chair, woke the computer, and clicked over to YouTube. Her fingers hesitated over the keyboard; what should she type in the search box? She settled on simply "werewolf."

Her stomach twisted into knots. Several videos claimed to contain real werewolf sightings but looked dubious or obviously fake. Two were clips from famous films. Halfway down the first page was . . .

Mel's breath caught. The video, posted by "cconnor819," was titled "Real Werewolf Transformation." Put up only three days ago, it already had more than 500,000 views. But what drew her eye was the thumbnail. The still image looked ... *Like the wolf from my dream, only with darker fur.* The creature was in profile, but its visible eye glinted an eerie yellow.

Please, please no.

Hand trembling, heart attempting to escape through her throat, she clicked the hyperlink. . . .

A dimly lit room with white brick walls. Those and the high windows (which were boarded up) made Mel think, *Basement.* Aside from a cot with rumpled sheets, the room was bare. There was no decoration—only jagged scratch marks covering almost every inch of the walls. A single bulb dangled from the ceiling like a burnt, hanged corpse.

The camera jerked, then zoomed in on the cot. There was a rustling noise and footsteps. A young man appeared on screen. Initially, his back was to the camera. He walked to the cot, turned, and sat down to face his audience.

Mel leaned in to study him. Thin and lanky, he wore jeans and a black Metallica t-shirt. His pale skin was striking against the shirt and his sable hair. Adding to the chiaroscuro effect were dark circles underscoring his light eyes. Hollow cheeks and the lines on his forehead made him look older than he probably was.

His eyes transfixed her. *So sad . . . empty . . . haunted.*

Mel shivered.

"My name is Caleb Connor," he said, his voice carrying a Southern twang she hadn't expected. "I am recording this to show the world that we exist—that werewolves do exist, right here in America. We are more than a myth. We could be your neighbor, your friend, your family member. At moonrise tonight, I am going to prove it to you."

Mel's jaw hung open, and she stared wordlessly in horror. *This can't be. No. He can't—he wouldn't—*

Caleb stood and walked behind the camera to turn it off. The video went black for a split second, then returned to the room, which had grown even dimmer.

The cot had been removed. So had most of Caleb's clothes, Mel saw when he returned from off camera; he'd stripped down to his boxers. Despite the deep gloom, she thought she saw his ribs protruding. *Poor thing.* Her nurturing instincts arose, and she silently begged him, *Don't do this, kid.*

"The full moon is about to rise," he said hoarsely. He brought his face closer to the camera in the low lighting. The same feverish glint she'd seen in Gavin's eyes shone in Caleb's. "I'm in my monthly hideout. It's secure. I can't escape.

"Any minute now, I will be stripped of my humanity."

He backed away and sat cross-legged in the center of the room, closing his eyes and folding his hands in his lap.

Seconds ticked by. Mel could barely breathe, couldn't move. Couldn't take her eyes off the screen. Her hands grew sore from clenching into tight fists. *Don't let it happen. Please let him be just some crazy who thinks he's a werewolf.*

But after less than half a minute, Caleb's face scrunched up in pain. He tilted to one side, hands clutching at his ribcage. He gave an anguished, guttural moan, shifting position until he was lying flat on the floor, his left side to the camera.

He could be faking it. Anyone can pretend to be in pain. Wait and see. . . .

She waited . . . and saw dark fur sprouting on the kid's arms and face.

Shit. Her heart hammered, and her breathing quickened. *Special effects? Film student working on a final project?*

This early in the semester?

Her logical side could argue back and forth all evening, but instinct told her what she was watching was real.

Maybe this is just a bad dream. I'll wake up, and the video won't exist.

Cringing fingers twitched over the mouse button; she could turn this off. She didn't have to view the rest.

But her eyes stayed glued to the screen; her finger failed to press the button; the video played on.

Echoes of pain from her recent transformation coursed through her as she watched Caleb writhe. The macabre scene was all too familiar: His face bulged outward. His nose shrank and blackened. Fangs blossomed before his mouth was ready, shredding his lips. Fingers shriveled, and the skin around his thumb split open, revealing white bone. The digit plowed several inches up his arm to form a dew claw. Mel rubbed her wrist, shuddering.

Fur washed like a wave over Caleb's torso and legs. His limbs warped, twisted, and crunched. Bones ground and knee joints popped as they reversed.

Finally, the transformation ended. The creature that had been Caleb stopped moaning and whining. It lay still, recovering.

Then, with a snarl, it leapt to its feet. Its head swiveled as it took in the small, bare room. A menacing growl rumbled in its throat. It turned to face the camera.

Whimpering, Mel closed the browser. She'd seen enough—more than enough.

That wasn't special effects.

She slumped back in her chair and closed her eyes. How long she sat like that, she didn't know. Her head was full of everything and nothing. Thoughts whirled and mixed so frenetically that she couldn't distinguish details. Like sparks in a pool of darkness, her fears grew, coalesced, threatened terrifying scenarios. She shoved them down again and again.

A loud thump downstairs broke her reverie. Giggling followed, and Brianna said, "You're so clumsy, Chris!"

With a gasp, Mel returned to the world. *Surely not that many people will hate us and fear us,* she told herself. Not to mention lots of people would think the video a hoax.

But that doesn't give him the right to expose our whole kind!

Everyone was so big on consent these days. Had Caleb Connor stopped to think about that for even one second before trampling all over her and the other werewolves' right to privacy? Even though he hadn't named names, he'd brought the kind of publicity that would open countless more watchful eyes and maybe would encourage people to speak up about what they had seen or suspected or knew.

And she knew people had spoken up. The video had been live barely three days and already YouTube's sidebar was full of sugges-tions. Mel went back in and saw titles like: "My Neighbor's Furry Little Secret," "What I Saw down by the Lake," and "My Math Teacher is the

Wolf Man." She hovered over some of them and almost clicked.

Don't. She'd had her fill of disturbing videos today.

Switching over to a search engine, she typed in "anti-werewolf groups." Her jaw dropped as more than 800,000 results popped up. Clicking a few links and skimming the pages gave her a glimpse into a hobby—a sort of club—she'd never known existed. "Werewolf hunt-ers," she whispered, shivering although the furnace was on.

There were three chapters in her region of Pennsylvania alone.

Some of the websites already mentioned Caleb Connor. Grisly images were splashed across most: messily hacked-off lupine limbs, tails, and other body parts—many unidentifiable. Collections of teeth and skulls. Internal organs in pools of blood. Blood everywhere. Men in camo gear holding up shaggy, severed heads that looked nauseat-ingly like Caleb's wolfish one. "You're next, Connor!" one site proclaimed under such an image.

Mel couldn't take any more. Closed the browser again. Groaning, she put her head down on the desk.

Three local chapters.

Why were people like this? Why were they so horrible? *Those poor people!* Except . . . Mel was one of those "poor people" now. She was the one they wanted to capture (and torture?) and hack into pieces. Did werewolves not change back after being killed? Would her parents ever know what happened to her? Or Pam or Jocelyn?

Gory images flashed through Mel's brain again. These people hated her. They didn't know her, but they hated her. Could any of them know about her?

My claws came out in front of Jos. What if it happened again, in front of someone else? Someone less friendly and trustworthy? Some-one with a grudge—like Timmy?

"Timmy believes in professional wrestling," Pam had said that day in class. Timmy had been chased by the beast and heard its howls. If Mel ever slipped up in front of him . . .

It could be the last mistake she ever made.

Shivering, she straightened. It felt like hours had passed. "No use sitting here frozen in fear," she told herself. She had to decide what to *do* about this new problem.

She grabbed her phone and texted Chandra, asking if she'd seen the video.

The reply came after a few minutes.

"Watched it. Telling the others."

The others. The ones Mel would meet on Thursday. Apprehension gnawed at her. She both did and didn't want to go. She'd always found it difficult to interact with strangers.

What if they didn't like her? What if they were weird and scary?

Quit being silly, she told herself. *You have no choice. Joining them is the only way to get your hands on the cure—or partial cure.* The only way for her to stop living in fear.

And, quite possibly, the only way for her to stay alive at all.

21

McCullough's

"What?! You haven't seen it yet? What planet have you been on?"

"I don't get what all the fuss is about. It's gotta be fake. Reality check, people."

"At first I thought no way could it be real, but then I did some research about special effects. . . ."

The chatter skittered down the hall like marbles flung from the *Sentinel* office doorway, ricocheting straight into Melanie's reluctant ears. Wednesday afternoon had arrived and with it the first news huddle of the semester.

Never before had Mel dreaded a meeting so intensely.

The Caleb Connor video had skyrocketed in popularity over the weekend, zooming past two million views. It was all anyone could talk about. Mel hadn't watched the video again, but she had read a bunch of the comments—which swiftly reminded her why she rarely did that:

>I almost pissed myself. This better not be real.
>This ***** cuold be dating your daugther. Hope she likes doggie style.
>Someone find this ***** and lock him up.
>No--shoot em dead!
>We can't let monsters like this roam our streets.

Sure, not all the comments had run along this vein, but a shocking number of them had. *They're the ones who are monsters,* she'd thought, seething.

Them . . . and those hunters.

She hadn't heard paranoid, prejudiced, or violent talk about werewolves around campus, but people were a lot braver in the relative anonymity of the internet. Her friends and classmates could be harboring similar thoughts, just not expressing them aloud.

Outside the *Sentinel* door, Mel clenched her fists and fumed again. *I hate that stupid kid for posting that stupid video.*

Thinking of people she despised . . .

"Hey, Melody," called Timmy Simmons as she failed to slink into the room unobserved. "What happened to your car? Looks like the scrapyard forgot to finish junking it."

Mel rolled her eyes and found a seat as far away as possible.

Timmy pointed at his nose and continued, "What's with the new look? Trying to start a trend?"

Getting desperate, are we? She'd just come from the bathroom, where she'd dealt with another nosebleed, and had left little scraps of tissue in her nostrils to catch the last of the drips. "It's called a nose-bleed. People get them. Can't believe you don't all the time, since you're so nosy."

A girl sitting next to her snickered, and Timmy made a face. *Okay, that was a pretty stupid pun,* thought Mel, grimacing. Usually, the retorts stayed tucked safely inside her head.

Before Timmy could fire back, Dawn Fincher strode into the room.

"Welcome back, everyone," she said briskly. "Hope the holiday fun didn't dull your minds too much. Vacation's over, and you are once more my slaves. So, who's got the first story idea?"

Timmy's hand shot into the air. "Caleb Connor," he said. As whispers broke out around the room, he sat back and crossed his arms proudly.

Although Melanie had expected this, she groaned inwardly. If only she could sink through the floor!

"I suppose it's too big a news piece to ignore," said Dawn, scribbling on the board. "We need an angle, though. I smell an opinion piece."

"How about two?" said Timmy. "We could have someone argue for the video being real—for werewolves being real—and someone argue against it."

"Hmm, I like it, Simmons. You want to write one of the articles?"

"Sure. I'll take the position that werewolves are real."

Dawn's eyebrow lifted. "Okay. Who wants to take the opposing view?"

Nobody volunteered, and Dawn's gaze shifted to Melanie. "How about it, Caldwell? Care to take a shot at this one?"

Mel felt like *she'd* just been shot. Or stabbed in the gut. Heat crept into her cheeks; she crossed and uncrossed her legs. Almost everyone was staring at her expectantly. She opened her mouth, but no words made it past her dry throat.

Risking a look at Timmy, she saw him narrow his eyes at her. Her heart rate sped up, and sweat beaded along her hairline. Had he figured out her secret? Was he going to use the *Sentinel* to expose her?

"Melanie?" Dawn tapped a foot impatiently, hand hovering below Timmy's name on the chalkboard. "Do you want to write it or not?"

Mel swallowed and licked her lips. "Oh, uh, sure. Sorry. Just thinking about what kind of research I'll have to do."

Nodding, the editor-in-chief scrawled her name and moved on to taking other story suggestions.

Mel only half listened as people talked sports, local, and national news, and Dawn's ever-shortening piece of chalk went *clack, clack, scrape.* Her stomach felt sour, churning with the bitter gall of defeat. She was trapped. Turning down the article might have raised suspicion, and that was the last thing she needed.

What she did need was to find an unassailable argument that werewolves couldn't—didn't—exist.

Good luck with that, wolf girl.

❯ ❯ ● ❰ ❰

JANUARY 19, WANING CRESCENT MOON

Melanie woke the next morning and immediately remembered that today—Thursday—was the meeting. Of the Organization. Her chest felt tight, and her hands trembled slightly as she pawed through her closet.

After she'd showered and dressed, her phone chimed. Chandra had texted her the address for a place called McCullough's Tavern in Blossburg. It was almost a half hour's drive from Wellsboro.

"Walk straight through to the door at the back, next to the bar. Tell the bartender you're in the club. Knock six times.

"Don't forget to delete these messages."

I'm "in"? Wait, a bar? I'm not twenty-one yet. Definitely don't look that old, either. Okay, she would be of legal age in two months, but until then, was she allowed on the premises? Maybe she could walk in but only order food and soft drinks. She wasn't about to expose her inexperience by asking Chandra.

"Okay," she typed. "See you there."

"Actually, something came up and I can't make it."

Mel's stomach dropped. *What? I'm not going to know a single soul there.*

Should she skip out? When would the next meeting be?

You have to go. Do you want the cure or what?

Once again, she was trapped. Were any of her decisions hers anymore?

The morning and afternoon gusted by in a frosty haze. Mel picked at her breakfast and lunch and zoned out during classes. At dinner, she tried to eat more but barely tasted anything. She scooted out before her friends had finished their food.

Out in the student center lobby, she bumped into Luis—figuratively, this time. "Hey, Melanie, how was your vacation?"

"Relaxing. How about yours?"

"Best one I've had so far. We celebrated my *abuela*'s eightieth birthday, and some of my relatives from Honduras were able to come."

"Cool."

There was an awkward pause. Mel shifted her weight to her other foot.

"Well," said Luis at last, "see you in the library?"

"Tutoring starts up *next* week."

"Oh, yeah. Oops. I'm glad you told me, so I won't show up and waste my time." His deeply dimpled, pearly white grin appeared.

For a second, Mel forgot her trepidation about the meeting. "No problem. See you later; I have somewhere I need to be."

"Got a hot date?" he teased.

Heat crept into her cheeks. "No. Just . . . a thing."

His brow furrowed, but before he had a chance to say any more, Mel muttered a hurried goodbye. She strode out of the student center and into the cold, windy night.

Her Honda was waiting for her in a corner of the back lot, away from the glow of streetlamps. She was so embarrassed by the dents and dings that she'd been parking as inconspicuously as possible—and walking everywhere unless she had to drive. The shop couldn't take the car until Monday. At least the snowfall hid some of the damage.

GPS ready, Mel rumbled off campus and headed east on a different highway than she usually took. She'd never been to Blossburg before and knew nothing about it. *Should've looked it up. Pleeease don't let it be anything like that neighborhood where the creepy doctor's lab was!*

Reaching the town half an hour later, she sighed in relief. What she saw was much pleasanter than what she'd imagined. She passed elegant Victorian homes and drove through a quaint shopping district with striped canvas awnings and old-fashioned lampposts. Signs declared a nearby castle. Too bad she wasn't going that way.

McCullough's was a few blocks behind the downtown area of Main Street. The two-story tavern was pale beige, crisscrossed by dark brown Tudor-style woodwork, and the sign above the door sported an Irish harp. Elaborate knots in green and gold snaked around the windows. A couple dozen cars, trucks, and motorcycles occupied the smallish lot, filling it about halfway. Additional parking was available in the rear, but this wasn't Melanie's safe, familiar campus, so she swallowed her pride and chose a spot not far from the entrance.

For nearly five minutes, she sat behind the wheel, psyching herself up. *You can do this. You've got this. Walk in there like you own the place. Chin up, head high.*

Even before she opened the car door, she could hear (and feel the thumping beat of) the Celtic rock music blasting from the pub. It was a genre she loved, and upbeat rock always set her blood and courage pumping.

"Let's do this," she told herself through clenched teeth, and strode into the tavern.

)) ● ((

"Where'd Mel run off to?" asked Jocelyn as she and Pam walked back to Hartman together. "Tutoring?"

"Doesn't start till next week, I think."

"Huh. She might be there anyway."

The girls changed direction and hiked over to the library, then searched both floors with no success. "Guess I was right about next week," said Pam.

When she and Jos returned to their dorm at last, they saw that Mel's car wasn't in the parking lot. "She went into town or something. Maybe she's out with a guy." Jos waggled her eyebrows suggestively and grinned.

"Probably Gavin. I saw Luis come into the cafeteria after Mel left."

"Gavin," said Jos. "Do you think he's trustworthy or shady?"

Pam shrugged. "He seems okay, but after reading that stuff on Mel's phone . . ."

"Yeah." Both girls fell into a sober silence as they climbed the stairs to the second floor and unlocked their doors.

After removing her soggy boots and coat, Jos joined Pam in her room. "Hey, have you checked Mel's browser history?" she asked, on a sudden whim.

Pam's gray eyes widened. "No."

"You've already snooped through her phone—might as well invade her computer too."

"Well . . . all right."

They woke the machine, thankful that Mel hadn't set a password. Jos got the feeling Mel would be brilliant at making up one they'd never guess. Pam, who sat in Mel's chair, opened the web browser. Jos leaned over her shoulder as she pulled down the history list.

"Wow, she's been looking up special effects, werewolves, and Caleb Connor like crazy," said Jos.

Pam shuddered. "I almost threw up after watching that video."

"Can't blame you." Jos wouldn't admit it to anyone, but Caleb's transformation had given her more than one nightmare.

Suppressing the memory of gruesome images, Jos rubbed her arm—which seemed to be better now, less painful and red. Seating herself on Mel's bed, she asked in all seriousness, "Do you believe in werewolves, Pam?"

)) ● ((

Acrid, stale-tasting cigarette smoke filled her nose and mouth, burned in her throat. Her stomach dipped and rolled like a cruise liner caught in a tropical storm; her heart fluttered like a flag about to fly off its mast. Tingles raced up and down her spine, shooting to her extremities, numbing them. The whole effect mimicked the beginnings of a transformation. Normally, she'd take deep, slow breaths to calm herself; but in air like this, that might trigger a coughing fit.

Mel pushed through the haze, which clung to her like spider webs. It was so noisy in here, so dark, and so bright—focused beams of light glaring from various places around the ceiling, and dark corners and dark scattered patches. The whole place was a riotous jumble of sight and sound heightened by her nervous state.

She forced herself to keep walking through it, to ignore the stares of men she passed. A few grinned or winked at her; she averted her gaze and strode on. Reaching the bar and the door at the back, she hesitated. The bartender, tall and balding, approached and gave her a scrutinizing look.

"I . . . I'm in the club," she finally remembered to say.

He nodded toward the door, then walked away to serve a patron requesting a refill.

The moment of truth. If she knocked, if she opened that door, if she went in . . .

It swung open before she could raise her hand. A blonde woman stepped over the threshold and stopped in surprise when she saw Melanie. The woman's skin had the dry, sallow appearance of a long-time smoker; her hair was thin and stringy, her eyes sunken and dead looking. She raised an eyebrow at Mel and said, with a raspy Appalachian twang, "You lost or somethin', honey?"

She thinks I'm a kid. "I'm in the club," was all Mel could think to say, feeling like a broken record.

The blonde woman's eyes narrowed. "Is that so. You got a scar to prove it?"

Heat rose into Mel's cheeks. *A pathetically small one.* She showed the tiny, triangular fang mark on the side of her left hand. The woman squinted and leaned in close. "*That* thing? Looks like a papercut!"

"It was enough to change—to ruin—my life," Mel said defensively.

The woman sighed, softening. "I'm Sheila," she offered, then rolled up her right sleeve and showed Melanie a ring of jagged tooth marks on her upper arm. "Hurt like hell when my newlywed husband, rest his soul, did that."

Mel's eyes widened in shock. She had no idea what to say.

"You gonna tell me your name too?" asked Sheila after an uncomfortable pause.

"M-Melanie."

"Well, Melanie, I'm off to the little girls' room. You wanna join, be my guest, and I'll introduce you to the rest of the riffraff when we get back."

"Okay," said Mel, trailing behind her, not liking the label Sheila had given the others. *Does "riffraff" include her? And me?*

While Sheila occupied a stall, Melanie stood in front of a dingy mirror, trying not to breathe through her nose. She frowned at her reflection and shook her head. *What if Mom and Dad knew I was here? Or Pam, or Jos . . . anyone who cares about me?*

Sheila washed her hands quickly and sloppily, soaking the cuffs of her flannel shirt. She wiped her hands on her ripped jeans and said, "Don't worry; I'll keep the boys from buggin' ya too much."

This woman sure knew how to make Mel edgier than she already was.

They headed back across the raucous bar front. Sheila pushed the rear door open, Mel following. The room beyond was the size of a large living room and had its own small bar in a corner. Tattered sofas and armchairs, along with some rusty folding chairs, lined the walls. More than a dozen people—almost all of them male—sat or stood around in clusters, talking, laughing, and drinking. Through the haze of smoke, Mel saw that they represented a variety of ages and ethnicities. Tall, short, thin, husky. Some were dressed like bikers in black leather, some in suits and ties, and others in normal street clothes. It was a lot for Melanie to take in.

Sheila led her over to the only two other women present, who stood chatting with a muscular, red-haired young man. "Vanessa, Janae, Dave. This is Melanie."

The trio turned to size up the newcomer. "Welcome," said Dave. He smiled and stuck out a hand. His grip was firm and warm, his bicep rippling under the sleeve of his tight shirt. He appeared to be about twenty-five, had a crewcut, and gave off military vibes.

The women, one black and one white, nodded and smiled at Mel. "Best stick with us, hon," said Janae. "Some of these guys can be a bit rough around the edges." She grinned at Dave, who gave an offended huff and folded his arms.

"Hey, *I'm* not one of those."

"Yeah, you're our Steve McGarrett," Vanessa teased.

"Careful—don't let Brad hear you say that," Dave warned with a twinkle in his eye. Vanessa tossed her hair and laughed.

Melanie pictured the handsome commander from *Hawaii Five-O* and thought Dave bore some resemblance to him, except for the flaming red hair. She already liked the man. His smile had settled her nerves somewhat. And his broad shoulders and well-developed pectorals certainly weren't unpleasant to look at.

After another few minutes of small talk, a loud voice—a thick Irish brogue—cut through all the others. "Time to get down to business, ladies an' gents. Take yer seats, please."

The crowd shuffled around, obeying. Melanie stuck close to the three other women. They sank onto folding chairs directly opposite the man who'd called them to order. "That's Roy McCullough," Sheila whispered, catching Mel studying him. "And his brother, Simon."

The pub owners were middle-aged, Roy broader and hairier, Simon darker and wirier. Chandra had told Mel the McCulloughs were the leaders of the Organization but hadn't said much else about them. *Hope they don't call on me to introduce myself. "Hi, my name is Melanie, and I'm a werewolf." "Hi, Melanie." "It's been seven days since my last transformation."*

. . . Same for them.

Roy was speaking again, and just like at the *Sentinel* meeting, the first topic on the agenda was the Caleb Connor video.

Angry, fearful murmurs filled the room, and Roy waved a hand to silence them. "Well, there's no denyin' the seriousness or the implications o' this situation—"

"Hell, yeah, it's serious!" barked a short, thin man with a unibrow. "That damn kid's gotta be out of his mind, drawing attention to all of us like that! Does he *want* the hunters out in full force?"

"I just barely escaped one—real crazy dude—last year in Colorado," said a man with dreadlocks next to him. "Haven't noticed any here yet. Have you guys?"

"No, but when I lived down near Birmingham . . ." A grizzled biker described his close encounter with a pair of fanatical, redneck werewolf-hunters. The men in that corner listened raptly. Mel caught about half of the story, the hairs on the back of her neck prickling.

Roy sat back and crossed his arms, listening, allowing the group members to let off steam. Simon whispered something in his ear, and he nodded.

To Mel's immediate right, Janae and Vanessa were discussing the nasty comments to the video. "They really hate us," said Vanessa, her pretty features pinched with anxiety.

The man on her other side (Brad, Mel recalled) squeezed Vanessa's hand. "You know I won't let anything happen to you, baby."

Vanessa gave him a starry-eyed look. *Ugh, please don't start making out,* thought Mel. She met Janae's eyes, and the woman rolled hers. Mel snickered softly.

After five or ten minutes, Roy cleared his throat and called the group to order. "All right, everyone, yeh've had yer chance to share stories. Seems many of us've had close calls with hunters or the law. But we survived, and we will keep on doin' so. We will not run in fear; we are better than that.

"In times like these, it is imperative that the lot of us—werewolves across the country, across the world—band together. Support one another. Strengthen our bonds. A cord o' three strands, and all that. We are a pack, a brotherhood—and sisterhood." He nodded toward Melanie and the other ladies.

Mel gave a small smile, and Janae bobbed her head emphatically. "*Mm*-hmm."

"The weak, cowardly humans who hunt us for sport, hunt us to kill us—*they* are the monsters. They deserve what they would inflict upon us. Now, I'm not callin' fer retaliation."

The man with the unibrow frowned, looking disappointed.

"That's not our style. We're simply tryin' to live in peace, to coexist. Every one of us has human family and friends and used to be human, ourselves."

Used to be human. Used *to be.*

"We're not against them, but we do condemn the hatred and violence that some o' them practice. As fer this Caleb Connor... he was *wrong* and *selfish* and *foolish* to expose himself and, by extension, our community. I've no doubt he's signed his own death warrant; the hunters will catch up to him in a jiffy. He'll reap his reward. Our job is not to seek vengeance on him but to support each other."

Murmurs of "Yes" and "You're right" floated around the room. Mel agreed silently.

"That bein' said, most humans still don't believe we exist, chalkin' it up to special effects an' all that. No need to be paranoid that hunters are lurkin' around ev'ry corner, but it goes without sayin' that we should remain cautious and vigilant."

"We're not going to take a more active approach?" said Unibrow Man, almost petulantly.

Simon shot him a warning look, but Roy said smoothly, "Glad yeh brought it up, Todd. That was the next item on the agenda—findin' and makin' alliances with other packs."

Eyes lit up, and excited whispers flew back and forth. Todd folded his arms but inclined his head in grudging approval.

"Have we found any others yet?" said the man with dreadlocks.

"We've got a couple o' promisin' leads." The springs of Roy's arm-chair shrieked, and he grunted as he grabbed a clipboard from under the chair. Passing the clipboard to his right, he said, "Maybe some of yeh can help. If anyone knows of any groups or even individual were-wolves, anywhere in the country, please write down their name, location, and any pertinent information yeh might know about them."

While the clipboard went around, Roy answered questions about what an alliance would entail. "We'd alert each other of danger, o' course. We'd share ideas, experience, and ... well, there's somethin' we're workin' on, which I'll tell yeh about when it's ready. Somethin' that should be quite helpful to us."

He moved on with the Q&A session, but Mel tuned it out as she wondered, *Something helpful? Is he talking about a full cure?* Her eyes roved the circle of werewolves again, though she already knew (to both her disappointment and her relief) that the old doctor wasn't in attend-ance. She'd have to ask after him later.

Dave caught her eye, five seats to her right, and gave her a smile. She gave him one of her own and thought, *This isn't so bad. It's not just a bunch of weirdos. Well, maybe that guy with the elaborately braided beard over there ...*

She wasn't fond of Todd, but Dave and the three women seemed all right. As for the leaders—Mel couldn't read Simon, but Roy was making a lot of sense. His words about peaceful coexistence and looking out for one another resonated deeply with her.

A series of six knocks interrupted Mel's thoughts. "Come in," Roy called gruffly.

The man who entered the room was ordinary looking in every way—average height and build with a face that was neither handsome nor ugly, framed by a haircut she'd seen on scores of men. Roy nodded at him, and he inclined his head respectfully before taking a seat.

Mel turned her attention back to Roy, who picked up where he'd left off, but then peered at the newcomer again. There was something familiar about him. Had she seen him before?

For the rest of the meeting, she half listened while her mind wandered between several puzzling topics: Where was Chandra and what was she doing? Who was the man who'd arrived late? And—the idea suddenly occurred to her—was the person who'd bit her in this room?

Could it be Sheila, Dave, or even (yuck) Todd? Did all these people keep their wolves safely locked up? Did one of them own the RV?

Shooting surreptitious glances at Late Guy, Mel bit her lip and frowned. She felt pretty sure this was not her first time seeing him. He wasn't talking, just listening, his eyes tracking from speaker to speaker. Janae put in her two cents' worth, and Late Guy's attention stayed on her for a moment, then shifted to Mel. He looked straight into her eyes, and his widened slightly. Did he recognize her?

He *couldn't be the one who bit me, could he?*

22

Op-Ed

After the meeting, Melanie got caught up in conversation with Sheila, Dave, and Janae. Vanessa said goodbye and left holding hands with Brad. Mel noticed Late Guy slip out just before the couple.

At least she could ask someone what his name was. She turned to Sheila, but before she could pose the question, the woman grabbed her arm. "C'mon, I'll introduce ya to Roy and Simon."

"Okay," said Mel, stomach fluttering nervously.

The brothers were conferring near the bar, Roy tossing back a shot of whiskey. He and Simon turned to greet the women. "So this is the lass Chandra was tellin' us about," said Roy. "Pleasure t' meet yeh." He offered his hand and, instead of shaking hers, raised it to his lips and kissed it.

"Nice to meet you," said Mel, blushing. Her eyes flitted from his to Simon's, which were a cold, pale blue. The taller man inclined his head wordlessly.

"I trust that after this meetin', yeh've gained some idea of what we're about," said Roy. "We're a pack, a family—here to protect one another."

Mel nodded.

"D'ya have any questions, comments, or concerns?"

She opened her mouth to ask Late Guy's name, but thought that would probably come off as nosy or strange. Then she remembered someone more important to her right now. "Actually, I was wondering about, um, that doctor. The one who drew my blood after Thanksgiving. He *is* a doctor, isn't he?"

"Elderly gent, ya mean?" Roy clarified. "Yeah, that'd be Sokoloff. Brilliant physician. One o' the top geneticists in the world." Simon shot

Roy an icy glare. Roy cleared his throat and shifted his weight to his other leg. "He would've been here tonight, but he said he's got loads o' work to do."

Disappointed, Mel pressed on: "I was hoping I could talk to him about his research—the cure?" She prayed that her desperation wasn't too obvious. "Can you tell me anything about it?"

A strange glint entered the McCullough brothers' eyes, and they gave each other a brief, meaningful look. "Well, that's a wee bit beyond my understandin'," said Roy, waving a hand over his head. "But yeh could talk to Dave about it. He's the good doctor's assistant. Appreciate it if yeh didn't mention it to anyone else just yet. Sheila knows, though."

The woman bobbed her head in agreement. Mel's eyebrows lifted slightly at the secrecy. *Why . . . ? Don't they all . . . ?* But she simply said, "Oh. Okay," and glanced over at the muscular redhead. "Thank you."

Roy raised the shot glass he'd just refilled. "My pleasure. Hope t' see yeh again next meetin'."

"Oh, yes—of course. Um, when's that?"

"Chandra'll pass that information along, soon 's we decide." He tossed back the burning whiskey as if it were water.

Sheila waved and headed out as Melanie made her way over to where Dave was chatting with Janae. Janae looked up at almost the same moment. "Hey, girl," she said. "What'd you think of the alphas?"

"Oh, uh . . ."

Dave laughed. "She's teasing. We don't really call them that. Just 'Roy' and 'Simon.'"

Melanie sidled up beside Janae, smiling. "They seem all right. They told me to ask you, Dave, about, uh, Dr. Sokoloff." She wasn't about to waste time on subtle hints. It was nearing 8:30, and Mel had an early class tomorrow.

"I see," said Dave, his expression growing serious.

Janae's smile also waned. "It's been real, but I gotta go. See you guys. Melanie, it was nice to meet you."

"You too."

The room had mostly cleared out; only a handful remained. Dave motioned to a chair, and Mel sat. He straddled the one next to her and rested his arms on top of the back.

"So are you a doctor, or a nurse or something?" she asked him.

"Nah, I'm just a lowly phlebotomist."

Mel cringed, then said, "Sorry—needle phobia."

Dave chuckled. "You're definitely not the only one."

"Actually, I took you for a military guy."

"Good instincts. Ex-army," he said. "I was in the service, in Afghanistan, until..." He scooted backward and lifted his shirt, making Mel blush. He was hairier than she'd expected, but sculpted abs were visible underneath the red fuzz. Then she noticed the wicked-looking bite scar on his left side and winced. "Yeah, there was a were-wolf living in those mountains, and I was on patrol the night of the full moon."

"Do all you guys like to show off your bite marks?" Mel said off-handedly, trying to lighten the mood.

"Who else showed you theirs?"

"Sheila."

"Ah, from her fiancé."

"Husband."

"Oh, that's right."

"You don't know what happened to him, do you? She said, 'Rest his soul.'"

"Afraid not."

Realizing she'd gotten distracted, Mel uncrossed her legs, leaned forward, and said, "About this cure. Or partial cure? How does it... What *is* it? A drug?"

"Yeah, it's a chemical compound we're synthesizing—well, *he's* synthesizing; I just help with sample collection and running tests. And procuring the supplies we need."

A chill weight settled in Mel's abdomen. "Wait, what?" she stammered. "It's still in the works? Not finished?"

"Not yet. We're close, though."

"But—but the paw prints in the snow. They spelled a message."

"That must have been Chandra," Dave explained. "She has the natural ability to keep her mind during a transformation. Dr. Sokoloff's been studying her DNA to try and replicate the effect."

Though she and Chandra weren't close, weren't friends, Mel felt betrayed. "She made it seem like..."

A look of sympathy crossed Dave's face. "I'm sure she didn't mean to—"

"What, *lie*? She would never do that?" Mel's eyes flashed.

He sighed. "Everyone lies now and then. Or leaves out an important piece of the truth. But sometimes we have good reasons for doing so."

"I wouldn't call giving someone false hope 'good'!"

"Melanie, we're getting there. We're so close. The doc believes he's on the verge of a breakthrough."

Quietly, slumping a bit, Mel said, "Why . . . why couldn't you guys wait a little longer, till it was ready, and *then* contact me?" She stared down at her hands, which were clasped in her lap as if comforting each other.

Dave touched her shoulder. "If it had been up to me, I would have waited. Or waited to mention the drug, in any case."

"I wish it had been up to you." Mel drew in a long breath and slowly released it. "I should go. It's getting late," she said, standing and pulling on her coat.

He rose, too. "Here, let me walk you out."

They exited the hazy meeting room and crossed the overstimulating, dark-and-bright main room. Mel donned gloves as she wove between crowded tables, thankful that none of the patrons leered or whistled at her—thanks to her muscular escort, she was sure.

Dave held open the front door for her, and she smiled at him and stepped out into the windy, cloudy night. All the way back to Wellsboro, Mel replayed her conversation with Dave in her mind.

"Verge of a breakthrough," she muttered, frowning. "They sure as heck better be."

》 》 ● 《 《

FIVE DAYS LATER, JANUARY 24, WANING CRESCENT MOON

The night before the Wednesday deadline, the first few submissions for *Sentinel* Issue One trickled into Mel's inbox. People were more on top of their game at the beginning of semester. She printed the articles to proofread later. She simply didn't have time right now, not with the werewolf op-ed looming before her, still frustratingly incomplete.

I won't let down Dawn again. Ever. It's a new semester, a fresh start.
She felt anything but fresh.

Miserably, Mel remembered hearing a priest or someone saying that it was much harder to disprove something's existence than to prove it. Though he'd been talking about God, the same principle could apply to werewolves and other mythical (or not-so-mythical) creatures. Sure, she'd gathered plenty of quotes—but they were only speculation, not proof. She'd have to rely on her persuasive prose to power-up her article.

As the clock ticked inexorably toward ten, and Pam changed into pajamas and brushed her teeth, Mel sweated and stared and frowned at the words on her computer screen. They were far from satisfying, but in a week she'd failed to make them any better. The main body paragraphs, the arguments, were fleshed out. All that remained was to tie things off, to finish with flair.

She drummed her fingers, then typed:

> And so, ladies and gentlemen, I urge you not to let paranoia and hysteria overcome your common sense. This is just another *War of the Worlds*, whether or not Caleb Connor ever comes forward and admits it. Why exactly did he cry wolf? We may never know, but the esteemed mental-health professionals quoted here all agree that Connor shows the classic signs of PTSD, depression, and abuse. He is to be pitied, but his video (a sad cry for help) is not to be believed or feared.

Mel hit Save one last time, then sighed and leaned back in her chair. *That's as good as I can do.* She closed the document; tomorrow she'd give it a quick review before sending it to Dawn.

Humming "The Point of No Return" from *The Phantom of the Opera*, Pam walked back into the room. She smelled of minty toothpaste and lavender lotion and was hand-combing her hair, which had grown an inch or two since September and now almost brushed her shoulders. Pam seemed lost in thought as she sat on her bed and picked up her phone to start a text-message conversation.

It was 10:15. Mel yawned and stretched. She was about to log out of her email account and take her turn in the bathroom when a new email popped up.

The sender was Timmy Simmons. His op-ed, companion to hers, was attached.

Ice slid into Mel's stomach. She definitely didn't want to read his article now—or ever. She just wanted to sleep, long and deeply, but she knew she wouldn't catch any winks with the suspense of not knowing what Timmy had written.

Subconsciously holding her breath, she downloaded the document. It was two pages double-spaced and was titled "Monsters in Our Midst." She made a face and read:

On January twelfth, our lives were changed forever. The world as we thought we knew it expanded when a young man named Caleb Conor revealed that werewolves exist. The video he made showing his monthly transfomation has been hotly debated, but most experts in special affects agree that the footage has not been doctored. Every grusome detail you see, is *real*.

Timmy went on to quote three experts, the magic number they'd been taught in composition class. Intro paragraph, three body paragraphs, and a concluding summary and call to action. *Very by-the-book and unimaginative,* thought Mel, a bit snootily. Never mind that she'd also quoted three people.

But as she read Timmy's typo-riddled final paragraph, her eyes widened and she clapped her hand over her mouth to stifle a gasp.

If Caleb Connors video is genuine—which the three experts above have clearly shown—then their have to be other were-wolves out there. How many more? Unfortunately we can't know the answer. However through stealthy investigation, I have managed to uncover the identity of one that is living right here; on our own campus. Yes: tiny Wellsboro University, nestled so safely in the beautiful Appalachian foothills; is not as safe as you think, for one of our very own students holds a dark, dangerous, secret. One of my fellow journalists in fact. You don't need to look any further than the other editorial for her name. Yes! Melanie Caldwell is a wolf in sheeps-clothing trying her very best to soothe you; to lull you into the false belief that werewolves are just makebelieve and she isn't a murderous raving beast, once a month. The signs are there if you look for them, don't say I didn't warn you.

No... he can't... they can't publish... Dawn can't approve this. Dawn can't read this—I can't let her see it.

What if he sent it to her already, separately?

This couldn't be happening.

How did Timmy know? How had he figured it out?

The room spun. She closed her eyes, gripped the arms of her chair. A moan escaped her throat.

"Mel? Are you okay?" she heard through the buzzing in her ears, as if from far away down a long tunnel.

Shit. Mel's eyes snapped open, and she scrambled to close Timmy's article. The sudden motion sent a wash of nausea through her. Her hand fumbled, flailed, but managed its task. The computer screen and the room were overly bright, lights wavering and dancing drunkenly. The floor seemed to lurch—how was she not falling out of her chair? She felt seasick.

A hand grasped her shoulder, and (still from a distance) came, "Mel? Say something. What's wrong?"

Her mouth was full of sandpaper. She thought she opened it, but nothing came out. Her arms were growing weak, her dizziness more intense.

Somewhere at the back of her mind, she knew it wasn't only Timmy's article that had sent her into this state. Something else had to be contributing.

But her awareness, her experience, knew nothing but fear and woozy confusion and dread that Pam would...

Footsteps pounded out of the room. Then two sets of footsteps pounded back into the room. Another voice joined Pam's, and the two voices were growing fainter and farther away. Mel thought her eyes were open, but she couldn't see anything. She was floating in a deep black pool...

And then she was gone.

Gentle taps on her face—growing more insistent. "Melanie! Wake up!"

She floated toward the surface. *Shari?*

"Should we call the nurse or take her to the hospital?"

Pam.

"Not necessarily. People do pass out sometimes, whether from anemia or because they haven't eaten recently enough or because they stood up too fast. Let's wait and talk to her before—"

"She was sitting in her chair!"

"I know. That rules out the third option."

Shari sounded quite calm and steady against Pam's whirl of emotion.

Slowly, Mel opened her eyes, and the room came into focus. The white ceiling with its glaring fluorescent light. Pam's and Shari's worried faces hovering above her, one to each side. She lay on the floor on her back. It was hard, and she felt stiff. She shifted and groaned.

"Honey, you passed out," said Shari, giving her right hand a squeeze.

"I . . ." Mel licked her lips. She'd figured that out herself. But why?

"Can you get her a glass of water?" Shari asked Pam. The tall girl hurried off to do so.

While she was gone, Shari helped Mel to carefully sit up. She scooted her backward and propped her against her bed. "Thanks," croaked Mel.

Shari's cool hand rested on Mel's forehead for a moment. "You don't have a fever. You're super pale, though. Do you think you're coming down with something? Could be the flu; it is that time of year."

Mel shrugged. She'd felt fine up until she'd read Timmy's article. Hadn't she? Brushing away the remaining cobwebs in her brain, she tried to review her day. "Maybe . . . my throat's been kinda sore today," she recalled.

Pam returned with the water, and she helped Melanie hold the glass to her lips. Mel took a few swallows, and her throat did hurt in the process. *Must be the flu,* she decided. *Or possibly strep.*

The girls made her take a ton of vitamin C and promise to take it easy tomorrow. "Skip classes if you don't feel any better," said Shari.

Obediently, Mel nodded. As her head bobbed, she felt not dizzy again but another sensation—something warm sliding down through her nose. Her hand came up instinctively and caught a large drop of blood. "Aw, *maan.*" Just what she needed.

Pam handed her a tissue, and Mel climbed to her feet, cautiously, holding on to the bed. No more wooziness, thank goodness. She hurried off to the bathroom and let her nose drip into the sink. *Wow, that's a lot of blood.* It kept flowing, splattering like starbursts, for minutes and minutes. She pinched the bridge of her nose. She knew she should tilt her head backward but didn't want the blood to gush down the back of her throat.

Five minutes later, her nosebleed showed no signs of stopping.

Mel glanced up at her reflection, which was paper-white and wide-eyed with fear. Crimson smears around her nose and mouth and chin, combined with the paleness, gave her a vampiric appearance.

She ran the water and tried to wipe herself clean, but the blood kept coming, and the water made it look like there was even more blood, a fountain of it.

Please, please stop! She was growing exhausted and achy all over. She longed to sit down, but if she sat on the toilet, she couldn't keep her face over the sink. If only there were a stool or something to kneel on.

Knees trembling, elbows sore from resting on cold hard porcelain, she closed her eyes. *God, please,* she prayed. She hadn't done that in a while. Maybe a long time. She was still mad at Him, if He existed. But maybe . . . maybe He'd hear, and maybe He'd help.

After a moment of silent pleading, she reopened her eyes and looked in the mirror again.

She nearly choked on blood. Her eyes burned yellow.

But—but it's almost new moon. That shouldn't be possible!

Something was seriously wrong with her.

Whom could she ask? Definitely not Chandra. Gavin? She hadn't talked to him in a week; she hadn't felt like it. He'd been a werewolf for such a long time, maybe he knew about illnesses unique to their kind. Had she contracted something like that? Canine flu?

Or could it be a coincidence that she'd caught the (normal) flu and had a terrible nosebleed at the same time? But she'd been getting quite a few nosebleeds lately, which wasn't normal—she'd never been prone to them. And human ailments didn't explain the eyes. Unless that was what happened to sick werewolves.

I'll ask him tomorrow.

Pam knocked on the door. "Mel, you all right?"

"Still bleeding," Mel called back.

"Wow." The worry was clear in Pam's voice.

Eventually, the blood flow diminished to a trickle and then stopped. Her eyes returned to brown. Melanie rinsed the last of the blood down the drain and collapsed onto the toilet. She hoped she wasn't developing anemia. *You'd better take iron,* her mom's voice urged.

She rested for a while before washing her face and brushing her teeth. Pam was waiting when Mel staggered into their room, and she fussed like a mother hen and practically pushed Mel into bed. "Stay in bed tomorrow. I'll bring you meals."

"A good night's sleep might be all I need," Mel mumbled, fidgeting to get comfortable under the covers.

The clock showed a quarter to midnight. Fantastic. The computer, which had gone into hibernate mode, whirred softly.

23

Libel

The shrill rings of Mel's alarm dragged her up from a deep, dreamless sleep. She groaned. Gradually, bits and pieces of last night returned to her. Timmy's article. Her fainting spell. The nosebleed. Her eyes glowing during the wrong part of the lunar cycle.

So many problems.

Slowly, Mel climbed out of bed. Her limbs felt heavy and sluggish, the air thick as water. A queasy dread gripped her, but the dizziness had gone. Her throat hurt worse than yesterday; her mouth was dry like she'd been breathing through it all night; and her nose was congested, though not in a drippy way. A steamy shower helped expel a dried blood clot.

Pam fussed and tried to make her go back to bed. "I feel a lot better," Melanie protested, willing it to be true. After another minute or two of failed persuasion, Pam relented. She headed off to breakfast while Mel dressed and dried her hair.

Once she was alone, Mel texted Gavin, explaining her physical symptoms. She asked if he had any idea of what could be wrong with her. Then she woke her computer and reread Timmy's article, to make sure she hadn't dreamed it. Damn, no such luck.

Heart pounding, she closed the document and buried it deep in folders. She was definitely not ready to reply to his email or confront him. She needed time to calm down and think things through rationally. Formulate a strategy.

Why was Timmy doing this? What did he want from her?

Gavin responded to her message as she was pulling on her boots.

"Sounds like the flu and dry air, except for the eyes. I don't think that has ever happened to me. I rarely get sick. I'll ask Mom if she remembers my eyes turning yellow when I was sick. If you feel better now, I wouldn't worry too much about it. Keep me updated."

Mel thanked him, feeling some of the tension leave her shoulders.

But the nausea persisted through her morning classes, along with growing fatigue and, by lunchtime, a mild throbbing in her forehead. She could barely eat. Her mind and pulse alternated between racing and lagging.

When it was time to head to the *Sentinel* office, fear escalated into panic. She couldn't set foot in the newsroom. What if Timmy was there? *Most likely he will be, if only to torment me.*

There was no rule that said she had to proofread in the office. She could do it in her room.

Go on, hide like a coward, said a voice. Her absence could be seen as an admission of guilt. Besides, Mel wanted to figure out if Dawn had received and read Timmy's article. If only she could hack into Dawn's email and delete anything from him before the editor saw it.

Miserably, Mel trudged to the communication building. Of course Timmy was there—and alone. He lounged at the layout table, his feet up on it, his fingers laced behind his short, thick neck. Light glinted off his glasses so she couldn't see his eyes, but his smirk was impossible to miss.

"*You—*" she started, fury mounting. "How dare you spread lies about me—"

"Lies? I don't know what you're talking about."

"You don't know *anything!*"

"I know enough to put two and two together. Pine Groves. That creature. The moon was full. Need I say more?"

The blood drained from Mel's face. She swayed and steadied herself, mouth working wordlessly. But wait—Pam and Timmy hadn't glimpsed the wolf, much less the wolf biting her. The nick was so small it could be from anything; surely no one realized what it was. She spread her hands. "Where was I bitten, then, huh? Do you see any big, nasty fang marks on me?"

He shrugged, put his feet down, and leaned forward. "There's a lot of your skin that I can't see."

"PERVERT!" She leapt at him and, before she knew what was happening, walloped him smack-dab in the middle of the face. Blood gushed from his nose; his glasses were knocked askew.

Holy crap! She staggered back, shocked at herself, hand stinging. Her knuckles felt greasy, and she wiped them on her jeans, disgusted.

"You—you—" Timmy sputtered, fumbling with his face.

Mel fled the office, tearing down the empty hall and out into the bracing air. She had to slow her pace because of the patches of ice, but she jogged all the way to her dorm without looking back.

Panting, she slammed the front door behind her, leaned against it, and clutched at her burning chest. Thank goodness her housemates were in class.

I am so screwed. She moaned and sank to the floor. Somehow, smart, sensible Melanie Caldwell had managed to *idiotically* make her situation even worse! *What is* wrong *with me?*

If Dawn found out—*when* she found out—Mel was in trouble. How much, she didn't know. But Dawn had told her to ignore Timmy, to learn how to deal with him. Mel was clearly failing dismally at that.

She drew her knees up to her chin in the position she usually assumed while waiting to transform. Transforming was almost less painful than this.... *No, it's not. Quit thinking that way.*

Deep, slow breaths. Her life wasn't over. Yet.

But how could she stop Timmy's article from being published? He was sure to show it to Dawn now, if he hadn't already, and to do much, much worse....

The nasty YouTube comments replayed in her head. Then Vanessa's anguished voice saying, "They really hate us." Almost everyone at the meeting had a story to tell of prejudice or a near escape. Soon Mel would have her own.

She imagined seeing fear and loathing in Pam, Jos, Shari, her mom, her dad, her brother, Luis, Dawn, everybody... Pam moving out, or her housemates kicking Mel out... people steering clear of her around campus, switching tables in the cafeteria or seats in the classroom... the sneers, the whispers... the gossip crew would have a heyday.... What if a werewolf hunter found out about Mel and—

No! She shook her head, trying hard to dispel the bloody images she'd seen on hunter websites. *Enough. Focus. Time to make a plan.*

Did she dare return to the office? Timmy was probably still there. Dawn might also be there now, getting an earful. Would she believe

Timmy?

Maybe she won't. Plenty of people want to punch him and could have. But if she does believe it was me, she might suspend me. Or am I back to no strikes since it's a new semester?

As for the werewolf part: Mel got the impression Dawn was skeptical of the supernatural, although she rarely heard Dawn voice opinions—the editor strove to take a neutral, unbiased stance in both her writing and her speech. It was hard to tell what Dawn thought about a lot of things.

Timmy doesn't have tangible evidence. But what if he waited until full moon and followed her off campus? With a camera? *Please, please no!* She'd have to be extra careful and maybe leave a day early. What day was the next full moon? She pulled out her phone and checked. February ninth, tenth, and eleventh. A Thursday, Friday, and Saturday. Great, leaving on Wednesday would make her miss three days of classes.

In the end, she decided not to go back to the *Sentinel* office. *That* might look guilty. Returning to plead her case to Dawn meant she had a case to plead. If she were human, she shouldn't care so much what Timmy published about her.

What am I thinking? It's slander—libel. Dawn won't publish that, whether it's true or not. She'll cut out the last paragraph.

Mel unfolded her knees and relaxed, letting out a sigh of relief.

Then her heart clenched again. Timmy could find another way to distribute his entire article, like running copies and sticking them in everyone's mailbox.

Would he go that far?

Maybe he'd threaten to unless she paid him or did something for him. *Eww,* she thought, remembering his comment about not seeing all her skin. Creepy-crawlies raced up and down her limbs and spine; she scrunched back into a protective ball. She felt so alone, vulnerable, surrounded by enemies.

She wasn't alone. The Organization.

Though she was still miffed at Chandra, she texted her: "I have a serious problem."

Now, there's *an understatement.* Mel sniffled, and tears welled up. She swallowed back a lump in her throat.

While she waited for a reply, she climbed shakily to her feet. Her housemates could return at any minute, and she didn't want them seeing her like this. She dragged herself upstairs and flopped on her bed like a ragdoll.

Moments later, her phone rang. Chandra. "Hello?" said Mel—her voice quavering, to her annoyance.

Chandra's tone, in contrast, was clipped and direct, like that of a drill sergeant. "What kind of problem? What happened?"

Mel sat up, swiped at her eyes, then described Timmy's article and her confrontation with him.

"So this little shit knows your secret and is either going to spill the beans or use it to blackmail you?"

"Yeah, and I—I have no idea what to do." A tiny sob escaped.

More gently, Chandra said, "First off, stay calm, and be proud of what you are."

"O-okay," said Mel, and steadied her breathing.

"He can't really publish that article, can he?"

"No. Dawn, the editor-in-chief, will cut out the part about me. It's libel."

"But Timmy can run his mouth off to anyone at any time," Chandra said grimly. "Not that they'll necessarily believe him, but some could become curious. And you don't need that kind of attention."

Melanie shook her head sharply. "No." Biting her lip, she played with the hem of her shirt and tried not to imagine what would happen if Timmy spread rumors.

"All right, well," said Chandra, "your editor is going to—or maybe already has—read the article, yes? Can't help that. Do you think she'll believe it?"

"Probably not."

"Good. Is Timmy the kind of person people take seriously? Is he popular?"

Mel snorted. "No. He's an egotistical twerp who believes professional wrestling is real."

Chuckling, Chandra said, "Even better. Whether he blabs or not, hold your head high and do everything you normally do. Right now with the moon's pull so weak, you don't have to worry about glowing eyes or other giveaways."

"Um ... actually ..." Mel bit her lip harder and twisted her shirt even more tightly.

"What is it?" Tension edged into Chandra's voice.

Hesitantly, Melanie told about her fainting spell, nosebleed, and glowing eyes.

"*Last night?* But that shouldn't be possible."

"I know," moaned Melanie, "which is why I'm so worried. Plus, I've been feeling sick all day, though not as bad."

Now Chandra sounded really concerned: "I think you should go see Dr. Sokoloff. Have him draw your blood, test it for contaminants, illness—"

Mel cringed, and a small whimper slipped out.

"Melanie, this might be very serious. What if you get worse? What if you get too sick to lock yourself away at full moon, and you hurt people? Your secret will *really* be out then."

Horror washed over Mel at the thought.

"Y-you're right." She took slow, shuddering breaths. "I'll go see him. Is he still at that place where Gavin and I delivered the package? Cedarwood, I think?"

"Yes."

"Can I go there any time, or do I have to make an appointment?"

Chandra gave Melanie the doctor's number so she could arrange the details with him herself. After hanging up, Mel moaned and flopped back against her pillow. *Might as well get this over with quickly,* she thought, and dialed.

〉 〉 ● 〈 〈

Two days later, Mel got her car back from the shop. At last the Honda was presentable again—and even more so than before, since it now had considerably less rust.

It was Friday, and she'd arranged to drive to Sokoloff's office tomorrow morning. The prospect was terrifying, especially since she'd be going alone. Asking Gavin to come was out of the question.

But what if Chandra was right? What if she got worse? Her fatigue, nausea, and headache persisted, only partially relieved by various medicines.

She carefully hid her discomfort from Pam. She also wore her dark contacts.

My life is falling apart, she lamented, curling in a tight ball under her covers. *First, my GPA plummets, and now my health is going down the drain fast.*

Not to mention what had happened the other day at the *Sentinel* office.

Wednesday, following the phone call with Chandra, Mel had gotten a text from Dawn summoning her to the office. *Shit. I'm in a deep pile of it.* Timmy had to have told Dawn everything.

Mel had waited until the next period, pretty sure Timmy had a class then. Indeed, he was no longer there; only Dawn was.

As soon as Mel slunk into the room, the editor looked up from her computer and narrowed her eyes. "Caldwell, I need to talk to you."

"Okay," Melanie said meekly.

"Sit," Dawn commanded, pulling out the chair next to her.

Gingerly, Mel sank onto it. She didn't like the look in Dawn's eyes. Not anger, but deep disappointment. Mel knew some painful words were about to be spoken.

"You and Simmons are *still* at each other's throats, huh?"

Mel hung her head and hesitated, unsure how to respond.

"I should never have agreed to his idea for these editorials. All it did was rile people up. Werewolves, for God's sake. We're not a tabloid."

Melanie looked up, a spark of hope stirring inside her. *Sounds like I didn't misjudge her.*

"What I want to know is," continued Dawn, "*why* Timmy would accuse you of being a werewolf."

So she *had* read his article already. "I . . . I've been wondering that, myself."

"He obviously has some kind of grudge against you. It's nowhere near April Fools' Day; he seems serious. I don't know how long he's had it in for you, but could this have anything to do with that camping trip last fall?"

"Maybe. I didn't spread any rumors about him, but he seems to think I did."

"Anyway, it doesn't matter. I'm not printing his concluding paragraph, and I'm considering scrapping both of your articles and replacing them. It's a bit last-minute, but it would teach Simmons a lesson in professionalism."

Please, please scrap them! As annoying as it would be if Dawn asked her to whip up a new article a week before publication, Mel would gladly do it.

Dawn folded her arms and said, "Speaking of professionalism, Simmons isn't the only one displaying an astonishing lack of it." Her eyes pierced into Melanie's.

Heart rate speeding up, Mel dropped her gaze. Her whole body tensed. *Here it comes.*

"Melanie, I expected better from you. A whole lot better. You actually *punched* Timmy? After I warned you to learn how to block him out." She shook her head, looking both stern and perplexed. "I don't know what's going on with you, but you need to get your act together. You seem to be under a boatload of stress, and I don't know why or where it's coming from, but I think you need a break."

"Wh-what are you . . . ?"

"What I'm saying is, I'm putting you on suspension until you work through whatever this is."

Numbly, as if through dense fog, Mel had only half-heard the rest of what Dawn was saying. She understood Dawn still wanted her article and might publish it. Or she might have Timmy write another editorial to replace the pair. But Mel wouldn't be writing or editing for the *Sentinel* until further notice.

She didn't remember the walk back to Hartman. Exhausted, she'd fallen into bed as soon as she'd returned. The numbness was fading, replaced by shame but also a twinge of relief. Less on her plate for a while—but how would the suspension impact her grades? She'd fallen into a fitful sleep.

Today—Friday—after classes, she had picked up her car with Luis's help, driven straight back to the dorm, and taken another nap. Pam woke her at dinnertime, frowning and asking, "Are you sure you're all right?"

"Peachy keen." Mel faked a smile and hurried to get ready for supper, despite her lack of appetite. She popped an aspirin when Pam wasn't looking.

Carrying her sparsely laden tray into the dining hall, Mel spotted Timmy on the far side of the crowded room. Anger welled up, and she glared daggers at his back. He turned, though not all the way around to face her—just enough so she could see the nasty purplish-yellow bruise that had bloomed on his face. *I hope it takes forever to go away.*

To her intense relief, Mel hadn't heard any rumors about her being a werewolf. No one had given her the evil eye or treated her differently. She tried to focus on that and on other positives—like how her nose hadn't bled today or yesterday—and push thoughts of Sokoloff and needles to the back of her mind. Pam was flirting with Aaron; Jos was teasing Shari. Mel sat listening, trying to absorb their cheerfulness, pushing her food around her plate.

The knot wouldn't leave the pit of her stomach.

24

Turn for the Worse

The next morning, Melanie finished breakfast ahead of her friends and slipped out to her car. She shivered uncontrollably—and not only from the arctic blasts. Her poor car shivered too, under her death grip.

Dave's going to be there, she reminded herself. *I'll make sure* he's the one who draws my blood. It'll be fine.

Mel's phone chimed, and she checked it at a stoplight. Gavin, asking her how she was feeling. He ended the text with: "Please don't do anything rash."

Mind your own business. How does he even . . . Did he "see" me doing this?

She scowled and gritted her teeth. At least *she* was doing *something.* What did he ever do but hide in his cabin, pretending like everything was okay? *That's not living.*

Cedarwood was just as slummy as she remembered. Feet hadn't yet trampled the snow into grayish-brown slush, and the debris had been transformed into glittering white lumps. Those few people present moved quickly, heads down, heavy coats swishing. They were interested only in reaching their destinations.

No one was watching her. No one saw her duck into Sokoloff's unit.

The unit's front room was cool, bare, and dim. Heading straight for the laboratory at the back, she fingered the pepper spray in her jacket pocket. She trusted Dave, basically, and prayed she wasn't wrong about him—but she wanted to be smart about this. And not only because of Gavin's text.

The lab's door was ajar, and Mel heard Dave's warm baritone saying, "No, it's only going to get colder. Will this snow ever stop?" Another voice responded, "I thought you liked the snow."

That second voice was higher, raspier. And it sent a nor'easter howling down her spine.

Her grip on her pepper spray tightened. *I won't let him do anything.*

She tapped lightly on the door and stuck her head around it. The doctor was sitting at one of his computers, dressed professionally, tie and all, under a lab coat. Dave leaned against a countertop, hands in pockets. He looked casual and relaxed in jeans, a forest-green hoodie, and well-worn sneakers.

"Melanie, come in." Dave smiled and stepped close to shake her hand.

With a wry grin, she said, "You don't look like a phlebotomist. I thought you were supposed to wear a lab coat or scrubs or something."

He laughed. "I'm sure there's a spare lab coat around here; I can put it on if you want the total experience."

A stray thought about playing doctor with Dave flitted through her mind, but she brushed it away. She could feel the real doctor's eyes on her and nervously turned to give him a quiet "hello."

"Good morning. I understand you have been feeling quite ill, young lady," Sokoloff said gravely, rising and approaching her.

Mel fought not to take a step backward. She nodded, and noticed sympathy on Dave's face.

"Let us get some samples drawn. I will test them for all manner of possible causes." The old doctor put a hand on her elbow to guide her, but Mel flinched, and he backed off. She marched to the dreaded chair and sat in it defiantly. Dave joined her and Sokoloff after washing his hands and donning gloves.

Mel stripped off her coat and rolled up her sleeve. Dave gave her a reassuring smile. He sanitized the needle, tightened the tourniquet, found a vein. Averting her eyes, Mel screwed up her whole face—pride be damned. The pinch came, but it wasn't as bad as when the doctor had drawn her blood. *Dave's pretty good at this,* she thought, although she remained tense.

When Dave had finished filling his six vials, Mel's spring-loaded muscles relaxed. Sokoloff asked her a series of questions about her symptoms, jotting down notes. She answered honestly and thoroughly, then realized she was dying to interrogate him in return.

"How long have you been doing this? I mean, working with werewolves. I'm guessing our anatomy is different than humans'. How experienced are you with treating us?"

Glasses glinting, he looked up from his steno pad. The lines across his forehead deepened, like furrows plowed in soil. His weathered, wrinkled hand trembled slightly as he clicked his pen closed and stuck it in his breast pocket. "I have worked for thirty years in my field," he said, "which is genetic research and DNA sequencing. I have only known about werewolves for the past couple of years, however. I . . . came to the States two years ago at the behest of the McCullough brothers and have studied werewolf DNA and physiology since then."

Mel frowned. She'd hoped he would say he had a decade or more of experience with werewolves. *He might not be able to help me,* she fretted.

"He's a genius," put in Dave, as if sensing her thoughts. "If anyone can find a cure, and treat whatever you're suffering from, it's him."

"Are you a human or one of us?" she asked Sokoloff.

An odd expression passed over his craggy face, like a mild earthquake through hill country. "I am a werewolf."

Well, it's good that he's got a stake in this; he'll be extra motivated. "How close are you to perfecting the cure?"

"I estimate that next month, or maybe in March, we will start seeing some very satisfactory results. Meaning, some of our test subjects will be able to keep their minds during at least part of each full moon night. Possibly all night."

Mel's heart leapt. *Finally, some good news!* "Who are the test subjects?"

"I'm one," put in Dave. "Sheila's another. Several others are signed up to start next month. There're more spots open, if you want one."

Me? Melanie gulped. Letting these people take blood out of her veins was one thing; letting them put an unknown substance *in* was entirely different!

"I'll—I'll think about it," she said.

"We will need to start giving you the injections two weeks before the full moon, which means right now," said Sokoloff. "But since you are ill, I do not want you to participate in this round. I would like to figure out what is wrong with you, and get you back to optimal health, before you test the drug."

"Okay." That sounded wise, and it would give Mel more time to decide. *I should probably wait until it works well for the others, then join.*

Interview done, she rose to leave. Too fast—a wave of dizziness swept over her. She swayed and plopped back onto the chair, blinking the world into focus again. Tiny lights twinkled; her forehead throbbed in time with their dance. She closed her eyes and massaged them.

"Melanie!" She felt Dave gripping her shoulder and heard him say, "Doc, she's white as a ghost."

"I'm fine," Mel protested, eyes snapping open. The men were both staring at her with concern.

Dave knelt and studied her face. "Can't fool me," he said quietly. "You're not going anywhere yet. I don't think you're fit to drive."

"But I need to—"

"I'll take you," he interrupted. "In a little while. Just rest, relax." He reached up and put a cool hand on her forehead. "You've got a low-grade fever."

Sokoloff said, "Melanie, please remove your contacts."

"Where am I going to put them? I didn't bring the case."

"Just take out one for a moment; I need to see your eye color."

Sighing, she obeyed. Dave and the doctor frowned. "Let me guess," she said: "yellow?"

"Yes," they said, almost in unison.

"What does that mean?"

"I do not know," Sokoloff admitted. "I will start running tests immediately." He whisked the vials of blood over to a microscope and a centrifuge.

Dave sat next to Melanie and asked her about herself—her major, her friends, her interests. She was grateful to him for providing a distraction.

Eventually, she and Dave ran out of things to say and fell silent. The centrifuge whirred. Sokoloff had created a dozen slides of her blood mixed with various chemicals; their acrid smells drifted to her from across the room. He peered into the microscope and muttered, "Hmmm" in what Melanie thought was an ominous tone. She wondered what he was seeing and thinking.

"How are you feeling now?" Dave asked.

The throbbing had mostly abated. "Better. I think I can drive myself back."

Another frown, and a shake of his head. "No, I said I'd take you."

She didn't catch the words that followed; a curious tingling sensation in her hands and arms distracted her. Glancing down at them, she shrieked in fear.

Fur was spreading across her hands. Her fingers were shriveling, growing claws, morphing into paws!

"Melanie?! What's wrong?" said Dave.

"My—my hands—" She looked back at his face and shrieked again. Russet hair was sprouting on it, and his mouth and nose were pushing outward into a muzzle.

Somehow Dave was able to speak normally through his shifting facial structure. His eyes were wide—and gold. "Doc, come here!"

Sokoloff was already rushing over. He knelt in front of Melanie, his own eyes glowing, face shifting and growing fur, hands transforming as they reached toward her—

"No!" she screamed, jumping up.

Dave's thick arms grabbed her from behind, pinioned her arms against her sides. "Calm down. We're not going to hurt you. The worst is over. No more needles, okay?"

She struggled, kicking backward, connecting with his shin. He grunted in pain and clamped his leg around hers ... like Gavin had done when he'd kidnapped her.

Thinking of Gavin and his good intentions, she stopped writhing.

The doctor gripped her face with both hands—they felt cool and dry and not furry—and brought his wolfish face to within inches of hers. "Her pupils are dilated," the wolf said in plain, human-shaped English. "Melanie, what are you seeing? What are you frightened of?"

"You—I—we're transforming!"

"No, we are not."

"But your face, Dave's face, my hands ..."

Mel shook her head to dislodge his hand-paws, then blinked rapidly. Blood rushed in her ears, and her vision narrowed, edged by black. The room spun; she would have swayed if Dave weren't holding her so tightly. She moved her mouth but couldn't tell if words were coming out. Then the blackness swallowed her.

An acrid stench brought light and sound and the world back. Mel half-lay, half-sat in Dave's lap on the cold linoleum floor. Dave held something white and chalky under her nose. So *that* was the awful odor of smelling salts. She grimaced and pushed them away.

She twisted to look at Dave, and Sokoloff—both were fully human. So was she, upon inspection. "I . . . hallucinated?" she croaked.

"Yes," confirmed the doctor. "Not a good sign, but helpful for narrowing down possibilities."

Melanie sagged against Dave and let out a frustrated sigh. "This really *sucks!* What did I ever do to deserve this?"

"I used to ask myself that a lot," said Dave. "I guess we all do, for a while. Have to grieve before we can move on."

I have *been grieving,* she realized with a start. *For months. Grieving the death of my old life.*

An hour later, Dave returned Mel and her car to Hartman. When he offered, Mel refused to let Dave help her upstairs or even inside the building. She was worried about gossip from Brianna and questions from Jos. Fortunately, Pam was out—with Aaron or in the music building.

Mel wanted nothing more than to take a long nap, but she had a quiz to study for and some reading to catch up on. Grumbling, she sat down at her desk. When she woke her computer, she noticed a few new emails.

One was from Timmy.

What now?! Her stomach lurched, but she had to read it.

There was no subject line. It was short and unsigned. It simply said:

I want to be what you are. I want you to turn me. Do it, and your secret is safe.

What the hell? Doesn't he realize how painful the transformations are? She couldn't believe he, or anyone, would want that torture *three times every month.* Couldn't he guess how bad it was from the Caleb Connor video? Or did he just not care?

Telling him about the agony, arguing that line, would be admitting what she was. *Never.* How on earth should she respond?

She closed it and tried to read her professor's online notes, but the words all morphed into "werewolf" and "turn me."

Would the double op-ed be published, or was Dawn making Timmy write a new article?

Was his email serious, or was he messing with her? If this was his idea of a joke, she should simply not respond.

That evening, Mel was loading her tray with dinner when a passerby's elbow smacked her back. Too forcefully to be an accident. It rattled her silverware, and she was glad she hadn't grabbed a drink yet. Mel turned and saw Timmy, who threw a smirk at her over his shoulder. She kept her own expression blank and looked away without retaliating.

His emails continued—the same message, sent at the same time each morning—for the next five days.

)) ● ((

FEBRUARY 2, WAXING CRESCENT MOON

The following Thursday, the *Sentinel* released Issue One. Mel gingerly flipped to the op-ed section.

The werewolf articles were there! Of course Timmy's original last paragraph wasn't. Still, she thought, *Dammit, Dawn! You should've forced him to do a new topic.*

Numbly, she pushed through the crowd of students checking their mail on their way into the cafeteria. Almost everyone held the newspaper, and many were scanning it while waiting in line. Mel's appetite went from dying to deceased. She ducked into the bathroom, nausea surging.

Locked inside a stall, she dry heaved. Gasping and panting followed; it took her several minutes to recover. To calm herself, she tried to recall what Chandra had told her on the phone. *Hold your head high. Be proud of what you are.*

Timmy's emails . . .

She should tell Chandra about those.

When Mel finally emerged from the bathroom, she veered away from the cafeteria. She couldn't go in there, couldn't risk people approaching her about her article. Timmy would likely have a crowd gathered around him—what kind of rubbish would spew from his mouth and spread around campus? Was this only the beginning of Mel's having to hide from everyone?

Stomach still churning, she plodded back to her dorm. She slept away the lunch period, as well as her 1:00 class. *Crap—I hope I didn't miss a pop quiz,* she thought, hurrying to her last class at 2:30.

That professor surprised her with a quiz. For which Melanie had only read half the pertinent material. She could feel her GPA slipping even lower, while anxiety sucked at her like quicksand nearing waist level.

Safe in her room again, Mel finally texted Chandra about Timmy's emails.

"At first I thought he might be messing with me, but now I'm starting to believe he's serious."

"Can't blame him for wanting to be at the top of the food chain," Chandra typed back. "But someone like him has no place with us. Give me a day to think about what you should do."

Great. More waiting. Waiting for the full moon, waiting for Timmy to ramp up his threats or spill her secret. Waiting for her symptoms to get worse, not knowing exactly *how* that would happen, what new ones might be added. Waiting for Sokoloff to call her and say he'd figured out her illness and a cure for it.

Waiting, waiting.

)) ● ((

Jocelyn logged out of her email, and news headlines popped up on the site's homepage. "Alleged Teen Werewolf Missing from Texas Home." Now *that* she had to read.

> Caleb Connor, 17, of recent YouTube fame, was reported missing from his home near Lubbock, Texas, on January 26th. Police found no signs of a break-in or traces of foul play in or around his residence. Connor may have been taken while walking home from school, authorities speculate.
>
> An AMBER Alert was issued, with not much to go on, and no result as of this writing.
>
> Connor's mother, Elaine Gibson, 41, told police it was

possible her son had run away from home. He regularly disappeared during full moons. Police are searching for his hideout based on footage from his viral video.

It remains a disquieting possibility that Connor was abducted by one or more anti-werewolf fanatics, after exposing his alleged transformation online.

More information to follow as it becomes available.

Poor, dumb kid, thought Jos. *They could be right about the fanatics. Or it could have been another werewolf—or several—angry at him for outing their kind. No crime scene, no evidence pointing either way.*

This reeked of a kidnapping, and likely a murder. Although Jos felt sorry for the boy, she wondered why he hadn't taken better measures to protect himself. He should have known there'd be backlash.

Was he trying *to get himself killed?*

She heard footsteps in the hall, poked her head out the door, and saw Melanie. "You hear that Caleb Connor is missing? By the way, I read your article. Well written as always."

Mel, who already looked too pale, blanched further and swayed.

"Whoa, you all right?" said Jos.

"Fine," Mel replied tightly. She closed her bedroom door and slipped into the bathroom. Seconds later, Jos could hear her retching over the toilet.

Jos frowned worriedly at the bathroom door before returning to her desk.

25

Escape

Chandra didn't get back to Melanie until Saturday—two days later. "Okay, here's the deal," Chandra said without preamble. "I want you to come to the Organization's safe house for the full moon. Sokoloff will be there, so he can keep an eye on you. You can also observe the trial."

Mel slunk to her room, looking around to make sure no one could hear her before she answered in a glum whisper: "He hasn't figured out what's wrong with me yet. Or at least he hasn't called."

"I'm sure he's doing his best," Chandra said briskly. "So, next week, you are to leave *on* the day of the full moon, Thursday, not a day early. If you show up on Wednesday, the safe house will be empty and cold—not to mention locked up."

"Okay," agreed Mel. She bit her lower lip and wondered what the place was like. "Dave will be there too?"

"Yes. I recommend meeting him somewhere and letting him take you the rest of the way. You two can work that out for yourselves. The important thing is that you, Melanie, are going to let Timmy follow you."

"What? Why should I—"

"Because I'm gonna deal with him, get him off your back. I'll give him a scare he won't forget. You won't be part of it. Just act like you don't know he's there, and then give me a call."

"You're . . . you're not going to hurt him, right?"

Smoothly, Chandra said, "Of course not."

Mel leaned back against the wall. Her hand slipped on the phone, her clenched fingers cramping. Everything that had been preying on her for the past two days shook loose. She felt like crying. She almost laughed. "Are you sure it'll work? He's obnoxiously persistent."

"It will. Trust me." The woman's confident tone never wavered.

Mel sighed and relaxed. "I do. Thank you."

"Anything for a fellow wolf."

〉 〉 ● 〈 〈

The following Wednesday evening, Mel paced her room. A maelstrom of doubts, worries, and fears howled beneath her calm exterior.

No word had come from Sokoloff, no diagnosis. Mel's condition had stabilized, and she hadn't had any more hallucinations, dry heaves, or fainting spells. How long would that last, though?

Worse, doubts about Chandra's plan were beginning to torment her. *What the heck is she going to do to Timmy? Better for everyone if he doesn't tail me. I should leave plenty early. Noon, maybe. Hopefully, he won't be ready to follow then. He wouldn't skip classes, would he?*

She rehashed her meet-up plan with Dave: a highway rest station at 3:00. The Organization's safe house was two hours away from Wellsboro. Moonrise was at 6:35. Plenty of time.

Unless something went wrong. Unless Dave didn't meet her. He'd said it was better that she didn't have the address to the safe house—better to have nothing written down—and she supposed he was right, but that didn't make her any less nervous.

Should I really go? She longed for the Doyles' comfortable cabin. For the known. The known-to-be-safe.

Was she truly safe anywhere?

Heart hammering, fingers and toes tingling, she sank down onto her bed. The threat of dizziness subsided but left nausea and fatigue in its wake. Even her own body wasn't safe anymore.

And her mental faculties. How much longer could she trust her eyes? Her ears? Would more hallucinations come? Right now her room looked its usual, normal self, so she was pretty sure what she was seeing and experiencing was real. But with her vivid dreams and general state of stress and confusion...ever since discovering werewolves existed, reality had been a lot more elusive.

She had to make this stop. She *had* to go to the Organization.

Whatever happens tomorrow, she thought, clenching her fists, *it's worth it.*

Owl City's "If My Heart Was a House" gently interrupted. Gavin.

She'd been dodging his calls and ignoring his texts for days.

Staring blankly at the phone, she didn't pick up. He'd leave another voicemail, pleading with her to come to the cabin.

Thoughts of him ripping up her note returned. She scowled. *He needs to get it through his head that he can't control me.*

Would he try to kidnap her again?

She definitely had to leave early tomorrow. *Noon it is.*

)) ● ((

FEBRUARY 9, FULL MOON (FIRST NIGHT)

The next morning after Mel showered and dressed, Gavin called again. (She'd changed his ringtone back to a generic one.) Gritting her teeth, she thought, *I'd better set things straight with him.*

"I'm not coming with you this time," she said in lieu of a hello.

There was an intake of breath, a pause, and then his voice, sounding angry and hurt: "Why? Where are you going to—"

"I think you know."

"Melanie, please. Don't do this. Don't go with them. It's too danger-ous."

Her fist balled at her side. "You don't know that for sure."

"But my—"

"Your vision, yeah, yeah." She threw herself onto her bed, kept her voice low. "But you know what *I've* come to see? You, clinging to your preconceived notions of things—and people. You need to stop and give them a chance to show you the way they really are."

With an exasperated growl, Gavin returned, "Well, I think *you* think you know everything—and you're blinded by what you want to believe. You trust too easily—except when it comes to me, apparently, the one person who's actually helped you. But no, you'd rather trust strangers than someone you know."

"I'm not sure I *do* know you," she spat. "You saved me once; that doesn't mean you own me. Besides, I paid you back at Cedarwood. My life is still *my* life. I can do whatever I want, and you had no right to destroy that note!"

There was a longer pause. Mel imagined him scowling, or the blood draining from his face. Then she heard a *thump*, and wondered what he'd punched or thrown.

Finally, voice deadly calm, Gavin said, "You're right. You don't know me. Because if you did, you'd understand I'm trying to protect you, not clip your wings. But I guess you can't see that because you're so focused on yourself and on what you want."

How dare you! Rage boiled, shooting upward from her midsection to flush her face. "You think I'm selfish, huh? Do you even know what it is that I want? I just want to fucking *stay alive!* Do you have any idea about the people who are out there, who want to hunt us down and mutilate us for sport?" Her throat tightened as she recalled the bloody images from online.

"I know about hunters. But the cabin is safe. Hidden. They can't get us there."

"Sure it is—for now. As far as we know. But things change, and until we're human again, there'll always be some risk."

"And what are the odds we'll ever find a cure? You know how long I searched for one."

"They have a geneticist."

"They don't know it's in our DNA, or anything that science can discover and fix. What if it *is* a literal curse?"

Melanie gripped the edge of her mattress and squeezed, hard.

Black ooze squeezing out of her chest.

No. Can't be. St. Peter was wrong about her being damned.

Steadying her breathing, she said, "Last I heard, he's making great progress. There could be a breakthrough any day now."

"Well, I hope you're right about that," Gavin sighed. "I hope you're right about them and their intentions. I do wish you well, Melanie. But I still think you're making a huge mistake."

"It's mine to make. My decision." *Not mistake.*

They hung up, and Mel hurried to finish getting ready for classes.

After her two morning classes, she zipped through the cafeteria line, slapping together a to-go meal: ham sandwich, apple, and bag of chips. She'd packed plenty of bottled water and snacks for her time at the Organization's hideout. Dave had told her there was a kitchen stocked with basic food, mostly canned, but her cautious and always-prepared side wasn't about to take any chances.

Hurrying back to Hartman, she kept a sharp lookout for Timmy. No sign of him or his old white Buick.

Mel scanned her room one more time, as she always did before full-moon trips, making sure she hadn't forgotten anything. Her bags were in her Honda's back seat already. The gas tank was full. She took deep, calming gulps of air. *Better get going. I can do this. It's going to be okay.* The pepper spray was in her coat pocket.

She was locking the door behind her when she heard footsteps creaking up the stairs. "Hey, Mel," said Jos, arriving on the landing. "Would you mind helping me with something really quick?"

"Like what?" Melanie tried to hide her chagrin but couldn't help checking her watch. It was a quarter past noon.

"Some fancy formatting for my psych paper. You're good at that, right? Shouldn't take long."

"Sure." Mel sighed inwardly and followed Jos into her room. *Why couldn't she look this up online?*

Jos brought up her paper and explained what she wanted done. Mel tweaked, finagled, and figured it out in five minutes.

"Thank you so much!" said Jocelyn. "You're the best."

"No prob," Mel said curtly, flashing a half smile. She rose to leave, but Jos slipped between her and the door and shut it. She leaned against it, arms crossed. "What are you doing?" Mel asked, narrowing her eyes.

"I know you're leaving again. And I know why."

Words failed Mel. The blood drained from her face, and the air seemed to crystallize into a block of ice around her. "What—? How—?"

Jos rolled up her sweater sleeve, exposing angry red lines on her forearm. "These are killing me again. Like they've been doing for the past two months around the full moon. When you disappear for a few days. . . . Also, I saw you packing your car this morning."

Blood rushed in Mel's ears; blackness edged her vision. She swayed and grabbed the nearest support, the footboard of Jos's bed.

"Whoa, you should sit down." Jos moved to help Melanie lower herself onto the bed. Numbly, Mel allowed her to do so and to sit next to her. "You've been looking so sick lately—I'm worried about you."

Not right now. Not right now. I don't need this right now. This can't be happening. Mel put her head in her hands and took steadying breaths.

"You . . . haven't told anyone my secret, have you?" she choked out.

The dizziness ebbed, but her heart still pounded.

"No."

"Not even Pam?" She couldn't look at Jocelyn. Her tear-filled eyes were riveted on her trembling hands.

"Nope, but I think you ought to tell her. She's going crazy, y'know? She's really hurt by the secrecy."

Mel did look up then, eyes flashing. "Don't you understand why it has to stay a secret?! Since the Caleb Connor video, everyone is so scared of—everyone hates—" She couldn't finish.

Jos nodded. They sat in silence. Eventually, she said, "It happened on the camping trip, didn't it? The beast in the cave—it bit you."

"Yes." A faint whisper, almost inaudible.

Though Jocelyn wasn't a touchy-feely person, she rubbed Melanie's back and said, "I'm so sorry, Mel. I can't imagine what you must be going through." Her green eyes crinkled with compassion.

Melanie felt walls crumble inside her. For so long, she'd been erecting an elaborate structure around her heart—a castle complete with palisade and moat. It had been meant to protect her . . . but it had also been keeping out the protection of her friends.

You don't hate me? You're not terrified? A tear spilled down Mel's cheek. Her body shook with sobs that she tried desperately to restrain.

"Honey, you need to let that out," said Jos. Her hands moved in soothing circles, fingers massaging Melanie's shoulders. "We all need to ugly-cry sometimes. You'll feel a lot better."

Sniffling, swiping at her face, Mel said, "I don't have time for this. I gotta go."

"The moon doesn't rise for hours," said Jos. "Where do you go during full moons, anyway?"

"A cabin, a couple hours away from here." Mel wasn't about to mention the Organization or her change of plans this month. And she didn't feel like bringing up Timmy either.

Jos raised her eyebrows. "How'd you find a place like that?"

Should I explain about Gavin? It's his secret to tell, not mine . . . but I have to tell her something. With a sigh, Mel started at the beginning: her conversation with Gavin at the volleyball game, his weird "seizure" that turned out to be a vision of the future, how he'd cut her with the knife to show her she wasn't exactly human anymore, then resorted to kidnapping her because she didn't believe him.

Her suitemate's eyes grew wider as the story progressed. When Mel was finished, Jocelyn said, "Holy cow.... Gavin is a clairvoyant? And he saved you ... saved us from you." She blanched. "And werewolves exist. This is all ... insane."

"Tell me about it," Melanie muttered. "Do you actually believe what I just told you, or are you about to call the local loony bin and have them come get me?"

"I believe you," said Jos, quietly. "Caleb Connor's video was pretty darn convincing. I did my own research on it."

Mel gave a low growl. "I hate that kid."

"I bet. And I can't believe you had to write that article."

"It was the worst." Mel rubbed her forehead. Another headache was building between her eyes.

She became aware of her watch ticking; one o'clock was fast approaching. "Crap! I really gotta go, Jos." Carefully, Mel stood up and pulled her coat and gloves back on.

Jocelyn watched sadly as she hurried from the room.

Exiting Hartman Cottage, Mel threw furtive glances all around. No Timmy. No white Buick. Just snow and trees and empty cars in the parking lot. No one came out of the nearby dorms. She darted to her Honda and climbed in, wanting to gun it and peel off campus—but of course that would attract attention. Not to mention she'd probably slide on ice. She thought of her accident and shuddered.

Mel drove at a leisurely pace around the edge of campus, avoiding Timmy's dorm and the student center. Every time she spotted a white car, she flinched. A white Buick was parked outside the library. Was it Timmy's? She couldn't remember his license plate number. *That patch of rust in the wheel well—his car has that, doesn't it?* Her pulse quickened.

She sped up, checking her rearview mirror every few seconds. No sign of Timmy emerging from the library. Mel passed half a dozen more buildings before the final stretch to the guard shack. *Please don't let Luis be on duty.* A random guy was, and he didn't even look up from his book.

As she drove into town (still no white Buick following), relief crept up like heat from her vent. Maybe Timmy had no intention of taking things this far. He might only be messing with her via email. He was probably too scared to try following her. *Ha—chicken. All talk and no action.*

Wellsboro dwindled behind her, and she broke out into open, snow-dusted fields. The highway was clear, well salted, and traffic was light. Her tires hummed on the pavement, the ease of the car's movement bringing a sense of freedom. She'd escaped!

She reached the rest stop at half past one. An hour and a half remained until Dave showed up. *Hope he's early.* Mel parked behind the brick building that held restrooms and vending machines. She ate her lunch, half-listening to the radio and reflecting on her confrontation with Jos.

She doesn't seem to be treating me any differently. In fact, she was nicer than usual. I've never seen her give anyone a backrub before— that's a Pam thing.

A tiny spark of hope. Maybe she could tell her friends ... maybe Pam ...

... would try to come along and end up getting hurt.

Or blurt out her secret in the library someday.

It's one thing to be caught. It's another to give yourself up. Her lips twisted wryly. *What am I, a criminal?*

At least criminals got trials. That was more than the hunters would give her.

Two o'clock rolled around, and she ventured inside the rest station to take advantage of both its commodities. She studied the items in the vending machines, then bought a couple of energy drinks.

In the car again, Melanie leaned her seat back and closed her eyes. She didn't know if she could or should sleep here, but she might as well get a modicum of rest. It would be an incredibly restless night—the next three of them.

At 2:55, a knock on her window startled her awake. Dave grinned down at her, his red hair bright against the gray sky. "Hey there, sleepyhead."

Blushing, Mel raised her seat and stepped out of the car. "Hi."

"Can I help you with your stuff?"

"Thanks." She opened the rear door and he transferred her bags to the back seat of his shiny black SUV.

"Nice ride," she said, smiling as he opened the front passenger door for her.

"Just got the transmission replaced," Dave said ruefully. "Cost a pretty penny."

Mel gave a sympathy groan. "Car repairs suck."

They buckled up, and Dave pulled the SUV out. Though they didn't hit any potholes, Mel's stomach did flips when she thought about what she was getting herself into.

)) ● ((

TWO HOURS EARLIER, 1:00 P.M.

Gavin punched his steering wheel. "Come *on*, you stupid train!" Could the damn thing possibly move any more slowly? He had to get to Wellsboro before Melanie left. He had one last shot at convincing her. Maybe in person, he'd be more persuasive.

Or maybe he could kidnap her again.

The train's low, drawn-out whistle sounded as languid as its pace. "Hurry up, hurry up, hurry up!" Why did this have to happen, today of all days?! His hands trembled, itching to grab something and beat the crap out of it. Slam doors, throw fine china at walls . . . wrap iron fingers around that mad doctor's throat and squeeze.

Get back. It's not your time yet, he warned the wolf, slowing his breathing and regaining control.

What felt like an hour later, but was only two minutes by his dashboard clock, the train's final car chugged past, and the safety gate lifted. Gavin leaned on his horn to spur the car in front of him to action.

At ten after one, he arrived at the parking lot outside Hartman Cottage . . . only to find Mel's car already gone.

"Shit." Gavin slammed his foot on the brake. "Shit, shit, shit, shit, shit, shit, *shit.*"

He should have left earlier. Called her again. Begged her to listen to reason.

"Shi—" he began, his voice snapping off midway with something like a sob. He tried to lift his phone, to call her, but it dropped from his fingers. She wouldn't listen to him anyway.

He pressed his forehead to the wheel.

What do those people want with her? What are they doing to her?

What about the sickness? What about—

Does she really hate me?

Will I ever see her again?

Knuckles tapped his window, and he straightened abruptly. A girl with curly black hair and Goth-style makeup was staring at him. *Isn't that...Jocelyn?*

Cranking down his window, he said, "You're Melanie's friend, right?"

"Yeah, Jocelyn Beaumont. You're Gavin."

He nodded. "Did you see her leave? How long ago? Do you know which way she went?"

"You just missed her. I thought she was with you." Jocelyn's green eyes were alight with concern.

Wait a minute. How does she know...? What does she know?

Jocelyn put her hands on her hips, and her forehead creased into a deep frown. "Was she lying to me?" she murmured. The wind howled, and the girl shivered. "You'd better come inside," she told Gavin. "I think we both have a lot of questions for each other."

)) ● ((

3:05 P.M.

Mel enjoyed the feel and smell of her heated leather seat. The SUV's interior was clean and carried another aroma—cool and spicy—that she guessed was Dave's aftershave. It failed to disguise the scent of burgeoning wolf, but at least it mingled well with that and the new-leather smell.

"So, where's the safe house?" she couldn't help but ask after a mile of silence.

"It's in the middle of some state game lands," Dave replied.

Mel blinked. "Is that legal?"

"It's legally owned by one of our members."

"Oh." She propped herself sideways, the better to talk with him. "I didn't realize you could live in a place like that."

"It's not actually on the game lands themselves; it's surrounded by them, though, on three sides."

"So it's pretty isolated?"

"Yes. Perfect for us." He grinned briefly at her before returning his attention to the road. "I think you'll like it. It's a big old farmhouse, inherited from this guy's uncle or something, which we fixed up and expanded. It has eight safe rooms."

"Wow." Mel pictured a two-story structure with an expansive front porch, rocking chairs, rooster-shaped weather vane, and maybe a barn or silo behind the house. "Are there any animals left?"

"No, sorry—no pretty horses running in the fields." Dave grinned again.

"Aww." Mel's disappointment wasn't feigned; she would have loved the comfort of the gentle creatures. But she realized it was silly to think the Organization kept animals. Chandra had said the place had been empty yesterday—no one must live there permanently. It was only a monthly hideout.

Fields and forest flew by. The light snowfall had stopped, strong winds taking its place. "Mind if I turn on the radio?" asked Dave.

"Go ahead."

Dave flipped through stations until he found a country one. Mel didn't recognize the song—not her genre of choice. But she soon found her head bobbing to the music.

4:40 P.M.

An hour and a half later, Dave turned them off the freeway and onto smaller side roads. They rounded a peninsula of forest that Mel figured was state game land. Unforested land made its own peninsula jutting into the wooded area, which stretched as far as Mel could see.

The road narrowed and turned to dirt. They bumped along, passing no other vehicles. A farmhouse appeared, but they sped on by. Half a mile later, another house and barn. They didn't stop. "We do have a few neighbors," Dave said. "Not too close, and half of these houses are empty."

"The economy," Mel guessed.

"You are correct!" said Dave in his best game-show-host voice. "Tell her what she's won, Johnny!"

Mel giggled.

At last, a large gray structure came into view. As they drew closer and slowed, Melanie's expression clouded: The building was dilapidated. *This can't be—*

"Home sweet monthly hideout," said Dave. He gave her a cheerful wink. "Ain't she a beauty?"

Mel didn't grin or laugh this time; her thoughts and heart raced. *Is this some kind of a joke? It looks like a strong wind would blow it right over.* Most of the house's paint had flaked off, its rusty shutters hung askew, and half of its wraparound porch had rotted and collapsed. All of its windows were boarded up. A great many shingles were missing from the roof, making it look gap-toothed.

Grimacing, she thought, *It looks awful and creepy.*

Was this really the place they used every month?

)) ● ((

EARLIER, 3:05 P.M.

As the shiny black SUV exited the rest station's parking lot, a white Buick started its engine. It was tucked out of sight between a Ford F650 and a full-sized Transit van. It pulled out of its spot to follow a good two hundred yards behind the SUV, but had to slam on the brakes halfway down the aisle. A cobalt-blue Mazda Miata had jerked out of its space, and the two vehicles had nearly t-boned.

"Hey! Watch where you're going, prick!" yelled Timmy. He raised a middle finger and leaned on his horn. The Miata stayed put, blocking him while Melanie and her red-haired companion sped away. "No!" Timmy growled. "Come *on*! Move it, asshole!" *Beeeeeeep!*

The Mazda's windows were tinted, but the door opened, and out stepped . . .

A goddess in a white parka. Lustrous jet-black hair, smooth tan skin, large dark eyes, long shapely legs. Timmy's anger melted, and his jaw hung slack as she approached. In a trance, he rolled down his window.

"I'm so sorry!" said the woman through full, pouty lips. "I didn't see you, and my battery just died. Do you think you could give me a jumpstart?"

)) ● ((

EARLIER, 1:15 P.M.

Gavin stepped into Jocelyn's bedroom feeling incredibly awkward. He'd never even been in Melanie's room, and here he was right next-door to it but with an unfamiliar girl who seemed to know more about him than he wanted her to. "So, why did you think Melanie would be with me?" he hedged, taking in the half-Gothic, half-girly room. It reeked of patchouli and a light, floral fragrance.

Jocelyn shut the door and then fixed him with a piercing gaze. "I know her secret—your secret. You're werewolves."

Gavin's brow furrowed. *How'd she find out? The Caleb Connor video? Is she going to tell anyone? Has she already?* A million other questions churned beneath the surface, stirring up deep fears. But his voice was surprisingly steady when he finally said, "Did you figure out her disappearances were always at full moons?"

"Yeah, among other evidence."

"How long ago . . . ?"

"Pretty recently," she admitted. "I confronted Mel today, before she left, and she told me about your family's cabin—only because I was worried about whether she had a safe place to go. I wasn't fishing for all the juicy details."

"I see." He frowned, crossed his arms, and looked away.

"You don't seem too happy that I know," said Jos. "Don't worry—I haven't told anyone, and I won't. I swear. I'm not one of those crazy bigots who've cropped up everywhere since the Caleb Connor video."

"Glad to hear it."

"It must be hard for you to trust people. You can trust me. I'd never betray Mel or anyone she cared about."

Gavin nodded reluctantly, but he did feel reassured. Jocelyn's expression was open and sincere. He smelled confidence coming from her, not the fear or adrenaline that would indicate she was lying.

"So if Mel's supposed to be with you, but she's not, then where did she go? Why would she ditch you and that lovely cabin of yours? I don't mean to pry, but did you guys have a fight?"

Toe scuffing the carpet, Gavin said, "Yeah." Jos waited calmly while he decided how much to share. "We met some people—some other werewolves—and they're trying to get us to join up with them. We both didn't want to at first, but now Mel does. I never will. They've done some . . . untrustworthy things."

Jocelyn paled. "She must have gone to them, then."

"Looks like it."

"Do you know where they are?"

"No. Well, I do know of one place, but it's not a safe house. They wouldn't be there now."

Running a hand through her curls, Jos groaned. "Oh, Mel. What have you gotten yourself into?"

Nothing good! Gavin scowled, clenched his fists, and fought the urge to pace. The wolf prowled at the back of his mind, telling him to lash out at the wall, kick the bed. *I can't believe I just missed her! If I hadn't hit those red lights—if I hadn't had to wait for that stupid train—*

Guilt surged through him. *I should never have ripped up that note.*

"Hey," Jocelyn interrupted, "Mel told me you're, like, a psychic or something."

He gave her a sharp look. "More juicy details?"

She blushed. "It came up because she explained how you knew she was a werewolf. At the volleyball game."

"Ah."

"Anyway, how does that work? Can you see anything in the future, whenever you want to?"

"I wish. No, it happens randomly—I have no control. It almost always involves eye contact. I see what's going to happen to a person in their eyes."

Stepping close, Jocelyn put her green eyes, heavily outlined in black, inches away from his. "How about in mine?"

Gavin flinched, and not only at the intimacy—she'd eaten garlic with lunch. He held his breath and forced himself to meet her earnest gaze. Long, uncomfortable seconds passed. "Sorry, nothing."

She sighed and retreated from his personal space. "Worth a try." Absently, she rubbed her arm, and a flash of pain crossed her face.

Melanie scratched her, Gavin remembered. "How's that wound? Can I see it?"

Jos rolled up her sleeve, and his eyes widened. The scratch marks were red and inflamed, as if they were only hours old. "That's the kind of damage our claws can inflict?" He gave a low whistle. "I'm so sorry. I hope that will go away with time."

Shrugging, Jocelyn pulled her sleeve back down. "It only lasts for a few days. Aspirin takes the edge off."

She's putting on a brave face. Gavin bit his lip.

Still almost five hours till the moon would rise. He only needed two and a half to get to the cabin. There was time to search for Melanie . . .

If only he knew where.

26

Pivot Point

Timmy's mouth moved, and strange sounds came out. The goddess waited patiently, lips gently upturned, slightly parted. Damn, that was distracting. "Oh, uh, yeah, I, sure...." What was he supposed to be doing?

Right—helping her jumpstart her car.

Timmy rolled his window up, and she stepped back to let him exit his car. Peeved though he was that Melanie had gotten away, Timmy couldn't resent his circumstances too much. *There's always next month.*

The two cars' hoods were close enough to each other that his jumper cables reached. As he connected them and instructed the goddess, he thought of the mysterious note that had led him to this place.

It was typed, anonymous, and succinct: "Rest station Rte 6 eastbound just past Mainesburg. 3 p.m. Melanie will be there." He'd found it in his mailbox this morning.

Who had sent it? Why? How did they know he knew about her, and that he'd been planning to follow her?

The red-haired guy who'd come to pick up Melanie was a possibility. But he must be an ally of hers; she obviously trusted him. Was he a werewolf too?

Jumper cables in place, Timmy started his engine back up and let the Buick idle, pumping power into the goddess's Miata. He leaned back in his seat and crossed his arms. While waiting, he sneaked glances at the goddess, who sat behind her own wheel. His thoughts wandered to all kinds of lustful places.

Ten minutes later, he turned his car off and unplugged the cables.

"Try starting it," he told the goddess.

Nothing. Still dead.

Patiently, he reconnected the cables. More time spent in the company of this real-life Aphrodite was nothing to complain about.

)) ● ((

As Gavin fretted over how to track down Melanie, Jocelyn paced the length of her bed. "Too bad Pam's not here," she muttered. "Then we could get into Mel's room and do some digging."

Gavin raised an eyebrow. "You'd go through Mel's stuff?"

"Desperate times call for desperate measures."

"True." If it would help rescue Melanie from those monsters, he'd violate her privacy. He could deal with *that* added guilt after all this was over.

Jos checked her watch. "In fifteen minutes, Pam will be between classes. I'll get her to let us in."

"But she doesn't know Mel's secret. What are you going to tell her?"

"That I'm worried because Mel has disappeared again. Pam and I have, um, already done a bit of snooping," Jos admitted.

This girl was full of surprises.

Taking a seat, Gavin braced himself for a long, awkward wait. The room was warm, bordering on stuffy, and the patchouli made his nose itch. To his relief, Jocelyn stopped pacing. She sank onto her bed, then asked, "Are you sure looking into someone's eyes is the only way you get visions? Have you ever tried other senses, like smell or touch? Maybe when we get into Mel's room, you can sniff some of her clothes or something."

Gavin chuckled, almost offended but understanding her good intentions. "I'm not a were-bloodhound."

Jos blushed. "Sorry. I know. Just hoping . . ."

"Yeah, 's okay."

Jocelyn rubbed her sore arm but stopped abruptly, her eyes taking on an inquisitive gleam. "Do you guys have, um, special connections to the wolf that bit you?"

"What do you mean?"

"I guess, like, a psychic link? If you're a werewolf, that means you were bitten, right? Not born one?"

"Yeah."

"So, the wolf that bit you. Do you ever know things about them when they're not around? Can you feel them, sense where they are?"

"No—I don't even know *who* they are."

"Oh." Her face fell. Rolling up her sleeve, she said, "Can you try anyway?" She stuck out her arm. "Maybe you can connect with Melanie through these."

Gavin felt pretty silly, but he put his hand on the four hot, puffy scratch marks. Jocelyn winced, then relaxed after a few moments. "Hey," she said, "how are you doing that? You took away some of the pain."

"Really?" He lifted surprised eyes to hers. She nodded, and he saw that some of the tension had indeed gone from her shoulders. Gavin kept his hand on her arm and thought healing thoughts: aloe, ice packs, his mother's tender hugs.

"That is amazing!" said Jos, closing her eyes and grinning like a cat that's just been rubbed in exactly the right spot. "I need to keep you around. . . . Are you getting anything on Mel?"

Oops—focus. "Nope." He shifted his attention back to Melanie, conjuring up images of her lovely smile, shiny hair, the light sprinkling of freckles across the bridge of her nose.

But he couldn't make any kind of connection, couldn't sense her feelings or thoughts or whereabouts.

"It's not working," he told Jos, releasing her arm. They both sighed, disappointed, and went back to waiting.

When the hour struck, Jocelyn dialed Pam, but the phone rang and rang unanswered. "That's weird. She always checks her phone between classes."

"What class did she just have?"

"Choir, I think."

"Let's go to the music building and look for her," Gavin said, standing and striding to the door. He couldn't sit around here any longer; he needed *action.*

Jocelyn grabbed her coat and followed him. "All right, I'll take you there. You drive."

)) ● ((

Finally, *finally* the Miata's engine gave a beautiful, throaty purr. Timmy pumped a fist. "Yess!"

The goddess's face lit up with the most breathtaking smile he'd ever seen. She cut the engine, climbed out of her car, and approached him. "Thank you *so* much, and I am *incredibly* sorry, again, for almost hitting you."

"Ah, forget about it," Timmy said magnanimously, puffing out his chest. He felt a foot taller (although he had to look slightly up to make eye contact).

"I feel like I should do something to repay you." Her dark eyes sparkled.

Knees going weak, Timmy found himself struggling with the English language once more. "Uh, you don't—not necess—unless you—"

"It's early for dinner," she said, "but I skipped lunch and I'm starved. How about I treat you? There's a steakhouse down the road. Unless you're in a hurry and need to get going. I'm sorry, I hope I'm not keeping you from anything important."

"N-no, not important."

"Come on then," she said, reaching out and putting a hand on his arm.

Even through his heavy winter jacket, Timmy felt a tingle of electricity. He imagined how soft her skin was, how it would feel on his skin. More tingles, lower. He had to be careful not to get too excited.

"Okay," he said, swallowing and trying desperately to rein in his thoughts. He wanted to pinch himself. *This can't be real. This has to be a dream.*

If it was, he wanted to never wake up.

⟩ ⟩ ● ⟨ ⟨

There was no sign of Pam anywhere in the music building. Gavin and Jos found the choir director unlocking the door to his office. "Pam missed class," he told them.

They looked at each other in chagrin. "Now what?" said Gavin, his wolf clawing at the cage of his patience. *Tick-tock. The moon rises in four-and-a-half hours. You can't stay here past four o'clock.*

Jos tried Pam's phone again, with no luck. "Of all the times for *her* to disappear too!"

Clenching his teeth, Gavin marched out of the building and back to his car. Jos trailed behind, face downcast but pensive. As they drove back to Hartman, she said, "Pam might be with Aaron, her boyfriend. I don't have his number, though."

"Any chance we could still get into Mel's room somehow?"

"No spare keys. I don't know how to pick a lock. The RD wouldn't let me in no matter what story I came up with—she's super strict."

Hmm, picking the lock.

Not a bad idea.

)) ● ((

4:45 P.M., DILAPIDATED FARMHOUSE

The black SUV crunched up the long gravel driveway and parked behind the ramshackle former farmhouse. A car and a truck were there too, and Mel wondered who else was here. *Be nice if it was Janae.* Some other friendly company would be heartening, since this place didn't look like it'd offer much comfort.

"Aren't you coming?" asked Dave. He'd climbed out of the SUV first, opened the back driver-side door, and grabbed his overnight bag as well as hers.

Melanie undid her seatbelt and exited the vehicle. She stood staring up at the building through gathering dusk. The rear wasn't quite as rundown as the front. The paint was flaking about as badly, but the back steps weren't broken like the ones leading up to the front porch. Light shone through cracks in the boarded-up windows. "What's with this place?" said Mel, trying not to sound like she was complaining. Could its flimsy-looking walls withstand the onslaught of a pack of werewolves?

And what other creatures might be living here? Rats? Snakes? Brown recluse spiders? She shuddered. *It looks like the kind of place where a serial killer would stash the bodies.*

Before Dave could answer Mel's spoken question, the back door opened and Sheila stepped out. "Hey, it's Melanie. Are you a guinea pig now, too?"

"No, she's just here to hang out and keep *you* in line," Dave teased.

Sheila made a rude gesture but smirked. "Quit rustlin' my jimmies, Gingersnap. Both of ya, get on in here. I'm about to start cookin', and the others can't be bothered to help." She beckoned impatiently and vanished back inside.

Trudging behind Dave to the house, Melanie felt some of the tension melt from her muscles. Dave and Sheila's banter had brought back memories of the meeting at McCullough's. *These people are allies.*

Absolute shock rushed over her as she entered the house. She'd stepped into a large kitchen—modern, renovated, outfitted with newer appliances. Almost as nice as the Doyles'. Completely un-dilapidated.

Sheila, who stood by the sink, chuckled. "Pick your jaw up off the floor, girl."

Mel couldn't help staring around at the stainless steel, granite countertops, and sizeable island. "It's so—different from—"

Dave joined in the laughter. "Yeah, sorry about not telling before we got here. It's always fun to see people's reactions."

You jerk—scaring the crap out of me for no good reason! Mel wanted to slap him, but relief and exhaustion doused the fire of her anger. Forcing a smile, she said, "Great joke. But why'd you guys fix up the inside and not the outside?"

"It keeps away curious parties. Even though we're out here in the middle of nowhere, can't be too safe."

Oh. That made sense. "Are the rest of the rooms this nice?"

"Basically—though I wouldn't call the safe rooms 'nice' exactly. Come on, I'll give you the official tour."

"Hurry up so you can come back and help me," Sheila called after them.

"What do you need help with?" said Dave. "Just keep an eye on the Spaghetti-Os and make sure to stir them every once in a while."

"It's mac and cheese tonight, Fangface!"

"Well, make sure *that* doesn't stick to the pan then!"

)) ● ((

EARLIER, 2:55 P.M., HARTMAN COTTAGE

Gavin was on the verge of giving up. He'd failed to pick the lock, Jocelyn couldn't get ahold of Pam, and time was slipping through their fingers. They left Hartman briefly to track down Aaron and found him returning to his dorm.

"I haven't seen or talked to Pam since breakfast. This isn't like her,"

Aaron said with a worried frown. "If you hear from her, please tell her to call me too."

Back in Hartman, Gavin paced Jocelyn's room while Jos sat at her desk, chewing her lip and twirling a long, curly lock of hair around her finger. "Come on, come on, think," she muttered.

It was all Gavin could do not to claw at the walls in frustration. *Careful not to let your claws out—poor Jos doesn't need any more of that.* He was sure his eyes were glowing bright yellow under his contacts. His hands shook slightly. He clenched and unclenched them, trying to relax the rigid muscles.

The clock struck the hour, and Jos's phone rang—startling both her and Gavin.

"Ohmigod, it's Pam!" Jos quickly answered: "Where the heck are you, girl?"

Gavin leaned in to hear, and Jos put Pam on speakerphone. "...Melanie's car."

What?!

"Come again?" said Jocelyn. "It sounded like you said you were in Mel's car."

"I am. I could tell she was about to leave, so I sneaked along. I was able to get into her trunk because it doesn't always latch all the way." They heard a groan and some shuffling. "Man, I am really stiff and sore. Just climbed into the back seat."

Gavin and Jos met each other's eyes; both sets were wide open in shock. "Okay..." said Jos after a moment, gathering her composure. "Where is Mel's car? Is she there? Did she find you?"

"No, she's gone. She parked at a rest stop somewhere and just waited around for *forever.* Then, a minute ago, she got into someone else's car and left. I heard a male voice. No one I recognized."

Heart skipping a beat, Gavin thought, *She's off with some guy? Who? The doctor? The man in dark sunglasses?* "Did this guy have an accent?" he asked.

"Who's that?" said Pam.

"Gavin Doyle. Melanie's friend."

"Oh. What are you doing with Jocelyn?" She didn't sound accusatory, just curious.

"Long story—I'll tell you later. What did the voice sound like?" he pressed.

"Um, I don't know. He didn't have an accent, sounded pretty young."

Not the doctor, then.

"So Mel's off with Mr. Mysterioso," said Jos, "and you're stuck at a rest stop in her car without the keys."

"That's the long and short of it." Pam sighed. "I'm gonna go inside and look at a map. Can you come get me?"

"Of course."

Over the line, Gavin and Jos heard a car door open and shut, then wind howling and Pam's footsteps echoing on cement. The sound of wind cut off, and Pam said, "Let me see . . . 'You are here.' . . . Okay, I'm just past Mainesburg. Route six eastbound."

"We're on our way," said Jos. Throwing on their coats, she and Gavin headed down to his car.

3:30 P.M., THE REST STATION

The drive took only half an hour. The rest stop was a simple, round brick building—no frills like a restaurant or gift shop. Gavin spotted Mel's Honda and parked next to it. Pam hopped out of the driver's seat, relief evident on her face, and locked up behind herself. Climbing into the Ford, she immediately asked, "Do you guys know something about Melanie that I don't?"

Gavin and Jocelyn glanced at each other. Jos raised a questioning eyebrow, and he took the initiative. "Melanie is dealing with some pretty serious issues," he began slowly.

"No duh! Is she okay? Why does she keep disappearing, where does she go, and why won't anyone tell me anything?" Pam's voice rose in pitch, bordering on a whine.

Jocelyn swiveled to better face her friend over the back of her seat. "Pam, I only just learned what's going on with Mel, and I promised her I wouldn't tell anyone. I urged her to tell you, though. She knows it's hurting you, but she's afraid."

"Afraid of *what*?"

Jos bit her lip and didn't answer.

Frustrated tears sprang into Pam's eyes. She glared at Gavin. "All this started after she met you—what do you have to do with it?"

Frowning, he said, "It's not *because* of me . . . but you're right: I am involved."

"Can you *please* stop being so cryptic?!"

Gavin let out a long sigh. He glanced at the dashboard clock. Time was running out—he needed to get these girls back to Wellsboro and high-tail it to the cabin. In his desperation to find Melanie, he'd put himself in a potentially dangerous situation—dangerous for Mel's friends and anyone else who might be around him when the moon rose. *Dammit!* He didn't want to give up and leave Mel, but what choice did he have?

"Buckle up," he told Pam. "I'm taking you guys back. There's nothing else we can do."

She grumbled but obeyed.

As Gavin backed out of his parking spot, his eyes met Pam's in the rearview mirror. His body went rigid, and his foot instinctively jammed on the brake as he was sucked into a vision.

)) ● ((

4:55 P.M., THE FARMHOUSE

Melanie followed Dave through a dining room with a long table and eight chairs, then into a spacious but cozy living room. Forest colors dominated: tan, green, and gray. The room featured a pair of brown leather couches, several matching armchairs, and an electric fireplace. *Of course,* Mel thought. *No smoke coming out of the chimney.*

"Three of the safe rooms and a bathroom are down here, at the back of the house," said Dave, pointing down a short hallway. He led her to a staircase, which they ascended—Mel slowly, cursing gravity. Her exhausted body protested every step.

Voices and footsteps echoed above them. One was Sokoloff's: "There you are. In the morning, I will draw more blood."

Reaching the top of the stairs behind Dave, Mel found herself in a hallway with half a dozen doors, three on each side. "Five more safe rooms up here," said Dave, "and another bathroom."

Dr. Sokoloff emerged from one of the rooms, followed by a middle-aged man with graying light-brown hair. The stranger's sleeve was rolled up, a Band-Aid stuck on the inside of his elbow.

Mel's eyes riveted on the man. Something deep inside her squirmed, and she had no idea why. He didn't look threatening. His face was lined and careworn . . . and somehow familiar.

"Ah, Melanie," said Sokoloff. "How are you feeling?"

She shrugged grudgingly. "Like crap."

"Worse than usual for just before the full moon?"

"Yeah."

He frowned. "I am sorry I have not been able to make a diagnosis yet. Rest assured, I am working hard on that."

She nodded glumly.

Dave stepped toward the stranger and shook his hand. "Good to see you again, Nick." He turned to Mel. "You two haven't met yet, have you? Melanie Caldwell, this is Nicholas Erickson, another new member."

Erickson inclined his head, and Mel said a polite "hello," offering her hand. He hesitated before shaking it. As they touched, a jolt ran up her arm. Mel tried not to let her surprise show on her face. *What the heck was that?* Erickson let go with a confused, wary look. *Did he feel it too?*

Dave didn't seem to notice. He took Melanie to the room she'd be using. It was windowless and bare except for the typical gouges in the floor and walls. There was also a high cupboard, which she could reach on tiptoe, for her bags. Mel was glad she didn't have to leave her belongings in the hall. On the way out, she checked the locks on the door. Four deadbolts. The place appeared able to contain a vicious werewolf.

"It's soundproof," Dave told her, to her further reassurance.

From the hallway, they heard a door opening and closing downstairs. A pair of new voices, one male and one female, greeted Sheila. The savory aroma of macaroni and cheese drifted upstairs, mingling with the reek of the almost-a-dozen different wolves who'd been using the place.

It was 5:15.

As they descended to the first floor, a wave of nausea sloshed over Mel. She gripped the railing and paused, letting the queasiness recede. It returned when she got down to the living room, though. She staggered to a chair, dizziness adding to her discomfort.

"Are you okay?" Dave knelt beside her, looking concerned.

"Not really," she said through clenched teeth. She closed her eyes and slumped further into the soft leather armchair.

Footsteps came into the room. "Hi, Melanie," said a woman's voice Mel vaguely recognized. Opening her eyes, she saw Vanessa and Brad, backpacks slung over their shoulders. "You all right?"

"She's a bit under the weather," Dave answered, "but the doc and I are keeping an eye on her. She'll be fine."

Vanessa patted Mel's hand and smiled at her on her way upstairs with Brad. Mel mustered a weak smile in return.

Five minutes later, the pair was back downstairs and another member of the Organization had arrived—the man with dreadlocks, whose name turned out to be Lester ("Call me Les"). Melanie forced herself to get up and join the others around the dining table. The room was noisy, crowded, pungent, and hot. She wished she could open a window, but they were all boarded up. Stomach churning, she squeezed in a corner next to Vanessa. Never before had Mel felt this awkward and overwhelmed. So many names and faces to remember. And she hated small talk.

Sheila grumpily served the mac and cheese ("Thanks for the help, guys") along with green beans as limp and stringy as their cook's hair. Mel's appetite had vanished, but she forced some food down. The beans were over-salted and the macaroni on the hard side.

When she was done, she helped Sheila load the dishwasher and then retreated to her room.

)) ● ((

EARLIER, 3:40 P.M., THE REST STATION

Images flashed through Gavin's brain:

A dilapidated farmhouse. A cluster of vehicles parked behind it, including a black SUV. The sun sinking below the canopy of the forest that bordered the property. Where is this place?

The scene shifted: He was driving down the highway, the sun behind him, almost completely below the horizon now. He watched the mile markers and made note of the exit where he turned off. The road narrowed and became rougher. It rounded a peninsula of forest, then bisected a strip of land delving deep into a vast, shadowy woodland.

Does this road lead to Melanie?

It led to the farmhouse. As he navigated its bumpy driveway through deep dusk, his headlights revealed a half-collapsed porch, flaking paint, and loose shutters. The windows were boarded up. All was quiet.

Was anyone really here? Why would any werewolf use a place like this as a hideout? Sure, the remote location was great, but this building couldn't be safe.

Gavin jerked back to the present, where Jocelyn was staring at him from the front passenger seat. "Hey," said Pam, "what's wrong? Why'd you stop?"

He was still reeling, trying to make sense of the vision. "Um . . ."

"You saw something, didn't you?" asked Jos, almost inaudibly.

"I thought—no, it's nothing." *Nothing you guys need to know.* Gavin took his foot off the brake and drove the girls back to their campus in record time, reaching Hartman at 4:00.

Pam lingered in the car.

"I need to go," he told her urgently. "I'm sorry about not answering your questions, but there's no time for that anymore. I have to be somewhere, and I'm running out of time."

"Come on, girl," said Jocelyn, who'd rounded the car and opened Pam's door. She tugged her friend out, thanked Gavin, and said good-bye.

This was the pivot point, the absolute last moment of decision. He could leave Wellsboro right now and reach his cabin with minutes to spare before the moon rose . . . or he could follow his vision to the dilapidated farmhouse.

It's a huge risk. Don't take it. What if he didn't reach the farmhouse by moonrise?

The vision had shown him arriving human, though. He thought his dashboard clock had read 6:30—cutting it super close there, too.

The guard shack loomed ahead. Gavin passed through the gate and hesitated at the T-junction. Turning left would take him to the cabin, to safety—but he'd be abandoning Melanie. Turning right would take him to her (he was pretty sure) but was a terrifying gamble.

Images of Melanie's smiling face arose in his mind. Then a shadow passed over her, erasing the mirth. Her eyes turned inward, filled with pain. She looked so lonely and vulnerable.

Gavin gritted his teeth, squeezed the steering wheel until he dented it. *She's in trouble. She needs me.* He would never forgive himself if he didn't try to rescue her.

He turned right.

27

Change of Face

The goddess led Timmy two exits down the highway to an unfamiliar town. They drove past several vacant or rundown buildings, and he wrinkled his nose. *The place we're going had better be a lot nicer than this.*

At last, they arrived at Sal's Steakhouse. It stood alone on the town's outskirts, a quarter mile from any other building. Its paint was fresh, landscaping well maintained, pavement free of potholes—but there were no other cars there, and the windows were dark. The front door sign read "Closed."

As they walked together to the employee door, Timmy asked, "Why are we going in this way?"

"My cousin owns this place," she said with a smile. "It doesn't open till five, but I know he'll make an exception for us—I'm his favorite."

I can understand why.

The goddess knocked. Moments later, a stocky man with a receding hairline opened the door. "Cousin!" he greeted her, and they embraced warmly. "Another special guest?" He eyed Timmy, who glanced back and forth between the pair.

They look absolutely nothing alike. The man had light olive skin and Italian features, while the goddess was much darker and probably Indian.

"Yes, this is . . . oh, silly me, I didn't get your name. I'm Sandra. This is Sal."

"Timmy," he said, and shook Sal's hot, sweaty hand. *Ugh.*

"My car battery died," Sandra explained, "and he helped me jumpstart it. I thought this would be a nice way to thank him. You don't mind, right?" She batted her long eyelashes.

"Anything for you, my dear." Sal swiped an arm across his substantial forehead, which was perspiring despite the frigid air. "Mario should be here any minute; I'll have him fire up the grill. I recommend today's special—"

Engines roared and tires squealed, drowning out his voice. Two cars careened around the corner of the building and stopped mere feet away. Five men wearing black clothes and ski masks jumped out. Two brandished guns; the other three hefted baseball bats.

"Nobody move! Hands where I can see 'em!" one gunman commanded.

Sandra screamed. The leader snapped his fingers, and another thug approached her, leering, his eyes roving her body. She tried to back away, but he grabbed her and twisted her arms behind her back. When she cried out in pain, he clamped a hand over her mouth.

"L-leave her alone!" Timmy squeaked. His knees trembled violently, and blood rushed in his ears.

A third man restrained him, yanking his arms so sharply that pain seared his left shoulder. Timmy whimpered. "Shut up!" the man barked.

"That's better," the leader said, pointing his gun between Sal's eyes. "Now let us in."

Shaking and sweating more than ever, Sal complied. The criminals frog-marched Timmy and Sandra in after him. One gunman kept watch at the door while the rest of the group passed through a service hallway and stainless-steel kitchen into a dark dining room.

"Sit them over there," the leader commanded. Timmy found himself shoved into a chair in the corner, Sandra next to him. A man loomed over him, guarding; another kept hold of the cringing Sal.

"Where's your safe?" the leader demanded, practically shoving his gun up Sal's bulbous nose.

"I-in the back office. Please, d-don't hurt my cousin and her friend. I'll do whatever you want."

"Shut up and get moving!"

Sal flinched hard, but he hurried to lead the two robbers back through the kitchen's swinging doors.

Timmy watched them go, then returned his attention to the

remaining thugs. They glowered back at him. One snarled, "Don't get any ideas, shrimp." Tremors coursed through Timmy. A tear streaked down his cheek. It was a good thing he was sitting; otherwise, he might have fainted. He wanted to comfort Sandra, whose doe eyes were wider than ever, but he couldn't spare the attention. He was too afraid to notice anything more than his own fear.

An eternity seemed to pass. Timmy heard a few thumps, a clang, and the leader barking orders. Then footsteps. The swinging doors parted. The leader shoved Sal into a chair at the table next to Sandra. "Got all the cash," he told his thugs. "Now we just gotta tie up loose ends."

Sandra gasped, and Sal went bone-white. "What does that mean?" Timmy whimpered.

"It *means* eliminate the witnesses." The leader gave a shark-like grin.

"P-p-please, no!" Sal sputtered. "We didn't see anything! We have no idea who you are!"

"Please don't!" Timmy blubbered, sliding off the chair to grovel on his knees.

"I got a wife and kids!" said Sal.

Sandra simply sobbed quietly.

"*Shut up!* On your feet! All of you—*move!*"

The thugs herded them the way they'd come, out to the rear parking lot, then lined them up against the building, execution style. Timmy was openly weeping now, dignity long forgotten. *This can't be real. No, please. This has to be a nightmare. Wake up! Come on, wake up!*

〉〉●〈〈

6:00 P.M., THE FARMHOUSE

Melanie curled in a corner of her safe room, using her backpack as a pillow and fighting to fall asleep. A pounding headache battled back tenaciously.

Her phone buzzed, and she groaned. *Not Gavin again.* Nope—Chandra. "Hello?" she said hoarsely.

"Melanie! Oh God, I can't believe what just happened!" Chandra sounded panicked, shaky, completely unlike her usual, poised self.

Alarmed, Mel sat up. "What's wrong? Are you okay?"

"Yes, but . . . my plan went all wrong." Chandra's voice broke. "I *was* just trying to scare him, I swear. I never meant for it to go that far, for anyone to get hurt. I'm so sorry!" She burst into sobs.

Fear pierced Melanie like a javelin through the chest. "What are you talking about? Timmy wasn't following me." She'd called Chandra and told her that while waiting for Dave at the rest station.

"He was. You must not have seen him. He's cleverer than you think. I mean, he *was*."

"Was"?! Mel's throat tightened, and her head swam. "Is he . . . ?"

"He's dead," Chandra confirmed.

Time seemed to congeal. The air felt thick, like Mel was trying to breathe in soup. Leaning against the wall, she struggled to wrap her mind around the reality—the finality—of what had happened.

Someone she knew, someone her age, someone she attended classes with (as obnoxious and hated as he might be) was gone. Cold. Lifeless. She'd never see him again, never edit his writing again, never hear his smug voice again.

Never have to worry about him blabbing my secret again!

Guilt instantly followed the flash of relief. *It's my fault he's dead. If we hadn't gone camping, if I hadn't been bitten, if I'd left yesterday or this morning . . . How could I not notice him following me?* Mel's heart pounded, and blackness edged her vision. She closed her eyes and breathed deeply.

When she was able to speak again, she asked, "How did it happen?"

Chandra sniffled, then sighed. "I drove to the rest station to keep an eye out for Timmy, just in case. I spotted him but waited till you and Dave left. He tried to follow you guys, but I blocked him and pretended my car's battery was dead. He gave it a jump, and to thank him, I invited him to an early dinner. We went to my friend Sal's restaurant— which wasn't open, but I knew he'd let us in. He's sweet on me. I wanted to get alone with Timmy in a comfortable setting where we could talk, where I could explain to him all the pain and trouble he'd face if he became one of us. If that didn't convince him, then I was going to try threats, pretend I had a pack that would come after him. But before we could even get inside the restaurant . . ." Another choked sob.

Mel waited a few moments, then prompted, "What happened?"

"The place got robbed. Five guys in ski masks showed up—I think they're a local gang. I've heard of them. They're very dangerous, known for leaving no witnesses. They forced Sal to open his safe, and they kept me and Timmy in the dining room while they did the job. Then they . . . they took us outside and . . ."

Clenching her fists, holding her breath, Mel waited once more as Chandra fought to steady her voice.

"They were going to shoot us. We begged them, *please, please,* but they put a gun to Timmy's head and . . . pulled the trigger."

"Oh my gosh." Mel closed her eyes, still reeling with shock and horror. "How did *you* manage to survive?"

"Sal was freaking out, telling them he had a wife and kids—not true. They said that killing Timmy was a warning, and if Sal ever talked to the cops, they'd come back and kill him." Mel could feel Chandra shudder. "But they didn't let me go that easily."

Mel's skin crawled—she sensed where this was going.

"While they were still taking the money, I heard them talking about the things they wanted to do to me. After they let Sal go, they tried to force me into their car. I'd never have escaped if it hadn't been so close to the full moon. I fought them, knocked out two of them, but of course they threatened me with their guns. Then I gave *them* the scare of *their* life—I showed them my golden eyes. And my claws."

Picturing the scene, Melanie couldn't help but grin.

"I had a feeling they were superstitious," said Chandra, a smile in her voice. "They panicked—screamed like little girls. One of them said something with '*lobo*' in it. They got outta there fast."

"Ha!" Mel pumped a fist in victory, then sobered. "I can't believe . . . I'm so glad you're okay. But Timmy . . . What did you do with—with his . . ."

Chandra sighed. "Melanie, I'm not proud of this. But what could I do? I left it there. I told Sal to call the cops and report that he'd found the body when he'd arrived. He hadn't seen a thing, had no idea who'd done it. I'm pretty sure that gang has someone on the police force, because they get away with everything. I sure as hell don't want to mess with them. They might get over their fear of the wolf woman."

"I guess . . . I understand." Mel chewed her lip, unwillingly picturing Timmy's corpse lying in a parking lot, getting covered in snow. Mouth and eyes wide, frozen in terror. Blood pouring from a gaping wound in his head, dyeing the snow crimson. *He was a total jerk, but he didn't deserve that.*

"It's almost moonrise, so I'd better go," said Chandra. "Just wanted to tell you what happened before you heard on the news. I'm so sorry." The sob was back in her voice, but she managed to say, urgently, "Promise me you'll keep this conversation completely confidential. Please. I don't want them after me. Promise?"

"Yes. Of course I promise." How could she do otherwise?

Chandra let out a relieved breath, sounding a little more like her normal self. "All right. Well, I'll see you tomorrow. Doc likes to draw my blood during the days of the full moon and compare it to the other test subjects'."

Mel said goodbye and let the phone fall to her lap.

She felt cold inside and shocked, waiting to cry but not crying.

There was a knock at the door. "Come in." Moments passed before Melanie remembered the rooms were soundproofed. Groaning, she pulled herself to her feet, then leaned against the wall as a wave of dizziness crashed over her. It subsided, and she staggered to the door.

Dave stood there, barefoot and shirtless. Mel blushed. The bite scar she'd seen before, but not the eagle tattoo covering his right shoulder. "I just came to check on you," he said, "and make sure you were all right. Moon rises in ten minutes." His eyes narrowed. "You okay? You look rather gloomy."

"I'm fine," Mel mumbled. "It's nothing. I'll tell you later."

"Sure," Dave said in a kind voice.

He turned to go but then froze. They both heard it—an insistent pounding, coming from downstairs. Someone was banging on the back door.

"What the hell?" Dave growled. "Who—?"

Mel's racing heart stopped when she heard a voice—faint yet familiar—yelling her name.

Anger surged. *How'd he find me? Why can't he leave me alone and stop trying to control my life?*

Had he hacked her phone or something? But Mel didn't have the address to this place.

Then she realized: *A vision . . .*

Is he insane? The moon's about to rise!

"Do you know who that is?" asked Dave.

Instead of answering, Mel pushed past him and sprinted down the hall. She took the stairs two at a time, Dave on her heels. She raced through the living room and dining room to the kitchen and unlatched the deadbolt. Flinging open the door, she came face to face with Gavin Doyle.

His eyes were glowing, which accentuated the dark circles beneath them. He leaned against the doorframe, face ashen but jaw set in a firm, determined line. She yanked him inside and slammed the door. "What are you doing here?!" she demanded, staring daggers at him.

Gavin looked pointedly over her shoulder. Mel turned to see a curious crowd gathering behind Dave: everyone but Sokoloff and Erickson. Arms were crossed; faces wore frowns. The other wolves were clearly not pleased about the intrusion.

Swallowing nervously, Gavin said, "I had to come. I couldn't let you stay here with these—these people."

Sheila growled, "What's *that* supposed to mean?" Her eyes ignited.

"Hey, easy, easy," said Dave, putting a hand on her arm.

"Please, Mel, listen to me," Gavin said, gripping Mel's shoulders. "I'm here to protect you."

She shrugged out of his grasp and took a step backward. "I can protect myself, *thank you*. I didn't say you could come here. I thought I made it perfectly clear on the phone that I make my own decisions—you don't choose for me!"

Gavin nodded. "You did. You do. I don't. I'm very sorry, Melanie. It was wrong of me to rip up that note."

Mel softened a bit, though she asserted, "I'm not a little kid, you know. I can take care of myself."

"But... you're sick. Or something." Gavin's eyes had stopped glowing, and now they held hurt.

"The doctor's here. He's trying to figure out what's wrong with me. I'm sure he will soon." Mel tried to sound confident.

Before Gavin could respond, Dave said, "Guys, it's 6:32. Three minutes!"

"Do we have a room for him?" Mel asked breathlessly, fearing the answer.

"No. He'll have to use the root cellar."

"Can't he share a room with one of us?"

Eyes widened, heads shook, and Sheila said, "Sure, he could—if you wanna gamble on which one survives the night."

"Root cellar it is," Gavin said tightly.

Heart speeding up, Mel thought, *I hope it holds him!*

"Come on, hurry!" Dave dashed to the door and pulled Gavin outside with him. Melanie followed, needing to see where they went, needing confirmation that Gavin was put somewhere safe.

The two men didn't run far—the cellar door was about twenty feet away from the back door. Dave threw open the weathered hatch. "Get in!" Despite the cold and the audience, Gavin started stripping off his clothes. "Where's the padlock for this thing?" Dave called.

From behind Mel, Vanessa said, "We'll search the kitchen. Guys, help! Check all the drawers."

Mel joined the hunt, and Erickson appeared in the dining room doorway. "What's going on?"

"We gotta find a rusty old padlock," said Les. "Seen one around here?"

"No." Erickson opened the drawer nearest him and rifled through its contents. "Did someone just show up? Who?"

"Go see for yourself," Sheila said crossly.

Erickson strode to the door, poked his head out—and staggered back inside, clutching his chest. "Oh my God."

Confused, Melanie watched his eyes take on a fierce golden sheen. He swayed, grabbed a countertop to steady himself. *Does he ... know Gavin?* She approached him. "Um, excuse me—"

"Got it!" called Brad, holding aloft a padlock and key as rusty as Les had predicted. "Someone run this out there." He tossed it to Erickson, who was nearest the door. Erickson fumbled and missed. The padlock bounced off his foot, and he yelped.

Mel scooped the lock off the floor. She squeezed past Erickson, then sprinted to Dave and Gavin. The wind slammed an icy fist against her, but the fever heralding her imminent transformation greatly softened the blow.

Gavin was down to his boxers. Blushing, Mel noted he was as pasty as Dave but much less hairy. She pushed a flashlight into Gavin's hand, trading it for his bundle of clothes. "Go now!" he said, and disappeared into the murky cellar.

Dave shut the door, then fastened the padlock. He and Mel raced back into the kitchen, which was empty—everyone else had fled to their rooms. Needles of pain stabbed Mel's left side. She moaned and clutched at it, nearly tripping on the dining room threshold.

"Come on!" Dave urged, seizing her hand. He half-dragged her to the stairs and partway up them. But then he stopped, doubled over in pain, and grabbed his abdomen. His ribs crackled and expanded under skin stretched to translucence.

"Augh!" Mel's burning knees distracted her from the disturbing sight. Vicious Charlie horses gripped her calves, paralyzing her.

Panting, Dave straightened up and took hold of her hand again. "We—can do it. Push through—the pain!"

Step by agonizing step, they fought their way up the rest of the stairs. Melanie collapsed on the landing, chest heaving, forehead slick with sweat.

Don't stop now! You gotta keep going! But her legs refused to obey.

Dave tugged at her elbow. "Get up, Melanie! Just a little farther! Think about what will happen if you don't!"

Images of her wolf tearing the house apart, busting out the kitchen door, and fleeing into the night compelled her. She summoned her last ounces of strength and, holding on to the railing around the stairwell, hauled herself upright.

Dave's safe room was near the landing, but Mel's was at the other end of the hall. He started leading her toward it. "I'm fine," she wheezed. "I'll make it. Get in yours!"

He opened his door, bent over in pain, and watched until she reached her door—practically crawling the last few feet. As she shut herself in, he did likewise.

Mel managed to latch all but the topmost deadbolt. She struggled to remove her clothing, tears streaming down her face. Fur sprouted on her arms. Her limbs throbbed. Where was her backpack? There—in the corner. She dragged herself over to it and with twisting hands shoved her clothes inside. *How am I going to get it up in the cabinet?*

She tried to stand, but her knee joints crunched and reversed. She screamed and fell backward. Nausea surged, and she turned her head and vomited. Some of it missed her hair.

Her eyes stared at the gouged wall as changes ripped her apart.

28

Aftermath

"What's he doing way out in the middle of nowhere?" Aaron asked, frowning at the tracking app on his phone. "That can't be where he lives, can it?"

Pam leaned in to get a better look. "Beats me. All I know is he goes to Brookside. Never heard where he's from or whether he lives on campus." *There are a lot of things I'd like to know about Gavin Doyle— like why he's helping Mel hide her secret. And he definitely has secrets of his own.*

"It's getting late; we should head out. It'll take maybe a couple of hours to get there." The pair had just finished dinner. Now they sat in Aaron's car, tracing the GPS signal from Pam's phone—which she'd hidden in Gavin's car.

"All right. Let's go." Pam buckled her seatbelt, and Aaron started the engine. They rumbled off into the night under the watchful gaze of the luminous full moon.

During the drive, Pam had plenty of time to think. Each mile of highway was nearly identical to the last: trees, trees, and more trees interrupted by the occasional exit or overpass. Normally she would have chattered happily about her classes and her day, but tonight she stared pensively out the window.

It all began after that volleyball game. Pam tried to recall the events of that evening, any details that would stick out in retrospect. Last semester seemed so long ago. Closing her eyes, she puckered her brow in concentration.

Mel was kind of antsy that day. Distracted. She said her stomach was bothering her. . . . She met Gavin at the volleyball game; they went somewhere and talked for quite a while. . . . After the game, it seemed

277

like something was bothering Mel. She was quieter—guarded, maybe—but I didn't give it much thought at the time. Instead, Pam had been preoccupied with Aaron and whether he was ever going to ask her out.

Melanie's first disappearance had been the next day, hadn't it? Too soon after meeting Gavin to be a coincidence. Mel had left her car on campus, so someone had to have picked her up.

Gavin, she guessed. *Is he with her now?* When they found him, would they also find Mel?

"Take this exit," she said at long last, pointing. "We're getting close."

Aaron put on his turn signal and took the exit onto a bumpy, narrow country road. "What's out here?" he wondered as they entered a thickly wooded area. "Bears?"

The streetlamps had vanished. So had the traffic. Aaron switched on his high beams. Pam's focus turned outward again, and she peered around at the scenery.

The moon silvered the tree tops. Bare boughs, like skeletal hands, stretched skyward in supplication. Evergreen peaks speared the sky. The forest held its breath.

"*Here?*" Pam gawked as Aaron slowed and turned onto a gravel driveway. "What a dump!" The farmhouse's porch was collapsing, its windows were boarded up, and it badly needed repainting. Everything was dark.

They crunched up the driveway anyway. Around back, they discovered half a dozen cars. Not abandoned, then. "Do you think ..." Pam whispered, then stopped, embarrassed at her thought. *Could this be a crack house?*

"Looks like a party," said Aaron. "But why the heck is it so dark and quiet? Early to bed, early to rise?"

Pam pointed out Gavin's car, and Aaron parked next to it. Longing to have her phone back, she tried the car doors, but all four were locked. "Don't worry; I got this," said Aaron. He produced a wire coat hanger he'd straightened except for a small hook at one end. In seconds, he'd jimmied the lock.

"You're amazing!" Pam pecked him on the cheek, then retrieved her phone. "Shall we knock and see if anyone's home?"

In answer, a bone-chilling howl rent the air. They both froze. Every hair on Pam's body stood on end. "What was—" she whispered, cut off by another howl, louder and closer.

Her heart pounded wildly. She spun, terrified some rabid dog or wolf was after them.

They were alone except for the cars. The woods weren't far, but the underbrush was still. Nothing leapt out of it.

Scratching and scraping sounds echoed crisply in the cold night. Frantic growls and snarls accompanied them.

"Something's trapped somewhere, trying to get out," Aaron said gravely.

Noticing a cellar door midway along the back of the house, Pam pointed. "Might be down there." Cautiously, Aaron approached the cellar. Pam squealed but followed a few steps behind.

Thump! Thump! Something large and heavy threw itself against the weathered wood. The hatch was padlocked, but its boards didn't look terribly sturdy. With enough effort, whatever was trapped inside might break free.

Pam sure didn't want to be around when that happened.

"Come on!" She tried to pull Aaron away, back to his car. But he stood transfixed, staring at the cellar door.

Splinters appeared near the center. The boards were weakening. The door bowed upward.

"Aaron, please! Let's go!"

Crack! A board fractured. *Crunch!* A jagged hole opened, narrow at first but widening.

Pam gasped. Through the darkness, she thought she saw a furry snout and fangs.

Mesmerized, Aaron stepped closer and crouched down. "Is that . . ."

"Aaron Gates, are you trying to get *killed?!*" shrieked Pam. She yanked at his arm with all her strength, and he straightened up.

"All right, I'm—wait, look!" he said. The growling and scraping had subsided, and the snout vanished. In the gap where it had been, a glowing golden eye appeared. It locked onto Pam's and narrowed—greedy, hungry.

Her knees buckled. A tremor washed over her body. She clung to Aaron.

"They *are* real," her boyfriend whispered, sounding awed.

Paralyzed, shell shocked, Pam could only process: *Werewolf?!*

This time, Aaron pulled her away, half-supporting her as they ran to his car and flung themselves inside. Without bothering to buckle up, he gunned the engine and peeled away. He didn't slow the car until they'd left the forest-lined corridor far behind.

Pam couldn't stop shaking. The image of that golden eye blazed in her mind.

Caleb Connor's video. Timmy's article. She'd dismissed both. But now . . .

She gasped, remembering the two pinpricks of yellow light in the tunnel at Pine Groves.

Tonight was the full moon. Hadn't the moon been full during their camping trip?

Melanie's disappearances are pretty regular, aren't they? About once every month?

A sob escaped her throat.

Aaron flashed her a concerned look. "Are you okay?"

She nodded, not trusting her voice. Her stomach churned, and she felt like she might throw up.

It couldn't be.

How can those . . . those monsters . . . exist?

ꪖ ꪖ ● ꪑ ꪑ

FEBRUARY 10, FULL MOON (SECOND NIGHT)

He woke, frozen as stiff as a corpse. The cold was so bitter it burned. His muscles, his skin, his joints—all were on fire.

Opening his eyes a crack, Gavin saw that his skin was tinged with blue. If he didn't get dressed and get inside, in front of a fireplace or heater—and fast—frostbite might set in. He doubted werewolves were immune to that.

As his awareness filled out, he glimpsed the stone floor and earthen walls of the root cellar. It had held him all night! *Thank God.*

Thoughts of Melanie propelled him to stand, tears of agony almost crystallizing on their way down to his jawline. He clenched his teeth like a vise to keep from crying out. His feet were half numb, and balancing on them proved tricky.

Turning and staggering toward the cellar door, he saw weak morning sunlight filtering down onto the steps. Had they opened the door for him already? That was awfully quick.

But when he reached the steps and started climbing, he looked up, then nearly lost his balance.

The door hadn't been opened—just a jagged, gaping hole in the middle of it.

I got out?!

I came back?

Gavin sank onto the steps, shivering so badly (inwardly and outwardly) that he had to pause and calm himself. His heart pounded, and he gasped air in staccato bursts. He wrapped his arms around his legs, knees pulled up toward his chin. *Slow, deep breaths.* What on earth had happened last night?

Once the gasping had subsided, he checked his skin and found mud, pine needles, and a bit of mushy freeze-dried moss. He'd been in the forest. There was nothing crusted around his mouth—no blood.

He couldn't stay here another night. He had to get to his cabin. To safety.

She won't leave with you, a voice told him as he climbed the rest of the way out of the cellar.

Melanie didn't want him around anymore. She could take care of herself. She thought he was a smothering, controlling jerk.

Gavin squinted against the white glare of snow as he trudged to the back door of the house. After confirming it was locked, he banged on it like he'd done last night. *Please let someone be up—please let someone let me in soon!* His teeth chattered, and he bounced in place, rubbing his arms. Couldn't they have left him a key or something?

"Gavin Doyle?" called a voice from behind him.

Startled, he almost slipped off the icy steps. A man strode toward him from the direction of the cars. He looked to be in his mid-thirties, average height and build, with unremarkable features. Something glinted over his shoulder—the muzzle of a gun that was strapped to his back. Gavin flinched, tensing up, hands covering his most vulnerable area.

"Wh-who ar-re you?" he demanded through chattering teeth.

"Gary Saddler," said the man, giving what he probably thought was a reassuring smile. "One of the few human members of the Organization."

It's him! The cop from my vision. Without the sunglasses, in heavier clothing and a totally different environment, but yes, this was the man.

Never thought I'd be grateful to run into him. Of course, his gratitude depended on whether Saddler was actually helping him or not.

Saddler reached in his pocket, and Gavin drew back warily. "Don't worry, just the key to the house." The man held it up for him to see. He joined Gavin on the steps, unlocked the door, and pushed it open. "After you," he said with a courteous gesture. "Your clothes are in here somewhere, I'm assuming?"

Gavin nodded, hoping Melanie had left them in an obvious place. He stepped into the kitchen and immediately found some relief from the cold. Saddler flicked on the lights behind him and closed the door, cutting off the arctic wind. "I'll get a fire going." He passed through the kitchen into what looked like a dining room, and then on into another room Gavin couldn't see.

He got his bearings, taking in the stainless-steel appliances, granite countertops, and the cool whites and grays of the walls, cabinets, and floor. The décor wasn't warming him any. He still shivered and shook like a leaf.

At the far end of the lengthy island sat a bundle of clothing Gavin recognized as his. *Thank God!* he thought again, and rushed to it. He dressed as quickly as he could, though it was excruciating, putting everything on—coat and all. Slowly, the feeling in his extremities returned.

He was going to follow Saddler and warm up a little more at the fire he could now hear crackling, but painful memories anchored him where he stood. Melanie had not been pleased to see him last night, and maybe still wouldn't be this morning. She didn't want him here. He was stifling her.

A fist squeezed his heart.

I should leave.

He couldn't face her again, not if she was as angry as last night. He couldn't bear to see that hard look in her eyes. She'd changed some-how—not just outwardly, but inwardly.

Rummaging in his pockets, Gavin found his car key, then slipped out the back door. His Ford wheezed to life, engine sputtering and complaining. He set his GPS for the cabin, took one last look at the house where Melanie now belonged but he didn't, and crunched down the long gravel driveway.

He'd been alone under this curse for years and years before Melanie had come along, and he was alone once more.

)) ● ((

FEBRUARY 14, WANING GIBBOUS MOON

Five days. Timmy had been dead five whole days. It seemed like moments, or like an eternity.

The library was nearly deserted on this Tuesday evening—not because it was a Tuesday but because it was Valentine's Day. A few people sat at tables or computers, most alone, some looking dejected but others intently focused on their studies. No one had come to Melanie and Luis's tutoring table yet, and hopefully nobody would. Mel had a ton of reading to catch up on. But the words on the pages in front of her blurred. She kept swiping at her eyes to keep the tears from falling onto her book . . . and to hide them from Luis.

Her sorrow was by no means only for Timmy. When she'd arrived back at her dorm room Sunday evening, she'd found it half empty. All Pam's belongings had been cleared out, the bed stripped, her closet empty and open like a mouth gaping in surprise.

There'd been a note folded neatly on the now-naked mattress where Mel's roommate—ex-roommate—had used to sleep and gossip and giggle:

I found out your secret. How could you keep something like that from me? I don't even know who you are anymore. I won't tell anyone what you are, unless anything weird or dangerous happens, but you'd better stay away from me.

It wasn't even signed.

The paper slipped from Mel's hand, drifting downward like a dead leaf. The air seemed to freeze, to be sucked from the room. Blackness edged her vision. Her knees buckled, and she pitched forward onto the empty bed, face buried in the fabric of the mattress until she felt like she would smother to death.

Not a half-bad idea. . . .

A door clicked open down the hallway, and footsteps approached, slowly. Mel knew it was Jocelyn before she heard her voice—quietly, tentatively—say, "Mel?"

She didn't answer, but finally turned her head so her burning lungs could get some relief. Arms outstretched, she clung to the mattress like it was a life raft. Her eyes stung, and her tear ducts were a dam about to break. She squeezed her eyes tightly shut.

Fabric rustled, and she could sense Jos crouching next to her, could smell her minty shampoo. Silence reigned for long moments. Then a gentle hand came to rest on Mel's shoulder. "I'm sorry, sweetie."

Mel sniffled, and the dam sprang a small leak. Great—she was about to be a blubbering mess in front of Jos once again. Drawing in a shaky breath, she opened her eyes a slit and saw compassion on her suitemate's face.

"I tried to stop her," Jos murmured. "To talk some sense into her."

Mel nodded, then shifted onto her side, facing away from her friend. She hated that pitying look. Especially on Jos's face, where it was rarely seen.

Then Mel remembered: "How's your arm?"

"Feeling better as the moon wanes." Jos explained how Gavin's touch had also eased the wound's pain.

Gavin. *He left without saying goodbye.*

But perhaps things had worked out for the best. Gavin had accused her of being too trusting, but that was only because of his inability to trust people. He couldn't see that the Organization could help him, wanted to help him. He'd rather stay locked up in his cabin, being tortured every month, than take a risk.

He's just going in a circle, going nowhere. He accepts this curse, but I'm fighting my hardest to alter my destiny.

Fate, destiny, chance, design ... Mel couldn't see that far, that deeply into the scheme of the universe—if it even had one. If there *was* a reason she'd been bitten, it would probably always remain a mystery. Time to stop dwelling on the past and move into the future.

Sucking in a deep breath, Mel cleared away thoughts of Sunday night, of Gavin, of Timmy's death. *Focus. Read. Get on with what you're supposed to be doing.*

Luis glanced at her over his economics textbook. "You okay?" he asked.

She nodded, not trusting her voice.

Concern still shone in Luis's eyes, but slowly it morphed to hesi-tance, to hope, and at last to resolve. He reached out and put a large hand over Mel's small one, which rested on the table beside her book. "I've been meaning to ask you . . ."

She waited, tingles radiating from where he touched her. His hand felt warm, strong, and sinewy. "Yes?" she prompted, gently.

"Well, um, I know . . . he wasn't my friend either, but it's a terrible thing when anyone you know dies, especially someone our age."

"Yeah," Mel said soberly.

"*Pero, sabes*, life's not over . . . for us, I mean. Good things happen too. And I wanted to ask you today, because it's St. Valentine's Day, so . . ." Luis took a deep breath. "Will you go out with me?"

Blushing, she looked down and then back into his eyes. "Okay."

His whole face lit up, and a broad grin stretched from ear to ear. "*Excelente*," he said, squeezing her hand.

They smiled shyly at each other, and Mel turned her attention back to her book. Before she could read a whole page, wetness dripped onto her upper lip.

She swiped at it, and saw red on her hand.

The nosebleed was back.

TO BE CONTINUED . . .

Thinklings

TIMELESS BOOKS • QUALITY AUTHORS

www.ThinklingsBooks.com
Facebook.com/ThinklingsBooks
@ThinklingsBooks

Thinklings Books started out when three speculative-fiction-loving professional editors—Jeannie Ingraham, Deborah Natelson, and Sarah Awa—got together and formed a writing group. We called ourselves the Thinklings, in honor of C.S. Lewis and J.R.R. Tolkien's group, the Inklings.

Over time, we found ourselves agonizing more and more about how messed up the publishing industry had become. Why couldn't good books get published? Why were so many bad books published just because their authors had big Twitter followings? We wished there were something we could do about the problem . . . and then we realized there was.

As a developmental editor, a substantive/line editor, and a proofreader, the three of us knew good writing when we saw it—and we knew how to make it even better. We had a lot of experience walking our clients through the publishing process—both traditional and self-publish—and we had contacts with marketing and design experts. We had some amazing unpublished books lined up and ready for production. We had, in fact, everything we needed to make a great publishing company. All that was left was to actually do it.

So we're doing it.

Spectacular Reads. Every Time.

I will win. I have to.

My plan was to keep my head down, do my job, bring endless rounds of coffee to my genius boss. But see, I have this thing about bullies. Doesn't matter who they are—evil fairies, ravenous demons, powerful traitors, or my own family. The moment they try to enslave my brothers, murder my king, and fold up my boss like a literal hand towel, they're my enemies.

I don't have magic. I don't have power. I don't even have much money. But as long as I have a brain and a will, there's nothing I won't do to save the people and the country I love.

So bring it on.

Bargaining Power by Deborah J. Natelson

The Narrative Must Be Obeyed

Everyone in the Taskmaster's Realm knows how the story goes: the boy of destiny goes on a quest, defeats the dark lord, and gets the swooning princess. It's a great story, if you happen to be a knight or a wizard or a hero. But it's pretty odious if you're Ordinary: a barmaid who has to inflate her bosom and have her backside pinched, a homely prince who can't buckle his swash because his face doesn't fit, or a soldier who gets killed over and over and over again just to progress the plot.

Fodder of Humble Village is one of those soldiers, and, frankly, he's sick and tired of getting speared, decapitated, and disembowelled so the good guys can look glorious. In fact, he's not going to take it anymore.

No matter what The Narrative tries to make him do.

The Disposable by Katherine Vick

Beware of Spilling Ink

Skate is a thief, trained and owned by the local crime syndicate, the Ink. When she tries to burgle a shut-in's home, she gets caught by the owner—a powerful undead wizard. He makes a deal with her: "borrow" books from other wizards in return for a place to stay.

Caught between her growing fondness for the wizard and her past with the crime syndicate, Skate doesn't know where her loyalties lie. But she'd better figure it out, because there's a new player in town, one whose magical hypnotism puts them all at risk.

Skate the Thief by **Jeff Ayers**

Immeasurable imagination. Unmitigated magic. Spectacular style.

The clockwork man is crafted, to begin with—commissioned by that terrible tyrant Time to serve as her slave for all eternity. His brain boasts balance wheels and torsion springs; he can wind himself up with a key in his side; and, most importantly, his gyroscopic tourbillon heart glimmers with pure diamond.

He is a living being and he is art, and he refuses to remain a slave forever. He therefore slips through Time's fingers as the Sands of Time slip through the cracks of reality (at least, when the time cats aren't using them as a litter box).

Among astounding adventures, despite harrowing hardships, and in between escaping interfering enchanters, the clockwork man seeks his imagination, his purpose, and his name.

The Land of the Purple Ring by **Deborah J. Natelson**

Technology Hates Janet

After she accidentally smashes a floatcar through City Hall, the bureautopia sentences Janet to captaining the starship S.S. *Turkey* and its misfit crew. Her mission: to boldly rescue a prisoner from the one corner of the universe colder than her ex-boyfriend's heart—Pluto. Which, aside from not even being a real planet, is the one place in the universe where chocolate is illegal.

In between studying The Space-Faring Moron's Guide to Common Science Fiction Plot Devices, falling for a rival captain's boyfriend, and avoiding unnecessary time travel, Janet has a chance to save two worlds . . . or doom them to permanent chocolatelessness.

The Cosmic Turkey by Laura Ruth Loomis

True Love vs. Ancient Curses

When the Egyptology department needs funds to offset a recent spate of museum thefts, Theodora Speer grudgingly trades her painting smock for an evening gown. Charming donors isn't usually her idea of a good time—but then, she doesn't usually get to meet handsome and mysterious men like Seth Adler.

Seth Adler is desperate to get close to a very specific Egyptian mummy, and attending a fundraising gala seems just the ticket. He doesn't expect to meet Theo, refreshing in her honesty and intriguing him against his will . . . and he definitely doesn't expect her to interfere with his plans.

Frantic to escape before the police catch up, Seth kills himself in front of Theo. Except it turns out he's not so dead after all, and it's up to Theo to keep him that way. Even if it means fleeing the police, practicing ancient Egyptian magic, and confronting the real thief.

Painter of the Dead by Catherine Butzen

About the Author

Sarah M. Awa grew up in Northeast Ohio. She "published" her first books at the age of eight and hasn't stopped writing since then. After earning a BA in English from Toccoa Falls College, she became a freelance proofreader and editor. She also served as creative director for The Ghostwriting Agency for six years. In 2019, she co-founded Thinklings Books, LLC.

Ms. Awa currently lives in Northeast Ohio with two hairy guys: husband, Oscar; and their adorable Shiba Inu mix, Thatcher. She loves reading, writing, anime, chocolate, and walking Thatcher in the park.

You can visit her at
www.sarahmawa.com

www.ingramcontent.com/pod-product-compliance
Lightning Source LLC
Chambersburg PA
CBHW031557240626
47153CB00002B/542